About the Author

Residing in the heart of the Midwest, Erin Tunney is a freelance writer and admirer of animals and fantasy. This admiration has inspired her to write fantasy novels of her own to share with the world. She draws inspiration from her work from animal care facilities and volunteering at an equestrian center. If you wish to see more of her work, please visit her website:
www.fantasyrealmbooks.wordpress.com

Beast Heart Series: The Wild Shepherdess

Erin Tunney

Beast Heart Series: The Wild Shepherdess

Vanguard Press

VANGUARD PAPERBACK

© Copyright 2025
Erin Tunney

The right of Erin Tunney to be identified as author of
this work has been asserted by her in accordance with the
Copyright, Designs and Patents Act 1988.

All Rights Reserved

No reproduction, copy or transmission of this publication
may be made without written permission.
No paragraph of this publication may be reproduced,
copied or transmitted save with the written permission of the publisher, or in
accordance with the provisions
of the Copyright Act 1956 (as amended).

Any person who commits any unauthorised act in relation to this publication
may be liable to criminal prosecution and civil claims for damages.

A CIP catalogue record for this title is available from the British Library.

ISBN 978-1-83794-350-0

This is a work of fiction. Names, characters, businesses, places, events and
incidents are either the products of the author's imagination or used in a
fictitious manner. Any resemblance to actual persons, living or dead, or actual
events is purely coincidental.

*Vanguard Press is an imprint of
Pegasus Elliot Mackenzie Publishers Ltd.*
www.pegasuspublishers.com

First Published in 2025

**Vanguard Press
Sheraton House Castle Park
Cambridge England**

Printed & Bound in Great Britain

Dedication

I dedicate this book to my mom, Yvonne, whose support and love had made this dream possible.

Acknowledgments

Many thanks to my teachers and the Pegasus Publishing Team for their support and guidance in order to bring this book to life. This wouldn't be possible without their support.

Prologue

The rain pounded on the roof of a small house outside of Snowdrop village. All the animals of a nearby forest huddled for warmth in the trees, bushes and warrens. Thunder rumbled in the distance. Faint light from crystal lamps hung along a window. The house held a woman and a man about to have their first-born child. The woman was crying out as she went through the last bouts of pain. Her husband was at her side, holding onto her hand as if she'd die if he let go. A handmaid with a white duck was in front of her, ready for the baby.

"Come on, dear!" The man in his early twenties held on to his beloved for dear life. On his shoulder, a black cat perched with ease. His hands held a few scars from battle but they did little to discourage him from his task. "Come on! You're almost done." He flinched as his hand was squeezed hard. His ears filled with her screams. He looked at his wife's damp face and smiled. "You did well, Mana." He moved a strand of auburn hair away from her blue eyes.

The wife laid on the bed. Exhaustion ruled her body. She felt her Bloodhound rest his large head on the bed. A soft whimper coming out of the big, square muzzle. Her breathing took some time to even out. Then, she noticed something was wrong. There was barely any noise, save for the storm outside. "Gabrialian? Why's my baby not crying?" She heard a few footsteps. Mana turned her head to see the handmaid holding the baby in her arms.

The baby was pale as snow. Her mouth formed a small "o." Only small gurgling sounds were heard. Not the traditional bawling that most couples would hear when their baby is born. Eyes sealed shut. The handmaid had a grim expression on her face. "The child is showing signs of a weak heart. She's not going to last long."

Mana got up. "No! No! No!" She flopped back down. Letting out a loud sob. Their first child was finally born and now she was being taken away from them by the God of Darkness. Her husband tried to comfort her, but his own tears burst forth. Her dog bayed constantly. "Oh, Goddess of Light…" she whispered in an almost inaudible voice. "Please… save my child."

Suddenly, a strange flapping noise was heard. Something was coming this way. Something large. Gabrialian ran over to the nearby window. He stared in shock at what he was seeing. It was snowing in the middle of spring. "What in the world…" A roar resounded close by Gabrialian burst out of the door. The handmaiden, who went by the name Rue, placed the baby by her mother's side and joined in the investigation. To their shock, a sleek creature of silver scales appeared before them. Blue, soulless eyes stared at them. A crown of horns graced its head.

"An Ice Dragon?" Rue gaped. "All the way out here?" She pulled out a charm made out of woven lavender. She muttered prayers to the earth god, Straneac. Her body shivered.

"No one make any sudden moves..." Gabrialian slowly backed away. He looked for a weapon on the wall. Sure enough, he found what he was looking for. On his shoulder, his cat's ears were pinned back eyes wide. He bit back a pained grunt as he felt claws dig into him through his clothes. Fingers wrapped around the hilt of a sword.

Without warning, the Ice Dragon stuck its snout into the doorway. A strange ribbon of light danced into the air. It fluttered for a moment. Then, it landed on the little baby. The baby glowed a bright light. Once the glow faded, the baby let out a loud wail. The dragon soon went up into the sky and the storm cleared away. Rue and Gabrialian stared off into the distance, unable to comprehend what had just happened.

Mana turned to gaze at her child. The baby's tiny fits waved in the air. Finally, a wail was heard. Mana picked her child up gently with all the strength she had. It was strange that her child had gained strength, but the sense of magic shimmered on her daughter. She looked up to the heavens. "Thank you... Thank you..." she glanced back at her child. "Welcome home... My Clara."

Chapter 1
Fright

Baaa!

Clara screamed in fright. She jumped away from the wooly creature. She snatched her shepherd's staff and swung at it. "Go on! Back! Back to your master." Clara wrapped her aqua shawl tighter around her shoulders. Amber eyes focused on the sheep. She managed to get it back to the herd with ease. She let out a sigh of relief. Her silver hair hung in a disarray. She rubbed her head. Sweat beading down her face.

"Clara!" A gruff voice got her attention.

"Uh oh…" She turned to see a man in his forties glaring at her.

His arms crossed. At his side was a black dog with floppy ears. "How many times do I have to tell you not to smack the sheep? Some of the villagers are bonded to them. If one feels pain, so do the others." He grabbed her staff.

Clara looked down in shame. "I'm sorry, Joseph. I'm really trying." She flinched as the staff was broken in two. She interlocked her hands together.

"You don't try hard enough!" Joseph hissed. He rubbed a hand to his face. "Just do some laundry, you useless girl."

Clara's heart burned at those words. How she hated them. Those were practically the mantra her village would say or whisper. *You had other sons to do it*, she thought bitterly. *I know you just don't like me.* The things she wanted to say swirled inside of her. However, the more she spoke, the more they laughed or punched.

Clara said nothing. She simply bowed her head and went over to the next task ahead. She picked up the clothes that were placed in the hamper. Clara felt her back itch. She refrained from scratching it. Her eyes went to the sky instead. Summer clouds hung in the air. Some even began to take the shape of dogs and foxes. Clara sighed. With a simple heave, she was able to lift the basket up. She wobbled for a bit. Her silent prayers to the Goddess of Air and God of Earth to make sure that she doesn't slip on some mud again. She reached the area where all the washing boards were set up.

She tossed in a few herbs and began to scrub the cloth. In a matter of minutes, she was able to clean the clothes little by little. The pile disappeared from the basket. Just as she hung up the last of the clothing, she heard a faint conversation. Clara flinched. She knew exactly what it would be about.

"That girl is so useless. She just keeps messing up. Every. Single. Task!"

"Joseph!" a harsh voice rasped. It was Rue. The old handmaid that helped Clara's mother give birth to her. "She's already going through enough as it is. Clara has been trying her best with her chores and working with you since her parents died in that Minotaur attack."

"That's only six years ago. She's sixteen! Her bonding ceremony will start soon. She practically freezes up when an owl flies by. It's a miracle that she can do laundry or make soup. I can't help but wonder if she's cursed."

A loud slap soon resounded. Clara flinched at the sound. If there's one thing Clara knows, never get Rue angry. "How dare you say such a thing! Clara may have her fears but so do we." A faint woosh of her cane only emphasized Rue's point. "Our duke claims that the wild creatures have uncontrollable magic and must be eliminated. Yet, they've barely done anything to us unless we provoke them."

"Dragons have been sighted more. Cockatrice attacks are getting to be far more common. Our crops are failing. Even the magic from the tamed beasts is the only thing we have left to keep our world from rotting. Killing those wild beasts is our only chance to survive the other monster kingdoms."

"Don't believe what he says. The mages may be under his thumb, but the gods know more things than we do. Clara is alive for a reason. What it may be, I don't know. However, never anger the path they've woven for us."

Footsteps were heard followed by a rustling of bushes. Silence ruled the forest.

Clara sighed. She hung up the clothes as delicately as she could. Once the work was done, Clara emptied the tubs and laid down the washing boards. She went over to a rock and sat down. She took note of her silver hair. She looked over to her right and saw some daisies. Clara picked some up. She split the stems and woven them together to create a crown. She placed it on her head. Clara gave a small smile. It was one of very few things she's good at. Suddenly, a sharp pain erupted as something hit her neck. She gritted her teeth as she rubbed the back of it.

Her hand had hints of blood on them. She turned as cackling was heard behind her. "Oh, no..." she softly muttered. Standing before her was a group of two boys and two girls. They each wore a special neckband of pure silver on it. All of them were nearly dressed in white. The lead girl was wearing a pale pink dress with frills at the hem. Gold rings ruled over her slim fingers. Her dark hair pulled up in a ponytail. Brown eyes staring at her coldly. It was the daughter of the village duke and the children of the mages. All of them watched her with wicked glee. "Lady Maroona. What do you want?" She slowly got up. Her body was already preparing for the worst.

Lady Maroona gave a nasty smile. "Where are your manners, Clara? Don't you know you're supposed to bow to royalty?" She walked up to her with a folded fan in her hand. She swatted Clara's face with it. She laughed as

Clara fell back. "Pathetic as always." All the other children began to laugh.

Clara slowly got up. She wiped her face. Her sad eyes turned to them. "Why are you always doing this?" Clara asked. "I've never done anything to you." She straightened her dress. "Besides, the bows are only for the High Duke and Duchess of the land. For nobles like you," Clara waved her hand and drew a flower in the air. "Is how we greet them? Depending on the mages and—" She was knocked down again. Clara gasped as they continually beat her.

"Shut up, you worthless freak!" One of the kids shouted. He stomped his foot hard on Clara's ribs.

Clara cried out. She rolled out of the way before another blow came to her. She ran as fast as she could. She dodged the punches of the other boy. She led them away as they gave chase. Her chest ached as her heart thundered hard. Her breath hitched. Eyes focused on the woods. She tumbled but kept going. Their taunting voices came after her. The more she ran the more it felt like she was flying like a bird. She sidestepped to the nearest bush that was large enough to hide her. Clara held back a yelp of pain as she rolled into a hollow. Footsteps thundered after her.

"Where did she go?" one of the girls asked.

"She couldn't have gotten far," one boy said.

"She's getting way better at hiding than ever before."

"Use your magic, Basilini."

Clara blinked. She felt her entire back shiver. Something was taking over her heart and mind. A massive pull. *Oh no...* she thought. *Not again.* Her heart thundered faster than before. Her vision swam. Suddenly, she saw things that were in green webbing. The moss and trees gave dark hues while the grass and flowers were brighter. Clara waved her hand on it. She saw several ripples. She knew what they meant. Basilini was using the plants to locate her. Clara dodged the spots that rippled. She picked up a thick, dark green thread and yanked hard. Her fingers interlocked on the trees like puppet strings. A few screams were heard in the distance. Followed by running. She laid where she was for a while.

The vision still swam in front of her, but it did help her know when it was safe to come out. It was always like this. Lady Maroona and her 'pets', as Clara would secretly call them, would come every afternoon to torment her. Even when her parents were alive. Her mother and father would easily drive them off, but it still continued to happen. Things only got worse when her parents died. They would hide her clothes. Tear up some books. One time, they beat her until she had bruises all over her body. She couldn't move for days.

Clara was thankful that Rue stood by her side when her parents were gone. She was the only adult who ever treated Clara well. Even going as far as sending complaints to the High Duke about the unruly children since Duke Averance only coddles his daughter and the mages barely do anything about their kin. Her rage is one that many of the villagers would be foolish to calm easily. Even her duck is a formidable foe.

After some time, Clara soon realized her tormentors were gone. She slowly crawled out of her hiding place. She flinched as a burning pain went through her ribs. She got up and made her way back to the laundry. *I hope they didn't destroy them*, she thought. Clara hugged herself at the thought of having to see a row of angry faces staring at her. To her relief, they were still there. Nice and dry. "Thank the winds…" she muttered. She folded them and brought them back to Joseph. The man was about to say something, but one look at her injury made him stop. He took the clothes and looked away.

Clara walked back to her house. She briefly glanced back at the forest. Her eyes caught sight of a golden building that stood out of the tree tops. The tip of it was like a golden needle in the sky. Ready to pierce the clouds. It was a tell-tale sign of Sky Needle city. It's only a few miles from her village and where the bonding ceremony would take place. Clara groaned at the idea of going there. It would mean having to be with her tormentors again. She went inside and began to boil some hot water. Clara flinched as she accidentally burned herself trying to get her fireplace alight. She flinched more frequently as she began to undress herself. She only removed her shawl when she saw the bruise on her neck. The purple mess going down her neck and almost hiding into her shoulder. She cringed. She undid her dress and let the cloth slide down her shoulder.

"Glad to see your back."

Clara froze in place. She turned her head to see Rue standing in the doorway. Her gray hair tied in a bun. The dark green dress almost blended her into the grass. Her duck waddled in slowly, age catching up to the both of them. Clara went red. "H-h-hi Rue... I got done with the laundry." Rue's gasp made her heart sink. It sunk deeper as Rue walked over to her with an upset look on her face. Clara moved her arm and soon realized that she was revealing her bruised ribs. "I can explain..."

Rue held up her hand. "No. I know exactly what happened. Maroona did it to you again, didn't she?" She sighed when Clara sniffed and nodded. She went over to the pot that hung over the fire. The sounds of bubbling water breaking the silence. Rue grabbed a wooden bowl and scooped up the water. She set it down on a nearby nightstand. She grunted as she sat down next to Clara. Her old bones began to creak. With ease she dunked a white cloth into it and applied it on the bruise. A tremor felt underneath her hand. The dragon mark on the girl's back gleamed silver in the firelight.

"Rue?" Clara didn't turn her head. She stared down at the ground. "Am I... really cursed?" She looked at her own hands. The comments of what the villagers say about her rang around her head. Her heart even hammered at the sight of Rue's duck. Bandages were soon tied around her waist.

"Don't believe those stupid words," Rue answered. She finished tying off the last knot that would keep the bandages in place. She lightly grabbed Clara's face so the girl would focus on her. "You've done nothing wrong. What happened on the day you were born is beyond your control. The death of your parents wasn't your fault either." She hugged Clara. "You've got a good heart, Clara. You made sure the elderly is well cared for. You try to complete your tasks. Even when they're difficult for you."

Tears streamed in Clara's eyes. She hugged Rue back. "I wish they'd stop. I don't want to go to the ceremony! They'll all just laugh at me." She flinched from the pain. "Worse, my bonded animal won't like me. I'm so afraid of animals." Clara broke away from the hug and turned her head to the window. "I don't know why that is… It just… happens." The stars were out tonight. The moon was full.

"Nonsense." Rue snipped. "Your beast will grow to accept you. As long as it isn't a wild creature, you'll be fine. The domestic help channels our magic. Maintain our connection to the gods better."

Clara didn't move her gaze. "What do you feel about the wild beasts? Will they truly kill us?"

Rue shook her head. "I don't know." She leaned away from Clara. Her bones creaked in protest. "For the longest time, the beasts such as dragons and basilisks are the result of unstable magic during the time where the gods have gone mad thanks to the god of darkness. They've attacked humans, but I believe it was because of human stupidity rather than pure cruelty on their end." She chuckled. "Lady Maroona and her foolish father being a fine example." She helped Clara put her dress back on. Rue got up from her spot and began to head over to the counter.

Clara got up quickly. "Please! Let me help you." She placed a hand on her side. She sat back down on the bed.

Rue shook her head once more. "You need to recover. I'll cook dinner. Just lay down for a moment. Besides, tomorrow is going to be a special day." She pulled out a bowl and a few eggs. She broke the shells, the yokes sliding out with ease. Rue stirred away. She tried to put on her best smile. "I promise. Once the ceremony is over, no one will make fun of you again."

Clara laid on her back and stared at the ceiling. "If only that were true…" she continued to imagine her life ahead of her after the ceremony. No one would be coming by to say hello to her. Rue being out of her life once she passes over to the Ethereal Rainbow. The heinous whispers. The ugly stares. Not even her own animal would look at her. Her future was going to be dark.

Chapter 2
Bonding Ceremony

She was running. Clara couldn't explain it, but it felt like she was on all four legs. The forest speeding past her. Faint sounds of howling and baying setting her into a frenzied panic. Suddenly, she leapt over a tree branch. Clara was only a few feet from where she was when a rope of bramble suddenly grabbed her by the neck.

Clara began to grow scared with every movement. The bramble threatening to crush her neck. Clara didn't understand why she needed to run or what made her so scared in the first place. All she knew was that she had to get out of the place she was in.

Heavy hoofbeats sounded to her right. She looked up to see a Shire Horse loom before her. Sitting on its back was a figure wearing a hood over their head. It was hard to make out the face. Even when the torch light of the hunters began to show up. The noises began to grow louder and louder.

Clara woke up with a start. Her heart hammered hard. Her silver hair matted from sweat. She slowly got up. Her ribs no longer hurt, no doubt the bruising had gone down. She hugged her knees. *What was that?* she thought. *I never had a dream like that before.* Her body shivered. Clara soon heard snoring at the other side of the house. She glanced at Rue. The old handmaid was in the corner of the room. Her duck nestled on her pillow. Clara was glad that Rue stuck around after her parents left her. The mere thought of the Minotaurs coming back to her village made her skin crawl.

Sunlight started to leak into the room. The signs of dawn reached her home. Clara sighed. "Time to get ready…" She went over to her drawer and pulled out a simple white dress. Clara went outside to pick up some flowers that lined her garden. Lavender and bluebells greeted her. Even a morning glory seemed an ideal flower for her. She put on her dress. As she did so, she noticed the bruising on her neck had gone down. She sighed at the sight of her silver mark that was peeking out. She continued her preparation when Rue finally woke up.

The elderly lady smiled at her. "Nicely done." She hobbled over to Clara. "And I love the choice of plants. Bluebells are believed to guide lovers to each other. Morning Glories symbolize seizing the day and lavender is always the popular choice among women. You're going to do just fine."

Clara wasn't so sure. She merely sat down as Rue tied her hair in a braid. Her thoughts were lost in the dread of meeting the other kids in the city. Her fingers interlock in prayer. She prayed to the gods that they would protect her from any more folly that would come her way. Clara heard a quack. She soon realized that Rue had already made her breakfast as well as finished braiding her hair. Eggs with a side of stale bread sat on a plate Rue was holding up for her. She tried to take the spoon from Rue's duck, but the shaking almost made it impossible. Clara snatched it quickly, politely took the plate from Rue, headed for the table and ate.

After her breakfast, Clara waited for Rue to get ready. It took a while, but Rue was able to wear a blue gown with a yellow shawl. A hiking stick in hand. Clara linked arms with her. The two women went down the field until they reached a main road that led them to their destination. Clara felt the wind blow through her braid. The flowers in her hair resembled jewels in the sunlight. Green grass gave way to a worn dirt road where several carts pulled by oxen, horses and mules lined the road. Some people walk beside their respective animals.

Clara tried her best not to draw attention to herself among the pedestrians. Some that had come from her old village. Her eyes turned to the sky or the dirt road whenever people had glanced her way. Her hands were pressed together. Her fingers intwined up until they turned stone white.

Before long, they soon arrived at the front of the city. Sky Needle City had several buildings in shades of light brown. Red bricked houses dotted some of the places. Several shops lined the streets. Signs of all the shops and taverns were displayed above the doors. The cobblestoned path was loud against the noise as each step is taken. Large crowds of people gathered around the great Sky Needle. It was a tower that had two large horses with their legs connected to each other.

Clara adjusted the collar of her dress. She prayed no one would see her mark. The cleavage showed some skin around her shoulders. However, people except Rue and her parents haven't known about her mark. If anyone found out... If Lady Maroona found out. She shivered. "Do I have to do this," she asked. Her stomach coiled like a dangerous snake.

"It's the only way to connect with the land," Rue answered. She gave a reassuring smile. "Now let's get to the square before anything else happens." She led the way, her eyes making sure that no pig or goat would make her trip. Several geese honked, drowning out whatever protest that Clara had. Clara even had to avoid a few animals that were about to cross her path. Sounds of children playing and adults talking barely gave her any comfort. Music blending into the madness.

As she walked past a stand, Clara soon overheard a conversation of four adults gathered around a fruit stand. "I heard that the Harpies tried to enter our borders again," spoke the owner, a young woman with black hair.

"Wretched monsters," hissed a man. His muscles rippled in fury. "You'd think by losing their precious queen, they would've learned their lesson by now."

"I heard that they've made an alliance with the Reptilia," said a thinner man. He stroked his dog's ears.

"Nah!" A cackling laugh from another woman with a round build broke through the noise. "The Reptilia are too cold blooded to care about an alliance. Rather roll in the mud and eat whatever's in their jungle."

"Crazy thing is I've actually heard their king tried to set up a meeting with our own Duke Morshar and Duchess Laning," the thin man mumbled under his breath.

"Bah! The chances of that are as slim as getting the selkies to stop attacking our boats and avoiding those dark elves." The muscle man rolled his eyes at the thought.

"The Dark Elf king truly is a nightmare. The way of controlling the Minotaurs after destroying that clan's king." The robust woman let out a disgust snarl.

"Shhh!" the shopkeeper hissed. "Not so loud. It may have been ten years but the pain is still fresh."

A sigh came from the muscled man. "True. Many lives were taken that day. Every once in a while, I still hear screams from my neighbors. Even a spark of fire gets them jumping."

"How long are we going to suffer like this?"

"Don't know… Hopefully the Empty can finish them off."

Clara walked away from the stand as fast as she could without drawing attention to herself. She soon arrived at the place she was at. Her palms lightly blanketed with sweat. She wiped them away as she made her way to the platform.

She tried to distract herself by going to the nearest stall. On display was a strange conglomeration of objects. Fans with strangely colored feathers. Metal bands with gemstones on them. Strange pelts hung around the stall.

Cow horns nestled in a basket. Her skin began to crawl as she read what was on display: Harpy Feather Fans, Selkie pelts, Sand Dwarf headgear and Minotaur horns.

Clara has heard of the process of getting these items. It was almost as bad as meeting the actual civilians of the savage kingdoms. She backed away slowly. *Why would anyone want to buy these?* With a heavy sigh, she walked toward the grand platform as Rue waved her over to a growing crowd.

The youth of the town gathered. They all wore white. All of them were crowned with flowers or jewels depending on what walk of life they come from. They all gathered around the building. Even Lady Maroona was wearing a regal white dress. Her hair wore a headdress of rubies and emeralds on her head. Pearls and diamonds were sewn into the fabric. Her followers had several insignias sewn into their clothes, showing their status.

At each corner positioned farther away from the platform, the domesticated animals were all penned. Symbols of the elements etched into the signs along the fencing. The fire symbol was a simple flame. The fire pen was comprised of cats and dogs. The water symbol was a water droplet that was held up by the crest of a wave. Sheep were the most common in that pen. The earth symbol was a large daisy wrapped around a tree. Its respective pen held an array of horses, goats, and ox. As for the wind symbol, it bore a bird gliding into the wind. Chickens, ducks and pigeons were clustered together.

Clara held her breath. Her heart turned to stone at the sight of them. Her world tilted. Her steps were rigid as if she stepped on glass. All eyes turned to her. She couldn't make out their expressions. Were they of fear, disgust, or laughter? Clara couldn't let these sorts of things get to her now. She just needs to get through this ritual as soon as possible. Clara straightened her back as best as she could. Her lips in a firm line.

Lady Maroona glared at her. "Well... If it isn't lady weak heart. I'm surprised you actually had the spine to show up here. So, where were you last night?"

Clara merely stared ahead. She wanted to give no mind. "I merely went home. The ceremony is going to start. If you wish to hold on to the title, I suggest not doing any more childish behavior. Or any monstrous brutality." She heard Lady Maroona scoff, but nothing more. She also whispered a few words but she ignored them. Clara knows what they are about.

A hush filled the air as a man in his mid-forties strode into the area. He wore a golden tunic with brown pants. Rings of silver and gold graced his fingers. A doberman close to his side. His black hair was tied into a knot. Four robed figures followed behind him, hoods raised to hide their faces. The green one had a shire horse in step with him, wearing a cloak of sage and lotus. The red one had a mighty wolfhound. The blue with a sheep while the light blue had a pigeon. They all went up to a podium where the tall horses were behind them. The cloaked figures pulled back their hoods to reveal their faces. Two men and women.

The man cleared his throat, "Greetings citizens of this fine city. I'm Duke Averince. My daughter is among the youth that is here on this special occasion. A long time ago, wild beasts roamed this land. The world itself plagued by the savage kingdoms. They forced humans to scrounge for scrapes. Their magic is too wild to control without compromising our souls. Then, one day, humans have found a way to tap into that magic." He waved his dog over. The Doberman walked over and sat down in front of him. In a matter of moments, the dog began to take on a red-orange hue. Duke Averince's eyes glowed in a similar color. "Through our domesticated animals, we've paved a way for our new way of life." He turned to the children. "Now it's their turn to have that experience. To be truly part of the world they were born in." Flames danced out of his hands and leaped onto the torches that were stationed around the area.

The crowd gave out gasps, a few even cooed at the sight. Young children with their mouths open into a small "o". Clara spotted Rue further away from the crowd toward the front. She tried to hold back her laughter as Rue rolled her eyes and snorted.

Before long, a silver light glowed on the children's wrists. The crowd watched in awe as the silver ribbons of the youth extended out like glittering tentacles. Guiding their children to their destined partners. Spreading out, the youths found their partners one by one. Even Lady

Maroona had found a basenji pup to be her partner. Everyone cheered at this marvelous sight.

Clara simply stood in her spot. No ribbon graced her wrist. A small smile crept onto her face. *At least one good thing happened today*, she thought. However, the stares of the crowd were starting to get very uncomfortable for her. She fought off every urge to run off the platform.

Suddenly, a whinny turned the crowd's attention away from her. She followed the direction of the noise. Her heart nearly stopped at what she was seeing before her. A group of men and their dogs were struggling to maintain control of a magical creature she never thought of seeing in her lifetime, a unicorn.

The pure white creature reared up. Silver hooves glittered in the light. Ears pinned back. A flowing white mane with a lion-like tail. Light blue eyes that matched the sky. Several horses shrunk back in pure fear as the white horn turned bright ivory. A few bystanders barely had enough time to dodge it. Muscles rippled against the restraints as it gave a wicked bellow.

Duke Averince marched over to them. His face turned red. His dog growling beside him. Fire waved in his pelt. "What's going on here?" He ducked as the horn swung at him. A loose rope dangled for a moment until the duke grabbed it.

"Apologies, sir," one of the men grunted. His hands began to burn with pain. "This one got loose. Just broke out of its stall before the ceremony started."

"Wasn't it fed sleeperlock?" Duke Averince shifted his weight as a hoof came right at him. His dog came around the back and bit its leg. Blood running down in a small trickle. A scream erupted from the unicorn.

"We did, but it just woke up without warning!"

Clara stood there frozen. Her heart was thundering hard. She could feel her body turn to stone. Tears went into her eyes. This felt like the invasion of her village all over again. Clara couldn't take her eyes off the creature even if she tried. "St-stop... please..." Her words were barely a whisper but it seemed to draw the unicorn's attention to her. Then, Clara felt something strange inside her. A strange pull. It felt like some lost part of her was coming over to make her whole. Suddenly, her wrist began to glow.

A silver ribbon slithered out of the sky. It danced and twirled. The flowers and water gravitated toward it. The crowd gasped. The ribbon soon touched the unicorn. Upon impact, the ropes vanished and butterflies fluttered around in their place. Light exploded around them. Clara covered her eyes for a moment, the sensation of her braid coming undone sent through her scalp. She opened them to see the unicorn stand before her. It stared at her. Nostrils flared. A strange sense of gratitude washed over Clara. A name etched in her mind.

Without even thinking, Clara raised her hand to the creature's muzzle. It sniffed it cautiously then nuzzled into it. Clara couldn't explain it, but a smile spread across her face. Far bigger than any she would give in a long time.

She felt… happy. The happiest she's been since her family passed away. Clara leaned into the unicorn. Her arms wrapped around it. Whatever fears she had of it just melted away. The soft pelt gave her comfort. "Thank you… Lotus." With that, the unicorn galloped off with light radiating on its body. Unaware that a second ribbon slithered after it.

Clara found herself going limp. All the human stares turned to her again. Whatever they were saying was drowned out by a ringing noise. She noticed Rue looking at her. Dark eyes wide with terror. Clara tried to reassure her elderly friend, but the words wouldn't come out. She took a step. Only to fall into darkness.

Chapter 3
Exile

Clara felt something wet on her face. Beneath her was the rough texture of dirt. Clara slowly opened her eyes to see that she was outside of the city. Faint drops of rain coming down. Several guards stood before the city entrance. All of them held a look of pure disgust. Rue standing behind them, a sad expression on her face. Confused, Clara slowly got up from her spot. Her legs wobbled underneath her.

"Rue?" Her voice rasped as she called out her name. Her tongue was dry as sandpaper. She walked over to them. "Rue? What's going on?" She flinched as spears were pointed at her. A sense of dread crawled over Clara.

Duke Averance walked up behind the men. He was a few inches shorter but he could be easily seen with his gaudy attire. Clara could also see Lady Maroona and her allies from a nearby building. They all had smiles like cats that devoured a field of rabbits. "Clara of Mana and Gabrealian…" His voice cut through the oncoming storm. "You've performed the greatest taboo that people hadn't witnessed for a hundred years. You bonded with a unicorn. A beast of corrupted magic." He raised his hand to the sky. "By the power of the gods, you're banished from the human kingdom. You'll never set foot in any village or city."

"But…" Clara took a step forward. She ignored the spears aimed at her. "I didn't do anything! Didn't the ritual rules say that it only happens when the magic inside of you is reflected—" Her voice died as she realized what it meant. *No… I'm really cursed…* She found herself unable to breathe. Suddenly, a rock was thrown at her face. It wasn't large enough to mortally wound her, but enough to leave a large gash across her face. She looked up to see that a boy with a round moon face, whom she recognized as Basilini, had rocks floating in his hand. More rocks began to pelt her. She backed away. Her body screamed of pain as more of them hit her arms and head. She looked at Rue for what may be for the last time.

Clara ran. This time, the rain came down hard. Thunder erupts around her. Whatever the other humans were saying to her, it was drowned out. Flashes of lightning blinded her at each turn. Her clothes hung on her body. A damp chill ran over her. "I have to fix this…" Clara muttered. "I have to fix this problem." She just moved, ignoring the warm lights and any house that was nearby. She kept running until the clouds cleared away and the night sky revealed itself to her.

Clara stared up at the moon. The night sky was a ribbon of velvet with diamonds scattered across the horizon. She jumped at a wolf howling in the distance. Lone and mournful like the empty life that she found herself in. Moonlight revealed that she managed to reach the Forbidden Forest. The one place that no human, unless a hunter, was allowed to enter. A chill clung to her body stronger than ever. She hugged herself, wishing that she had brought her shawl with her. She froze as she felt a sensation along her back. It felt like a small tear. She ran her hand along her hair and back. Clara's heart jumped to her throat. The length of her hair was cut short and the back of her dress was torn.

She soon added up what happened. Her dress must've torn when she fell and her hair was brushed away when they lifted her. They've seen her mark. Tears returned to her eyes. She got down on her knees and cried. Her hands covered her eyes. Sobs wretched out of her throat. *How could've this have happened?* She never complained. Never fought back against the children and adults who've bullied her. She helped out the elders. Yet, they've done nothing but just sneer and laugh at her. Even Rue can't help her out of this one. She had to go find the unicorn, Lotus, and undo their bond. She looked at the path that led her back to her village. Her home.

She got up and tried to take a step. Her feet froze in place. "What am I doing," she asked herself. Her heart was heavy with sorrow. The warm smiles of Rue and her parents vanished before her eyes. "I have no home to go to. Not anymore." Tears ran down her cheeks. Gazing at the forest, Clara gulped. She walked onto the moss-covered ground and into the darkness that awaited her.

Owls screeched in the treetops. Bats fluttered through the darkness like dancers. Wyverns curled in dead tree hallows to sleep off their last meal. The mere sight of these creatures made Clara's heart race. Each sound forced her muscles to tighten. Her steps are difficult to even try. The wind whistled in her ears. Clara sneezed. She looked around quickly. Suddenly, a rustle in the underbrush alerted her to a creature nearby. Clara covered her mouth to keep from screaming.

The rustling continued. It only grew louder with an unfamiliar growl. It sounded reptilian, but a faint sound of a chicken. She slowly turned around to see a pair of glowing yellow eyes staring at her. The creature rose out of the underbrush. Its head resembled a rooster, but the lower body was that of a serpent. Wings of a bird flared out, with several spikes hidden underneath the feathers. It walked on chicken legs, sharp teeth shown through the beak. This was an extremely dangerous creature. One that the hunters were ordered to kill on sight.

"Cockatrice…"

Chapter 4
The Unicorn and the Wolf

Clara gulped. She's heard stories of these monsters. Unlike the basilisks that could kill anything upon a simple gaze, this creature breathes a poisonous gas. The moment it breathed in, Clara ran in the other direction. Her hands covered her mouth as it breathed its deadly poison. A purple mist surrounding the woods. She ran to put distance, but the cockatrice was much faster. It ran beside her, its massive tail knocked her down to the ground. The air was knocked out of her. Her fear kept her moving as the creature tried to pin her down.

Her body rolled instinctively. Her memories of dodging hooves of cows and horses were vivid. The ground thundered with each impact. She got up and was only a few paces when the cockatrice appeared in front of her. It knocked her back down, successfully pinning her. She struggled to move under the talon. Her eyes looked up at the creature. Slivers of moonlight showed its bright red crest and mighty beak opened for one more attack. Clara closed her eyes. She let out an ear-piercing scream.

A neigh echoed in the forest. A bright beam of light zapped the cockatrice, causing the creature to back away. It looked toward the direction where it was just attacked.

Lotus stood there. The unicorn's ears were pinned back. Muscles taught around the legs and neck. Her horn glowed. Eyes focused on her opponent.

    Clara saw this as an opportunity to get away. She scrambled to her feet. She ran as fast as she could and ducked behind the nearest trunk of a tree. She poked her head out from behind. Lotus was only a few feet away from her. If she could just ask the unicorn to break their bond, it might reverse the burden on her. She flinched as the cockatrice let out a noise that was a mixture of a serpent hiss and a rooster crow. It coiled its tail and sat on it. In one, smooth motion the cockatrice leaped at Lotus. "Watch out!" Clara couldn't explain why but the urge to warn the unicorn rattled in her bones.

    Lotus ducked away. The cockatrice hit a nearby tree with a sickening snap. It hissed and turned toward Lotus. Wings flared. Spikes hardening, becoming more visible. Lotus pawed the ground, a puff of steam rising out of her nostrils. Her horn still glowed. She let out another beam again, this one hit between its eyes. The cockatrice screamed. Lotus kept her footing along the forest floor. The tree roots are barely an obstacle for her.

    The cockatrice looked at her once again. Neck arched. Then, it let out another screech. Lotus also lowered her horn in a fashion similar to the swordsman. The two great beasts cried out and charged at each other. Everything moved slowly at that point. Each movement was slower than normal. Only a heartbeat could be heard. Then, it was over. Lotus' horn was buried deep into the cockatrice's body. The rooster head bowed, eyes glazed over. Wings began to lax. Then, it collapsed with a soft warble. Lotus backed and raised her head high.

Clara found herself shivering. She backed away slowly. Everyone had told her that unicorns are the third most dangerous wild beast due to their magic. Dragons being the first and wyverns being second. Now, she had seen it for herself. It must be the reason why they wanted to kill them and banished her. Clara was about to run, when her foot tripped over a root. She fell hard. "Ow…" She rubbed her face and decided to crawl. She was only a few feet away when a shadow loomed over her.

Clara froze in place. She looked up to see the unicorn loom over her. Lotus was surrounded by a halo of light. Clara laid where she was as she lowered her head. Suddenly, she felt a weird tingling over her. She couldn't explain it but it felt like something of curiosity and recognition. Clara flinched as she felt Lotus' muzzle along her back. Hot air against her silver mark. She realized light began to surround her. It was like the one from the ceremony. Clara tried to move but her body refused. This sensation was like being wrapped in a warm blanket.

Clara got up slowly. As she did so, she noticed that her cuts and bruises from the stones had healed. She was on her feet when Lotus was facing her. Blue eyes meeting with amber. She stayed where she was. "N-nice, unicorn… Don't hurt me… I just need to retract the bond…" *Even though I have no clue how*, she thought. Now that she's thinking about it, no human ever broke their bond with their respective domestic animal. The only way it was done is if the animal partner dies. However, the backlash of a severed connection with the world causes a human to go slowly mad. *Probably not a good idea.*

    Lotus tilted her head. Her ears flicked slightly. A strange ripple went between them. She took a step forward only for Clara to back away in fear. Lotus simply nickered. She was about to go when movement got her attention. Nostrils flared. She tried to move closer to Clara. She began to trot. Clara stared in confusion. Before she could say anything, Clara was lifted into the air. She hovered as the unicorn began to run into a gallop.

    The forest zipped around Clara. Hues of blues and greens almost melded into one. Scattering leaves could be heard slightly over the galloping. Clara looked around for the source but all she could see were creatures of the night moving out of Lotus' way or going about their routine. Trees and bushes rustling fiercely. It was as if Clara's presence barely did anything to them. "Wait! Where are we going?" Her question was quickly answered when Lotus made a stop at what looked like a meadow. Several goldenrods waved in the breeze. Queen's lace turning white under the moonlit night. The night sky opened once again. Clara's eyes stared in amazement. A small watering hole stood there. She was soon set down to the ground.

    Thirst came to Clara's throat. She crawled over to the water. She put her head close to the surface. Large gulps that could be heard from miles around. Clara couldn't stop herself. Once she got her fill, she found a spot in the grass and curled up. Clara felt her back and realized that her gown was fixed too. She was stunned. Clara wanted to ask Lotus questions, but sleep finally dragged her down to a quiet place she needed to be.

The next morning, Clara felt stiff. Sleeping on grass was far different than that of a bed. It was much rougher. She stretched, arms raised high toward the sky. Her stomach growled fiercely. She moaned. Clara placed a hand on her stomach. "Why me?" she said, her voice barely heard by anyone. "I'm exiled, bonded to a unicorn and have no means of anything to eat. What am I going to do?" Suddenly, an apple rolled to her side. She looked into the direction of where the apple rolled from.

Lotus was by the water. Her neck twitched with each gulp of water. Once she was done, she turned her head toward Clara. Her head tilted. A small ripple was given off. It was almost as if the creature was going to ask: Well, aren't you going to thank me?

Clara simply stare, "Uh... Thank... you?" She took the apple and bit into it. A hum escaped her throat. Normally, she would have to ask farmers to borrow food from their orchard. However, they'd say no mostly because there were few crops that were harvested. Some wound up being bad. This one may have been from the wild, but it felt like the best feast she's had in a long time. The juices were sweet and perfect. Each crunch was crisp like autumn leaves. She kept eating until the core was only left.

She went back to glance at the unicorn. Clara got up. However, a heavy reluctance hung onto her like a thick cloak. Clara needs to figure out how to undo the bond without harming herself. The words she needed to say were stuck in her throat. "Um… IIII… Uh…" Clara swallowed hard and tried again. "Could you please undo the bond?" She covered her mouth in horror. She rarely was the type to shout.

Lotus stared at her. A little stunned but a ripple of being impressed with Clara's politeness. She walked over to Clara. Her nostrils twitched, taking in the scent of the human. Her blue eyes were gentle. Ears twitched to any sound that was being made. Then, she licked Clara's cheek.

Clara blinked. It didn't hurt. Normally animal licks would make her cry and an unsettling sensation would crawl over her. Even a wolf howl made her wail as a child. Now, it felt different with Lotus. It felt calm. As if Lotus was acknowledging how scared she was. A glimmer of intelligence. Before Clara could stop, she cried. Overwhelming emotions rattled in her body. Loneliness. Pain. Anger and sadness.

Lotus was a little hesitant. Startled by Clara's reaction. However, the emotions made the unicorn draw herself a little closer to Clara. She knickered again. The sound started to ease Clara's sorrow. Then, Lotus moved closer. Her head over Clara's shoulder. A soft puff of air caused the silver hair to rise briefly.

Clara instinctively wrapped her arms around Lotus. A strange relief washing over her. "Please..." she whimpered. "I want this bond away. I don't care if it hurts me. I just don't want to deal with this anymore." Suddenly, she felt something that made her shiver. Another presence was close by. This one had a heavy disdain over her. As if her presence sickened the mysterious being to its very core.

A low growl was soon heard. Clara let go of the embrace and gasped. A large black creature, far bigger than a dog, stood before them. The head could reach Clara's chest. Lips pulled back into a fierce snarl. Its fangs gleamed in the light. A pair of mismatched eyes focused on the two. One was silver while the other one was violet. Hackles raised as it crouched.

Clara froze. "N-no... Not a wolf. Anything but that..." She immediately got behind Lotus. Wolves were one of the wild beasts she feared the most alongside dragons. Her fingers sunk deep into the pelt. She recalled how Rue said that seeing a black wolf is considered a bad omen. That death will most likely follow her. *As if my life is plagued with enough misfortune,* she thought. "Go away!" she shouted as loud as she could. She ducked as the wolf growled at her again. This time, a wave of hot anger flashed into her soul. Clara clutched her chest in pain. A realization slowly came to her. *Wait... If I'm sensing these feelings...* Clara looked back at the angry wolf. A brief flash of silver was tied on the wolf's foreleg.

Clara gaped. "O-oh no... There's no possible way." She waved at the creature. "Nice wolfy... can you s-sit so we can have a nice talk?" She was only met by another growl from the creature. A slight formation of words came to her. It was in a similar fashion to when she learned Lotus' name. She also began to recall how everyone in town had said that when you bond with creatures, their name is the first thing that comes naturally. "O-Onyx?"

The wolf stopped growling. It sat there, stunned by hearing its name. The fur was still raised but ripples of confusion were sent to Clara. The tail laid on the ground. Heterochromic eyes staring at her. Ears perked upright.

Clara took a deep breath. She refused to move from behind Lotus but she had to think of something. "H-hi, Onyx," she said. Her voice gave off a nervous laugh. "Thank you for not tearing me to shreds... Already had a cockatrice chasing me last night." Her throat tightened as she sensed no amusement from Lotus or Onyx. Both beasts stare at her. Clara tried again. "W-well... dooo any of you know where I can find someone who knows how to do this sort of bond?"

The wolf snorted as if to say, "How should I know?" Then he, Clara was sure that Onyx was a boy based on his firm frame, started to walk somewhere. He took a few steps then looked back. A small growl rippled his throat.

Clara flinched. She's been around enough humans to sense irritation. "Okay... Then... Following you it is." She stiffly walked with Lotus close behind her. They journeyed back into the forest. As they entered, a few pairs of eyes watched them from above.

Chapter 5
Forest Harpy

Clara found herself munching apple after apple. Lotus being kind enough to hand her some. As they continued down the path that Onyx led them, Clara soon began to notice that her vision began to change. The hues around her took on more vibrant shades of green around her. Her body didn't ache like it did before when Basilin cast his spells. It felt safe. Like she was truly part of the trees now. No one to yell at her or angry faces. The exile felt more like freedom than anything. Well... Almost freedom.

Clara shrieked as a snake slithered on her foot. She wheeled away only to crash into a nearby tree. A bird nest fell from its branch onto her lap. A few baby birds popped their tiny heads out. Their mouths open for food. The parents soon arrived screeching and pecking at her. "I'm sorry," she yelled. "I'm sorry!" Clara used her arms to cover herself. Her arms stung from the beaks.

Suddenly, Lotus let out a neigh. The birds took notice and flocked over to her. Their nest went from Clara's hands back into the branches. Clara stood there. Stunned by what she had just witnessed. Onyx merely looked at her. He didn't growl this time but his lip was lifted into a snarl. He continued walking on.

Clara sighed. She simply walked in silence. *Not only a day and already they think less of me.* She tried not to cry as she rubbed her face. The mysterious sight still lingered for a bit. Clara first looked at Onyx. The wolf's body looked to be on fire. It was so bright and intense that it nearly blinded her.

Then, she turned to Lotus. The unicorn giving off swirls of blues and yellows. A flash of pale blue flashed above her. Clara froze in place. "Did anyone see that?" She blinked and her strange sight was gone. She let out a groan. "Of all the times when I actually need it!"

A laugh echoed along the forest. Lotus stopped, head raised high. Onyx sniffed the air. He simply gave a snort. A loud whoosh sounded overhead. Shadows falling on top of the trio.

Clara looked up. She gasped. "Harpies!" Hovering above them were four human-like creatures with bird wings and feet instead of human limbs. All of them were wearing loose-fitting tunics around their torsos. The pants that the harpies wore were also loosely fitted. Tail feathers jutted out from the back.

The leader had mottled brown feathers that spread out wide like a hawk. A mixture of feathers and hair rained down his back. On his left were two harpies that resembled bluebirds. His right had a sparrow harpy accompany him. Cat-like eyes focused on her. Grins showed rows of sharp teeth.

"Well," the hawk harpy said. His voice was shrill. "Look, what we've got here." He landed in front of Clara.

His figure towered over Clara but he looked to be a few years older than her. He took one step forward. "A stinkin' human has wandered into our territory." He flinched when Lotus flashed her horn at him.

"Woah!" The sparrow harpy gasped. "Never seen a unicorn get that protective before." She tilted her head. "Especially over a human." She nearly jumped at the sight of Onyx. The black wolf growled at them.

"It's the wolf!" One of the bluebird harpies fluttered toward Onyx with curiosity. She kept a good distance from his jaws. "What's he doing here with a human?"

Clara gulped. "Uh... Onyx has been trying to help me." Clara's heart jumped as they all stared at her. She fiddled her fingers together. "You see..." *I can't believe I'm having a conversation with creatures that are going to rip me apart in a matter of seconds,* she thought. She raised her arm. "I'm bonded to the two of them."

Shrill laughter burst out of the Harpy group. Their leader took to the air and snatched Clara. "That's a laugh! Humans don't bond with wild beasts. They would rather die or kill them for their magic."

Clara stared up in surprise. Kill beasts for magic? "That doesn't make any sense. We get magic by tapping into the animals we've bonded to." She yelped as the talons tightened on her shoulder. She looked below to see Onyx and Lotus below her. Their worry rippled through her.

"You mean those empty headed plague bringers?" The leader Harpy scoffed. "They could only give a small drop. You've survived so far by the beasts you kill."

"B-but..." she shrieked as she was suddenly tossed over to the next Harpy. Her teeth gritted in pain as another set of talons clawed into her. She kicked and waved her arms. The pain was only getting worse. Laughter only filled the air. Her thoughts only continued with dread as she recalled the stories of Harpies carrying away humans and bringing them into their nests to tear them apart. Her screams grew louder and louder.

Nothing hindered the mad group. Suddenly, a large Harpy with eagle wings appeared. A stern look on his face. "What is the meaning of this?" His eyes narrowed with great scrutiny. He looked a bit like Clara's father.

The Hawk Harpy stopped in his tracks. He almost dropped Clara. His talons grabbed arm. A loud pop was soon heard. "S-sir! We were just about to report this to you." His wings beat hard as he lifted Clara up for a better view.

Clara struggled. Her fingers scrapped on the hard surface of scales. She pried at them but they refused to open. She formed a fist and banged on it. "Ugh! Let go of me! I don't want to be ripped apart!"

The Eagle Harpy grimaced. "You know we only send them back. Or leave them in the Darklands." Then, his eyes widened in shock as he took in Clara's silver hair. Her birthmark glimmering in the leaking sunlight. "What...

That can't be possible." He ran a talon through her hair. "We must bring her to the village. Now!"

Clara's mark began to shimmer. Her eyes glowed. Clara's vision soon began to glaze over. Sparkling white-blue threads appeared before her. She reached out to the threads that wrapped around her arm like vines. A loud snap was heard followed by a loud screech. Clara's body dropped but was only saved by Lotus in a matter of seconds.

Hooves hit the earth, dirt flew everywhere as Lotus put on running speed. Onyx beside her. The wolf barked non-stop. Lotus neighed and bellowed back. Their argument went through Clara like waves. They continued like this until a large rock began to move in front of them. One green eye the size of a small cart staring at them.

Lotus reared up. Clara slid off her back and landed with a thump. Clara got up and coughed. Lotus kept neighing, her hooves almost hitting Clara. Clara leapt out of the way. A low rumbling was underneath her feet.

The mound before them rose. Green scales rippled as muscles stretched beneath the stocky build. Curved horns that resembled an Addax graced the creature's head. The head resembled a sheep. Ears flicked. Bat-like wings flared out. It let out a low roar. Animals scattered about beneath it.

"Earth dragon!" Clara ran away only to be halted by the Eagle Harpy. She tried to run in another direction, but all sides were blocked by Onyx and the other Harpies. She felt a hot breath along her back. Clara cast a sidelong glance. Her own breath in her throat. Warm scales touched her back. She could feel magic slowly flow out of her. The colorful threads vanished again. Flowers began to grow underneath her.

Suddenly, a voice entered her mind. It was soft. Female. An invitation to speak. *Hello, Clara... I've been waiting for you. Wild Shepherdess...*

Clara turned and saw that one eye was scarred. Another nick was along the direction of her snout. Clara stared at the creature. Her fear hung onto her, but the curiosity came into the mix. "H-how do you know my name?" Fear betrayed her voice. "What's a Wild Shepherdess?"

Chapter 6
Wild Shepherdess

I recommend that you go to the Harpy nest, the Earth Dragon responded. *I'll meet you there.* She flared out her wings and took flight. Her body weaved through the trees with ease despite her giant size.

Clara stared in surprise. She recalled her storybooks her parents would read to her. The dragons in the pictures were always dangerous. Menacing beasts with no emotion. Eating humans left and right. However, this one had no interest in it. She placed a hand on her mark.

The Harpies walked closer to her. The Hawk Harpy was reluctant to get close but the Eagle Harpy grabbed her shoulders. His talons took great care not to touch the dragon mark. His mighty wings lifted the two of them with ease. Before long, the other joined them.

Clara's heart thunder hard in her chest. The ground below her grew smaller. Lotus and Onyx both ran after her once again. Trees stretched out in the sunlight as they flew by. Animals came out of their hiding place to glance out. Birds fluttered out to join the procession. Before long, Clara gasped at an immense sight before her.

A large tree sat in the forest. The largest tree she's ever seen. Several large huts dotted the tree. A few of them were nests that had branches tied in a tent-like fashion. Harpies of every color and size were there. Flying around the trees. On one platform, some young Harpies were trying to fly.

They soon arrived at the biggest hut made from pine wood. The Eagle Harpy set her down on a small platform. Clara looked over the side to glance at a nearby nest. She saw that there were no signs of bones in them. *That's weird*, Clara thought. *I thought they used human bones to decorate their nests for victory.*

"What... are you doing?"

Clara jumped. The Woodpecker Harpy was at her side. She wrapped her wings around Clara's abdomen to prevent her from falling off. Once Clara was balanced again, she noticed that they managed to get Onyx and Lotus up with her. She fiddled with her fingers. "Well... I was looking for... some bones... in your nest." Her face turned a bright shade of red as feathers on their heads were raised.

"What?" The Hawk Harpy marched up to her. His eyes blazed with fury. Brown feathers flared out like earthy spikes. "What ludicrous notion did you get that from?"

"Enough Shard!" An ancient voice cut through the group. It sounded like a raspy old woman. All eyes turned to a Harpy that wore a tattered cloak. Her wrinkled face with milky brown eyes stared out at the group. Grey feathers stuck out of her hood. "Our hatred with humans has gone far enough. Besides, I see no evil in this child."

Shard growled, "I beg to differ! She nearly killed me!"

Clara looked down in guilt. "I'm sorry. Y-you were holding me so tight." She rubbed her shoulders in pain. Blood soaked through the fabric. She looked at the Elder Harpy. She curtsied with a slight wobble. "M-my name's Clara."

"My name is Gales. Elder of the Harpies here." Gales moved slowly, each step taken with care. When she reached Clara, she brushed the child's face up to the silver hair. "So… You've received a Beast Heart." Gales turned to the Eagle Harpy. "So, the time has officially come."

Clara looked on in confusion. "I'm sorry… I don't understand…" she gulped. Her body began to grow weary. "What's a Beast Heart? Better yet, a wild shepherdess?"

"Come inside." Gales guided her to the entrance to her hut. "You'll have a better understanding once you get inside." She suddenly let out a strange whistling noise.

Clara walked in. Smells of flowers and fresh herbs hit her nose. A sense of relief flooded in her. She saw a cluster of leaves that seemed to resemble seats. Clara was reluctant, but the sting in her shoulder forced her to do so. She quickly went to her seat. However, she found herself unable to avoid seating next to Shard and the Eagle Harpy. A strange hum entered the room.

"Hello Elder!" A dainty figure entered the room. Her feathers were a shade of emerald green. Her movements were a bit faster than the flight of the others. Her wings moved fast enough to create a humming sound. Her green eyes were filled with excitement. "You called for-A human?"

Clara gave a crooked smile. She waved, "Hi... I'm Clara..." Clara regretted it as her shoulders began to sting again. The Hummingbird Harpy was in her face quickly. She flinched. "W-wow... You're pretty fast."

"Name's Twitch," the Hummingbird Harpy said. "I'm not as fast when it comes to hunting but I don't fool around when it comes to flowers and herbs." Hung over one side of her hip was a brown leather satchel. She opened it and began to dig into it. Then, she pulled out a vial. Twitch observed the wounds, lightly pulling away some of the torn fabric. Her expression soured. "Shard! You did it again!"

"Shut it, Twitch!" Shard hissed. "She almost killed me with her magic! Haven't you forgotten what humans have done to us? Even after we just sent them home?" His feathers raised high. Eyes ablaze with rage. His talons dug into the ground.

Twitch was silent for a moment. She opened the vial. The smell of aloe drifted into the air. A bowl of water was handed to her by one of the Bluebird Harpies. With dainty pressure, Twitch applied the soaked cloth onto Clara's shoulder.

Clara bit her lip in pain. Her mind thinking back to the cruel treatment she received from her fellow humans. The jeering faces. Angry comments over the slightest mistakes she makes. Even the whispers of her hair. *I wonder if that's why they cut it,* she thought. *Because they just had enough of it.*

Lotus soon came over and only laid down only a few feet away. She was soon given a bowl of water and grass. Onyx laid at the entrance, looking at the treetops. Gales slowly went over to them. She brushed her wings against them. Her milky eyes staring into theirs. Onyx growled but snorted after the experience. Lotus blinked directly at the elderly Harpy.

"My my…" Gales said as she hobbled over to her spot. She grunted at her attempts to sit down. "In all my years, I've never felt an exquisite bond made by a human. One that is willing to say the least."

Clara felt even more confused by this. "I… don't understand. Willingly? As if… Lotus and Onyx chose me?" She glanced at the unicorn. She tried to ask for an explanation but nothing came to her. "But why? What possible reason is there to bond with me? I'm a human. Their sworn enemy."

"Perhaps you may have more in common with them than you've realized." Gales took a sip of tea that was provided by the Woodpecker Harpy. "Your kind has bonded with animals, true, but the thing is that your relationship with them may not be as pure as you think."

Clara flinched as bandages were wrapped around her shoulder. Blood no longer flowed out, but the sting of the ointment was there. She leaned back slightly. Clara was always warned not to hit the animals because some of their pain would be reflected back to them. Then, she remembered Rue's duck. Rue had complained of arthritis to her, but her duck seemed to have no trouble getting around as much as she does. Even her parents' dog and cat were taken away to make sure they weren't a danger to themselves or humans. Clara gripped her dress. Eyes to the ground.

"Tell me child," Gales asked. "What did you see?"

"Um… Currently?" Clara looked up. Her back hurt from trying to straighten herself.

"Any detail."

Clara nervously held her hands together. "Well, most of the time it's just ordinary human vision"—she cleared her throat—"but sometimes… I see colorful threads. Mostly greens. Then, I saw light blues coming off all of you. I'm able to touch them somehow."

The Harpies remained motionless. Their expressions were almost hard to see. Shard moved away from Clara. Eyes glazed over. Feathers raised in fright. Mouths formed into a hard line.

Clara felt a solid lump in her throat. The words brought her pain as she spoke. "I-I'm sorry for hurting you… I just wanted to get down…" she cleared her throat again. Her hands were unable to stop shaking. "I'd also like to know if you have any idea how to sever the bond between Onyx, Lotus and me." She looked up to see a shocked response from Twitch.

"Why would you do that?" Twitch was in her face in a matter of minutes. Shard was knocked onto the ground. "What you're doing sounds amazing! I've never heard of a human pulling off that sort of magic as a child. Let alone pull off a Mage Will of that level."

"Mage?" Clara blinked. Then she got up. Her shoulders burned as she did so. "No! No way. I was never taught magic. That kind of thing is only passed on from birthright. Normal folk aren't allowed to use that sort of magic. I mean farmers and weapon makers can use a little of it. However, Mage Will is for a Mage of an elemental stage. By adulthood, the elemental properties become more apparent."

She looked at her hands. "If this is causing harm to all of you... I'd best stop before I become this 'Wild Shepherdess' you speak of."

Gales sighed. "The Wild Shepherdess is one who has the power to control the elemental properties around her. She's the connection to the gods and our world." She raised her wings. "You see child, the magic you see around you is connected to one another."

Clara nodded, "I'm familiar with the story of the threads from the gods of our world." She picked up a leaf and held it up. "The gods and goddesses used special threads that came from their very souls to create our world. They wanted to make sure it didn't unravel so... they entrusted humans with their gift." She was met by a disgusted snort from Shard.

"By enslaving the very animals you've bonded to." Shard dodged Twitch's wing as it swung at him. "Apparently, your greedy parents left that little detail out since you've been a babe." He was tackled to the ground by the Eagle Harpy. "OUCH! Tornado!"

"Forgive him," Tornado spoke. "He's hated humans since his parents were killed by them." Tornado grimaced. "Along with several others from an ambush."

Clara gaped. She recalled that incident. Several of the royal guards along with the mages had staved and slain at least ten Harpies. Her eyes glowed with tears. *No...* she thought, *there's no way they'd do that sort of thing. Beat me up is one thing, but killing Harpies that didn't do any form of attack?* "I'm... sorry to hear that. But there's no way I can possibly be this Wild Shepherdess."

Gales pulled out several seeds from a pot that was sitting next to her. She set them down in front of Clara. "Try growing these. Then... We'll let you leave."

Clara's throat went dry. Her hands clenched so hard that her knuckles turned white. "Really? Y-you'll keep your word... Can you break my bond?" Tears formed when Gales only looked at her. She took a deep breath as she tried to get her vision working. Her eyes kept staring at the seeds. However, nothing happened.

Seconds to minutes. Minutes to hours. The seeds were still where they are. Their shells barely showed so much as a crack. Some of the Harpies began to fall asleep. Even Lotus and Onyx drifted off to sleep. Finally, Clara let out a sigh of frustration. "I can't do it."

"I knew it!" Shard got onto his feet and grabbed her by her hair. "You're just another—"

"Knock it off!" Twitch pushed Shard away. They faced each other off. Hissing and feathers flared. "This isn't going to help us! Maybe Clara is just tired. She's been through a lot! I can see it through her gaze!"

"So what? You're taking the human's side now, traitor!"

"Enough!" Gales slammed her wings down. The vibration of the floorboards startled everyone awake. Onyx was on his paws with a fierce growl while Lotus let out a neigh. "This is no time to fight amongst ourselves. We need to resolve things before the next black moon."

Clara let out a sob. "It's not fair!" Her delicate hand formed a fist and slammed it into the wood. "It's not fair! It's not fair! It's not fair!" Her fist kept slamming into the wood. "Why did I have to be so different? I never asked for this!" She kept slamming until her knuckles bled out. Clara leaned forward, hands covered over her head.

"I never asked to be bonded. I didn't want to be bonded to animals." Her sobs wracked her body. She paid no mind to both Onyx and Lotus coming over to her. "They scare me to know end. Even Rue's duck would scare me silly." Her arms covered her head. "I don't blame Lotus and Onyx if they want to get rid of me. Or you for that matter."

Suddenly, Clara felt a soft ripple. She looked at Lotus. The unicorn had her horn glow with a white-silver light. Then, Clara could see images of humans that were cruel to Lotus. Calling the unicorn names like "horned parasite" and useless mule. Humans laugh as they strike down an innocent unicorn foal with a sword. An image of Clara being at peace and talking to Lotus despite her fear.

Clara sniffed. She wiped her tears away. "You… want to know me?" Suddenly, her vision began to change and distort. A field of threads came into her view. In front of Clara was a mass of pure light. She could make out Lotus' shape from it. She turned to the seeds.

Tiny green orbs sat in the middle of a frail web. Clara moved over to it. Hands outstretched to it. Her fingers lightly touched the threads. It was just five years ago when she first came across this power. Maroona and her friends were picking on her after she tripped with a basket full of tomatoes. A few got onto Maroona's dress. Clara tried to run only to get beaten up. Then, Basilin was about to perform magic upon Lady Maroona's command, Clara saw it.

She touched it. The thick thread that influenced a tree that was nearby. Clara yanked and the tree creaked to life. Its branches knocked her tormentors over. It gave her a strange sense of power. Like the tree was willing to listen to her than Basilin. A sense of worth.

Clara wrapped her fingers around the lowest part of the web. She could feel the tiny presence of the seeds. Specks of life waiting for their purpose. A command. She pulled on it. Then, she spoke. "Grow…" Light flooded around her. She could feel some of Lotus' strength lent to her.

Clara gave the command again, "grow." The orbs began to take shape. Rising out of the strange haze of color. The shapes began to form and solidify into large flowers. Clara smiled. Her body ached again, but it was a wonderful ache. She let out a laugh. She could even feel Lotus' laughter and relief flowing. Suddenly, the whole thing started to have more webbing growing around her.

That's enough Clara.

Clara froze. She turned to the Earth dragon. Her hand let go of the thread. Her vision returned to normal. The Earth dragon had her large head poke into the entrance. It was hard to see the expression, but Clara could've sworn there was gratitude in them. She soon felt Lotus' muzzle on her shoulder. Even Onyx snorted, unimpressed by what was witnessed.

Gales chuckled, "Took you long enough." She had Twitch and Tornado help her up. She stumbled for a moment, then hobbled over to Clara. "Still don't believe you can't do it, child? The powers of the Wild Shepherdess are within you. Your connections are genuine and Lotus knows it."

Clara gulped. "I… I only—" she stopped as she looked at the flowers in front of her. The Sunflowers had only grown a few feet but their blooms were absolutely perfect and healthy. She had never seen something like that before. Not even when she saw a demonstration of Mage Oak's powers. Her back began to tingle. Clara glanced over at the dragon.

Clara, the Earth Dragon's voice entered her mind. *You must understand your magic, if you wish to find the answers that you seek.*

Clara laced her hands together. She turned to the gaze of the Harpies. Mixtures of caution and curiosity ruled over them. Her right hand stung as her fingers brushed against the knuckles. She took a deep breath. *I'm going to regret this.* "What do I have to do?"

Gales put a wing on Clara's shoulder. "Rest here for the night. You'll begin your training at dawn."

Clara's heart stopped beating. "Um…" she glanced around. Tornado and the Bluebird Harpies seemed neutral. Shard was ready to destroy her where she stood. Twitch was brimming with excitement. "Is that a good idea?"

"Yeah, is it?" Shard flared his teeth out as he asked the question. He was soon met by a smack to the head by Twitch. "Ow!"

"Don't worry, child," Gales said. "Gaia and I will make sure they don't hurt you."

"Gaia?" Clara tilted her head.

That would be me. The Earth Dragon let out a puff of smoke.

"Oh," Clara's eyes went wide. "What?"

Chapter 7
Dragon Teacher

Clara was nervously holding onto Tornado. Her arms wrapped around her neck. Onyx and Lotus were being carried over to Twitch's hut by Gaia. Gales thought it was best for Clara if she rode on Tornado's back since she needed to recover from her injuries. Clara tried her best at not looking at the other Harpies. They probably know by now considering all the shouting Shard made.

Before long they made it to a small hut, it had a few morning glories laced around it. The sweet smell of sweet peas drifted into the air. Tornado landed with ease despite the fragile platform. Clara slid off, her cheeks flustered from exhaustion. "Uh... Thank you," she said. A small bow nearly had sent her falling backward. Tornado's firm wing on her back kept her in place.

"I appreciate your patience." His yellow eyes softened. "You're a lot braver than most humans I've seen."

"I don't know about that"—Clara pointed out—"I ran away like a coward."

"Yet... You willingly went with us."

Clara sighed. Her eyes to the floorboards. "Only because I have no home to go to now." Tears welled up in her eyes again. She rubbed them away and cleared her throat. "I better go inside before I make a scene." Clara quickly went inside before Tornado could say anything else. Onyx and Lotus at her heels the moment Gaia set her down.

Clara was welcomed to a sight that seemed a little familiar to her. A room that was similar to the size of her family's kitchen. Two nests were nestled in a corner. One larger than the other. A table was littered with a few vials and herbs. Hanging above her head was a strange lantern made from thick leaves and fireflies. Her ears picked up a faint hum. She turned to see Twitch making her way to the entrance.

Twitch only hovered a few seconds. Her bird feet lightly touch the boards. As she pulled on full weight, she wobbled a bit. A smile spread across her face. Her satchel draped over her shoulder. It slid down to the floor with ease. "Welcome to my home," she said, spreading her wings wide.

Clara tucked her lips in briefly before she said, "Th-thank you…" She went over to the table to help clean up the mess. Her stomach growled. Her legs suddenly wobbled. She knocked over a few vials. None had managed to hit the floor. "Sorry! I have a tendency to be clumsy."

Twitch merely smiled. "It's okay. I knocked a few things too. I can easily find a few ingredients in the woods." She put away the vials and cleared the table. She then pulled out a strange drink, bread and a jar of honey. Twitch soon prepared the meals for her, Lotus and Clara.

Clara was very surprised that Twitch used clay plates instead of leaves. Even the hot mugs of tea were also made of clay. "How are you able to do pottery?" Clara's cheeks flushed. "With your... wings and all." The words just felt wrong to say.

"Just takes a lot of skill." Twitch grabbed her chair with her leg and sat down. Her tail feathers flared. She began to eat her fill. "*Mmmm!* Honey is the best next to nectar!"

Clara nervously sat down. Her body shivered violently. Her eyes were on the table and the food that was on it. Her hand shook as she picked up the bread with the honey poured on it. She tried to take a bite, but her mind went back to what Rue and the villagers told her: Never eat honey for they are part of the wild.

But... I'm not one of them, she thought bitterly. *So... why should it matter to have honey or not?* Clara took a bite. She nearly choked at the taste that she felt. The sweet, sticky sensation of honey in her mouth brought her a strange sense of joy. One that she hadn't felt since her parents went away. Tears rolled down her face.

Twitch looked up from her meal. "Hey... are you okay?"

Clara could only cry. Her mind was unable to speak. Emotions spilled out. Her body began to lay down. Clara soon went over to the nest, ignoring the Hummingbird

Harpy's gentle touch. She curled up and the world vanished before her.

A gray fog settled around her. She couldn't explain it, but it felt like that she was in an unfamiliar plain that was not of the material world. Suddenly, she heard a whimper. *A puppy?* She followed the noise until she was on the forest floor. Clara was shocked to see a little wolf pup surrounded by dead wolves. A little clump of black leaning against a wolf with a pelt as gray as a storm cloud.

Clara glanced around to her horror, there were swords and spears littering the ground. No dead human or domesticated animal in sight. Her stomach churned at this sight. Shadows began to appear in the fog. Clara grew frightened. She knelt down and didn't move. As the shadows began to come into the light, they were revealed to be wolves that survived a massacre. A dark brown wolf, no doubt the alpha, growled at the little wolf pup with fury.

"Run!" Clara's scream echoed. However, the pup didn't listen. The menace in the alpha's eyes only made her more afraid than ever. Without thinking, she ran over to the pup. "Run! Run! They're dangerous!" The terrified wolf pup did as she said. As it turned around, Clara saw the familiar heterochromatic eyes. It was Onyx.

Young Onyx ran away from them as fast as he could. The tiny paws trying to outrun the long legs of the adults. He couldn't get far. Then, to Clara's horror, the alpha grabbed him by his neck. The pup cried as he was clamped between the two fierce jaws of a monster. Onyx gave one mournful howl.

"No!" Clara couldn't bear to watch this anymore. The image of her own dead parents swam in her head. She reached out. To her surprise, her hand touched soft fur. Clara opened her eyes and soon realized that she was resting her head on Onyx. The wolf's whimpers escaped his muzzle. Clara jolted upright only to find her back against Lotus'. *What is it with me and animals?*

Onyx let out another painful whimper. His body shivered violently. Clara gulped. Her hand hesitantly hover over the wolf's neck. Her entire arm vibrated. Once her fingers lightly touched the soft black fur, a violet eye snapped open. Clara snatched her hand away as Onyx raised his head. "Please don't eat me."

Soft peeps were heard next to her. Clara turned her head to see Twitch resting in her nest. A soft white blanket wrapped around the Harpy. The frail form was in an upright position. Head raised upward as if she could see the sky. Eyes closed.

Clara rubbed her neck. *Is this how all Harpies sleep? Must be painful.* She felt something nudge her shoulder. She turned to Lotus. The unicorn's pelt turned golden in the pale sunlight. Lotus tilted her head in curiosity. Clara simply got up and went over to the entrance of the hut.

The early dawn gave the forest a soft touch. The leaves slowly turned from dark green to a nice shade of peridot. Trees and soil turned from a dull brown to gold. Faint sounds of songbirds fluttering in the treetops could be heard. Their songs of the morning drifted in the wind. Chittering of squirrels echoed to the morning melody.

Clara found it strange. Stories of the dark woods filled with Harpies that would tear humans to pieces and adorn their nest with skeletons began to die in her mind. Their wings and claws made her nervous. However, questions had begun to swirl in her head. A Harpies life. Their beliefs and sorrows. Did they have songs to play?

A yawn interrupted her thoughts. Clara turned to see Twitch wake up from her sleep. Twitch was wearing a simple white shirt and pants. A big grin was on her face. Her voice took on a sing song voice as she spoke, "Goood Morning! Feeling any better?"

Clara was silent for a moment. Her eyes turned back to the sunlit forest. One question left her mouth. "Twitch... Why are you being nice to me? Shard said that humans did awful things. However, you and the elder have been nothing but nice to me? Why?"

Silence filled the air. Fluttering noises filled Clara's ears until claws hit the platform beside her. "Well... Because I never really met a human before." She gave a sheepish grin as Clara gave a wide-eyed glance at her. "I've only heard stories about you guys... not very good ones."

Clara's throat tightened. "Like what?"

Twitch's mouth formed a thin line. "Well... That you guys would cut our wings off and take them as trophies. Sometimes our talons."

Clara's mind went back to the markets. Some of those stands had large feathers that were made into fans. Talons arranged into necklaces. They were far too expensive for her family, but they did look a little pretty. Now that she thought about it, Clara's stomach threatened to drop to the floor. "O-Oh... I'm sorry to hear that."

"I wasn't sure what to think. As horrible as it sounds, I wanted to meet a human so I would know what they're really like."

"Aren't you worried about what others might think of you for what you say about the enemy?"

Twitch shrugged. "My parents passed away when I was an egg... So... I'm kinda an outcast myself." She looked at Clara. "Do all humans have your kind of hair color?"

Clara rubbed her hair. She shivered in the area that was cut. "No... I'm the only one that has it." She pointed to her marking. "And this... No one likes it."

"What?" Twitch laughed. "That's crazy! It just makes you even more adorable! I'm surprised no man has swoon over you. Most of the females and males here would practically want to have a color like that."

"R-really?"

Twitch nodded. "White is considered a mystical color around here." A soft breeze whistled through the trees. Twitch hummed and raised her wings. "You know... our people believed that the winds carry us to our destinies. The melodies that are carried through them connect us to the entire world."

Clara stared in amazement. A winged creature of massive power having a belief. *I wonder if all the other civilizations have that capability*, she thought. Suddenly, she heard her stomach growl. Her cheeks flushed. Hands on her stomach.

Twitch gave a grin. "Breakfast time! Hurry! Eat something before that grumpy Shard comes to you!"

"What?"

"Don't worry. Tornado will be with him. Right now, get some strength to handle your magic."

"Um... What about Ony—" Clara soon realized that the black wolf was nowhere to be seen. Then, she saw a shadow jumping from one tree branch to another. She felt Twitch lightly pushing her back into her hut. Her connection to Onyx faded to a brief hum. However, her mind couldn't help but think back to what she had just witnessed. Clara soon sat down and began to eat her fill as she was bombarded by questions.

Clara finished her cup of water along with the sweet wildflower nectar that Twitch offered her. Then, she heard wingbeats coming closer. Her heart began to jump at an uneasy pace. Clara hesitantly got up from her chair. Legs taking on a stiff gait as she went to the entrance. Her hands weaved together.

Tornado and Shard stood on the platform. Shard looked tired and annoyed. His eyes were trying to hide how tired he was. Tornado stood tall and regal. "Good morning, Clara." Tornado's voice was smooth. "How are you feeling this morning?"

"Uh..." Clara cleared her throat. "Aside from being terrified of working with an ancient dragon that'll kill me,

I'm doing great!" She tried to give a smile, but it came out crooked. Clara frowned as Shard simply laughed at her.

"How pathetic! She's so scared that she can't even have a proper smile!" Shard laughed again. Claws soon entered his shoulder. The Hawk Harpy grimaced.

"Have you learned nothing, you dense fool?" Tornado released his grip. He sighed. Being so close together, Clara could now see that Tornado tower over Shard. "Only seventeen but still childish."

Clara turned to Twitch. "Uh... How old are you?"

Twitch grinned, "Seventeen too!"

"Come on, Clara." Tornado turned his attention to Clara. "Let's get you ready with Gaia."

"What about Lotus?"

"That's where me and Twitch come in," Shard grumbled.

Clara glanced between Lotus, Twitch and Shard. Twitch and Shard are a bit bigger than her. However, the claws were a different story. A wave of apprehension shimmered down her spine. No doubt from Lotus. "W-will Lotus be okay?"

"Calm down, human," Shard answered before Tornado could answer. "Your... unicorn will be fine. I've carried heavy things plus, Twitch, is only used to keep her from stabbing me with her horn."

"That's because you're too rough!" Twitch's feathers flared up. A warning hiss escaped her throat. "You'll never find a mate with that attitude!" The two growled for a moment.

"Stop it," Tornado commanded. His voice threatened to shake the leaves off the branches. "Help Lotus down now, while I take Clara." He turned his back to Clara and lowered himself. He waited until Clara was able to wrap her arms around his neck. He spread his wings out wide. He jumped off and began to glide.

Clara clung on for dear life. The world didn't spin around her like last time, but the pull of the ground made her feel a little nervous. She took a deep breath. The wind was nothing more than a gentle breeze. She looked over the nests and huts that hung along the trees. Several younger Harpies fluttered around to try to get their wings working. Flowers decorated some of the roofs. Several birds were perched on the branches.

"Do you bond with birds," she asked. "I just noticed you have a lot of them around you."

"No," Tornado answered, "not in the way that you do." He banked right. His tail feathers flared out slightly. Then, he soon arrived at a grove where Gaia was waiting. The green dragon curled up in contentment. Onyx licking the bone of an unknown animal. Tornado lowered down once again as Clara slid off.

Good morning, Clara. Gaia gave off a strange rumbling noise. She turned her head to Clara. Her green eyes focused on the small human form. *I see you're starting to get a better understanding of Onyx.*

"Understanding?" Clara looked at Onyx. The wolf looked away from her. Ears pinned back to his head. "You mean... some of the images I saw in my dream?" She began to go over the details of what she saw. She could feel a strong sense of intent from Lotus. By the time she reached the end of it, Onyx gave a low growl and stormed off. Clara only stood in place.

Don't force yourself, Gaia spoke. *He'll come back eventually. He can't ignore you forever.* She clawed the nearest tree. The bark breaking and cracking away. It even forced several birds to fly out of their hiding place. She set the bark down in front of Clara. *Now, you're more familiar with earth magic since you're able to see their soul threads first. So we'll start with that.*

"Soul threads? Is-is that what they're called?" Clara was thinking back to the story Rue told her. "Oh, right! Since it was considered within the belief of how life is formed—"

Yes. You've also seen the dangers of what happens when you're handling more fragile soul threads. She gave a brief image of Shard screaming.

Clara looked away. Her cheeks flushed. "I didn't mean for that to happen."

I know, but it doesn't change the fact that you must be more careful now that you have two creatures in this bond. Gaia placed a claw on the stripped tree. *For now, focus on healing this tree. It's a simple tactic along with growing seeds.*

Clara stared at the stripped bark. It looked naked and painful. Clara gently placed a hand on the tree. She shut her eyes and tried to concentrate. She tried to feel for any threads or a ripple, but there was nothing. Not even a hint of green in her vision. Clara opened her eyes again. Clara turned to the dragon. Her lungs tightened. "I-I'm so-sorry... I can only do this when I'm scared..."

Hot breath touched her back. Gaia's head hovered over her in mere inches. Clara shivered. Her whimper betrayed her. Fingers curled into the wood. For some reason, she was able to feel the dragon going through her head. *Why are you afraid of dragons?*

Clara was silent for a moment. Her eyes refused to move to her "teacher". Her lips formed into a thin line. "One time... a dragon came to my parent's house. An ice dragon. It was on the day I was born. For some reason, it kept me alive..." she touched her chest. "For now at least. A few villagers said that the dragon cursed me. M-my mother said it wasn't true. But..." tears began to run down her face. "I can't help the feeling that one of the other dragons might eat me because I'm not one of them."

Suddenly, her vision changed. Green threads of all shades appeared before her. She touched the nearest one and pulled. A sliver of bark moved up an inch. Clara shivered at the sensation. She repeated the process, her body slowly falling apart. Another power crawled into her. The silver ribbon on her wrist soon appeared. It weaved into the green. The bark soon grew back faster making the wound non-existent.

A soft muzzle pressed against her back. Clara found herself wobbling. She slunk down. Her forehead against the bark. She let out a soft sigh. Once some of her strength returned, Clara got up onto her feet. Her vision returned to its normal setting. She slowly got up. Her foot slipped. She fell but was caught by Lotus. Her frail arms wrapped around the unicorn's neck.

Nicely done. Gaia let out a low thrumming noise. *Normally, I've seen humans around your age passing out from doing one of these tricks. Barely could form a proper ring.* She looked at the tree. *Not even a hint of a scar.*

Clara looked up stunned. *Did... she just compliment me?* "Uh... Thanks." Her arms never let go of Lotus. The warmth comforting her and slowly giving her strength back.

The only thing that you should work on is how to activate your powers without being triggered by your emotions. It makes you more dangerous. The world is far more fragile than your kind will ever know.

"How do you know so much?"

Gaia turned to the sky. *Humans used to come here to train their young ones. I would see it from time to time. However, dragons and the beasts that reside out of your human culture have a better understanding of magic than any human would obtain in their lifetime.*

"Why's that?"

Because the gods and goddesses of the world had created us with their elemental threads.

"But... the god of night was the one to create all the wild beasts here!"

Gaia shifted her glance to Clara. A spark of rage in her eyes. The human shrunk away in fear. *Did your parents and caretaker tell you that? Along with the ridiculous notion that my kind would do that?* She huffed when Clara nodded. *Oh child... You have so much to learn about this world and the kingdoms that reside here.*

Chapter 8
Want to Ride a Wild Beast?

Clara sat on a tree root. Her strength slowly returned. Her mind went back to Gaia's words. She watched a few squirrels in the trees jumping from one branch to another. Birds chirped above her. Even a faint cry of an elk caught her attention. She looked at Lotus. Her unicorn nibbled at the grass. Her cheeks burned with shame at what she said. Lotus had far too much light in her to be associated with the god of night. *I wonder if Onyx was made by the god of fire?*

Faint sounds were heard on the bark. Clara looked up to see Onyx staring at her. His mouth was clean of the blood he had on his muzzle earlier. He sat down. Ears upward. Ripples of annoyance filled him.

Clara tried to give her best smile but her mouth was frozen in a grimace. "H-hi! My name's Clara... Diiid my magic bother you?" She was only met by a stern look and an unamused sensation in her spine. She cleared her throat. "I'm sorry... If I may have looked into a scary memory..." She hugged her knee. "I lost my parents too. When I was only six..." Tears stung her eyes. Memories of fire and pain roared in her mind.

She shivered at recalling the one thing that scared her the most. A lumbering Minotaur with blood red fur. Eyes the color of molten lava staring down at her. In its hand was an axe that was stained with blood. It let out a loud bellow before disappearing into a veil of smoke. Clara let out a soft sob and buried her face in her knee.

Onyx stared at her for a little while longer. Then, he laid down and crawled. He inched closer until he was able to put his snout on her arm. As Clara glanced up at him, he gave a soft whine. A brief image of Clara's dead parents alongside the dead wolf that was no doubt his mother went into Clara's head.

Clara felt something tickling her. It felt awkward. Awkward but gentle. Looking at his eyes, it reminded her of her father's Bloodhound when he tried to comfort her. *He's trying to make me feel better...* Clara tried to move her hand but it refused. She simply sighed. "Well... I guess I should get back with my lessons with Gaia before I have to eat again."

She slid down from her spot. Onyx jumped down after her. She only took a few steps before wingbeats were heard. To her shock, Gaia landed before her. In her jaws were an array of apples, herbs and pears. They were set down in front of her. "Is this... for me?"

Gaia nodded. *You may have rested but your strength still needs time to return.* She tilted her head. *Better yet, it would be best if you return to the harpies with your current form of magic.* She lowered her head to Clara's level. *You see, the Wild Shepherdess has the power of all the elemental gods, including light and darkness. It's part of the balance that forms our world.*

"But humans can only do one form of magic," Clara protested, "that's why we have only one partner to bond to." She looked at her beasts. "I don't know why I bonded to two. I feel like I can barely sense them. Maybe vice versa…" Suddenly, she felt something pull at her dress. Clara shrieked as she was being picked up again.

Her feet dangled in the air. Her arms swinging wildly. "P-put me doooown!" Then, she was dropped onto Lotus' back. She froze. Even Lotus let out a startled whinny. Hooves stamped on the ground. "W-what are you doing?"

I think the only way you'll ever get better at magic is to have a better connection with Onyx and Lotus. Explore this region and learn more about these two and the Harpy Kingdom.

Clara gulped. "I… I'm not really good at talking. Plus… Shard really hates me. I can't imagine what the other Harpies are like." She bowed her head. "I've only gotten lucky so far."

Just try your luck further out. You might find you have more in common than you realize. Gaia flared her wings out. She was in the air in a matter of minutes. Leaving Clara alone with her beasts.

Clara was stunned. She and Lotus looked at each other. Her heart hammered hard. Her fingers immediately curled around Lotus mane. Clara could feel every inch of her wanting to get off, but her legs refused to move. She tried to take a deep breath but the air was stuck in her lungs. Her limbs were shaking.

"C-come on, Clara," she said to herself, "t-try to remember what Rue told you... If bonded to a horse, you need to be firm." Clara cleared her throat. She tried to straighten her back. However, a strange vertigo rushed into her. She went back to her crouching position. "It's hopeless! How can I fix this if I can't stop feeling scared?"

Sobs wracked her body. She shut her eyes. Fingers curled in. Suddenly, her cheeks were nudged by Lotus. Clara opened them. A wave of reassurance wrapped around her. Clara sniffed, wiping her tears along her sleeve. "C-can you try going forward? M-maybe it would allow me to be scared enough to get off."

Lotus stared at her for a moment. Then, she began to put one hoof in front of the other. A slow gait that matched with the quiet rhythm of the forest. It was a simple circle with each step. Onyx was soon at their side. The wolf gave a reluctant huff as they continued to circle for a bit.

Clara still felt stiff with each rocking motion. However, her heart didn't thunder hard as much. "Okay... Let's try walking around for a bit. I'm sure it's getting a little boring for you to go in circles."

Lotus was still for a moment. She looked back at Clara. Her body was a little stiff as Clara's. Her neck muscles taut. Ears threatened to pin back. Then, she laid herself down. A ripple of acknowledgement sent between them. It was soon followed by a spark of encouragement.

Clara slowly slid off. Her feet were trying to get their bearings. She stumbled and fell on her knees. She was soon able to get back up. She took an apple and bit into it. The hard, green surface crunched under her teeth. She flinched at the sour taste. "What kind of apple is this?"

Onyx wagged his tail. A simple woof followed by a wide smile. Ripples of laughter going down their connection. Then, it died immediately the moment Clara glanced at him.

Clara blinked. *Onyx... was laughing?* She continued to eat her fill. Finally, she got up just as Shard and Twitch flew above their heads. Her heart sank at the sight of the angry Hawk Harpy. His scowl made her stomach churn, threatening to force her food out of her. "Um... Did Gaia send you?"

Shard hissed. "You wish. We were asked by our elder to see what you were doing. You were gone for so long, I thought the beasts of this forest would finally eat you." He folded his wings. "Personally, I think we need a proper monarch. Not this nonsense." He was earned a heavy smack in the face by Twitch's wing.

Twitch turned her attention to Clara. "I wanted to see if you got better with your magic. Did you succeed?"

Clara was silent. Her eyes stared at the ground. Hands folded. Lips tucked inside with teeth bit the skin deep inside.

"Oh... Clara." Twitch sighed. She hopped to Clara and hugged her. "I'm so sorry." She backed away to let her friend have breathing room.

Clara wiped her eyes. "Um… I have to ride Lotus to help me with my magic." Her cheeks went red. "The thing is…" she gulped. "I'm deeply afraid of animals!"

Shard barked out a laugh. "You! A human who's scared of animals?" His teeth flashed in a bright grin. That's rich!" His grin grew menacing by the minute. He dodged as Lotus charged at him with her horn. Even a growl from Onyx put him at an unease. Twitch's glare ready to melt him on the spot. "Okay… I seem to be outnumbered."

"As you should be!" Twitch hissed. "I don't care what the others think. Plus we're better off without a queen anyway! The last ones were nothing but cruel. No wonder they hated us."

"Queen?" Clara glanced up at Twitch. "Y-you have monarchs?"

"Used to," Twitch corrected. "We used to have queens that are through birthright. However, the last queen was mad beyond belief. She led Harpies on a suicidal mission against the human king of your land. Cost both Human and Harpy lives." Twitch's mouth went into a deeper frown. "Since then, I don't feel the least bit sorry about not having a queen."

"Our elder is getting old," Shard argued. "It's only a matter of time before she dies."

Twitch's feathers ruffled in fury. She took a deep breath. As the green feathers settled on her body, she turned to Clara. "Let's try riding on Lotus. How about the unicorn grove. That might help you two to get comfortable."

Clara sighed. She looked at Lotus. "D-do want to try again?" Her heart thundered hard. She soon retreated to her own thoughts. The tree bark growth was a great success, but she needed to find a way to control her abilities without getting herself or anyone else killed. The last human who was unable to control their magic was incinerated because they failed to connect with their beats. However, Lotus made her stiff.

Lotus gave a soft nicker. Her soft muzzle nudged Clara's arm. Waves of reassurance crept in. She laid back down. Her head arched. She looked like a regal steed belonging to the Royal Knights. Her eyes focused on Clara.

Clara gulped hard. Her hands were shaking hard. Her feet shuffled. "Oh-okay. Let's try again. It's time to fix the magic!" She slowly got one Lotus' back with ease. Her heart thundered hard in her chest. Eyes focused on the horn. The moment she sat on Lotus' back, Clara clung the white mane. A brief click escaped her mouth. Something that she remembered seeing when the other villagers were riding their horses.

Lotus moved forward. Each gait was stiff. Her nostrils flared as she heard Shard laugh. Her hooves stamped hard into the earth. Ears pinned back once again. Muscles rippled.

Then Clara felt it. A strong wave of determination rushed over her. It didn't remove her fears completely but it was enough to get her limbs to stop shaking. The ache of her stomach began to go away. Her once pale face started to have more color. She held onto the mane tightly. She leaned forward. "T-trot…"

Lotus soon began to increase the speed in her steps. Her legs lifted higher. It was almost as if they were ready to leave the ground. She led the way with Onyx beside her. Plants began to move slightly. The ground leaves different prints going from one at a time to a foot at a time.

Clara could feel her breath even out. A strange sense of calm rushed over her. Then, she saw a few deer at the ravine. The horned grazers were having their grass. Her body began to become less rigid. Muscles unbinding themselves. "Um… C-can we go see the… whatever the Harpies do when they're not flying around?"

"You mean patrolling?" Shard gave a hard grimace.

"Sure!" Twitch began humming an excited tune. "Come on, Lotus! Let's give Clara a ride to the arena." She only fluttered a few feet when Shard stopped her.

"Are you out of your mind?" His head feathers flared out. "Do you have any idea of the trouble she might cause there?"

Twitch glared back. "I'd rather help Clara with her magic than having to put up with your attitude." She flapped her wings hard. A tornado soon appeared, causing Shard to be flung into the air. Once Shard crashed into a bush, she turned to Clara. Her grin returned to her face. "Follow me!"

Clara briefly looked at Lotus and Onyx. Small waves of confusion were felt. They continued on their gait. The trot was taking them a while to get where they were going. Impatient, Lotus put on a full gallop. Her mane flew out in the wind. Clara instinctively held on for dear life. Screams filled the air.

"Lotus!" Clara found her spine vibrating up and down. "Slow down. Slow—" She ducked as a tree branch was about to hit her. She tried to find the link once again. However, they soon reached a river. Twitch was on the other side. Twitch only waved them over. Clara tried to squeeze the stomach and tried to yank Lotus' mane, but to no avail.

Lotus jumped over the river with ease. Onyx close behind her. As they did, time began to slow. The river gleamed brightly in the sunlight. The wind seemed to lift them high over the current.

Clara felt her body having to be thrown back. Arms flung out wide. A rush of wind covered her. Once they reached the ground, Clara managed to snatch a handful of mane before she fell off. She regained her balance as Lotus continued to gallop. For a moment, she was stunned. Her cheeks were flustered. Amber eyes wide. Then, a smile came to her face. Laughter escaped her throat.

Lotus let out a neigh. She jumped over a log, earning a loud whoop. Lotus began to pick up the pace. A ripple of happiness started to link between them. Twitch was only a few feet above Clara.

"Good job, you two!" Twitch chimed. Her smile was wider than it was ever before. Her wings weaved the air currents with ease. She turned around. "We're almost there."

Clara soon noticed a strange arena before them. It had four large pine trees looming out. Branches twined together like braids. Distant voices were heard. Faint shapes were made with what looked like a few Harpies carrying an orb. Her fingers dug into Lotus' pelt. She tried to even her breathing as Lotus slowed her pace to a small canter.

Twitch landed with ease. She looked at Clara. "Clara! Try some magic now. Any connection to Lotus or Onyx?"

Clara looked at her hands. They weren't shaking. The last time she's been on an equine was when she was four. Rue tried to place her on a horse. Clara wailed for some time until her parents had her get off. "Well… I felt excited for a moment. Like me and Lotus were enjoying the jump. Her heart was my heart." Her eyes began to glow a faint green hue. Shades of green surrounded her once again.

Clara slid off Lotus' back and knelt down. She put a hand on the ground. A light that resembled an emerald was beneath the woven material. *A seed?* Her hand began to sink deeper into the thick layers of brown and green. Fingers locked on, she felt her will on the seed thrust into it. *Grow.*

Without warning, the seed began to expand. The ground shook beneath her. Clara tumbled back a few feet as the stem of a young tree shot out of the ground. She watched in shock as the tree grew larger and larger. The brittle green skin turned into a dark brown color. Dark green needles shot out. Soon, it was as tall as the trees that were at the arena.

"Woah!" Twitch exclaimed. "I've never seen a human pull of that sort of magic before." She shivered when a strange tune played in the air. A sweet melody that belonged to a man. An ethereal that seemed to hide in the trees.

Clara heard the song as well. Her eyes laid on the trees. The threads faded and only a strange man stood before her. Light green skin with amber eyes like his. A placid smile graced his lips. Clara reached up to her, but the man vanished without a trace.

Flapping soon replaced it. The Harpies that were playing earlier soon arrived at the scene. One of them was the Woodpecker Harpy from yesterday. His dark eyes flashed upon recognizing her. "It's you! The human girl from before!"

Clara got up. "Did anyone hear any singing?" She could feel Lotus and Onyx confirming what she had just seen. "O-or the Earth God?"

A Sparrow Harpy glanced at his teammate, a Cardinal Harpy. "Did… She hit her head or something?" His answer was met with a shrug.

Shard flew over them at breakneck speed. "Why in the world would the Earth God sing?" He landed with grace. Muscles rippled along his arms. "The gods haven't sung since the great war between the monarchs." He then took notice of the tree. He crossed his wings. "So, the little human finally learned magic after all?"

Twitch growled. "Her name is Clara!" She marched toward him. Feathers raised. Muscles taut. "I know you can't stand humans, but grow up! Our survival depends on it!"

Shard glared back at her. "You have no say in this Clutchless!" He was about to shove her when the Woodpecker Harpy stepped in.

"How about we cool our heads with a game of Snatch?" A heavy silence filled the air. The Woodpecker feathers ruffled slightly.

Clara tilted her head. "Snatch? What's that?"

The Cardinal Harpy was the first to reply. "It's an age-old Harpy game we play." He leaned forward. "First time I've ever met a human who would inquire about the game. After all, you guys consider our behavior savage."

Clara fiddled with her fingers. "Um... I-I just saw your flying and it looked like you were trying to catch something. I wasn't told any of that." She bowed. "Please forgive me. I didn't mean to be rude."

The Cardinal Harpy simply grinned. "This is a first. Many humans would insult us and never apologize. Never had I met a human this humble." He turned to the others. "All right everyone! Let's show this human-excuse me! Clara how Snatch works." He gazed at Twitch and Shard. "You two pair up!"

Twitch and Shard stared at each other. Then, they looked at the Cardinal Harpy. It only earned a laugh.

"Are you out of your mind, Happy," Shard protested. He glared at the red harpy.

"Oh, come on," Happy replied. His body relaxed. No ounce of fear was found in his voice. "I personally want to see the best Snatch players again. You two make an awesome team. If not, I could make Twitch my—"

"Challenge accepted!" Twitch burst out the words before Happy could finish the sentence.

Clara stared in amazement. Onyx huffed and sat down. Lotus nickered, ripples of laughter coming out of her mind. Clara watched the Harpies gather into two teams. Shard and Twitch already set up with the Woodpecker Harpy, who goes by the name Elm. Happy and his Sparrow Harpy friend were joined by a young Barn Owl Harpy.

"Okay, everyone," Happy said, "you know the rules." He rolled a strange looking leather ball in the middle of the court. It had a strange resemblance to a large mouse. "The main goal is to get the 'mouse' in the opponent's 'nest'." He pointed to what look colored sticks nestled in the branches of the large trees. "You can steal the ball, but you can't draw blood or severely injure those that you're stealing from."

Clara raised her eyebrows. She's never heard a rule that sounded so civilized. The words that the villagers and Rue used back home echoed in her mind. Savage. Uncouth. Mindless. Each of those words slowly broke away one by one. They didn't even sound the least bit like the Harpies she sees before her. She leaned forward.

"Also," Twitch added, "we have a special scoreboard that was enchanted to take our goals." She pointed to a large stone slab that hung over the arena by a thick set of vines. A flash of pale green danced around the board. Two symbols were drawn into it. One resembled a wing with jagged edges and the second had a pair of wings with a happy face on it. "Whoever scores the most points wins!"

Shard groaned. "You always get way too excited for these games."

Twitch glanced at him. "Yet you want me to be on your team every time." She tilted her head. "What's wrong, mighty Shard? Afraid I'll kick your tail feathers like we used to do as kids?"

Shard's face went beet red as everyone laughed. "J-just start the game already!"

The Harpies lined up. Wings flared out. Body lowered. "Ready!" A long pause hung in the air. Eyes focused on the opponent. "Fly!" In a flash of feathers, the Harpies took to the skies. The ball was lifted up by a small tornado made by the Sparrow Harpy. However, Twitch snatched the ball before he could get his talons on it.

Her wings let out their usual hum. She dove and cartwheeled with ease. Her stops even held much grace. She tossed her ball over to Shard. Her smile never left her face as she watched Shard perform sharp turns before dunking the ball into the nest.

Clara watched with amazement as the Harpies swooped and dived. A few of them almost crashed into the ground. Colors flashed around. Feathers flared out. The score was a tie between Twitch's team and Happy's. Suddenly, just as Twitch made for the last goal, a large gust of wind from the Barn Owl Harpy knocked her back and made her crash into a tree.

"Hold!" Happy shouted. He glared at the Barn Owl Harpy. "How many times do I have to tell you not to use that much wind magic?" He flew over to Twitch but Shard was much quicker.

Shard had his back facing her. His wings spread out as she dropped onto him. "Are you all right?" A soft tone was taken in his voice.

Twitch shook herself. "I'm fine. Not the first time I got hit by wind magic gone amok." Then, as they got closer to the ground, Clara saw a strange gleam in those green eyes. "You know... One good thing about this game... Is this." She kissed Shard on the lips.

Clara stared in shock. *W-wait a moment! Didn't they just hate each other earlier?* Suddenly, she heard Onyx growl. An unsteady wave of emotion crept over her. She looked at the black wolf. His hackles were raised. Lips drawn back so tight that his teeth were showing. Ears pinned back. Even Lotus let out a harsh neigh. Hooves pawing at the ground. Clara followed their direction of where they were staring at. She gaped in horror. "Shard! Twitch!"

The two Harpies turned their attention to the sky. A faint sheen of smoke surrounded them. A grayish black hue blinding them. Smells of burning wood hung in the air. Everyone coughed slightly. Clara froze. She clutched her arms, fingernails driving into her dress and skin. Memories of screams and blood wracked her mind.

"No…" she whimpered. "M-Minotaurs…" She shut her eyes. Hands to her head. "No. No. No. No." Clara crouched down, her body rocking back and forth.

Chapter 9
Minotaur Fires

Shard let out a hawk-like cry. "Everyone! To the village!" He looked at Twitch. "Can you fly now?" The moment Twitch nodded, he tilted and allowed her to fly off. He unleashed several bursts of wind. "Be careful! We don't need any flames growing higher than they need to be." He led the way.

Clara was still crouched down. Whimpers left her lips. Arms tucked in. Memories of what happened to her ten years ago filled her mind. The once sunny sky turned into night. Fire scared the horizon. Lumbering shapes moved forward like living boulders. Screams of maids and children filled the air. Blades splintered about. Her parents were lying dead on the ground. Tears stung her eyes. Her body refused to move.

Something tugged at her sleeve hard. Clara looked up to see Onyx pulling. His teeth sunk into the white cloth. Clara shrieked and frantically tried pushing Onyx away. Her hands frantically slapped his muzzle. "Let go," she screamed. "Let go!" With one hard shove, she was able to break free from Onyx's grasp. Her sleeve ripped in the process.

She sat there. Her breathing began to intensify. Her vision began to turn murky. Clara got up to her feet quickly and began to run. She didn't know where she was running but she didn't care. All she knew is that she wasn't safe among the Harpies any more. She could imagine the fearsome bovine heads arched. Wicked horns curled upward to the sky. Bellows were soon heard as she made her way to a sloped path. Pebbles skittered across the ground.

Clara looked over to her left and saw several shapes. Three pale blue shapes and five bright red shapes. "My magic…" The whimpering grew louder from the blue forms. One of them was kneeling.

"Please! Please spare us!" A female voice broke through the noise. It was fragile and pleading. A baby's wail soon followed.

Clara's heart froze. *There's a family here*, she thought. Her fingers dug into the ground. Her mouth went dry. She shivered as a heavy snort reached her ears.

"Why should we spare the likes of you?" A gruff voice asked. It sounded like boulders rumbling down a mountain. "We have orders to find the Wild Shepherdess. At any cost." One of the larger red shapes lifted something.

Clara's fingers dug deeper into the ground. She could feel all the plants around her. The fear of the Minotaurs roaring in her mind. They were masters of blacksmithing. Weapons large enough to cut humans into. Servants to the heartless Dark Elves. Then, she saw the shape raise it high in the air.

"Where's the Shepherdess?"

"We don't know!" Another voice blurted. "We only heard that she was in our village, but we don't know what she looks like."

"Then it just gives you more misfortune," the gruff voice said. The red shape sung his weapon.

"No!" Clara dug into the threads. Her anxiety mixed with determination. She grabbed a handful and pulled the ones that were beneath the Minotaurs. The earth moved like an ocean wave. It knocked the attackers down. Clara got up from her hiding place. "Run! Run now!" Without thinking, Clara got onto Lotus. She held on as Lotus began to run at full speed. She took a quick look over her shoulder to see Harpies flying away as the threads began to fade once again.

Onyx was close behind. Muscles rippled with every movement. He let out a loud howl. The sound echoed along the trees. Birds, rabbits, foxes and deer ran out of the brush. Several Harpies could also be seen flying out. Their shadows were like large birds. Onyx ran faster until he was at Lotus' side. Suddenly, he veered away.

"Onyx?" Clara tried to look around for signs of a black pelt. Nothing. Suddenly, there was a jolt that hit her line of connection. A massive figure was at her right. She instinctively pulled Lotus' mane. A gleam of steel made her duck. Her heart skipped a beat as a Minotaur rose up and bellowed. Onyx clinging to the monster's back.

Clara froze in fear. She forced Lotus to turn around just as the Minotaur grabbed Onyx. Clara gaped. *Lotus!*

Her fear and words vibrated over their connection. *Do you have any power to use?* As if to answer her question, a flash of light erupted around them. The Minotaur roared again and dropped Onyx. "Let's go! Hurry!"

Clara didn't know where to hide or find a place to evaluate the situation. All she knew is that she wasn't safe. Right now, she had to let Lotus guide her to a safe place. Her eyes were focused on the road. Suddenly, a wall of fire blazed out before them. Clara shrieked and fell backward. As her head hit the ground her vision swam. Black dots jittered around until her vision cleared again. Clara froze.

Looming above her was another Minotaur. This was different though. It was dark brown with a white crescent moon on his forehead. In his hand was a large halberd. The metal gleamed in the light by the fire. Clad in thick armor that spread from his chest to his hooves. His lavender eyes focused on Clara. He sniffed the air. A steam billowed out of his nose. "So, you're the dragon blessed."

Clara clenched her fists. Eyes wide with terror. "Y-you! You're the one w-who killed my mother!" A flash of blood came into her mind. Tiny hands opening the door to her mother dead on the ground. The Minotaur loomed over the lifeless body. Her breathing intensified. Something inside of her burned. Not fear or hesitation. Hatred. "Go away!"

In an instant, Onyx was at her side. His black fur glowed with an orange tint. Clara could see the fire in him. It was matched to a fury of his own. Cautiously, she reached out to touch him. She stared in wonder as the soft fur laced against her fingers. She wasn't met with hostility. Right now, they could feel their own pain and loss ripple between each other. Onyx briefly looked at her with molten orbs.

"Impossible…" The Minotaur took a step. A burst of flame appeared before him. A ball of blazing gold. His eyes widened in shock. "A fire in your soul? How can that be?"

"Get out of here!" Clara's voice started to become raw. The marking on her back glowed. "I don't want to hurt anyone, but I will use my magic if I have to!" Her body felt contorted. The invisible strings of the earth and fire tied around her body. Two enormous beings were at her side in an instant. One of them she recognized from earlier. "You took my mother away. I won't let you take the Harpies as well." She pulled on the strings around her left arm.

Chunks of earth began to move, creating several pitfalls. Bellows could be heard from a distance. The earth churned again, smothering the flames that were causing smoke. Smaller flames shot out in front of the Minotaur.

The Minotaur growled. He summoned his own wall of fire. "Be careful you fool! You might burn the things you're trying to protect. You might extinguish your own life."

"Why do you care? You never gave my mother or the other humans you have killed any warning. You butchered anyone you wish. Your kind is just as heartless as the Dark

Elves." With a wave of her hand, she created another fireball.

The Minotaur lowered his head. In a matter of minutes, he charged. His horns missed Clara, but they scooped her and Onyx up. He tossed them into the air. They crashed down.

Clara gasped. She felt like a puppet with all the strings cut from her body. Needles of pain radiates down her body. The mysterious figures that were at her side vanished into thin air. Her limbs were unable to move. She could hear Onyx whimper in pain. "Onyx... I'm sorry..." Every word she spoke gave pain to her lungs. The Minotaur loomed over her. Clara wasn't sure if she was seeing things, but his gaze held some form of regret as well as recognition.

"I remember your mother well... she loved you very much." He reached out toward her. "Time to end this foolishness." A blur of feathers came into his vision as Twitch and Shard attacked him. Claws raked his back. He let out a loud bellow and backed away. A sharp pain entered his lower back. He turned to see an angry Lotus, her horn embedded in his thick armor. He tried to push, but the unicorn backed away. Trickles of blood seeped out of his armor.

"You've got a lot of nerve to come into our territory, Promoths," Shard hissed.

Twitch leaned over Clara. Lotus at their side. "Clara? Are you all right? Can you hear me?" She gently placed her hands on Clara's limbs. She grimaced. "Your bones are broken..." She reached into her pocket and pulled out an unusual dust of a pinkish green. "Don't worry. This'll help with the pain. I'm sorry we left you alone."

"N-not your fault..." Clara wheezed. "Wanted... justice for family." The powder was soon blown into her face. The world began to grow dark around her. She gave one more try to reach for Onyx. The wolf's mind was as foggy as hers.

Chapter 10
A Small Moment

Clara found herself in a strange world. It was warm and sticky. The humidity clung to her hair. The trees were also different, branches covered in thick green ropes. Harpies of more brighter color fluttered in the treetops. She walked further into the trees. Smells of strange spices hung in the air. Mud squelched underneath her feet. Suddenly, Clara spotted something move in the underbrush. "Hello?"

Before she could do anything, Clara found herself laying in a bed of leaves. She tried to get up, but her body screamed for her to stay down. A moan escaped her lips. Memories of what happened earlier came flooding back. "Onyx? Lotus?" She used her mind to reach them. The link was met with two responses. The one from Lotus was a little far away but she could sense relief ripple away. Onyx's response was a faint growl met with a huff.

Clara turned her head. Onyx was by her side. His legs and side were bandaged, but it didn't seem like he wasn't severely injured. "Onyx... How are you feeling?"

A moan reached her. He moved his head. Eyes focused on Clara. Ears flicked forward.

Clara sighed. "I'm sorry... I was being stupid... and useless..." Tears stun her eyes. "Just like I've always been."

"Crazy maybe, but not useless."

Clara gasped as Twitch loomed over her. Her cheeks burned. "H-how long was I out?"

"A few hours." Twitch pulled out a vial and uncorked a cap. She pressed it against Clara's lips. "You should consider yourself lucky Promoths missed. Being struck by a Minotaur's horns is a lot more painful than you think."

Clara choked for a moment. She coughed. The liquid tasted bitter in her mouth. Then, she soon noticed that the pain in her limbs had finally stopped. Clara slowly got up from her spot. She looked at Twitch. "What about Onyx?"

"His legs are a bit broken. Thankfully he jumped on the horns before he was flipped. You two will be fine in a couple of days."

"That's not enough to get her out of here." Shard's voice was soon heard. His head loomed over the two. His eyes burned with fury. "A lot of our flock are injured. The Minotaurs just stole half of our food supply. We're lucky that the fires didn't destroy too many of our homes."

Clara frowned. Tears stung her eyes more as they rolled down her cheeks. "I'm sorry. I... The Minotaurs killed my parents. I... they..." Her words were soon drowned out by her sobs. She wiped her tears away, but they only flowed out more. Suddenly, Clara felt a wing patting her head.

Twitch gave a sincere smile. "Don't be too hard on yourself. We ran into the family you saved back there."

Clara sniffed. "Huh?" Then, she remembered the light blue shapes. "Are they okay?"

"Just rattled," Shard explained. He sighed. A warble escaped his throat as he sat down. "They thought the gods had actually heard them and that the winds had brought them good fortune." He crossed his arms. "I think it's—" His words were cut off by a pillow thrown at his face.

Twitch let out a hiss. "Don't you ever shut up?" She turned her green eyes to Clara. "Our elder said that she can discuss other things with you when you're able to walk again." She got up from her spot and handed Clara a bowl. There were several apples and berries nestled in it. "Eat these. I'll come back later to look at your injuries." Twitch was only a few steps to the door when Shard caught her attention. "Aren't you coming?"

Shard gave a soured look. "Whenever she's alone, trouble seems to find here. I'll stick around in case anything else happens."

Twitch sighed. "Just try not to be too rough on her. She's already feeling bad about Onyx's state as it is." With that, Twitch left the room.

Clara and Shard sat in silence. Onyx's occasional huff filled the room. Clara looked down at her hands. She pressed her lips together. She took a deep breath. "Um... I know it might be a little late to say this, but... I'm sorry for what I did to you back there. I didn't mean to. I thought I was only going to do some kind of command." She folded her hands. "No one back home taught me magic properly. Rue told me some of the basics, but everything else... I had to figure it out on my own."

Shard blinked. "Why are you so weird with animals anyway? Most humans would get all huggy with their corrupted beasts."

Clara's heart twisted hard. "I... really don't know. With wild animals, they just look so strange to me. For the domestic..." She hugged herself. "It always feels like needles when I touch them. Their gazes can sometimes... feel empty." She shivered at the mere thought of being near a regular horse. The draining sensation.

Shard's face downcasted. He took a deep breath. He ruffled with his hair. "You really are a strange human. Plus... I saw how you were using two elements at once. I don't do fire magic but I heard that along with wind, fire is the most difficult to control. Minotaurs are masters when it comes to it, used to be honorable too." He looked at Clara. "I don't... blame you for hating them. I hate them too."

Clara sniffed. "Yeah... I do. The elves too." She wiped her tears. "However... I don't hate you guys." She hugged her knees. "At least you get to fly around freely. Me... I'm stuck on the ground."

Shard looked up at the ceiling. "There's an old proverb one of our old monarchs used to say. Hate and fear are like ropes. The more they bind you, the less likely you can fly freely."

"Sounds accurate…" Clara's stomach growled. However, her mind went back to the strange jungle. The colorful feathers that danced in the trees. "Do… you travel all the time?"

"Since the last queen fell to the hand of humans," Shard said. His voice began to grow more bitter. "We basically scattered. A few of our jungle blood would fly over here every now and then. Thanks to the humans hunting us though—"

"I get it." Clara reached out a tender hand to Shard. "I don't like being a human either. With my weird hair and all."

"Weird as you are… You seem to be the only savior we got." Shard laughed at Clara's shocked expression. "It may not look like it, but our world is rotting away. Plus the empty are on the loose."

Clara swallowed hard. She found her hand lacing in Onyx's black fur once again. "I-I thought those things were a fairy tale." Rue had once told her about them. Neither human nor beast. Shapeless creatures that devore hearts just to feel whole. A never ending quest of despair. They would appear on a moonless night.

Shard shook his head. "I saw one myself. I made the mistake of going out where there was no moonlight." His feathers raised up along his back and wings. "I made Twitch come too. She's always at my side when we were little. Gave each other dares that most Harpies would never do. However, it was the most reckless mistake that nearly ruined both our lives." He pulled up his shirt to reveal a thin, jagged scar along his side. There was another one where it sat in the center of his abdomen.

"Don't Harpies see in the dark?" Clara tilted her head. Onyx lifted his head up, eyes focused on the Hawk Harpy.

Shard put his shirt back on with ease. "Mmm... We do but it varies depending on the kind of birds we're connected to." He raised his wings. "I'm a hawk as you already know. So, my night vision is decent but only when the moon is present."

Clara wrapped her arms around Onyx. Her skin felt cold even after talking about those monsters. She almost imagines the mere idea of two young, foolish Harpies playing out in the dark forest. The empty chasing them the moment they come close. Iridescent bodies that could be barely seen. Dead bodies with holes in places where they should be. Clara tried to get up. Pain came to her. "Is it dark out now?"

Shard turned to the windows. "Yeah. Don't worry, there's a moon out."

Clara thought for a moment. Then, she took a risk. "Why do you let Twitch be around you? Even though you called her clutchless."

Shard sighed. He rubbed his temples together. "Loneliness I guess. You already heard about me losing my parents." His eyes softened as Clara nodded. "Well... After losing them, I just shut down. I found no reason to fly any more. My parents weren't liked. Mostly because they once served the mad queen. So, I was looked at as the chickling that's spared of the pain. One day, I was crying by myself by a river. Suddenly, I was hit by a moving object." He laughed. "I was so mad, but Twitch was alone and crying too."

"Aww... Are you telling her the story of how we first met and nearly died because of that dare?"

Shard and Clara looked up to see Twitch looking at them with an amused expression on her face. Elder Gales and Lotus were at her side. Both held baskets of fruit and fish. They set it down on the nearby table.

Shard turned beet red. "I was trying to pass the time!" His face turned redder as Twitch draped her wings around him.

"I like you too, you big grump." Twitch nestled her head against Shard's chest for a moment.

"Ahem!" Elder Gales cleared her throat. "Perhaps we should discuss Clara's magic and what to do next." She groaned as she set herself down on the floor.

The air around them was heavy for a moment. Then, Clara was the first to speak. "U-um... Well... I just made the earth move and created a few fireballs." Her cheeks flushed. "Gaia warned me that my emotions can have a negative impact. I met with Promoths and—" Tears stung her eyes. "He-he took my mother away from me. I wanted him to hurt so bad, but I hurt myself and Onyx instead." She pressed her hands into her eyes.

Elder Gales gave her an acknowledging look. "At least you understand the consequences of your magic better. You still need to learn how to handle fire. However, you should practice your earth magic here."

Clara sniffed for a moment. Suddenly, she received a kiss from Onyx. The large warm tongue licked away her tears. Ripples of comfort went between them. Her body shook for a moment. "Th-thank you, Onyx." She shifted for a moment. She ignored the protest of pain as she tried to crawl out of her nest.

Twitch was at her side, handing her an apple. "Don't push yourself. You're lucky that you weren't paralyzed." She walked over to the table. "Let's just get everything set up for you."

Twitch and Shard began to prepare the meal while Clara and Elder Gales sat across from each other. Clara stared at the elderly Harpy for a moment. Her fingers were absently stroking Onyx's fur. Her heart was steady. The memory of her dream came back to her. "Elder Gales... Does the Wild Shepherdess have the power to see places she's never been to?"

Elder Gales stared at Clara. "I've only heard stories of the Goddess of Light bringing travelers to their destiny and the people that are connected to it. Why do you ask?"

"Well... I had this dream that I was in a forest." Clara munched on her apple before she could continue. "It wasn't like the forest around here. It was hotter. There were some Harpies there, but brighter. I heard a noise. I tried to see the shape, but it was gone before I could see anything."

Elder Gales was silent for a moment. She sighed. "It's the outskirts of Scalem, the capital of the Reptilia Kingdom."

"The Reptilia?" Clara sat upright. The color drained away from her face. She's heard stories of them. One even escaped her village. Her heart thundered as memories of a scaly creature hiding in her house. She gulped. "Um... do you have any political relations with them?"

"Our tropical flock has some trading over there. It's mostly to reach places that the lizard blood or snake blood can't reach."

"Lizard blood?" Clara cringed at the word. It sounded rather unfavorable.

"It's a term used to classify Reptilia," Twitch explained. She handed Clara a fried fish on a stick. Shard handed her a goblet of nectar. "Lizard blood are for those that resemble lizards. Gator and croco blood are those that resemble alligators and crocodiles. Turtle blood—" She was cut off as Shard pushed her cup into her mouth.

"Okay wind tongue," Shard grumbled. "I think she gets the point."

Clara gulped. Being around Harpies was one thing, but Reptilia were by far the most unknown creatures of this world. She only knows that they were cold-blooded beasts that were just as cruel as the empty. "S-so... I have to go there? Alone?" She looked at Lotus and Onyx. "No offense."

Elder Gales gave a soft rumbling laugh. Her eyes were soft. "No, child. I'll have these two accompany you."

Shard spat his water out of shock while Twitch abruptly looked up from her cup. Shard coughed a few times before he could speak. "What? You can't be serious. Twitch… Sure. But me? I have a place here."

Elder Gales gave an annoyed huff. "Your skills are needed beyond this forest. Our kind needs to be safe again. The world is dying."

"But how can going to see the Reptilia clan help?"

"Our worlds have been divided for too long," Elder Gales said. "It's time that the matriarchs and the beasts become one again." She raised a wing before Shard could protest. "True unity."

Clara looked down at her food. She took a bite of her fish. It was a little crispy but it felt like meat underneath the scales was tender. She continued to eat. However, her skin prickled with cold. This was going to be a long journey for her. Especially, if Twitch and Shard are being dragged against her will. She briefly looked at Onyx. Nervous, she peeled a piece of her fish and handed it to Onyx.

Onyx looked at it for a moment. His mismatched eyes tried to understand what was happening. Then, he opened his mouth. His teeth gently took the piece from Clara's hand. The fish was gone in seconds. He then sniffed Clara's fingers. Onyx licked them without a moment's hesitation.

Chapter 11
Unicorn Herd

Clara began to be accustomed to her time with the Harpies. Twitch stayed by her side. Happy was also there to show a few things about their customs. Her favorite was their way of fortune telling. She was amazed that they would read one's destiny just by placing a few feathers into a bowl of water, speak a few words and let the wind blow on them until an image would show. When she was well enough, Clara took the time to gather her courage to ride Lotus. Each ride slowly began to become easier from mounting to dismounting. Onyx also grew accepting of her by allowing her to touch him. Her meeting with Gaia was still a bit overwhelming, but her earth magic began to grow stronger.

 The next morning, Clara was now dressed in a pair of soft brown pants and a white shirt. Her feet felt strange without any shoes on, but then the sensation of bark and grass on her toes gave her a little relief of anxiety and her feet in general. Her hair was still cropped short. Clara turned to Onyx and Lotus. Their eagerness to go out ran through her spine. She twirled her fingers as the invisible strings caused the branches to form a ladder for her to climb down. Clara was about to take a few steps when Twitch stopped her.

"Hold it!" Twitch loomed over Clara. She tried to look menacing but it only made Clara giggle. "You still have a look at your bones, young lady!" She fluttered her back in.

Clara laughed only harder. Her cheeks turned a bright pink. "I'm fine. My bones don't hurt. Even Onyx was just ready to jump down the branches." She glanced over as Onyx barked in agreement. His tail wagged strongly.

Twitch ran her wings along Clara. She even looked at her face. "Okay. One more question. How are you with the animals now?"

Clara was silent. "Well… I still find it to be a bit nerve wracking to be around… Dragons especially—" She held up her hands. "No offense to Gaia!" She folded her hand together. She looked at Onyx and Lotus. "I'm starting to feel better being around Lotus and Onyx now."

Twitch smiled. Her eyes held a playful gleam to them. She briefly looked at Lotus. "Okay. Then, I'll take you somewhere special today! Hop on Lotus and follow me!" Twitch took off before Clara could say anything.

Clara sighed. She slowly got onto Lotus' back. "I hate it when she does that." Her hands clasped onto Lotus' mane. "I hope Gaia doesn't scold me for it." She willed her connection for Lotus to go. Her body lurched slightly as Lotus began to go. Her heart leaped with joy as Lotus made her way down. The rocking motion felt far lighter than the horses that her parents would have her ride on.

As they went along, Clara smiled and waved at the Harpies. Most of them were still cautious of her, but they still waved her hello or a simple bow. She saw Happy overhead. "Good morning, Happy."

"Good morning, Clara!" Happy let out a chirp that was in sync with the birds that resided in the trees. "Twitch is taking you somewhere?"

"I have to hurry or I'll lose her." Clara then noticed Lotus' ears perked. Nostrils flaring out. "What is it, girl?" She soon felt a wave of familiarity and excitement rippled down their link. Even Onyx raised his nose to the air and took in the strange scent. Instinctively, Clara clung tighter to the white mane. Lotus reared up, neighing.

The unicorn took off like a bolt of lightning. Her hooves churned up the vegetation as she followed Twitch. Onyx kept with the pace. Muscles rippled with each movement. Fallen trees and large bushes were no match for this duo. They soon reached a clearing. Oak trees formed a ring around them. In the center of the clearing were other unicorns.

Clara stared in amazement. She's never seen a herd of unicorns before. Her mouth formed a small "o". *They're like the horses and sheep back home*, she thought. An indignant snort broke her train of thought. She leaned over to see that Lotus was giving her an annoyed look. "Sorry." She slid down from Lotus.

The unicorns were like a living snowstorm. The white pelts stood against the greenery. A few had some scars along their flanks. Some had horns that were chipped.

They soon raised their heads. All eyes trained on the unexpected guests. One of them took a few steps forward. This one was an older version of Lotus. Blue eyes with a far longer mane.

Twitch landed beside Clara. "Found this herd just a few days ago. They like to graze here now and again." Her mouth formed a grim line. "Never realized that it was getting really bad out there."

Clara turned to her. "Why's that?" She watched Lotus. A wave of uncertainty rolled between their link. Her own stomach was also twisting in knots. She held her breath as the two unicorns were only inches away from their faces.

Despite the clear sky above them, a heavy chill hung around them. The silence felt like an eternity. Suddenly, Lotus and the older unicorn nuzzled. The other unicorns come and join in. The foals stayed close to their mothers. Neighs filled the air. Horns touched in a gentle manner.

Clara soon realized what Twitch was talking about. Several unicorns had black markings on their flanks. Some of them had black ooze seeping out of their wounds. Her face soon paled. Hands grasped each other at the disturbing sight. She's seen those wounds before on some horses. The curse of the Empty.

Twitch gave her a sideways glance. "I wanted to show you this. Not only for Lotus' sake but for what lies ahead." She looked up at the sky. Three wingbeats were soon heard above them. She giggled as the unicorns scattered as Gaia, Elder Gales and Shard landed in front of them.

Clara stared at them in surprise. "Gaia!" She bowed. Her cheeks flustered. "I'm so sorry if I kept you waiting." She watched as Lotus came over to her. She gaped as the other unicorns began to approach her as well. Clara froze in place. Her throat constricted. All eyes focused on her. Her skin ran cold. Her heart jumped out at the sight of the unicorn that Lotus was with being close to her.

Lotus let out a soft nicker. Eyes soft. She nudged Clara's shoulder. A soft sense of reassurance went over the bond. Images of Lotus as a foal followed by the unicorn before Clara. Her eyes flicked down to Onyx. She snorted. The unicorn was met with a mutual snort.

Clara gulped. "So… This is your mother…" She gave an awkward smile. Her palms began to sweat. She tried her best to wipe them, but uncertainty ruled over her heart. Clara shut her eyes as Lotus' mother moved in closer. Then, she felt a warm muzzle against her cheek. Clara opened her eyes. She looked back at Lotus' mother. With shaky hands, Clara placed them gently on the soft white muzzle. Her fingers glided smoothly. Slowly, but surely, Clara's anxiety began to melt away. As she continued to pet the unicorn, memories of her own mother filled her head.

The fun spring days where they would garden her precious sweet pea and tulips. Watching snow fall in the winter. Drawing the deities on the holidays. Tears stung Clara's eyes once again. This time, she couldn't hold them back. Sobs wracked her body. Her arms instinctively wrapped around the creature's neck. Her cries continued as Twitch rubbed her back. The others gathered around her. Other unicorns rubbed their muzzles on her face.

After what had felt like forever, Clara took a deep breath. She was sitting down against a tree. She rubbed her eyes free of tears. Onyx was curled up next to her. Lotus on her left. The Harpies and Gaia were simply watching her. Gaia lowered her head to Clara's level. *Feel better child?*

Clara nodded. Suddenly, her eyes began to glow again. The colors around her were brighter than before. Even the smallest of threads in the sky started to become visible to her. "Uh… I see threads in the sky."

That's wonderful. Gaia purred at the news. *It means that your connection with this world is getting stronger by the day!*

Twitch and Shard looked at each other then back to Clara. "Try this spell," Shard said. He raised his wing up for a moment. He moved his wings in small, circular motions until a small tornado sat in the center of it.

Clara mimicked his movements. To her surprise, the threads from the sky began to wrap around her hand. She continued this motion. The image of the tornado in her mind. As she relaxed her hand, a tornado smaller than Shard's appeared in the center of her palm. A smile appeared on her face. It felt weird, but it tickled with each movement. Her joy vanished the moment it went away.

Shard gave a teasing grin. "Looks like you need some practice… Clara."

Twitch gave him a light slap on the back. "Don't try teaching without me." She turned to Clara. "Let's try out your Earth magic now."

Clara looked at the ground. Her eyes focused on the grass beneath her. She tried to focus. The green threads danced in bright shades of green. Even the brown threads began to resemble a more bronze color. She could see her hand sink into the tangled haze. She tried to sense any seeds nearby. Clara found one. Her fingers twirled along the threads. She pulled them up along with the seed, her will pressed on it.

Gasps and surprised grunts were soon heard. A soft rumble vibrated around her body. Threads began to move upward as if wanting to touch the threads in the sky. As threads began to vanish and her vision returned to normal, she saw the tree growing before her eyes. A small twig with branches sprouting out. Finally, the tree rested to a height where it was no taller than Lotus' knee.

"Amazing!" Twitch gasped. Her eyes sparkled with joy. Shard leaned forward, eyebrows raised. Elder Gales smiled.

Gaia purred. *You're ready.* She raised her head high. *Go Shepherdess... The Reptilia Kingdom awaits.*

Chapter 12
Night of the Empty

The next day, Clara, Shard, Twitch, Lotus and Onyx readied for their trip to the next kingdom. Clara set up a few packs that Lotus would be able to carry without having to put a strain on her back. Shard and Twitch had a few satchels packed with food and herbs for their trip. The sun was beginning to rise as they stood by the entrance of the village. Elder Gales and Gaia approached the two.

Elder Gales handed Clara an amulet. It was hung by a twine string. The stone had a raven with its wings flared out, mouth out in an eternal call. "Take this with you. It'll warn you if any of the empty are nearby. Remember: Fire and Light are the only things that keep The Empty at bay. Just stay with Lotus and Onyx until you can master them properly."

Clara nodded. "I know. I'll have to master the other elements..." she gulped. "With other dragons. As well as deal with the Reptilia." She was suddenly met by a few young Harpies that went to hug her. One of them was a young Nuthatch Harpy that she saved from the Minotaurs. She gave a small smile and pet their heads. *Who knew Harpy babies have such soft heads?* Clara found several Harpies brushing against her skin with feathers. In Harpy

Culture, it was a gesture of wishing someone well along their travels.

"May the winds guide you," Elder Gales said.

Clara waved them goodbye. She hopped onto Lotus' back. She could hear choruses of "goodbyes" behind. Clara looked ahead of the trail. She clutched at her heart. Tears stung her eyes. She shook her head. Onyx woofed softly at her. Comfort wrapped around her body. Clara held onto the mane and they marched on.

The group was silent for a while. They all kept eyes on the bushes and trees for Cockatrice. So far they've only seen tracks and scales. Clara didn't mind that, but the night of her first encounter with one did leave her with a sense of unease. What disturbed them the most were the dead animal bodies they would find. Their chests opened and lifeless eyes staring at them. Clara and Twitch tried their very best not to vomit at the sight of the dead animals, but they would hug each other as Shard buried the beasts.

Night crept in. The sky turned dark blue. Small stars began to appear as the sun began to rest from a long vigilance. Owls hooted in the treetops. Sounds of raccoons and opossums echoed through the leaves. Other wolves were heard in the distance. Onyx howled every once in a while, making his presence known. Lotus fidgeted at every sound, ears pinned back.

Shard and Twitch began to fly slower. They soon landed and began to collect some wood to make a fire. Clara had to watch her step, Onyx being her eyes. Every sound put everyone on edge. A small fire was soon made once the forest was pitch black. Everyone huddled closely to the light.

Clara flinched as a scream was heard. "What was that?" She hugged her knees tightly. She raised her hand, reaching her threads in case the matter arose.

Shard briefly looked up from the fire. "Cockatrice screams... There must be more in this area." He turned his gaze to Clara. "Clara, you've been in these woods long enough to recognize one, right?"

Clara looked down in shame. "I'm sorry... I'm still not used to being away from shelter this long. My nursemaid, Rue... She would tell me to stay inside after dark. Mostly to make sure I don't go into the woods or stray from the village." She gave a hollow laugh. "Yet I'm still the stupidest human in existence."

Twitch walked over to her. "Now don't say that. You've pulled massive feats with your magic and you were able to get on Lotus' back without freezing up."

Clara looked at Onyx and Lotus. Her lips formed a thin line. "It won't be like that forever. I have to free them. Lotus needs to be with her herd again." She put a hand on Onyx. "I'm sure Onyx would appreciate his freedom too."

Shard raised a brow. "I thought humans have a permanent connection with their beasts. And something about going mad when that bond is severed."

Clara nodded. "It's true. I've actually seen it happen before. One man lost his cat in the Minotaur attack and babbled nonsense for months." She looked up at the sky. "But that's all right... I'd rather have everyone live a happier life if I wasn't bonded to any animal. Even to be a little normal." Clara ran her fingers through her hair. "Maybe lose the silver hair when it's over."

Twitch frowned deeply. She hugged Clara. "Noooo!" She whined. Her voice made Shard and Onyx flinch. "Don't lose the silver. It's adorable on you!" Her hug only grew tighters, Clara having a hard time breathing. "Besides, do you honestly want to break your bond with them?"

Clara stared at the flames. Her lips drew into a thin line. Her fingers curled into Onyx's fur. A heavy silence filled the air. The power. The thrill of riding, she never had before. Was she willing to give that up? A loud snap broke out of her train of thought. Suddenly, her spine went cold. Her heart was heavy in her chest.

Shard and Twitch got onto their feet. Feathers raised. Even Onyx let out a low, warning growl. Slithering noises soon followed. Shard turned his gaze toward the dark haze that surrounded them. He narrowed his eyes for a moment, then they went wide with fear. "Get in the trees…" he said through gritted teeth. "Now."

Clara followed his gaze. She soon saw a brief glitter in the underbrush. She activated her powers once again. The threads were still bright, but a few broken patches were there. Suddenly, a gray mass soon came into view. Even though it didn't have eyes, Clara could feel the weight of its gaze. She grabbed a few threads of green and pulled.

A wall of rock soon surrounded them. Clara got onto Lotus' back and willed the trees to lower the branches. Onyx stayed for a moment, barking reverberated through the chaos. "Onyx let's go!" Clara felt a stubborn streak reach between her bonds. Clara let out a frustrated growl. Lotus also shared her frustration. Their connection formed a ribbon of silver. It tied around Onyx's middle and was lifted up. Protest rattled in their link, but Clara simply ignored it.

As they made halfway up the tree, a glittering slime leaked between the rocks. In the firelight, it became clearer. The body was shapeless, iridescent. It slithered only a few steps before it shrunk away from the flames.

Clara could feel the branches falter. Her fingers curled into the mane. Muscles tensed as she tried not to panic. It took a while to find her voice. "Sh-Shard… The Empty can't climb trees right?"

"Being on higher ground is the only thing that kept us alive." Shard's breathing labored. "We had to bump into a few trees just to avoid being eaten."

"It was eating the threads…" Clara gulped. Her mouth went dry. Many of the villagers had spoken about how The Empty simply devoured everything insight, but Clara never imagined something such gluttony. "How long do we have to be up here?"

"Until sunrise," Twitch answered, "or until it finds something else to chase after." She leaned forward as she dared. "At least it's scared of fire. Plus it can't stretch very far, so we have a good chance of making it through the night."

A weird scraping noise turned their attention to the ground. The Empty was doing something strange to the ground. To their shock, a chunk of dirt flew into the fire. Then, it started to climb. The bark begins to break and rot away. Suddenly, more slithering noises were heard below.

"No way…" Shard's voice could only be heard. Fear betraying his voice. "There's no way it should climb."

Clara immediately activated her magic. The green threads around her began to fade to a duller color. She frantically looked around. The world started to drop slightly. Lotus' fear and panic entwined with her own. *Lotus,* she tried to form words in her connection. *I'm going to need your help, but I need you to calm down.* Clara began to frantically grab whatever threads she could and formed a bridge just as Gaia taught her. "Come on!"

Lotus let out a small beam of light from her horn. The thick bridge of branches getting them from one tree to the next. The group made their way as quickly as they could. They barely made it as the first tree they were on collapsed. Suddenly, a screech was heard. It was coming from The Empty that had managed to reach the branch of the current living tree. Squelching was soon heard. Something glittered below the group, the strange mass clumped together and made its way up the trunk.

"What the—" Twitch let out a wind attack. It knocked their assailant down. However, it continued to crawl right back up. "I didn't think they'd actually travel in packs!"

"There must be something special with this one!" Shard pointed to the lead Empty.

"What do we do?"

Clara thought for a moment. She soon recalled how unicorns were part of the element of light. She looked at Lotus' horn. Her fingers lightly touched the spiraled surface. She could feel its magic flow inside her. Clara moved her hand back onto the mane. Clara allowed her plan to be extended to Lotus and Onyx. Lotus sent her reluctance. A loud cracking noise was soon heard. Clara swallowed down her fear and tried to send her reassurance.

Onyx also felt the link for he was a bit calmer, but his lips never left their original snarl. He was soon placed on Shard's back.

"What the—" Shard stared at Clara. He wobbled for a moment. His wings spread out for balance.

"Shard, Twitch, Get ready to jump to the next tree."

"What?" The Harpies screeched in unison.

"But Clara—" Twitch barely had enough time to dodge as a tentacle went for her face.

"There's no time." Clara tightened her grip. She activated her powers again. The silver ribbon soon wrapped around her arm. Her eyes and hair began to take on a white glow. A light that was so bright that it would've rivaled with all the stars in the sky. Clara and Lotus formed a lance together from the silver threads of their bond.

M-make...

Clara stopped momentarily as a strange voice entered her mind. Her arm was raised, her lance aimed at the lead

Empty. She shivered at the voice. It was emotionless. Yet... It held a sense of longing. A longing to exist.

The voice spoke again. *M-make m-me whole...*

Clara was stunned. She's never heard of The Empty of being able to speak. The lead Empty sprung at her. Clara thrusted her lance at it. She and Lotus unleashed a burst of light that shook the forest. Blinding everyone and everything. Clara felt something slam into her face. Her hand pressed against. Her mind was screaming for some form of balance.

"... Clara... Clara!" Shard's voice broke free of the fog in her mind.

Clara soon found her waist being wrapped around by Shard's strong wings. Lotus's leg caught in his talon. Clara looked down to see that The Empty was now gone. Their only known evidence of their attacks left scars in the bark. "I... I'm okay..." She slowly raised her head. "Thank you for catching me, Shard." She moved her arms around his thick neck.

Shard flew down and set Lotus. He gave Clara a stern look. His eyes burned with fury. "Of all the crazy things I've seen a human do, yours was the craziest! You created a bridge of branches. Managed to use light magic even though you had now clue how to use it! Take on the Empty almost by yourself. That was reckless as it was stupid."

Clara looked down in shame. She gripped her pants. Clara was prepared for the "useless" to rain down on her. Clara heard a laugh. She felt wings wrap around her.

"And I have never been happy to have a reckless soul join us!" Shard held her tightly in his embrace. "You did good today. Most humans would run and hide, but you held on."

Clara's eyes grew bright. Even Onyx's pride riddled her. Slowly and awkwardly, she hugged back. "Thank you…" she whispered. Her words barely escaped her lips. Throat turned raw. She soon felt Twitch, Lotus and Onyx join in her embrace. Clara allowed this to continue until the golden rays of the sun gave way to the morning that they needed to see. A small tree started to grow in place of the one that was knocked down.

The group had a small breakfast. Their bags had miraculously survived the night's attack. However, sleep was something they couldn't afford right now. Even though The Empty were gone, they still had to deal with possible Cockatrice encounters and possibly hostile Grizzly Bears. They continued on until the heat began to be uncomfortable. The trees went from being pine and oak to palm and ficus. Smells of spice hung in the air.

Shard cleared his throat. "Ladies and Onyx, welcome to the Reptilia Kingdom."

Chapter 13
Into the Reptilia Kingdom

The group began to hear and see strange creatures they've never seen before. Frogs and birds with more colors than ever before. Large cats with stripes and spots moved in the underbrush, resulting in a few close calls. Long limbed creatures with tails chittered in the treetops. Rodents swam in the water alongside crocodiles and pink fish with a hole in their head.

Clara took a deep breath. Beads of sweat ran down her face. Her clothes clung to her. Her hair stuck to her face. She had never felt such heat. Even though there was water nearby, it felt hotter than the summer days back home. A twig snapped, catching Clara's attention. She looked into the distance. A brief shadow flickered by. A lean shape. Even Onyx and Lotus grew uneasy.

Twitch took notice of Clara's gaze. "Clara? Are you okay?"

Clara turned to Shard and Twitch. "I think someone is following us. Don't any of you feel eyes staring?"

Shard turned his head. His sharp eyes scanned the area. "Let me go up. It could be just our cousins. They… have a tendency to play hide and seek at times. Plus you're a human so…" He took off under the glare of Twitch.

Twitch moved closer to Clara. "Maybe now would be a good time to practice sky magic."

"You're sure?" Clara wiped the sweat off her brow. "Shouldn't we find some water first?"

Lotus snorted in agreement. Her body glistened like pearls. Head slightly lowered. Onyx laid on the ground beside her. The black wolf moaned and rolled onto his back.

"I'm sure." Twitch set her bag down. She stretched her wings out and leaned against a tree. "Besides, my wings and feet are tired."

Clara slowly sat down. Onyx was already asleep by the time he laid his head on her lap. Lotus on her belly. "I don't exactly blame you. I can't really sleep on Lotus' back. I even really didn't feel safe back there." She fiddled with her fingers for a moment, her mind going back to the lead Empty. "Did… You ever hear The Empty speak?"

Twitch tilted her head. "No… Not that I'm aware of." Her eyes lit up as she thought of something. "Actually, there was supposed to be an omen about those that supposedly hear them."

Clara leaned forward. Her throat tightened. "Good or bad?" She could feel Lotus slowly stir beside her. Onyx merely flicked his tail.

Twitch bit her lip. The jungle grew silent all around her. "Bad. It means that grave misfortunes will be bestowed on those that hear them." She immediately leaned forward the moment she saw her friend distressed. She gently patted Clara's head. "I'm sure that you're fine.

You've been through a lot. I'm sure things are going to look up for you in no time." Twitch gave a soft smile. Suddenly, rustling was heard in the distance. Twitch froze, feathers raised. "Stay here. I'm going to go check it out."

Clara watched Twitch vanish. Clara leaned against Lotus. The heat and exhaustion finally settled into her body. Her eyelids began to droop. Screeches were soon heard causing Clara to bolt upright. She tried to activate her power but nothing worked. She frantically got on her feet. Lotus and Onyx following, anxiety rippling between their bond. Clara glanced around. She saw several wings pop in and out of the trees.

Instinctively, Clara was about to reach for Lotus' mane when she noticed movement from a nearby ficus. A slim shape. One that was similar to what she saw in her dreams. She slowly walked toward it. "Hello…" Clara flinched at the rustling. She could feel a pair of eyes staring at her. "Please… I-I mean you no harm. My name's Clara. Are…" She dreaded to say the next words but she had to say them. "Are you Reptilia?"

A shadow briefly made its way up the tree. A pair of eyes looked over the branches. Back arched. Faint hisses heard.

"Wait!" Clara tried to reach out. Her frail hands grabbed the knot and knob that resided. She was almost up where the mysterious stranger was, but she slipped. Clara landed on her butt. She let out a frustrated sigh. "Look… I'm really tired—" A frantic sensation of fear and anger hit her soul. She turned just in time to see two Harpies that resembled parrots standing over a bellowing Lotus. Onyx laid on his side, unmoving. "Hey!"

Her scream brought the attention of the two Harpies. She steadied herself. "Stop it! She's a unicorn! Don't you even—" A soft thump resounded behind her. Something stung her neck. She let out a cry. Then, her vision began to blur. The heaviness in her limbs began to increase. It felt like people strapped sand onto her body. *Th-this is way stronger than what Twitch uses.* She was on the verge of collapsing, but something held her up. Cool leather pressed upon her cheek, easing the oppressing heat that riddled her body.

Chapter 14
Meeting Helios

Clara couldn't explain it, but something felt soft under her. It felt smooth against her fingers. She sighed and slowly opened her eyes. Curtains of satin blue hung around her. Faint lights from a lamp hung on the left. Clara tried to see where it was, but the exhaustion and cool night air lulled her back into sleep.

Clara was five years old. Winter had come to her world. White powder kissing the houses and fields. Her village was in chaos. People running around. Children scream. Men cursing under their breath. Women frantically trying to get their loved ones inside. All were trying to avoid a Reptilia that escaped from imprisonment. It was being displayed throughout the human kingdom before it was delivered to the king and queen.

"Did anyone see it?" one man shouted.

"No," a gruff man spoke.

"Let's get everyone inside," an old woman spoke. "It'll be dark soon. The ugly thing won't last long anyway."

Clara merely watched the adults in the distance. Her mother came and took her hand. They made their long trek back along with Rue. By the time they were home, the sky was already pitch black. Clara sat by the fire as her parents were discussing what to do. She wrapped a blanket around herself.

After Clara went to bed, she heard something. A soft thump resounded. Clara bolted upright. "D-daddy? Did you hear that?" She looked in the direction of where her parents were. They slept away, barely noticing their daughter's voice. "Mommy..." Another thump sounded again. She slipped out of the covers.

Clara fumbled in the dark for something that she could use as a weapon. A stick was the only thing she could find. With a shaky breath, she went over to the door. Cold air hit her face as she tried to find the source. She soon noticed a still form lying in the snow. It was hard to make out from underneath a burlap cloth but she could make out muffled noises. Worried that it was some lost child, she brought them inside. Her hands clung to the damp cloth of burlap. "Can you stand up?"

Light flooded in. Something wet slapped against her face. Clara woke with a soft groan. In front of her was Onyx and Lotus. The two creatures stared at her, relief pulsing between them. Onyx placed his large head on her chest. He gave a whine. Clara patted his fur. She soon found that it was shorter than normal.

Clara lifted herself up. She was stunned to see that Onyx's fur had been trimmed neatly. She had only seen that with those that were able to afford filers or groom blades. Clara then noticed that Lotus had been groomed as well despite having been draped by a net. Her mane was braided. Tropical flowers woven into the white. Smells of spice hit her nose. To her surprise, she found a tray of food placed on a small table. Several fruits and a strange soup sat there. A large fish with pink scales took up half the tray. A goblet of water gleamed in the day.

"What's all this?" Clara got onto her feet. She walked slowly to avoid falling. Pillows littered the floor. Each with a strange image of giant lizards and dragons sewn into them. A regal tapestry hung against one side of the wall. It held a strange gray lizard holding a sword. She reached the table. Her hand reached for a fork, but hesitated. She tried again with her fingers firmly around the cutlery. She decided to try the fish. Her throat clenched as a piece sat on her fork.

She looked over at Onyx and Lotus. Waves of reassurance rippled through. Onyx went over to a bowl that held what looked like slabs of meat. Onyx gently took one by the corner and ate it whole. He met his gaze with hers. Nothing happened.

Clara took a deep breath. "Okay… If I was able to befriend Harpies… then I think the R-Reptilia won't be as bad." She took a bite. The tender meat of the fish fell apart in her mouth. Warmth pooled into her stomach the moment she swallowed it. She soon began to eat her meal with ease. The fruit was far bigger than the ones in the forest, but they were far sweeter. Except for a green one with fuzzy skin.

The door opened. Twitch and Shard came rushing in. Two other Harpies came in with one Reptilia behind them. One of the Harpies was the Macaw Harpy from before. The other resembled a Quetzal, two long tail feathers trailed behind him like ribbons. Golden eyes cold with anger. The Reptilia was leathery, the coating resembled armor. A long mouth with rows of teeth showed he wasn't one you shouldn't trifle with.

Twitch hugged Clara. "Are you okay?"

Clara hugged her back. "Yeah. I feel a bit better after having something to drink and some sleep." She looked at Shard. "What happened?"

"They saw you among us and thought you were threatening us," Shard answered. He glared at the Macaw Harpy. "Apparently, they just received a prophecy from their elder. Saying a human girl was going to destroy our world. However, this fool decided to go out before getting all the details!"

The Macaw Harpy gave a soured look. "Oh, forgive me for wanting to protect my home! Plus, King Helios was acting super weird." He flinched as he was met with a firm stare.

The Quetzal Harpy bowed. His dark green hair flopped around. "Forgive us Wild Shepherdess, our elder told us that the human maiden that we should fear had dark hair. Not silver."

Clara grew silent. She could only think of one girl with dark hair. *Lady Maroona,* she thought. *Her destroying the world?* She shook the thought away. She tried to do her usual curtsy, but she couldn't shake the feeling of how awkward it was. "That is all right. It was an honest mistake. You've hated humans for a long time." She looked mournfully at the floor. "It couldn't be helped." She cleared her throat. "Anyway, I'm here to learn how to master the magic of air. Even fire as well."

Clara decided to show her earth power. She took a few seeds out of the strange green fruit. Palm outstretched, the seeds nestled in the center. Her command over the threads started to pull. The seeds soon twitched. Their hard covers gave way to green vines and fresh fruit that was ready to be picked.

"Impressive…" Rumbled the Crocodile-faced Reptilia. "For a human. Our king wishes to have an audience with you. As well as a personal apology for what happened yesterday."

Clara tilted her head. "Whatever for? I've yet to meet him."

"Best head on over to find out," Twitch said. She lightly pushed Clara to the door. The others soon followed. They all went down a hall where the walls turned gold in the light of the sun. A variety of Reptilia guarded the doors or walked past them. Some resembled lizards. Others were snakes and alligators.

Clara could feel their unblinking eyes at her. She couldn't help but feel a little naked. She looked at her feet. They looked a bit calloused and bare. The shoes she once wore in exile were long gone. She discreetly sniffed her clothes. Clara cringed at the stench. She soon arrived at the throne room.

The throne was six feet away from them. Two statues that resembled mighty lizards stood on each side of it. Their heads raised high they could be mistaken for wingless dragons. The throne itself was made of pure sandstone. Several emeralds and sapphires graced it. Sitting on top was a Reptilia with a bizarre coloring.

His scales were silver with white spots that ran along his body. Blue eyes with pupils that resembled an hourglass placed horizontally. His frame was lean but held some muscle. He wore a crown that was made of pure ebony. Garnets made it look as if there was blood dipped on the tips. Cloth draped from his left shoulder to his right hip. A loin cloth draped over his legs. His tail was long with a slight bulge toward the end.

The Crocodile-blood Reptilia walked over the throne. He bowed to the crowned lizard then turned to the group. "Clara of the humans… Shard and Twitch of the Harpies. I wish to present, his majesty, King Helios." He gestured toward the throne.

Clara stared at the king for a moment. She had never seen a Reptilia like him. Yet, there was a strange air about him that made her stomach turn. Her heart leaped as King Helios got up from his throne. She could feel his eyes on her. Her throat was constrained. The world started to wobble as he was only a foot away from her.

"Clara." His voice was surprisingly smooth compared to the earth rumbles of the other lizard guards. He bowed his head. "I would like to apologize for not revealing myself to you when you were exhausted. As well as for knocking you out." He gently took Clara's hand and kissed it.

Clara's face went beet red. She could feel her whole body vibrate. His lips felt like silk against her skin. Her heart hammered so loud that she swore everyone would hear it. Lotus knickered, her head moved up and down. Onyx glanced between King Helios and Clara with great confusion. "W-where did you learn to do that," she asked.

"I've observed your customs from afar and from some humans that pass by here."

"How were you able to do that without conflict?" Twitch asked. She blushed and moved away slowly.

"I have my ways." King Helios backed away from Clara. His gait held reluctance. It even took forever to remove his hand from Clara's. He slowly glanced at everyone. "I welcome you to my kingdom. More importantly, the capital." He walked over to a balcony and waved them over. Everyone walked over to the edge and found what they were looking for.

Clara and the others gazed at a strange city. Buildings of clay rose out of the ground. Huts dotted the outskirts. Camels and ox roam freely among the market stalls. Colorful Harpies flew to and from nests. Further out of the expanse, desert sand spread out of the left while the jungle loomed on the right. It was as if the two lands were trying to live in harmony with each other. Music and spice filled the air. Drums vibrated. Flutes hummed ancient tunes.

Clara's eyes widened. A civilization that was supposed to live in mud and filth had made all of this. Her mouth formed a smile. However, anxiety reached her as she saw a statue that sat in the middle of what looked like the market square. A lizard that rode on an elephant. Heavy power emanating from it. Her hands began to shake as elephants began to appear as well. Their massive gray forms move out of the jungle.

"Welcome to Reghila," King Helios spoke. He stood beside Clara. Almost as if he knew she was about to faint at any moment.

"W-what a mighty kingdom!" Clara had a hard time opening her mouth to say those words. She turned to look at King Helios. "So, you let some of the Harpies live here?"

King Helios nodded. "There's a story that your people don't know. I'm afraid that the Minotaurs, the Sand Dwarves, the Selkies and even the Dark Elves have forgotten it." He turned to them. "The gods and goddesses including the Night God created this world together. However, the Night God had gone mad from the harmonious sanctum. He wanted to bring chaos. So, he created the Empty to fill the void. The other deities tried to stop him, but to no avail. He was eventually locked away by the threads that held him together. So, seven kingdoms were made to protect life and make sure the threads were woven to keep it in place."

"We heard a story similar to that," Twitch said. "However, no one really knows how the collapse happened. All I know is that the story changes amongst the kingdoms according to our elder."

King Helios gave a small smile. "I see you're quite knowledgeable. Indeed, it—"

Shouts were soon heard from below. A Snakeblood Reptilia hissed at a small Harpy. His hood extended outward. The other Harpy was shouting something at the snake. Before long, several guards were trying to cool down the situation.

King Helios sighed. "I'm sorry you had to see that. We've had a few disagreements ever since I've allowed Harpies to live here."

Clara turned to him. "Why is that?"

"The last Harpy Queen sent her army here to kill the Reptilia in hopes of gaining the Earth Breath Jungle and Bone Scorch Desert. Mainly for their supplies." King Helios pulled his lips into a grimace. "It led to a deadly massacre and nearly destroyed both races. Thankfully her followers went against her after the incident with the humans."

Shard and Twitch looked away in shame. Clara could only express sympathy for them. She then noticed that King Helios' eyes held sorrow for a moment. Something about the pain that she felt most familiar with. "Um…" Clara was reluctant to ask this question but it would bug her if she didn't ask. "W-where are your parents? The previous rulers. Are… they around?"

King Helios tightened his grip on the rail. His tail twitched.

Guilt twisted Clara's heart. She bit her lip. She could feel the same heaviness as his. "I'm so sorry." Clara wanted to put a hand on his shoulder. The comfort she wished she had when her parents died. "It must've been so hard for you to run this kingdom by yourself."

King Helios cleared his throat. "Well, then. Enough about my kingdom. It'd be best if you take some time to rest before you continue where you need to go."

Clara reached for him. "Wait!" Her hand touched his shoulder. Her cheeks went red once again. She pulled her hand away. "Your Majesty. We need your help. I can't really explain it but I have a feeling the Empty is getting stronger. Also… If the vision about someone destroying our world is true, then we… have to…" Her words died as she felt King Helios and the others stare at her. She bowed clumsily. "I'm sorry!" She slipped and lost her footing. Clara was about to fall forward when King Helios held her up by the arms.

"Clara. It'd be best if you focus on your mission. You're the Wild Shepherdess. You need to practice your powers. The Beast Heart is the only thing that can protect this world." He left with his guards before Clara could say anything else.

Clara stood there. Stunned by what was happening. Even though King Helios wasn't a cold blooded monster as previously described, there was something about him that was distant. An unnamed fear that Clara wanted to understand. "I'll talk to you again," she whispered. Her heart fluttered in ways that she never thought possible.

Chapter 15
Ways of the Air

Twitch and Clara were in a small courtyard. A fountain stood in the center of it. It was mostly empty save for a few birds and rats that scattered across the grounds. Clara looked at them nervously. "As if the Empty were bad enough…"

"Oh, come on," Twitch said. "You've been able to handle a unicorn herd and a large wolf. Plus a Forest dragon taught you earth magic. Also—" She rotated her wings at Clara. "You're friends with me and Shard. Kinda. How can you possibly still be afraid of these guys?"

Clara gave a soured expression. "First of all, they're a lot smaller than me. More susceptible to climbing on me and taking my eye out."

Twitch tilted her head. "Is that what your village said about them?"

Clara pouted. Her eyes to the ground. "Maybe."

Twitch groaned. "I think I should head over to your home and teach them a thing or two about wild beasts."

"I'm sorry for being impatient but can we get started?"

Twitch took a deep breath. "As you and your fellow humans have already figured, Air magic is really tricky to master. The threads are a lot harder to obtain. Plus they have a dual function. You need to be relaxed and have no care in the world." She took off to the sky. "Yet you can't be silly all the time either. If you want to make a whirlwind or have it blow in a certain direction, you have to keep an image in your mind." She soon spun in a circle. The air currents were slowly becoming visible. Before long, a whirlwind covered Twitch and the leaves in the courtyard started being pulled into the vortex, forming a ring around it.

Clara stared in amazement. Her hair whipped around. Onyx whined nervously, ears pinned to his head and tail tucked. Lotus simply huffed in annoyance that her mane was starting to come undone. Suddenly, a black scrawny rat hit her on the back of her leg. Clara shrieked and fumbled backward in her attempt to shake it off.

Twitch ended her display and helped Clara with the rat. She gently swatted it away. She held out her wing to lift Clara up. "This is why you need to have concentration. Don't mind the things around you and focus on small tasks first. Start by creating a gust of wind." She pointed to a pile of leaves.

Clara gazed at the pile. She lifted her hands, concentrating on finding the threads in the sky like before. Her vision clouded again to several colors. Then she noticed several specs floating around the space. The bundle of threads were the rats and birds of the court yard. She shook herself. She turned her head to the sky. The threads were a jumbled mess. Her fingers twitched. Then, a few spindles of thread came toward her hand like thin spider silk. They slowly wrapped around her hand. She took aim at the leaf pile again. With ease, coiled her hand and flicked it.

The leaves scattered around in a loud whoosh. A few birds and rats scattered away. Startled by a sudden change in the air. Clara gave a small satisfied smile. She looked for another pile to cause them to scatter. Little by little, she soon was able to produce gusts of wind with ease. Her arm got tired after a period. Suddenly, she smelled something. Clara picked up a piece of cloth and sniffed it. "Augh! Now I really reek!"

"Then you're in luck."

Twitch and Clara turned to Shard. He was accompanied by the Macaw Harpy, who introduced himself as Juanito, and a Reptilia with bulging eyes that rotated around every once in a while. A placid grin on his face. "They just got a bath for you already. I think you're going to like it."

Twitch looked at him suspiciously. "What are you hiding, Shard?"

"Nothing. I just figured she needed one after our adventure last night."

Twitch narrowed her eyes. Her mouth formed a pout. "I know that look. You always had that look when you're up to your tricks. Like the one time you put switched dye berries for black berries. Edli had a purple tongue for a month. I remember you had to carry buckets of water and deer dung for a month."

The Reptilia turned orange as he tried not to laugh. He was clothed in a few pieces of armor. Mostly arm guards. A dagger at his side. His tail was prehensile, held in a curled form.

Shard turned bright red at this. "Twitch! It's nothing like that. I promise. Clara will love it."

Clara laughed. "I'll take it. Just as long as I don't smell of despair and urine." She slowly went up to the Reptilia. Her stomach felt a little uneasy with this colorful stranger. "H-hello. What's your name?"

The Reptilia bowed to her. "Names Iridescent. Scout to the king. I'm a Lizardblood like his majesty. More specifically, a Chameleon." He flashed his colors with ease. "The Crocodileblood that you saw earlier is Aquir. He's stern but had been a longtime friend to the king. You'll meet Orobus, he's a Snakeblood. A little scary but you'll grow to like him." Iridescent gestured to the halls. "Follow me. I know the way to the bathing halls."

Clara sent a signal of invite over to Onyx and Lotus. They looked at her for a moment but sent her an eagerness to follow her. Clara waved her friends goodbye and followed Iridescent. After some time, they soon arrived at an immense room that had large pools of water. There was no roof above them. Stone walls raised high. Slabs of gray stone riddled around the rims of the pools. Waterfalls poured out of the mouths of mighty elephants.

Clara's jaws dropped. "This isn't a bathing hall. It's a massive room." She ran over to the nearest pool. "Hello!" The walls echoed back her greeting. She giggled with joy.

She was about to take off her shirt when she stopped. Her cheeks flushed. "Um… W-will there be fresh clothes for me when I'm done?"

Iridescent nodded. "Yes. The king has set up a few handmaids to be at the ready with fresh clothes. We had to make sure they were of your… human standards…" He went slightly black after saying those words.

"That's fine." Clara gave her best smile to reassure the Reptilia. *He's trying so hard. I'm sure that he just feels awkward about having a human here as much as I do.*

Iridescent nodded. "Very well then. Good day to you. I hope you arrive for dinner with the rest of us." He bowed. He soon vanished behind the doors which gave a heavy slam. It echoed for a moment before it settled.

Alone with her beasts, she soon began to undress. Her shirt was the first thing to go. It felt strange showing her mark in a different place. She only changed once in the Harpy village, but she had to do it in privacy that Twitch was kind enough to provide. Her pants were the next to be removed. She slowly entered the water.

The water felt cool against her skin. Flower petals tickled her skin. The ache in her feet faded away. She looked at Onyx and Lotus. "You can join me if you want to." She felt a few nos in her mind. "Okay then." She submerged into the water. It was a little deep. Deep enough for her to have some swimming room, but not deep enough where she would drown. The only time she ever swam was with her mother in the river.

Each stroke eased the ache in her body. She continued to swim until she was able to surface. After resting against some rocks, she soon saw a few things left out for her. A towel and a few bathing oils. She picked them up and began to use them. *I hope they don't make me itch.*

To her surprise, they gave off a sweet smell. Jasmine tickled her nose. It gave her skin a sense of comfort she never felt before. Just as she was heading over to the nearest waterfall, Onyx began to growl. There was something in the hall with them. She turned to see Onyx barking at something. It skittered onto the rocks before entering the water with a soft plop.

Cautious, Clara backed into the waterfall. Several birds began to descend into the open mouth room. She stared in shock as Flamingos and Ibis appeared at the rim. The skittering only grew loud. Onyx barked at the mysterious intruders. Then, he sent an image of what he was trying to catch. A rat.

Clara froze. She recalled the sound she heard earlier. She made a frantic attempt to reach the nearest stone slab. Suddenly, she felt something crawl onto her shoulder. Her heart stopped beating. She glanced to her right and saw a rat resting on her shoulder. Clara screamed. She tried to swim but the little creature swam closely beside her. The moment she reached the edge, the rat was at her side. Onyx tried to grab it, but fell in.

Lotus neighed in distress. Her horn glowed with light. The birds, rats and other small creatures that snuck in were gathering around Clara's pool. Bearing witness to the chaos before them. Clara's frantic swimming. Onyx's frustrated chase. The rat followed Clara wherever she went.

Finally, it ended with Clara hiding in the waterfall. She curled up, knees tucked into her chin. "It's hopeless. How can I be the Wild Shepherdess if I'm so scared?" Tears ran down her cheeks. *I wonder if shard did this to hurt me. I guess he still thinks little of me.* The rat stared up at her. Its tiny paws lightly touch her feet. She sniffed. "What do you want? Aren't you planning to eat me?"

The black rat, its body thin and damp, clambered up Clara's leg all the way up to her head. It took a strand of her hair. Instead of eating it, it began to groom. Licking in places that Clara missed. Paws stroking the hair. Clara shivered but no pain came. She held out her hand. The rat went down her arm. Sitting in the middle of her palm, it looked up at her.

Taking a deep breath, Clara ran a finger down its back. It gave a grateful squeak as she felt the soft fur. When she pulled her finger away, she could see that there was no dirt at all. She could feel Onyx peering at her through the waterfall. Clara waddled over to where he was. The wolf sat there. He looked like a damp dog.

Clara placed a hand on Onyx. "I'm okay now. Just…" She looked around at her new audience. "Not used to this kind of attention." The rat suddenly jumped out of her hand. She thought it was going to swim back to shore. Then, it turned to her. Beady eyes focused on her. A strange sensation came over her. It didn't feel as strong as

Lotus or Onyx, but she could feel a mischievous desire. "You... want to play?"

Onyx sniffed the rat. He stiffened as it clambered up. He tried to shake it off but it held on. Onyx tried shaking the creature off, but it only held on or hopped into the water.

Clara smiled and laughed. "Okay then. Let's play."

With that, Clara played with the rat and Onyx. Lotus simply trotted to a nearby corner to avoid being wet. Other animals started to join in the excitement. Her laughter echoed along the walls. She soon discovered Koi fish in another pool. She placed her hand in the water. Their smooth scales greeted her touch. Once the sun began to set, she was soon met by two handmaids that gave her a dress. It was indigo with light blue lizards crawling around the hem of the dress.

She waved the other animals' goodbye and went to the dining hall with Iridescent. The Lizardblood looked embarrassed the entire way over. Onyx and Lotus were at her side. Both animals give off contentment. She soon arrived at a large room with a long wooden table. Sitting at the head was King Helios. On his right was Twitch and Shard.

Twitch's feathers were flared out. They could be easily mistaken for green spikes. Her pale face was red as an apple. Sharp teeth glinted from her mouth. Her face was so close to Shards, it looked like she was ready to bite his head off. "Did you realize what you've done? If Clara comes out like a pale mess—" Twitch then noticed Clara heading toward their table. Her wings flung up in the air. "Clara!" She ran over to her friend and hugged her. "Are you okay?"

"I'm fine," Clara answered. She looked around. "What's going on?"

Twitch glared at Shard. "Want to tell her of your latest scheme?"

Shard's face was pale. His feathers ruffled with great distress. Even an unfeeling glance from King Helios made him uncomfortable. "W-well... I uh... About that bathing hall. It has a tendency to let other creatures bathe as much as other Reptilia and Harpies that reside here." A look of guilt radiated off his face. "I just wanted you to work past that stupid fear of yours. You can't do your magic if you're so afraid of animals and other things all the time."

"That's not how you handle it, dummy!" Twitch turned her glare to Iridescent. "He was involved too."

Iridescent turned black. He gripped his tail. He leaned against the wall, but he was stopped by a Snakeblood Reptilia that resembled a cobra with molted brown and green scales. "I... just wanted to help."

King Helios glanced toward him. "I'll have a word with you later." He went back to Clara. "How are you feeling, Clara?"

Clara looked at him. She tried to quell the beating of her heart but it was ready to burst out of her chest. Pink slowly creeping on her cheeks. "I'm doing well. The bath was refreshing." She gave a mocking look at Shard. "Even if someone didn't bother to tell me about what was going on with those pools." She went to her seat which was located to the left side of King Helios. Clara felt stunned that she made such a bold move.

King Helios faced her. "I'm glad that you're doing well. I would like to show you something once dinner is over." He clapped his hands and the servants soon arrived with their plates. Smells of spices hung in the air. Fish and vegetables were arranged in a manner that was fitting to them. Next to them, a small bowl, no bigger than a human finger, sat next to King Helios.

Clara took notice of this just as Onyx was given his bowl while Lotus was given trough. "What's that?"

King Helios tilted his head away, but Clara could've sworn that he looked a little embarrassed. "Oh... Just a friend coming over for a visit." Before long, the very same rat Clara met was on top of King Helios' head. It squeaked a greeting. The rat clambered over to his bowl and began to nibble.

"Oh!" Clara pointed at the rat. "You're the one I met in the bathing hall!"

King Helios glanced at her. He tried to move his head slowly but surprise gleamed in his eyes. "You did? Were... were you afraid?" His voice held a sense of nervousness.

Clara was silent before she responded. "Yes. I was. But..." She picked up a piece of fish. She leaned forward and handed it to the rat. "I saw that it didn't want to hurt me. It was a little weird, but a bit fun too." She giggled as the rat graciously took the fish with its paws.

King Helios was impressed. He gestured to the rat. "This is Mors. He's been a dear friend of mine since my parents' passing." He stroked the creature gently. Then, he went to eat his food. His cutlery was made out of pure bronze. Each movement was smooth. Even the muscles rippled with each motion.

Save for only the clinking of dishes, silence ruled the remainder of dinner. Twitch would occasionally glare at Shard. Shard would try his best to eat without the urge to shrink away. The other servants and guards also had a few moments to eat before they went to their duties.

Clara found her meal to be the most enjoyable. She found it weird that she would be eating inside a noble's home. Let alone a castle. Her eyes wandered from the tapestries to the chandelier hanging above them. She began to recall the game her parents used to play with her. Imagining what it would be like to be such a high-ranking member. However, it began to become a disgusting reminder of Lady Moorna, her pets and her parents' death.

An eerie sense of calm washed over her. Once she finished, she decided to try forming a tornado like before. Clara took a moment to close her eyes. Then, her vision warped again. The threads appeared once again in the distorted darkness. She looked to her right to see that King Helios had a mixture of water, fire and sky. The light within him swirled around like summer clouds. She turned to the window that was above them. A few light blue threads were leaking out of it.

She lifted her hand and beckoned them to come. They stretched and twisted. They clumped together, turning into a bigger ribbon. The ribbon twirled in her hand. A spiral that kept turning on her command. She turned her vision off for a moment to see that a whirlwind was now sitting on the palm of her hand. It was bigger than the last one she created the first time. The wind was ready to jump out and dance on the table.

Everyone turned their attention to the wind. They all gasped in shock. Even Onyx let out a yelp of surprise at the sight of the tornado. The plates rattled. The remnants of their meal slowly being pulled off.

"Clara! You did it!" Twitch grinned. "Now, do you know how to turn it off?"

Clara nodded. "I think so… You just have to be a little firm, right?"

"Do it gently." Twitch's grin grew nasty as she looked over to Shard. "Shard did it one time and he made blackberries fly all over the place." She laughed. "You should've seen the number of black bears and deer that came by to lick them up." She continued laughing until everyone but Shard laughed with her.

The night sky soon came. Twitch and Clara continued their lesson a little longer. Each task began to become easier for Clara. The winds can now be at her command. She was even able to create a tornado large enough to rival Twitches. Twitch couldn't be much happier. Once they were done, Twitch hovered down to Clara.

"Okay." The Hummingbird Harpy yawned. "We'll practice more tomorrow. This time, I'm going to make Shard teach you a few tricks! A special punishment for his little scheme."

"I wouldn't say his scheme wasn't too awful," Clara said. She gave a sad smile at Twitch's head tilt. Onyx and Lotus trotting over to comfort her. "I've been through worse."

"What do you mean?"

"I'm sorry. I shouldn't bug you with my past."

Twitch lean forward. Her eyes shining with concern.

Clara sighed. "There were some children in my village that hated me for some reason." She lightly ran her fingers through her hair. "M-maybe it's my hair or the way I speak. No matter what I did or didn't do, they would always find some excuse to hurt me. They had a tendency to pick on others too but they picked on me the most."

"Why didn't anyone stop them?"

"They were children of our mages and Duke of our village. Like your elders, they play a big role in maintaining things. So the adults barely do anything." Clara soon went into details about her torment under Lady Maroona and the other villagers.

"That's horrible!" Twitch hugged. "Clara. You did nothing wrong. Those… humans aren't worthy of what you offer. You try and that's what matters." She backed away. Her yawns were growing more frequent. "I better get some sleep before we get to the next steps." She waved goodnight and flew down the halls.

Clara decided to go find King Helios before she turned in for the night. Lotus and Onyx at her side once again. She asked Iridescent. After following a few instructions, she soon saw King Helios talking to several guards. They all looked tense. Their grip on their weapons was so tight that their knuckle bones were visible. She could barely make out what they were saying but their tones suggested that it might be the conflict from earlier.

Once the guards left, Clara approached King Helios. "Your Majesty, good evening." Her smile came naturally as he turned to her. She could feel tension breaking away. Her eyes wandered to all of his features. Mostly the scales. They turned to silver under the light of the moon. The white spots mimicked the starry sky.

King Helios gave a humble bow. "Good evening, Clara. I see you're doing well. Have you mastered your air spells?"

"Twitch said, I still had to learn a few things from Shard." She crossed her arms. "Though she's mostly doing that as a form of punishment. I'm sure she would want to beat him up, but he's way too strong."

King Helios let out a laugh. "You seem to have acquired some good company." He glanced up at the sky. "You know… I was once afraid of humans."

Clara stood there stunned. A Reptilia that knew fear? Reptilia were supposed to be unfeeling. *Then again*, Clara thought. *I met a Reptilia that changes color based on his mood.* "What made you stop?"

King Helios let out a low whistle. Suddenly, heavy grunts and grumbles echoed through the jungle. Onyx growled. Lotus merely stepped back at the sight of an enormous creature before them. Ears large enough to be fans. Thick gray skin that looks like a spear would bounce off it. Ivory tusks gleamed in the light. Another creature stood beside it. A golden cat with a black mane the size of a horse.

"A lion? An elephant?" Clara's eyes grew wide at the sight. Two giant wild beasts that would rip a human in two if she wasn't careful. "Uh… They're your friends as well." She gaped at him. "How many friends are beasts?"

For the first time, King Helios let out a joyful laugh. He went over to the elephant. The large creature gave her trunk to the king. A low rumbling echoed in the night sky. It kneeled and lifted King Helios onto her back. King Helios held out his hand. His eyes sparkled with an unnamed joy.

Clara gulped. She tightened her fists. She walked over to the elephant, her legs turning stiff with each step. Clara soon noticed something in the elephant's dark eyes. They held a gentle gaze. The skin was rough but almost felt so delicate that it might break. She climbed up, her feet feeling strange underneath. Clara slipped for a moment but regained it thanks to the trunk holding her hip. Her hand touched King Helios'. Warmth crawled into her stomach as she sat down.

"Ready?"

Clara nodded. She gasped as the elephant began to move. The motion had more rocking than it did when she was on Lotus. Her body tensed up. Hands immediately gripping the ears. Her breath hitched for a moment. Once they started moving, she began to calm down. The swaying motion of the elephant soothing her with every step. She could see the world becoming smaller before her. Even Lotus and Onyx could be mistaken for toys from where she was.

"Amazing isn't it?" King Helios gently slung his arm around her waist. His tail wrapped around her. He immediately pulled it away. "Sorry! That was a bit rude. Let's be off."

With that, they went deep into the jungle first. The moonlight bouncing off the trees. A weird cry ran out. Hollow and mournful. Large eyes peered out of the darkness. Small shapes leaping from tree to tree. One river held a large creature that sprung out of the water. The rubbery skin was pink as a rose. Spotted and striped creatures came out to greet them.

Clara stared out in wonder of how they looked dainty and strange under the light of the moon. "It feels like a dream."

King Helios nodded. "I used to walk in the jungle as a child. The birds here have a tendency to hold concerts with their respective Harpies. Right now it's their time to rest. Most of the creatures here have different elemental properties. The ones who stay awake in the night have far stronger power here due to their ties to the moon. That's why some humans would risk coming here. The magic is far too rich to resist." His limbs began to shake. He cleared his throat. "I've seen some Reptilia being slaughtered for no reason by human hand."

Clara turned to him. "Is that why you're so afraid of them?"

King Helios nodded again. His eyes were filled with sorrow. "My parents were doing a patrol of the territory upon hearing the word that some Slave Traders were spotted here."

Clara's face paled. "I thought that practice was gone years ago." She recalled that the recent decree by King Amen and Queen Witney along with the mage council slave trading was banned after the war with all the creatures of Weavaura. There were still a few operations made in secret, but she never thought it would happen here. Let alone have a bunch of Slave Traders being foolish enough to go after Reptilia. "What happened?"

King Helios absentmindedly strokes the elephant ears. "I tagged along because I was curious. However, those Slave Traders had prepared an ambush. They killed my parents with some form of magic I've never seen before. Next thing I knew…" His words began to weaken as he trembled. "I was being shipped off to human villages." His hands began to shake. He rubbed them against his head. "They made fun of me through a cage. A few of those wretched traitors—"

Clara soon noticed tears streaming down his eyes. They looked like diamonds gracing his scales. She reached up to him. Her warm hands tenderly cupped his face. She rubbed away the tears. Never had she ever seen a Reptilia cry before. Nor had it been so beautiful. She hugged him. Her embrace met with his. Their pain taking a moment to intertwine.

After taking a deep breath, King Helios continued. "The next village I went to was going through the early throngs of winter. I've never heard of such a thing. The cold was terrible even during the night. I curled up and prayed that the Goddess of light would come and warm me."

"How were you able to escape?"

"One of those fools passed out next to my cage. His keys were close enough for me to reach. However, I was underprepared for the cold. The only thing I could find was some burlap cloth. I was out of it. When people saw me, they shrieked. I ran a couple of times but I did get a few scratches and cuts. By the time night rolled in, I was alone." He pulled Clara in a tighter embrace. "Next thing I know, someone dragged me inside their home. I don't remember much but I was able to get home. As well as becoming king in a matter of days."

Clara gave him a sympathetic look. "I'm sorry about your family. It must've been so hard to get the others to…" Her cheeks went red. "I'm sorry again! I probably stepped out of line—" She fidgeted, her whole body was on the verge to slide off. To her surprise, her wrist was held gently in his fingers. The claws at the end barely touch her skin. Her face turned bright red.

King Helios hugged her. "No. I appreciate the gesture. Yes, the road for me being king is not an easy one. However... It was the mere idea of meeting the human who saved my life would be enough to get me here." His tail coiled around Clara's waist once again. This time it held on longer.

They were soon interrupted by the same mournful noise and a tiny mass of black fur jumped out. It had scraggly fur. More mussed up than that of a rat's. A long finger gave it a monster-like appearance. It was followed by several other furry creatures. All of them with large eyes and long tails.

Clara gasped as the little creature decided to climb onto her shoulder. "What are these creatures?"

King Helios laughed. "They're called Lemurs. The one on your shoulder is called an Aye-Aye. They won't hurt you. Just don't scare them." He lightly tapped the elephant and they continued on their journey. King Helios told them all the names of the creatures that were unknown to Clara.

The desert was also a strange treasure trove of life. As they went along the sand that was part of the Reptilia territory, Clara witnessed far more bizarre creatures in the sand. Camels with their big humps. Hairless rats that burrow down and have their own monarchy. Addax running alongside a Basilisk. A strange harmony found in an empty place filled with nothing but sand.

Clara could feel a contented exhaustion fill her. She slid off the elephant's trunk with ease. Her landing was graceful. She turned to King Helios. "Thank you for a wonderful time, Your Highness. I hope we can have more of these nights."

King Helios leaned forward. His face mere inches from hers. His eyes filled with a longing that Clara couldn't name. The silver along his body seemed to grow brighter than ever before. He leaned in and kissed her forehead. A strange sensation came off his lips. A soothing sensation that wanted to caress his human. He pulled away from her and gazed at her once more. "Perhaps we will one day. Good night, Clara." King Helios walked away with the lion close behind him.

Onyx pawed at Clara. A wave of confusion sent through their bond. Clara gave him a gentle pat on his head. "I'm okay. Just… a little surprise." She looked in the direction to where he walked. "I wonder why he looks at me differently." Something in her heart screamed of a familiar memory. However, her cheeks went red as she went to her chambers.

Chapter 16
Sand Dwarves

Clara found herself sleeping in more than normal. She was used to the early arousal that Rue would give her to do the chores. Sometimes, it was the singing of the Harpies and birds that would wake her. The soft feeling of the sheets dragged her to a nice deep sleep she hadn't experienced before. By the time that she was able to wake up, a servant came in with a tray of food. Instructions were also laid out next to the platter in where to find Shard and what her next lessons were going to focus on.

    Dressed in her now clean shirt and pants, Clara went to see Shard. Onyx merely stayed behind to eat his bowl of meat. Lotus was more than eager to be involved in more wind spells. Especially ones that might make her fly like a Pegasus. Clara laughed at the mental images Lotus sent her. The young unicorn prancing in the sky with no wings did seem a little funny. Almost as much as seeing the shocked look Shard would have if it ever happened. She was almost to the west side of the palace when she noticed something in the window. A strange cloud of dust was heading toward them.

Worried for Shard, Clara ran as fast as she could. She nearly bumped into Iridescent as she finally made it. "What's going on?"

"The Sand Dwarves are coming over here to… make an alliance." Iridescent went into a dull brown coloring as he said those words. He gripped his tail.

Shard walked forward. "Oh, great! Those dirt digging dolts are coming." He turned to Iridescent. "How long has this 'arrangement' been going on? Don't you think it's stupid at this point to convince their king?"

Iridescent glared at the Hawk Harpy. His colors shifted to a bright orange. His dewlap flared out. "You dare doubt our king's judgment?"

Clara got between them. "I know you two have conflicts but why form an alliance? Don't the Sand Dwarves have all that they need in their homes?"

"Not everything." Iridescent turned his attention to Clara. "They can't grow plants well in their desert home. The succulents that grow there contain water and some ointment but not enough for other ailments. Let alone be able to have proper crops. They are forced to eat unfertilized Basilisk eggs in order to survive."

Clara stared up at him in surprise. "I thought Basilisks were too dangerous to be near. Let alone look at them properly." She then remembered what King Helios said to her. Basilisk gaze only gives off a death-like state to a creature for only a few hours.

"Don't ask me how, but the Sand Dwarves are the only ones brave enough to do it."

Clara turned to the direction of the dust cloud seen earlier. *I wonder, if King Helios would be up for it*, she thought. *We had been up for a long time last night.* Her mind went back to that night. The tender kiss hovered in her mind. Cheeks flushed at the mere thought of how close she was at being kissed on the lips.

"Hey, Clara," Shard said, "are you okay?"

"Yes." Clara took a moment to calm herself. "Let's get to the lesson. I'm sure everything will settle down eventually."

Shard looked a bit confused but he shrugged. "As long as I can get out of my punishment and not infuriate Twitch further." He led the way to a part of the wing to use for some of the more complicated lessons. The moment he began he didn't take it easy on her. He told her how to make the tornadoes bigger. Turning wind into blades. Then, how to use your own breath as a form of defense.

Clara took each task without complaint. Even her own body began to call down the threads of the sky to give her power to her spells. Lotus assisted with the more trickier ones. Their excitement grew with each spell they accomplished. By the time the noon sun rose, Clara's face was beaming. Even waves of contentment rippled in Lotus.

Shard gave her a smile. "Nicely done, let's get some food before we get to the one that gives levitation."

Clara laughed. "This is one of a few times I hear you give me a compliment." Her stomach growled fiercely. She laughed again. She walked on with Lotus happily walking beside her. Lotus nudged her, an image of a carrot popping into Clara's mind. "I don't know if they have carrots, but we can ask."

Shard walked beside them. Wings hung limply from his body. He tilted his head at her. "For someone so keen on figuring out how to break the bond, you sure are attached to Lotus."

Clara fiddled with her hands. "Well... It's just... I guess I was getting comfortable." She turned to Lotus. "Lotus, would you like to be free of me?"

"For the last time, that can't be possible."

Clara, Shard and Lotus turned their attention to the commotion that was coming from their left. A giant door was open to reveal King Helios talking to a tan skinned humanoid. His beard was black as night and a long braid came out of his crown. He was at least four feet. His crown was made of pure silver. Garnets and emeralds were set into the metal. Red and sandy yellow robes clothed him. An image of a basilisk woven into the fabric. Crude armor was placed on his chest and arms. A short sword attached to his belt. His golden eyes looked at the Reptilia in disdain. Several guards were at the king's side.

Shard stared in surprise. "That's King Oberon. He leads the Sand Dwarves."

Clara turned to him. "Have you heard of him?"

"Nah. Just heard he's got a temper meaner than any storm."

The two noticed Twitch and Iridescent standing on the side. The group soon went over them. Twitch was the first to take notice of them. The Hummingbird Harpy was distressed. Feathers raised up. "You shouldn't be here!" She hissed. Green eyes feral. Iridescent nodded behind her.

"What are they arguing about?" Clara's question was hushed, but she still prayed it didn't carry down.

"The Sand Dwarves want a double of what was originally given in their trading, however, King Helios isn't giving them an inch."

Clara was about to lean forward to listen in on the conversation clearly, but Iridescent stopped her. "Best to stay hidden," he warned. "I heard King Oberon has a great disdain for humans. Harpies are second." He looked at Twitch and Shard. He held up his hands. "No offense."

"None taken," Shard said flatly.

Clara kept her eyes on King Helios and King Oberon. Two clans that only want what's best for their kingdoms. Yet, Clara was worried if things were going to get out of hand. She gripped the stone tightly. She silently prayed to the gods of Earth and Sky that nothing bad would happen.

"Bah!" King Oberon threw his hands up in the air. "I shouldn't expect any less from Reptilia. Cold-blooded and selfish. Bad enough those arrogant Harpies think they're so good just because they can fly around this cursed world with ease. At least they find a way to stay safe from The Empty!"

The group went still at those words. Even the guards behind them were nervous of how their king spoke of them. Clara wanted to explain the dangers of The Empty.

The things that she witnessed two nights ago were still fresh in her mind.

King Helios merely stared at King Oberon. His eyes held a brief flash of disdain and anger that he was holding back. "The only reason we can't give you any herbs is because the plants have been wilting faster than normal. Even some of The Empty had been spotted by the scouts. There wouldn't be enough medicine for both Reptilia and Harpy to survive. Let alone your people."

Clara held her breath. She could feel the heaviness increase. She looked at the warriors of each king. Hands placed upon their weapons. Ready to battle at any sign of a scuffle. She even began to notice a few Harpies gathering around them. One of them was an old man with black feathers with tips of gray appearing at the end. Feathers raised. Clara absent-mindedly took a step forward. Lotus' sending her warning signs through their link.

"It's your fault that they existed in the first place. If your ancestors hadn't hogged up all the water, we wouldn't have to use the last remnant of our reserves. Even the cursed Slave Traders wouldn't come after us. Some king you are. Can't even share with the likes of us but willing to give it to these birdbrains."

Clara marched forward. A strange burning took over her heart. "That's enough!" The words came tumbling out of her mouth before she could understand what was going on. "You have no right to talk like that. His struggles are no different from your own. I'm sorry that The Empty are making things different for you, but you have no right to take your anger out on both the Reptilia and the Harpies."

King Oberon stood there flabbergasted. He soon drew his sword. The metal aimed at Clara's throat. "A human? Here?" His eyes went back to King Helios. "What is the meaning of this Helios? Are the humans siding with you now?" Behind him, several Sand Dwarves drew out their swords.

Clara's face paled. She could feel Lotus' anxiety. A ferocious growl sounded behind them. Onyx appeared out of the shadows. His lips drawn to a snarl. Hackles raised in fury. Teeth glinted in the light. He stalked over to Clara. Fury running down her bond. The Sand Dwarf warriors backed away in pure shock, their weapons almost dropped to the ground.

"A black wolf!" one of them shouted.

"An ill omen!" A second one cursed under his breath.

"I've never seen one with those kinds of eyes before."

King Oberon didn't falter. He slowly pulled out a small dagger that was hidden in his boot. His eyes shifted to Clara and the wolf. He soon began to notice Lotus lowering her head, ears pinned back. His grip on the sword grew tighter. He moved it closer.

Clara's heart thundered in her chest. The heat of both the jungle and desert ruled her body. She balled her hands into fists. She had to calm down. However, the blade only made her voice quiver when she spoke her next words. "M-my name's Clara. I've been banished from the human kingdom." She slowly turned around. The dragon's head peeked out of her neck. Several gasps were heard. She turned around to face the King of the Sand Dwarves.

"Th-the Wild Shepherdess is real?" King Oberon took a step back. "What kind of madness is this?" His sword lowered slightly.

Clara took a deep breath. "I assure you that I'm not lying." She faced Lotus and Onyx. She sent soft waves of comfort. She sent it to Onyx first. "Onyx… I'm okay. You need to calm down." She could feel the stubborn determination. A brief image of a sword at her neck flashed. Clara glanced at King Oberon. "Drop your sword."

King Oberon pressed the metal into her skin. Droplets of blood slowly seeping out. "I'm not going to fall for those foolish tricks. You humans think you're clever of gaining magic. Well, I know why you're so cowardly with the beasts out here." The rest of the words came out through gritted teeth. "It's because you can't harvest their magic properly. Control is all a human ever wants."

Clara looked him square in the eye. "No… I never wanted that." Her right hand began to glow. Silver ribbons popped out and tied around her beasts. There were no signs of fear or anger. Just two beasts who wanted to protect their friend. Suddenly, several other beasts gathered in the courtyard. Rats and birds. Camels that were their steeds groaned and began to knock away the Sand Dwarves. Honey Badgers growled. Hyenas gave their unnerving laugh, followed by lions and leopards. Elephants trumpeted in the distance. Several Harpies flew out of the way to avoid getting trampled.

"I merely want to break Lotus and Onyx free of their curse," Clara's voice began to ring clearer. Fear slowly dripped off her body like melted ice. "I still fear beasts both here and in my human kingdom. However, it won't stop me from controlling this magic I have." With a slight flick of her wrist, a nearby palm tree creaked to life. Its trunk stretched out to give Clara a palm leaf. The wind around them twirled until they became small tornados, making the flowers dance in the sky.

The crowd backed away. The unnerving energy of the magic rippled through the earth.

King Oberon soon shook himself. He raised his sword high. "I won't be cowed by this power. It's done nothing for this world!" He brought his sword down. The blade was about to make an impact on Clara's soft skin. The blood on the blade began to form a webbing around the metal. It hummed. The light turned bright red. It broke into a million pieces, fluttering about like a crimson butterfly. At this, King Oberon was on his knees. His breath heavy.

The other Sand Dwarves were stunned. They tried their best to hide their fear, but one look at Clara made them drop their weapons. Almost at once, they fled. Sand tornados flashed out before them. Large, dark shapes popped out of the ground and snatched the warriors. They were gone in an instant. King Oberon raised his head to Clara. "D-don't think you can win us over that easily. The last Wild Shepherdess failed to save this world. You will too." He soon vanished into a wisp of sand.

Clara stood where she was. Her fingers tenderly touched the spot of where the blade had cut her. She flinched as a pinprick sensation went down. She groaned at the blood. "I just had this cleaned." Onyx and Lotus were soon at her side. Concern rippled Clara's core. She gave a soft smile. "I'm all right." She turned to King Helios. Her cheeks flushed the moment she realized what she had done. She bowed. "F-forgive me, Your Highness."

The Reptilia King walked toward her with ease. He lightly touched her face to have a better look at the wound. He pulled out a silk scarf and placed it against the wound. "You must be more careful, Clara. You're lucky that King Oberon didn't cut you down so quickly the first time he saw you."

"He shouldn't be giving you a hard time because he thinks your struggles are no less bad than his." Clara put her hand against the waded-up scarf.

King Helios glanced over to the nearest guard. "Find me some clean bandages for me, will you?" Once the guard left, he scanned the ground and sky.

The animals soon left. Their task already done for the day. High above the sky, a faint shape appeared above them. A roar echoed around the courtyard. Everyone looked up to see two dragons in the sky. One dragon was red as a untarnished ruby while the second held every color in existence.

"A light dragon and a fire dragon," Shard spoke. His feathers were raised slightly at the sight of them. He looked at Twitch. An unspoken notion set between them.

King Helios faced Clara once more. "Let's talk more inside. Perhaps it's about time I explain the Beast Heart to you more."

Chapter 17
Beast Heart

Clara's neck felt sore with each gulp she took. The bandage managed to stop the bleeding but there were enough herbs to allow healing. Clara offered to grow more for the kingdom but King Helios refused. He told her that it'd be best not to exhaust her power. The display she did earlier caused her to feel fatigued. Even hungrier than ever before. By the time she was able to sit down, her limbs threatened to fall off.

"Woah! Slow down!" Twitch handed her a pitcher of water as Clara was going after another mango.

Iridescent gazed in awe at the astounding sight while the Snakeblood, now known as Orobus, laughed as his hood flared out. "Never in my life have I ever seen a human actually devour four plates of food in the same manner as an anaconda with a capybara."

Clara took a few more gulps of water before she was able to settle down. "I'm sorry. I... I've heard that you can suffer severe fatigue after using that level of magic, but I never knew it was going to be this bad."

"Levels of magic?" Twitch raised a brow at this quizzical comment. "What is that exactly? Is it a human thing?"

Clara glanced at her right to where Twitch sat. "When a human wants to be a mage, they have to do it at a young age. That's vital because the magic is more unstable at that age, especially those gifted with it." She picked a few fruits from a bowl and set them down in a linear row. Her hand gestured to each fruit. "For example, if you're doing Earth magic, you start off as a seedling. Then, sprout for your adolescent age. Finally, you have the ultimate level. Flower if you're female and Tree if you're male."

"You've seemed to reach—" Shard snickered. "The Flower level for sure. If anything, King Oberon was ready to wet his pants." Shard was only met with heavy silence. He went back to the sliced meat on his plate.

Twitch rolled her eyes. A heavy sigh left her lips. "As much as I hate to admit it, he's right. You've come a long way with your magic." She took notice of Lotus nudging Clara for a date. She chuckled as Clara handed Lotus one. "And having a nice relationship with Lotus and Onyx."

Clara gave a half-hearted smile. She turned to King Helios. She couldn't help but notice the troubled look in his eyes. "Your Majesty, are you okay?" Clara's heart skipped a beat as King Helios looked at her again. "You-you wanted to talk about the Beast Heart?"

King Helios was silent for a moment before he could speak again. "Yes. You're probably aware of the story of how our world came to be?"

Clara nodded. "Elder Gales told me."

"Well. Beast Hearts are said to be the tears of the gods and goddesses. Each beast is to hold elemental threads that had been tangled tightly into a thick cluster of magic. However, human hearts were altered differently after Nixon tried to twist them into his own image. Due to that flaw, humans couldn't bond with beasts of the wild because it didn't fill the emptiness the same way the tame do."

"Tame?" Clara tilted her head. Then, it hit her. "Oh. The domestic animals that live back in the human kingdom."

King Helios nodded. "No one really knows how it happened, but it is believed that the first humans warped the souls of the tame to obey their beck and call. Even if it means death for them."

Clara looked over at Lotus and Onyx. Then, she thought of the animals back at the courtyards. They all surrounded them. As if she silently screamed for help and they heard her. Wanting to protect her from King Oberon. Somehow two dragons sensed her. She hugged herself. The mere idea they would die for her even if they're driven made by her death was far too staggering to imagine. "So... The Beast Heart not only contains strong magic, but could control any animal at will?"

King Helios tried to reach out for her hand. Then it froze for a moment in midair before he pulled it back. "No... I don't believe it does. The dragons and other creatures of Eldritch Magic are the source of the Beast Hearts."

Shard blinked. A bit of meat dangled from his mouth. "Hearts? As in... there's more than one?"

"But that's just a rumor," Iridescent protested. He looked at Orobus. "Isn't it?"

"We can't say for sure," Orobus spoke. "There aren't many stories about the Beast Hearts."

Twitch and Shard both sighed. "So we're not getting anywhere with how Clara is connected to the Beast Heart."

Clara thought back to what the Macaw Harpy had said earlier. Her skin crawled as she thought of Lady Maroona with a Beast Heart. The cruel acts she might do with that kind of power. Would she be heartless enough to even burn the world? "Can we ask the Elder around here?"

King Helios nodded again. He turned to Orobus and Iridescent. "Join Clara and her Harpy friends. Make sure that no hostility breaks out." Once his warriors nodded, he turned to Clara. "Be very careful. What you saw was just the tip of the iceberg of the unease here."

With that, everyone left the dining hall and went back out into the afternoon sun. The humidity seemed to intensify around the parts of the jungle. As if the land was angry about the recent encounter with King Oberon. Clara wiped her head of the sweat that began to bead down. They soon came across several huts that were in the treetops. Before long, a Bird of Paradise Harpy poked his head out of one of the huts.

He flew down with grace, the tail feathers trailed behind him like ribbons. He soon saw Clara. "I've seen you before. From earlier with King Oberon. You've become quite the talk around these parts. A fearless human that was able to stare down a sword like that." He gave a grin. "Impressive."

Clara's cheeks flushed. "I wouldn't call that bravery. More along the lines of helping someone else out on mere impulse." She cleared her throat. "We've come to see your elder. There's something that we need to ask him."

The colorful harpy nodded. "Elder Summer thought as much. He's in that hut on the ground." He pointed his wing to a run-down hut where a small fire pit stood just a few feet outside.

Clara bowed. "Thank you." She walked toward the direction with the others in tow. As she got closer, she could smell tropical flowers and burning incense. The palm leaves tried their best to provide shade. Several holes were shown on the roof. Her eyes laid on the doorway. In the darkness, she could make out a sleeping form that was no bigger than Twitch. She was about to take a step closer when a wheeze softly reached her ears.

The form slowly moved. A pair of pale eyes looked back at Clara and her group. Shuffling sounds echoed through the hut as the old Harpy came into the light. He struggled to get onto his feet. The Harpy had ashy brown feathers and a muted brown cloak to cover his body. Gray hair flowed all the way down on his back. The head was far rounder than Elder Gales. Large eyes taking up the majority of his skull. The thin mouth set into a permanent grimace. "Hello… human…" His voice graveled greatly. Each word made his whole body vibrate. "What color is your hair?"

Clara blinked. She cautiously waved a hand in front of Elder Summer's face. To her surprise, the elderly Harpy didn't respond to her movement.

"You're not the first one to act like that. Even a few youngsters kept fanning me just to see if I'll react." Elder Summer laughed. "I may be blind but I've yet to have the winds claim me! So, what's your hair color?"

Clara made a crooked smile. "Silver... My hair is silver. Also, my name's Clara."

Elder Summer stared up at the sky. "The prophecy... Did your elder tell you about it?"

"M-my village elders never mentioned a prophecy to me."

"Elder Gales only peeked and only knew that the Wild Shepherdess would be seen with silver hair," Twitch said.

"It was only a few days ago that we just found out about a human girl destroying our world," Shard said. He glared at some of the Tropical Harpies nearby. "We could've found that out in a less painful manner."

Elder Summer sighed. "I apologize for the assault. Our homes have been shrinking. The humans have taken more than they need since the war ended."

"But all the mages and knights have been saying that we've been having small plots to own. Most of them have gone to royalty."

Elder Summer grew silent. He patted his wings around until they hit a wooden bowl. Small satchels of various colors soon appeared from underneath a pile of palm leaves. He lowered himself and held the bag in his mouth. He shook it left and right. Then, the satchel was taken from him.

"Would you like some help?" Clara asked. The satchel nestled in the palm of her hands.

Elder Summer gave a thin smile. "I would appreciate that." He soon began to give a few instructions of which ingredients were needed to be placed in the bowl. Twitch helped get the ingredients that were low on. He sat down once the ingredients were mixed into the bowl. He moved his wing in a circle. Feathers around him began to be lifted into the air. The powdered materials went into the air. A faint howl resounded around them.

Clara watched in amazement as the winds used the feathers to solidify shapes. They almost moved into a life-like manner. As if a tiny world was being formed before them. It settled on several humans in robes. Eyes flashed with an eerie green color. Something about those gaze made her skin crawl.

"A terrible evil has plagued this world. Even before the great war. Its greed has consumed everything left and right. If the clans don't unite, all will be lost to the monster queen." The shapes changed to a human girl with blood red hair. Warped creatures stood at the sides of her throne. Her eyes were cold and unfeeling. Only one human stood at her side.

Clara gripped her arms tightly. "So… What about the Wild Shepherdess? There was one, right?"

"The previous Wild Shepherdess... No one knows what happened to her. Even the dragons themselves couldn't do much."

"But... Why me?"

An image of a girl similar to Clara appeared before them. She held what looked like a staff. "Clara... I know it is too much to ask for a broken child such as you. However, the Wild Shepherdess is the only one who can guide the magic back into our world. You see..." Animals soon surrounded the girl. "The beast contains multitudes of threads. They are the closest to the gods. Your kind bond because they want that power. The Wild Shepherdess guides them and protects them from being unraveled. If they die, no life would remain." The images faded.

Elder Summer got onto his feet and tried to walk forward. "Clara... You must—" An arrow hit his throat. He coughed, blood pouring out of his lips. The Harpy fell backward.

"No!" Clara screamed. She tried to lean forward but another arrow appeared, barely missing her.

"There!" Iridescent's colors went bright orange with brown speckles trailing his body. He pulled out a bow and arrow. In a matter of minutes, something fell out of the tree. He turned to Shard. "Keep Clara close to you. There might be more of them. Avoid flying!"

Shard kept Clara close to him. He saw the helpless look in Clara's eyes as they laid on Elder Summer. "There's nothing much you could do for him. We need to head back to the palace." Shard unleashed a gust of wind as a shower of arrows headed straight for them. The gales blew into nearby palm trees. Several figures fell out. He used his wings to force Clara behind him.

The figures rose from their spots like ghosts. Their mottled green and brown cloaks made them almost camouflage into the jungle brush. In their hands were crooked swords, bows and sickles. One had their hood fall back to reveal a face, a human one. Dark with a jagged scar that went from his scalp to his lip.

Clara's heart almost stopped beating at once. They were only stories, but here they were. Weapons drawn with a blood-thirsty desire in their gaze. One word escaped Clara's lips. "Slave Traders…"

Chapter 18
Slave Traders

Why? Clara's head could only be filled with questions. *They were supposed to be illegal by order of the monarchs! Why are they here? What's going on?* Clara decided to reach for Onyx and Lotus. Their anger blazed into her body like a wildfire. She gazed around to see several more Slave Traders coming out of their hiding places. Some even began to throw nets at the unsuspecting Harpies that were too late to react. Even some were downed by arrows and swords.

Shard threw a few more gusts of wind. He sharpened a few of them to cut through his opponents as well as the nets. He then turned to Clara. "Clara, try to see where Onyx and Lotus are. Use your Earth magic to guide us out of this mess and into the palace." He cried out as an arrow hit him in the shoulder. "Thundering thieves!" Shard snapped the feathered end off, but the rest remained embedded in his shoulder.

Further away, Twitch and Iridescent attacked a few Slave Traders that were trying to make off with a Harpy that was only a toddler. Twitch moved as fast as she could. Her wings barely missed the blades. Iridescent changed his scales, his body melting into the scenery.

"Where did he go?" one of the Slave Traders asked. Suddenly, an invisible force knocked him over. The second had his chest slashed as Twitch was able to break the netting.

Twitch guided the toddler Harpy to its mother. "Get to the palace." She turned to a nearby Slave Trader. A whip snapped in the air as it tried to come after her. Twitch grabbed it with her teeth. Her neck moved violently upward as the shockwave caused the Slave Trader to go flying. Suddenly, Twitch had a net draped around her. She tried to break free but a thick rope was tied around her neck. She was brought down to her knees. She tried to flare her wings but the netting prevented her.

"No!" Shard went flying over to Twitch. His eyes held a fire that Clara had never seen before. Clara watched in amazement as Shard grabbed the swords and avoided the sickles. He even slashed open a chest of one of the Slave Traders. His teeth flared out. Feathers arched almost as if they were spikes. He bit into arm. Screams resounded.

Suddenly, Clara felt something grabbing her hair. She kicked and screamed. Her eyes caught a glimpse of the man that held her hair. It was the scarred one from earlier. She smacked him before he could put the flask to her face. A brief scent hit her nose. Clara ran, her bond rippled down. She could feel Lotus' rage. *Light magic is not possible to humans*, she thought. *But, Lotus, if you can hear me, I want to do that spell we did on the night that the Empty attacked us. Onyx, I'll need you.* A brief flash of pain entered her body. She looked at her leg and saw that there was no blood on it. She did notice a strange lion approaching her.

The pelt was pale gray. A mane black as night. The body was so thin that every bone was visible underneath. However, the milky eyes were its most disturbing feature. Haunting and empty. It seemed to be more of a lifeless puppet. Even worse, it could be mistaken for an Empty.

"Wh-what on the great earth are you?" Clara soon saw several other Slave Traders began to notice her. She looked around to see that the others were too busy fighting and saving the Harpies. While I barely do anything. Tears stung her eyes. The fury of the situation burned. The Harpies and possibly the Reptilia. Everyone hurting. Clara gritted her teeth. She could see Lotus appear coming around the corner, but Onyx was nowhere to be seen.

One Slave Trader grabbed her wrist and hair. Beside him was a scrawny dog that she'd never seen before. Fur matted to its body. "You're quite a pretty one. I'm sure the king and queen will be ecstatic to have you as a maid or maybe a concubine to our chief."

"Get... Your hands... Off of me!" Her free hand picked up the threads that were in the sky. Tornados soon appeared. The twisting gales were only as big as elephants, but the force was strong enough to pull the weapons into the vortex. Several animals that were associated to the Slave Traders whimpered and ran. The Slave Traders tried to stand their ground but it allowed the Harpies to have their opening. Dogs and cats yowling in pain. Ducks were flushed out of the brush. Even some goats and sheep were picked off.

Clara used this distraction to pull away from the man and made a run for it. She activated her vision again. This time, it laid on the gray lion. She gasped. The creature was made out of black and purple threads. A dog yelped away, threads twisted into knots and spikes protruding out of it. Her stomach twisted in horror. Onyx! Lotus! Help me! Her terror thrashed out as the lion made its way toward her. She heard footsteps and barely had enough time to set up a wall of stone in front of her attacker.

"You think your magic will work on us?" Clara could now see it was the scarred man. His scar acted like a jagged crack as a purple thread leaked out. "You don't even have a proper beast."

Clara was frozen in place. The sky threads began to break one by one. The tornados slowly faded. A howl resounded around them. Clara felt a sense of reassurance. Pain riddled around the bond, but it was strong. Lotus bumped her nose against Clara's hand. The unicorn's own comfort laced with fury. A refusal to leave Clara's side. Onyx was at her side. His black pelt was slick with blood and he seemed to limp. Clara could feel her own fury.

The bandage that covered her wound fell away. The wound raw. Fresh blood seeped out. Clara remembered how tugging on Shard's life caused a negative effect on it. Reluctantly, Clara soon grabbed the scarred man's threads as he rushed toward her. She could hear his cry. Her fingers tightened, refusing to let go. The urge for Onyx and Lotus to use their power rippled along her body.

Onyx grew brighter as his red threads of fire burned in the darkness. He arched his back. He launched himself at the lion, who was in a bowed position. His jaws locked on to the mane. His grip grew tighter. The dark threads of the mane breaking under the bite.

Lotus charged at several men. Her horn stabbed several Slave Traders with ease. She bucked and reared. Her light never faded. A flash of light exploded from her. Cries resounded as men collapsed.

Clara couldn't believe what she was seeing. The Slave Traders had similar threads to the scared man. Clara felt a burning sensation at her side. Her vision faded to see Onyx had a set of claws rake against his side. She watched helplessly as Onyx was tossed away. Then, her chest hurt as large paws went on the black wolf's chest. Her mouth opened but only soundless rage came out. She twisted her fingers violently upon the green threads that covered her hand. Spikes of rock jutted out, killing the gray lion.

Spikes soon jutted out of several locations. The surviving Slave Traders ran in several directions. Harpies and some of the Reptilia that arrived dodged them. Only a few got injured. Elephants bellowed in fear. Toucans and macaws screeched into the sky. Lemurs frantically leaped from treetop to treetop to avoid getting crushed.

Clara marched over to Onyx. She ignored her screaming prisoner. The tornados vanished, a faint breeze billowing in their wake. She knelt down beside Onyx. Her hand lightly touched his side. Blood soaked between her fingers. Tears welled in her eyes. "Onyx… No… Please… Be okay…" she sobbed. Her other hand shook. A rough sensation tenderly touched her hand.

"Clara… Let go…" King Helios' voice broke through the madness. He kneeled next to her. His claws lightly pull her into his direction. Eyes filled with concern. "You're going to hurt everyone…"

"But—" Clara protested. Her voice raw. Cheeks tender from the tears that went down in rivers. Her ears felt unusually wet. "The scared man… He-he can't… He'll hurt everyone if I do."

"No, he won't." King Helios pointed to the Slave Trader. The human was looking up at the sky. His mouth was frothing. Eyes rolled into the sockets. "He's too incapacitated to do anything. We'll take care of the rest."

Clara's breath hitched. She slowly let go of the threads. Cuts soon appeared along her arms. The moment they were released, she collapsed onto Onyx. She weakly lifted her head to look at Lotus. "L-Lo-tus… Help me… heal…"

Lotus bowed her head. Horn lightly touching her fallen companion. A mournful knicker came from Lotus. Eyes closed, a bright light was once again released. Shimmering colors danced around Clara as they stitched up Onyx's wounds. The flesh sealing away the deep gaps.

Once it was done, Clara was now soaked in blood. The wound on her neck is slightly larger than before. Her hair matted to her head. Her arms looked as though she was sliced up by several daggers. She briefly turned her gaze at the scared man once more. She could barely feel King Helios' strong arm wrap around her waist. Though darkness seemed to creep beneath her vision, she noticed something fell out of the man's pocket. It was a seal. On the crest was a wolfdog, thin as a rake, holding a dagger in its mouth. *The seal of Duke Averance's... What's it doing here?*

Chapter 19
Meeting the Gods

A strange palace stood before her. The walls seemed to be a mixture of cooled magma with trees. Orbs of light danced around the grounds. The door was made entirely out of wind. Singing echoed inside, ethereal and sweet. Above it was a sky that held the moon, stars and sun in a bizarre arrangement.

Entranced by the sound, Clara went over to the entrance. She was only a few feet from the entrance. Suddenly, a female face appeared in the wall of wind. Clara nearly screamed and stumbled backward. She could only stare as the mysterious woman began to take on a solid form. The woman had wings on her back and smiled at Clara. "F-forgive me... But... um... Who are you?"

"Oh, Clara,"—the woman sighed—"I thought you would know by now. Especially since I've seen you study magic so strongly back in your village." She adjusted her hair as feathers peaked out. Suddenly, a pair of feathery antennae curled out in front of her. "Then again... those foolish teachers always drew me wrong." She pouted. "I'm Ventus, goddess of air."

Clara gasped, she momentarily covered her mouth. "I'm so sorry!" she bowed. "Please don't unleash your wrath on me!"

"I think you did that on my behalf with those Slave Traders." Ventus' eyes went cold with silent fury. She took a deep breath and smiled again. "Would you like to come inside and meet the others?"

Clara nearly fell backward on the spot. "Me? They all want to meet me?" She folded her hands. Her thoughts went to the god of night. "Will... Nixon be there too?"

"No. He's been missing I'm afraid. So is the goddess of light."

"What? But... I thought... I was told that the goddess of light killed him and restore this fragile world."

Ventus turned to Clara and took her hand. "There are a lot of things you don't know about this world, Clara."

Clara sighed. "I know. A lot of creatures of this world keep telling me that." She rubbed her temples. "I can't believe I'm getting the same lecture from a goddess. If Rue could see me—" Suddenly, a realization hit her. "Wait! Am I dead?"

"No... Your soul is just visiting for a bit. The other souls of humans have been lumbering around our borders for some time however." Ventus waved Clara over. "Come in. Come in."

Clara hesitantly walked through as the door creaked open. Their footsteps echoed across the hall. She soon glanced around. The muted and bright colors swirled around her. A few statues stood tall. Various dragon statues stretched their wings and tails. Before long, she came across a council room where three other characters stood behind a large, oak table. Above the table was a tall chandelier. She recognized the two gods from before. The other goddess wasn't one she'd seen before. Her head was that of a marine creature known as a dolphin. Her skin was smooth and gray. Dark eyes watching her eagerly as if she expected Clara to play with her for a long time. She wore a dress of light blue. The cloth free-flowing.

"U-um… Hello…" Clara gave an awkward wave. Her smile revealed her teeth. Eyes wide with fright. They all head toward her. She felt like a Sand Dwarf being surrounded by these giants. Up close, they seemed to be a few feet bigger than Gaia. *If Rue and the others back home would see me now.*

"Good to see you again, Clara," spoke the green man. His mouth had tusks jutting out of his lower lip. Flowers, vines and leaves went down from his head to his hips. A muscular build that a farmer would envy. He wore a green cloak with a green vest underneath.

The fire God had molten eyes. Hair made out of pure flames that changed to a mixture of green and purple. His frame was a bit thin, but held some muscle to him. Ears pointed out and made him resemble a Dark Elf. Horns curved into a spiral like that of an Addex. He wore more armor around his chest and legs. His arms held a scale-like pattern similar to Reptilia.

"It's um… nice to meet you all." Clara felt the silence hold her and the others down. She looked at all of them up and down. "I do wish it was under better circumstances. Also, you're all a little… different from what I imagined."

"I blame Aruin for this folly." The fire god, who Clara recognized as Mueric, growled. "He just had to make all of us look human just for his silly little game."

"The first human king?" Clara has heard of this story before. Aruin was the first human king during the times of chaos. He guided the other humans to prosperity by finding the threads that controlled the domestic beasts. Forming a permanent bond with them would allow them to control them.

"He's not human, I'm afraid," the water goddess answered. She lowered herself. "He's Nixon's jealous brother."

"What?" Clara rubbed her temples. She bit her lip. She shut her eyes in frustration. "This is just so much to take in. Why am I here? What's going on with my parents?"

Ventra sighed. She looked at the others. "We need to tell her this."

"Clara," the water goddess spoke, "the reason why you're here is because of your power."

"My… power…" Clara rolled her eyes. "It's the Wild Shepherdess thing again isn't it?"

"Yes and no." Ventra knelt down to Clara's level. "Clara, you were the only human that saw the warped threads." His frown deepened. "However, you are the only human in existence to learn how to pluck a life thread. We know you're only doing it for protection, but you mustn't let your soul become tangled with another. It can corrupt you in ways that you can't imagine."

Clara's skin went cold as she recalled what she did to the Slave Trader. Tears stung her eyes. "What can I do now? Can I see my parents?"

"In time," Ventra said, "all we can say right now is that since humans have been making false connections to the beast, it made it difficult to find the path to find The Road."

Clara gaped. Her heart began to sink in sorrow. The Road was supposed to guide the souls to the afterlife once both beast and human have perished. Now knowing this…"You mean my parents… They're…" Her throat constricted at the word she didn't want to say.

"No entirely," the Fire God spoke. "Let's get one thing clear. You must restore the power of this world. Or no soul will be made into existence. Beast, human or any other clan."

Clara looked at the Fire God in the eye. "Why don't you do it?"

The gods raised their arms and a glow surrounded them. Before long, wounds soon appeared. They criss-crossed along the length. The skin looked slightly pale. Even the fingers were almost ready to fall off at any moment.

"Our war with your 'king'," the Earth God said. His words soon began to drip with venom. The leaves and petals that formed his hair began to look extremely withered. "Nearly took everything from us. Even our own existence."

"But I'm nobody," Clara spoke softly. "I can't even protect Onyx from a lion. Let alone heal him properly." She looked at all of them. "I'm sorry. I can't help you. I need to free Lotus and Onyx from this curse before they wound up like that lion. They'll never be happy as long as I'm with them." She walked away for a moment and turned to them. "Take care. I'll find my parents when this is over."

A whirlwind of whispers entered her ears as she walked on. One of them was a voice that rang loud and clear. "Clara…" A warm sensation came to her upon hearing her name. Her limbs started to feel a scaly hand hold her carefully. Before she saw a beam of light, she heard Ventra's words.

"Clara, go to the kingdom beneath the sands. Bring King Oberon's love back to him."

Chapter 20
A Kingdom beneath the Sands

Clara found herself in bed. A gray shape looming over her, but her eyes were able to focus and King Helios came into view. His kind eyes looked down at her. A cool night breeze entered the room. He wore a tunic of simple brown colors, but it didn't hide his pleasing frame. "Welcome back." His voice was smooth and comforting.

"Onyx..." Clara flinched at those words. The pain in her throat radiated. She tried to move her hand, but her arm burned as if it caught on fire. She briefly glanced down to see her arms were heavily bandaged. Clara felt embarrassed and frustrated with herself at that point. "I'm sorry..." She turned her head away. Then, her head turned back to King Helios.

"You did what you could for him and the rest of us." King Helios gently pressed his head against hers. He moved away and soon pulled out a vial. A lavender-colored liquid swirled in his gentle fingers. King Helios carefully tilted her head, his fingers cupping her chin with great care. He placed the now open vial onto her lips.

Clara instinctively took in the liquid. She shivered as it went down her throat. Disgust ruled her mind, but she bit back the urge to spit it out. Clara could feel some of it numbing the pain. She carefully experimented with her fingers one by one. No pain so far. Then, she tried moving her hand. Not as bad. She wanted to speak, but her throat gave a dull ache. A warning not to even utter a word.

Suddenly, several shuffling noises were heard right beside her. An enormous head popped into Clara's view. It was none other than Onyx. The giant wolf looked like a heartbroken puppy. Heterochromatic eyes bright with worry. A soft whine came out of his muzzle. His sorrow and guilt rippled in the bond.

Clara slowly moved her hand on top of his head. She slowly went into his mind. She sent reassurance between the line. Her apologetic voice went into it. *It's okay, Onyx. I was the pathetic one to let you get hurt again. You're only following me because of my bond. You deserve so much more.* She slowly stroked it. Her mind went to find Lotus. It was a dull hum. However, Clara could make out the anger and frustration that radiated off of it.

A faint whinny was carried over the night breeze. Before long, hooves were thundering in a distant courtyard. Shouts and screams echoed out. King Helios turned to the window. His smile radiated in the silver light. "Looks like Lotus found out that you're awake."

A heavy bang of the door made Clara jump out of her skin. Lotus knickered as she moved over to Clara's bed. Relief washed over the two. The young unicorn was worn down. Lotus brushed her muzzle against Clara's forehead. Her neck was bandaged.

Clara turned to King Helios. Her eyes burned with many questions.

King Helios sighed. He rubbed his temples. "Where do I even begin… Let's just say that we were able to round up the living Slave Traders that hadn't escaped us. The Harpies are currently holding a ceremony for Elder Summer. His death is called for human blood. Right now, they're being held for questioning. As in terms of possessions… it seems that one of those rock spears hit a nearby cart that had some slaves stashed away." His face began to take on a grimmer look. "They've also taken the Queen of the Sand Dwarves, Arebella."

Clara tilted her head. "I thought all Dwarves were male." She flinched and cursed out to the gods for her damaged throat.

"No. There are females, but they mostly hide out or hunt close to the perimeter of their territory. Especially, if…"

"What?"

"They're carrying a child."

At those words, Clara's heart froze in place. She could hardly imagine a woman being able to survive Slave Trading. Let alone when carrying a child. She recalled one woman who lost her unborn babe to the trade and went insane. Clara's fingers curled into Onyx's fur. The words that Ventra had said to her about the kingdom of the Sand Dwarves. *Is this what she meant?*

"Right now... Queen Arebella is in stable condition. However, I need to send her back or the Sand Dwarves might wage war on us."

Before Clara could ask the question, the answer rang in her mind. The Reptilia refused to give medicine. Their supplies are already thin as it is. Now here she was taking the last of it.

King Helios tilted his head at her. He gently stroked her head. "Don't be hard on yourself, Clara. That medicine was worth giving to you."

Clara felt heat crawling up in her cheeks. She gulped hard. However, the dryness of her throat only made her more thirsty. She watched as he left. Her eyes never took off his sleek yet muscular form. Once King Helios was gone. She fell back to sleep with Onyx and Lotus curled up by the sides of the bed.

The next morning was surprisingly dark. As if the sky mourned the loss of a dear Harpy. Clara wasn't able to attend, but she heard an eerie tune. It felt mournful. The same heaviness she felt when her parents left her. The pain was still there but not as bad as it was earlier. Her limbs were now free to move as they wished. She was even able to sit upright to eat.

Her fill was nothing more than water and a few mangos. Clara took in the strange, sweet taste of the fruit, but she noticed that it was a bit bitter. Even the water itself had a tinge of dirt that didn't feel right. Clara slowly got out of bed, Onyx supporting her side. She looked at him.

"You don't have to do that, you know." Her voice was still raspy, but didn't cause much pain as before.

Onyx looked up at her. A sincere gaze in his eyes. In a matter of minutes, the bond between them soon gave way to a memory. It was similar to the dream that Clara had before. A puppy Onyx being rejected and picked on by the other members of his pack. His mother being dead on the ground. Wolves from other packs snarling at him each time he had to introduce himself in the pack. Humans hunting him every time he got close. Dogs barking at him. Weapons pointed at him.

Clara's own memories soon began to mingle with his. Lady Maroona's taunts. The villagers all giving her angry looks. Her falls sparking more rage. The wary eyes that follow her strange hair among the black, brown, a few blond and red hairs. No matter how many bruises and cuts she took, Clara was somehow able to find the reason to live. A hidden plea from this world not to go.

The moment their mental exchange ended; Clara found her cheeks wet with tears. Her heart didn't feel as heavy. It felt strange, but the pain they share seems so similar in more ways than one. She swallowed hard. Her fingers tightened her grip around Onyx's black fur. Her feet began to grow steady as they made to the doorway and started to head down to the bathing hall.

Twitch and Shard soon met her halfway. The two were quite shocked that she was out of bed and in a disheveled state. They also weren't in the best spirits. Their wings looked ruffled. Shard had some bandages around his midsection and legs. As for Twitch, she had some cuts along her wings.

Twitch gave a sympathetic stare and helped Clara to the wash halls while Shard stared at them silently. The two went inside and silently began to clean themselves. A few birds and even an Indri joined them. Water flowing and smacking against the rock was the only thing that could break their silence. Even Clara took great care of cleaning Onyx's fur and Lotus' mane.

Once they were done, the servants soon arrived to hand them their towels and were asked to join King Helios. Everyone soon arrived into another large room. It was just as spacious as Clara's. Green and bronze silk scattered across the floor. Smells of incense flooded the room. In the farthest corner of the room sat a large bed with black curtains drawn. Sounds of shuffling and whimpering echoed. A nightstand was knocked over. Shattered remains of a jar were against a wall. One Reptilia servant was even plastered to a nearby window.

Twitch turned to Iridescent. "How long has she's been like this?"

"For a day and a half." Iridescent took on a few notable shades of brown. He rubbed his chin. "I don't know if we can get her out of there."

"Did she eat anything?" King Helios focused his eyes on the curtains. His body taut, but it was shaking a little. He tried to maintain his head.

"She drank her water like a crazed lion," Iridescent said. "When it came to feeding her though… Well… half of the servants had to run for cover. She was throwing things at them."

"What about her baby," Clara asked. Her fingers went cold at the mere idea that the Sand Dwarf Queen carrying a dead baby inside of her after what happened. "Is it okay?"

Iridescent gave Clara a grim expression. "It's hard to tell at this point. Her stomach is extremely swollen, but the bruises indicate that she was beaten just for sport."

Clara clenched her fist. Her amber eyes began to glow briefly almost there was a fire inside of her. Ready to burst out at any moment. Her throat clenched hard. She took a deep breath. *Rue always said that they were ruthless, but this is too much.* Clara walked over to bed and gently pulled away the curtains.

In the bed laid a Sand Dwarf. She had a muscular build, but hers were more feminine. The queen was the same size as her husband. Her hands were on her swollen stomach. She was curled up, tears in her eyes. Her black hair was short, almost non-existent. Her dark skin made her blend into the darkness around her. Whimpers of pain didn't die away.

Clara got on her knees and nervously laid her hands down on the side of the bed. Being careful not to touch the distressed Dwarf. "Your Highness… Queen Arebella," Clara managed to keep her voice soft, but her shyness betrayed her. "Can you hear me?"

Queen Arebella stopped her sniffling. She looked up. Her dark eyes stared at Clara. She slowly got up from her spot. Queen Arebella snarled and hit Clara in the face. She spat in her face. "Go away! It's all your fault. M-my baby is gone. Gone because of your kind!" She threw another fist and a ferocious kick. "I wish all of your stinking kind was dead."

"Clara!" Twitch tried to move forward but was stopped by King Helios. His arm raised in a gracefully manner.

"Let's see what she can do." King Helios focused his eyes back to Clara. His hand gripped tightly around the pommel of his sword.

Onyx whimpered. He nudged his muzzle against Clara's head. It was met by a hand that rubbed his muzzle.

"I'm okay, Onyx..." Clara got up. Her face revealed a bruise on her left eye and her nose broken in a few places. She wiped the blood dripping from her nose with the sleeve of her tunic. "It's not the first time I got punched in the face." She chuckled. "I just got healed too." Clara tried her best to hide her tears. No isn't the time to cry.

Clara managed to dodge another punch that came to her. She lightly clasped the queen's hand. Thick fingernails dug into her skin as a second hand clamped around hers. Trying their best to pry them off the first one. Clara grimaced, but held her gaze to Queen Arebella. "Your Majesty, I'm sorry that it happened to you and your baby. I know it must be so frightening. Why can't you let the healers have a proper look at you? Maybe your baby is still alive in your belly."

Queen Arebella hissed. "My baby is dead. I know it to be true. I felt no movement after a few days of being punched and kicked around." Her hand pulled harder Clara's hand. Then, it slipped and pulled on the sleeve. A blank stare replaced that rage.

Clara stared at her scars. "I just got these just yesterday. I nearly died of the magic I was using to save both Harpy and Reptilia alike." Her grip slightly tightened. "Little did I know that I was also saving you in the process." She rubbed her thumb against a callous surface. "However, I still have a long way to go with this magic. I know deep in my heart that your baby is still alive."

"Why? Because of your accursed magic, human?"

Clara shook her head. "No. I've heard stories from some of the war veterans of how hardy the Sand Dwarves are. I had no idea about that until I met your husband."

"Oberon?" Queen Arebella began to relax slightly. Her eyes held a sad glow. Tears threatening to return. "Did… did he look for me?"

"I'm sure he was. He kicked up a fuss at the negotiations. He even raised his sword against me. I think part of the reason he was cruel was because he was worried about you. It won't help him if you're like this. Please, let us help you."

"Why should I believe a word you say?"

Before Clara could answer, she soon found herself diving into her special sight once again. A bunch of red and green threads laid before her. Its smaller tendrils curled up on her. Underneath, further down where the abdomen was to be, a small light vibrated. Clara slowly let her hand reach to the spot. She nearly jumped out of her skin at the contact. Life. A tiny spec of life that had yet to be born.

Clara gently touched some soul threads of Queen Arebella's. She could hear a startled gasp, but was not met with any resistance. They touched and a soft voice reached them. "Hello…"

Clara's vision went away. The threads faded away and was replaced by furniture and solid shapes. She sank to the floor. She cupped her hand as bile made her way to her throat. Iridescent and Shard helped her off the floor. Vertigo caused her legs to wobble until she was able to reach a nearby chair. She set herself down. Cold sweat beaded down her brow.

"My baby…" All eyes were now on Queen Arebella. Her eyes were filled with tears again, but there wasn't a spark of anger like there was earlier. It was as if the fears and anxieties that plagued her went away. She gently rubbed her hands against her stomach. "I felt my baby. They're alive."

Clara gave a weak smile. "I knew it was so. Can you please eat? W-we can help you get home."

Queen Arebella looked up at Clara. "D-do you mean that, human?"

Clara turned to King Helios. "If it is all right with you, Your Majesty."

King Helios nodded. His eyes went back to Queen Arebella. "Queen Arebella, now that you know that we mean you and the baby no harm, I will assist you on bringing you back home." He bowed. This statement earned several gasps in the room. "I know that you're in dire need of medication, but the only reason that we can't give you any is because our supplies are being dangerously thin. Let this be a chance to have a proper alliance."

Queen Arebella thought for a moment. Her hands on her stomach once more. Then, she turned her attention to a bowl of dates. She plucked one and bit into it. She turned to him. "The alliance isn't my call alone. However, if you can get me home safely, then we might consider something."

Clara straightened. Her hands balled into fists. "If there is anything we should be angry with, it would be The Empty. Ever since they appeared, they've ravaged the land. We need to stop them before it gets out of hand."

Onyx let out a small bark in agreement. Even Lotus moved her head up and down wildly. They went over to Clara. Their muzzles lightly touched her. They licked her hands, earning her a laugh. A soft glow soon radiated off the three of them. Lotus' horn glowed a soft shade of blue. The light landed on Clara's nose just as it had started to bruise.

Everyone stared in shock at what they were witnessing. Plants began to grow underneath the trio. Ferns and tiny palm trees peeked out of the floor. Once it was over, Clara was now able to stand. Gasps filled the room. Queen Arebella's was the loudest.

"It can't be..." Queen Arebella looked at Clara. "A-are you... are you bonded to them, human?"

Clara nodded. She felt her skin tingle. Her eyes went down her arms to see the scars from earlier beginning to fade. Her cheeks flushed. "W-well... I am... I'll fix it."

Queen Arebella slowly got up from the bed and walked over to Onyx. She raised her hand to let Onyx sniff it. She soon stared at his eyes and ran her hands around it. Queen Arebella backed away. Queen Arebella turned her attention to Lotus. The unicorn eyed her warily. Her ears pinned back slightly. Queen Arebella raised her hands, her belly revealed to Lotus. Lotus only touched her stomach before she backed away. She wobbled for a moment before she went into the bed. Her glance turned to the wolf. Queen Arebella simply laid down.

King Helios gestured for the servant nearby to come toward him. Once the servant did as he was told, King Helios leaned forward. He relayed a few instructions. The servant bowed and began to gather a few extra sheets that laid on an ottoman.

Clara gently gripped Onyx's fur and Lotus mane. She slowly got up from her spot. She couldn't explain it, but it felt like her own core was being explored by Queen Arebella as much as Lotus and Onyx. Her legs were unsteady but they didn't threaten to collapse under her weight. She was a few feet from the door when the tired voice of the Sand Dwarf queen reached her.

"Human..." Queen Arebella spoke. "What name do you go by?"

Clara slowly turned to see the queen resting comfortably in bed. The teal sheets wrapped around the small frame. "Clara. My name is Clara."

As the night began to draw out, Clara found herself having dinner with King Helios. Twitch and Shard were helping get a few things prepared for their next leg of their journey. Iridescent was also asked to join them. The other Reptilia guards were to stay behind and make sure that there was no uprising while their king was gone.

She gingerly ate her small plate. It mostly contained raspberries and a few edible succulents. Onyx was out hunting for his food while Lotus grazed outside the palace. Clara tenderly checked her link to make sure that nothing happened to them while she was away. Her fingers held her fork in a vice grip. Her nerves rippled slightly. She glanced over to King Helios.

King Helios was eating his piranha. Its red belly cut open. A few candles burned around him, making his scales look as though they've been forged from steel. His gaze held immense concentration. His tail thumped on the ground.

"King Helios…" Clara spoke. Her heart nearly jumped out of her chest as King Helios looked at her. "Why would you want to join me? Wouldn't you risk your throne for my sake?"

King Helios put down his fork and stared at her. His blue eyes held a soft gaze when they land on her. It's as if he knows something about her in a way she doesn't. He suddenly got up from his chair. He vanished for a minute.

King Helios soon came back with a brown cloak. It was made out of thick wool. On the center of it was embroidered dragon. The gray threads turned silver in the light of the nearby torches that lit the room.

Clara leaned forward. Her fingers lightly traced the threads. It was slightly crud. Some of the stitches made the shape come off a little jagged. Even the mouth was shaped wrong. Her skin was riddled with goosebumps. *Why does this feel so familiar?* Her eyes went back to the Reptilia King.

"I got this from a human in a small village." King Helios' eyes went dark as he spoke. "When I was captured by Slave Traders, they took me to the Human Kingdom. I saw trees and animals that I've never seen before. Furry creatures so burly and ferocious. White powder that was cold to the touch." He gripped his hands tightly.

Her throat constricted. "W-what was the name of the village?"

"Snowdrop village."

Clara's skin went pale at this. "That's... the name of my home. Or was..." She looked down at her hands. She soon recalled a crowd gathering around a carriage. A lock that broke. "How did you escape them?"

"One of them got too drunk." King Helios' lips curled in disgust at the memory. "He tried to splash some in my face, but I dodged it. I had never been thankful for a large cage. He fell asleep. The stupid fool had his keys in a place where I would reach." He sat down. His elbows probed him up as he leaned onto the table.

"I... remember the panic that happened. Everyone had to get inside because rumor has it that younger Reptilia would vicious eaters. Not hesitant to eat anything that moved." Clara wanted to throw up after saying those words. Her fingers curled into the fabric.

King Helios sighed. "I only had a few clothes on me, but it wasn't enough against the cold. It felt like an eternity. I wasn't even sure I was going to make it. I came across a house that was far away from the madness. I didn't want to be anywhere near a human after everything but... I didn't want to die in the snow. I knocked and got dragged inside." He placed a scaled hand on the cloak. "The human gave this to me before I went away."

Clara shivered. Her heart raced immensely. She snatched her hands away. "I-I see... So... You're doing this in honor of the human who helped you."

King Helios nodded. "Yes. If it weren't for her, I wouldn't be here. Worse yet, I would've been just as spiteful as King Oberon is right now."

"Well... That is until we get Queen Arebella home." Clara quickly got up from her seat and bowed. "Thank you for the dinner, Your Majesty. I best pack for the journey." She went away before King Helios could say anything else.

Once she arrived to the room, she slammed the door shut. Clara sat on the bed. Her hand grasped her shirt tightly. The other hand went into her hair which had grown a little longer than it had for a long time. *No...* She thought.

NO! NO! NO! It can't be! It can't be him! Her breathing hitched. She went over to her bed.

Her mind went back to the memory of what happened when a Reptilia was loose. The night when a young boy came to her house. A knock resounded on the door. Her parents were fast asleep. Clara tried her best to stay under the covers. The knock came again, weaker this time. It was soon followed by a groan.

Clara couldn't help but feel concern hit her stomach. What if someone was outside because they got locked out in a panic? It wasn't the first time her village witnessed a death of someone who was locked out of their house during a cold winter. Clara gulped. She grabbed her pillow and walked over to the door. She had to stand on her tiptoes to reach the knob.

The moment she opened the door, a scrawny figure flopped into the doorway. It was a little hard to see who it was due to the lighting. Even the crescent moon's light didn't help. The only thing that could be made out of the mysterious stranger was that he, Clara was sure it was a he, was small. No doubt to be around her age. A big burlap cloth was the only thing covering him.

Clara immediately pulled him inside. She shut the door, but it slammed shut. She looked to see that her parents were still asleep. Clara managed to grab the stranger and dragged him to her bed. She pulled down the sheets with ease. More groaning was heard. She knelt down before the shivering shape. "I'm sorry," she whispered. "I can't use the fire. I'll burn the whole house down."

"M-mother…"

Clara nearly jumped back in shock. The shape shifted. She looked into a wicker basket. She pulled out a small cloak from it. It held a misshapen dragon sewn into it. Clara tenderly placed the cloak on top of him. "This should make you feel better." She went back to her bed and curled up. For a while, she tossed and turned for some time. The cold touched her feet. She huffed with frustration.

Clara looked down to see the bundle sleeping peacefully. The breathing evened to a soft lullaby. It was still hard to make out what his hand, but it seemed inviting. Clara blushed. She never slept next to a boy before. However, he had all the blankets. If it would stop from getting colder… Clara slid off her mattress. She slowly laid down against the boy. To her shock, something firm wrapped around her. It was no doubt the boy's arms. She froze. However, it did feel really warm.

"W-why are you helping me?" The voice that came out of the little boy was raspy.

"Well…" Clara hesitated to answer. "You needed help. My parents taught me to help those in need. No matter what."

Her eyes began to close. The last image was a pair of blue eyes staring back at her. A soft "thank you" tickled her ears. The next morning, there was nothing left of the mysterious stranger. Her hand make cloak gone.

Now, here she was. Her mysterious stranger that ever showed her gratitude in her life was now a king. The escaped Reptilia. She gave herself a moment to cry before she went back to packing her things for their trip. Her heart trying not to break. *Why?*

The morning came. Clara managed to pack whatever was needed. Twitch, Shard and Iridescent were equipped with pieces of armor. Iridescent and King Helios both had long swords. Queen Arebella was simply given a cloak and a saddle made out of scrapped cloth so it wouldn't hurt Lotus' back.

They didn't get much detail out of the Slave Traders. Whenever they were asked about who their master is, they simply chuckled and gave wicked grins. Their leader was a babbling mess. He even screamed unintelligible words the moment Clara walked into the room.

Clara stood out in the afternoon sun with Twitch and Queen Arebella. She was dressed in a pale blue tunic with a pea green skirt. Her white hair waved in the small breeze. Onyx sat beside her. The large wolf let out a yawn. He was eager to start the journey before it was too hot to do anything. Lotus was being patient, her ears pricked forward.

Twitch sighed. "Too bad we didn't get any answers from those slave traders. It would've saved us a lot of trouble." She looked at the treetops that bordered the jungle. "Well. Not all the trouble. I just hope the Jungle Harpies aren't going to proclaim war on the Reptilia."

"I'd be more concerned of the state of the slaves that were still alive," Queen Arebella stated. She held her belly. "This morning I heard Iridescent trying to convince the slaves to return home…" her eyes narrowed. "They were far more broken than I was."

"You mean by all the beatings and being cut up by a sword?"

Queen Arebella shook her head. "No. It's much worse than that."

Clara went pale. Her skin bringing out her shadows from last night. Her mind went back to that off-colored lion and her incident with Shard. "The threads in their bodies…"

Queen Arebella grimly nodded. "Yes. The more specific term is Life Threads. To a regular human, they wouldn't be easily distinguished between the threads of regular plants. However, they do have a brighter light."

Clara nodded. "I've seen it before. Usually when I activate my power."

Twitch glanced at Clara. "Now that I think about it, I do recall Elder Gales said your ability went by a name. I… think it was Soul Eye."

"Soul Sight," Queen Arebella corrected. "You were close though. A very rare ability. Even one is born every century in my clan."

Clara looked at the sky. *I wonder if King Helios has it too and… that Slave Trader.* Her thoughts were interrupted by the sound of footsteps. She turned to see King Helios, Iridescent and Shard. Her cheeks flushed instantly.

King Helios was dressed in his traditional attire but he had arm guards made out of pure silver. His green cape billowed in the breeze. His blue eyes sparked with sincerity.

Clara was about to say something but the knot in her throat stopped her. Emotions swirled around her like threads being tied together. Anger. Confusion. Her fist tightened. Knuckles turning white.

"Clara?"

Clara turned her attention to Twitch's concerned face. "I'm okay." She felt Onyx nudge his muzzle against her hand. She sighed. *Maybe not.*

With that, everyone immediately began their journey. With Queen Arebella's help, they were able to get through the golden sands. The heat began to increase by the minute. As the sun reached its highest peak, the group went to a cactus to have a drink.

Lotus laid in the sand, her body curled up, supporting Queen Arebella. Clara handed her a flask of water. Onyx laid down by the Sand Dwarf queen. The large wolf gave a soft whimper. His large head nestled against her swollen stomach. For a while, the group just simply laid down in the dunes.

Twitch and Shard tried to groom themselves. Their talons gently going over their feathers. Wings flared out; they could be easily mistaken for kites. Smiles were soon on their faces. Twitch sang a soft tune of her people.

Clara watched King Helios. Her eyes focused on his movements. She wanted him to actually look this way. The words jumbled in her heart. She gripped her pants hard. She tried to get up but her legs weren't moving.

"Good grief," Queen Arebella huffed. "You're moving like you've been stung by a scorpion. What's eating you child?"

Clara tucked in her lips. Normally she would tell Rue about certain problems. However, she's never dealt with the feelings that swirled inside of her. Her nails dug into her knees. "W-well... I... I just... have these feelings I just developed."

"For who?" Queen Arebella asked. She tilted her head. Her lion-like gestures made Clara even more nervous.

"Just... for someone in... the Re-Rep..."

"Someone in the Reptilia Kingdom?" Queen Arebella was dazed for a moment. Then, a sly smile was on her face. "Ah... I see. You've got a fondness for a Reptilia haven't you?"

Clara's face got redder the moment she followed Queen Arebella's dark eyes. Once there was a brief exchange, she covered her face. "Of all the men in the world, why did it have to be him?"

Queen Arebella smiled. "You kind of remind me of myself when I was younger."

Clara moved her hands slightly from her face. She gave a puzzled look. It felt strange having the queen be this friendly toward her. Only yesterday, the queen punched her nose. She only stared at her.

"I wasn't much of a magnet for Sand Dwarf men at sixteen." Queen Arebella let out a laugh. "The looks weren't much of a problem compared to my prowess. A lot of men were intimidated by my strength and skill. Even the other women teased me about it."

Clara tucked in her knees. "Yeah, I know how that feels," her mouth went dry as she's said them. "I... got teased by everyone for my hair. They'd say I would never get married because my hair has a wicked spell on it."

"So, one day, King Oberon was in search of his bride. You wouldn't believe how many maidens practically swoon and fought tooth and nail for him!" Her laugh grew louder. It was up to the point where even Lotus lifted her head in shock. "I, on the other hand, didn't think I was capable of winning him. Plus, at the time, I thought of him as a big ol' blowhard."

Clara couldn't help but giggle. She could even feel Lotus and Onyx laughing in their bond. All the twisted feelings slowly unraveled inside her. She began to ease a little. "So, what made you change your mind about him?"

Queen Arebella glanced at the cactus that we were nearby. Sitting on top of its head was a small white flower. She gave a sweet smile. "He approached me one day. He asked me where I could find blood diamonds."

"Blood diamonds? What do they do?"

"Whoever wears them are said to heal instantly. In some cases, it's said to turn our body to stone. Making us a formidable force."

Clara lowered her knees. "Do they?" She tucked in her lips. Regret clung to her stomach. "Sorry…"

A soft glow went over Queen Arebella. "I gave him directions. He was stunned that I didn't act like a star-struck meerkat. Sometime later, he came back and demanded that I duel with him."

Before long, Clara hung onto every word about Queen Arebella's engagement with King Oberon. Their fights. Their wishes. When the Sand Dwarf queen talked about marriage, Clara's heart began to sink. Her eyes began to sting with tears. "Th-that's a nice story… I wish that could happen to me." Clara dug her nails in her pant leg. Her lips formed a deep frown.

Before Queen Arebella could say anything, King Helios walked over to the group. The Reptilia King looked down. "Clara, are you okay?"

Clara wiped her face. "Yes," her voice crackled slightly at the lie. "I'm fine. The heat was a bit much." She took a handful of water from the small well they dug up. She wiped her mouth. She got up and helped Queen Arebella onto Lotus.

By the time, they were on the road again, the sun was an angry orange orb. The sand turned golden against the sunset. A few oryx were seen. However, a camel carcass with a large gap in its chest told the group that the Empty were close by. Even the vultures were reluctant to even try to eat it. All eyes and weapons were on display as they watched closely.

Night finally arrived. The blanket of stars did little to put their fears at ease. Clara glanced around nervously. She even activated her vision to make sure the black masses don't appear. Her mind went back to those voices. Her ears strained to listen to that haunting request. She tried to hide the fear in her bond, but she could hear Onyx growl and Lotus snorted. She was so focused on finding them that she nearly jumped out of her skin by a light tap.

She turned her attention to Twitch. Clara didn't realize she was holding her breath until she let it out. "Sorry…"

Twitch lightly patted Clara's head. "It's okay. I don't blame you." They both glanced at Shard. His head swerved from side to side.

Clara soon turned her attention to Queen Arebella. Her heart twisted as the queen put her hands on her stomach again. *She almost lost her baby to the slave traders*, she thought. Her skin began to show goosebumps. *We need to get her back home soon.*

Suddenly, King Helios came up to her. She was surprised to see him hold up something in his hand. It was a dagger. The sheath was made out of wood with lizards carved into the wood. The pommel was made out pure bronze, shaped like a lemur's head with emeralds for eyes. "Something to protect you."

Clara was stunned. Her hands shook at the sight of the elegant weapon. She was never given a gift before. Sometimes Lady Maroona would hand her a toy sword only to beat her with it. Clara wrapped her fingers around it. She shivered. Her skin didn't feel cold. She looked up at King Helios. "Thank you," she whispered. She took a moment to set up the dagger around her hip. The thick strap was a little snug. She bowed slowly, trying to hold back tears.

Suddenly, Lotus whinnied. Clara felt a ripple of panic sent through her. She had a brief image of something moving. Lotus whinnied again. Her hooves stamped hard in the sand. She weaved slightly to avoid knocking Queen Arebella off.

Clara turned her attention to the sand. She activated her vision once more. To her horror, there was the Empty. Black writhing blobs slithering toward their direction. She instinctively went for her threads. "The Empty. They're coming…"

Twitch and Shard flared out their feathers. Their armor gleamed in the light. They both took to the air.

Iridescent went from green to brown. He pulled out his weapon. He was at King Helios' side in an instant.

Clara gazed at Queen Arebella. "Queen Arebella… please tell me we're closer to your kingdom's entrance."

Queen Arebella was silent for a moment. Her face paled. Her hands to her stomach. Then she said, "I… didn't expect them to reach this far out…" Her eyes met Clara's. "Yes… Just a few feet north of here."

"They're coming from all sides!" Twitch's voice was on the verge of a shriek. She lowered down to be seen by everyone else. Her wings hummed as she hovered. "The only option we have is to run!"

"Then let's use a tornado to buy some time," Clara said.

"Too risky," Shard protested. He lowered down, but his eyes remained on the Empty. "We need to create a sandstorm. We're less likely to get sucked in."

Before Clara could ask further questions, large sand clouds rose. Her heart sank. She soon began to run in the direction where Queen Arebella indicated. Onyx and Lotus followed behind her. She looked to see that the others were as well. King Helios the closest to her side. She summoned the winds through the threads she frantically plucked. It formed a small shield, but they found themselves barely seeing their entrance.

Clara heard a loud bellow. She briefly saw Lotus speeding by with Queen Arebella holding on for dear life. "Lotus!" Her voice could be barely heard over the wail of the wind. "Come back!" She ran faster. Her knees picking up the pace. To her horror, she saw a shimmering shape that was chasing after Lotus. A tentacle wrapped around the leg. An Empty was trying to attack Lotus. "No!" She stretched her hand out.

Colorful threads soon appeared. The Empty that was trying to attack Lotus screamed. Clara gritted her teeth and pulled hard. It fell back and fled. Clara ran closer to Lotus. She soon let out an angry gale that pushed away any of the Empty that was hiding in the sand. The more she ran, the more her lungs screamed in pain. She continued to let loose several more gales, each one stronger than the last.

"There!" Queen Arebella's voice was barely heard over the din. She pointed in the far distance. "The entrance is just through that rock."

Clara squinted her eyes against the sand. She could see a boulder that resembled an oxen. She lowered her winds and summoned the green threads. Clara felt Lotus trying to help her. Clara ignored it. A shard of rock broke free and hit the ground. Swarms of the Empty gathered around it. She reached for Lotus. Onyx leaped forward. The rest was a tumbling mess.

Sand swamped the group for a moment. Clara struggled to move but the sand seemed to toss her deeper into the pile. She soon felt strong arms wrapped around her and pulled her out. She coughed hard. She heard a few snorts. Clara briefly turned to see Onyx and Lotus surging forward from the sand. Queen Arebella still on top of Lotus. The two creatures shook off the sand, disgruntled complaints went down her bond.

She shifted to realize that her head was against his chest. Clara gazed up into King Helios' eyes. Her cheeks went red. Before she could even utter a single word, she was set down. Her heart thundered hard. She began to shake the sand off her body. Suddenly, she heard a groan.

"Twitch!" Shard's voice echoed through the caverns. It was followed by Twitch grunting in pain.

Clara glanced at the group. Her face paled at the sight of Twitch being supported by Shard. Blood oozed onto the floor. Twitch had a stone shrapnel impaled in her leg. Every ounce of blood left Clara's body as she walked toward Twitch. Her knees buckled beneath her. Tears stung in her eyes. "I... I... I didn't mean..."

Shard was in Clara's face. His eyes blazed with rage. "You stupid! What were you thinking? Didn't you see we were right behind you?"

Clara just stared at the wound. The pain in her stomach tearing her apart. Tears began to stream down. She tried to speak the words, but they just died. She began to sink. Words from her time in the village danced in her head. Worthless. Clumsy. Scaredy. Cursed. Clara began to tremble as Shard continued to yell at her.

"Shard!" Twitch's voice seemed to break out of her spell. Clara felt something brush against her forehead. Clara slowly lifted her head. Twitch was staring hard. "I know what she did was reckless, but you saw how fast the Empty were going in the sand."

"Well, yeah," Shard admitted, "but Gaia—"

"Gaia would've understood the situation." Twitch went to Clara. "Clara, you need to be more aware. I know you were only trying to protect us, but be more careful." She slowly sat down. She simply stared at it. "Don't worry. It's not even that deep anyway."

"A little—" Shard's teeth flared out.

Twitch hissed back. "Just... Help me get this out before we get any deeper."

Clara tenderly wrapped her hand around the stone. She watched as Shard knelt beside them which was a little tricky due to his armor. Clara flinched as she felt the warm blood on her fingers. A cold sensation rippled against her spine. She bit back the urge to vomit. Clara tightened her grip and pulled it out. She froze in place as the blood poured out faster. An image of her mother laying in a pool of her own blood invaded her mind.

Onyx's soft whine snapped her out of her scared state. She stared at her hands and frantically wiped them against her pants. Clara hugged Onyx. Her legs felt weak as she got up. Most of her village would be happy at the sight of the enemy's blood. For her... It was as if humanity was turning almost as monstrous as the empty.

Clara saw Lotus and Queen Arebella head deeper into the cavern. Clara walked briskly over to them. She wobbled. Her hand instinctively went to the dagger. For some reason, it gave her comfort. She gazed at the queen. "Are you okay?"

Queen Arebella turned her head to Clara. She still had her hand on her stomach. "I'm doing okay. Though my baby is really mad over the ride."

Clara blushed. "I'm sorry. I just wanted to make sure that you and Lotus were safe." She stared ahead. "Ar-are you nervous? About being a mother?"

"I'm more nervous of my baby coming out safely."

"Hopefully, it doesn't come out while trying to find your... possibly angry husband."

Clara tried her best to peer into the darkness. However, her vision wasn't the best right now. Even with Queen Arebella's directions, Clara still struggled going into dark tunnels. A few times she hit a wall. Even crashed into Shard and Twitch. Finally, she had to hold on Lotus just to avoid being a nuisance any further.

Darkness seemed to have swallowed up time. There was no beginning of their path. Nor their end. All the group knew was that they were only a few feet closer to where they need to be. Suddenly, a soft hiss reached Clara's ears. She stopped Lotus and gently felt along Queen Arebella's body. There were no signs of labor, but the muscles around the body were beginning to twitch violently.

Clara tapped Lotus. The unicorn kneeled down to let Clara slide Queen Arebella off. Clara helped her to the nearest wall. She knelt down. "Are you okay?"

"My-my baby might be kicking up a bigger fuss than I thought," Queen Arebella grunted.

Clara felt her hand being lifted. Her fingers formed a point. She followed it to see faint glowing in the distance. She slowly got up from her spot. Clara bumped into King Helios. She felt his hand gently holding her up.

"Let's go together," King Helios spoke. "The rest of you, stay here and guard Queen Arebella. We'll have a talk with King Oberon."

"But—" Clara was about to protest, but Onyx's reassurance rippled between them. His large nose nuzzled against the dagger. She took a deep breath. "Okay... Twitch will you be okay?" She felt feathers brush against her. A Harpy gesture for reassurance. Clara plastered a smile and went with King Helios. She could faintly hear Onyx at her heels.

She and King Helios walked together for a while. Heavy silence between them. Clara tried opening her mouth but the words she wanted to say were hard to speak. Her heart thundered hard against her chest. Her lips went inward. Before she could even utter a sentence, King Helios was the first to speak.

"To be honest Clara. I also wanted to talk to you in private." His stride evened with hers. His tail wrapped around her waist. "I've noticed that you were quiet for some time. I'm… sorry about our discussion last night. Truth is…" He gave a soft laugh. "I knew you were the girl who rescued me from the snow all those years ago."

Clara's eyes began to burn with tears. "Why?" She sniffed. She tried to wipe her eyes, but water soon dampened her face. She stopped walking. She faced him in the dim light. "Why didn't you tell me from the start? Did I embarrass you?"

King Helios let go of Clara's arm and slowly touched her head. He easily pulled her close to his chest. "No. I simply didn't want to startle you or put you in a position that is more difficult than you were in now." His lips gentle brushed her hair. "I've always missed your silver hair. Your soft voice. I wanted to know about you but I was in more danger staying if your parents saw me."

Clara was silent. Her mind went back to finding the blankets empty on that day. Her parents found traces of snow but nothing else. She sighed. "I guess that makes sense." Her fingers dug into her arm. "Still, you should've told me!"

"I know… However, I wanted you to know that I thought of you every day. You were the best thing that ever happened to me."

Clara's tears broke free, running down her cheeks. Suddenly, she heard a noise. A chink of iron echoed down the halls. She felt her hip being freed from his tail. She saw several Sand Dwarves coming toward them. The smell of blood soon hit her nose.

The Sand Dwarves soon came into view. Some held lanterns shaped like owls. Their weapons were dented. A few cradled bloody stumps of where their hand should be. Their expressions were grave. At least twenty of them stood before them. Among them was none other than King Oberon.

The Sand Dwarf King held fury in his dark eyes. His lip curled upward into a snarl. His sword held menacingly in his hand. "What are you doing here, Helios? You've made it clear that we can't have your supplies. Come to gloat of your riches? Or witness what the Empty have done to us?"

King Helios took a step forward, but he was stopped by raised spears. He held up his hands.

Clara cautiously stepped forward. She looked at Onyx who was growling. "Onyx, calm down. We can't afford any casualties." Clara cleared her throat. "King Oberon. We know about Queen Arebella. The Slave Traders came and attack the capital of the Reptilia. I've witnessed a Harpy Elder die." She shook away the tears that threatened to return. She took another step forward. Her heart jumped at the sight of the spears, but something in her told her to remain by King Helios' side. "Queen Arebella is alive and we came all this way to bring her back to you."

King Oberon roared, "Lies!" He slammed his sword down into the stony floor. "I've seen many returned slaves wind up dead. Most of my men were empty husk or had their hearts taken by Empty! Humans, Reptilia, Harpy... They all hold nothing but worthless promises. My wife was hunting. I told her not to go. I told her to stay." Each word he spoke only dripped with sorrow. Tears began to leak in his eyes. "But no... She went against my wishes, the stubborn fool."

Clara stood there in silence. Stoic. Unfeeling. Those were the words humans spoke of when they described a Sand Dwarf. Not for Clara. Stoic was indeed a word for Sand Dwarves, but another word entered Clara's mind. Fragile. They had lost so many of their own. Their own king on the brink of madness. Clara found herself holding onto King Helios' hand. "Your Majesty... We only want to create peace between you and the Reptilia."

King Oberon stiffened at those words. A shadow fell across his gaze, making him more menacing than an actual Empty. "Peace?" He spat the word. Behind him, the other Sand Dwarves began to circle around them. Their weapons raised to form a spiky ring of iron. King Oberon took a step forward. "You expect me to believe that? After all you've said? After all you've done?"

Clara barely had enough time to speak as King Helios shoved her away just as King Oberon's sword came at them. The gap was dangerously thin. Clara landed hard on the ground with a thud. She heard Onyx gave a bark. Flashes of steel made her roll out of the way. The air around her caused her to feel every swing and movement. She pulled out her dagger as one blade came at her.

She turned her head for a small moment to see King Helios standing his ground. The Reptilia King had his sword out. Sparks flew as it collided with King Oberon's. Clara scrambled away after she missed an oncoming axe. Her heart raced in her chest. *King Oberon's madness will destroy everyone,* Clara thought.

Clara took in a deep breath and turned back to the direction of where she came from. Tightening the grip on her dagger, Clara charged forward. She knocked over a dwarf that was about to land a final blow to Onyx with his axe. She made her way down the tunnel of darkness. Hands scrapping against bared rock.

Clara soon tripped and her knees scrapped against the rock. She heard movement. She swung her dagger only for it to be caught by none other than Iridescent. She could barely make out his scales in the light. "Iridescent! Sorry! Sorry!" She slowly got up. Her feet moved forward."

"Clara?" Twitch's voice was heard in the darkness. "What's going on?" Even though she couldn't see it, Clara pictured Twitch having her feathers raised.

"King Oberon!" Clara could barely hide the panic in her voice. She tried to reach out for Queen Arebella. "He's gone mad! The Empty have attacked him and now he's trying to kill King Helios! He needs his wife!" Warm, ruddy hands suddenly held hers. Lotus's muzzle nestled against her forehead.

"Then, let's hurry," Queen Arebella said. Her voice sounded tired, but determined.

Clara was able to lead the way. Her steps still quickened. Lotus' hooves shared the same pace. She held on to the mane with one hand. The dagger in the other. Sounds of blades and marching feet soon filled the tunnel. As they got closer, Clara's grip on her weapon grew tighter.

Suddenly, the steps stopped. Shuffling and whispers were heard. Clara didn't care what was going on, but she had a good idea why. She marched until the lights were clear. Clara's heart nearly dropped out of her chest as she saw King Helios on the ground, clutching his wrist. King Oberon ready to give the final blow.

Clara let go of Lotus. She sent a mental command to Onyx. Clara was surprised to watch Onyx do as she asked. The black wolf bounded toward King Oberon. Clara ran behind him. She summoned several threads of earth. In an instant, she created a stalagmite that knocked the sword out of King Oberon's hand.

Onyx tackled King Oberon to the ground. He snarled and bit the thick arm. His large paws pinned the arms down.

"Onyx," Clara said. She helped King Helios get on to his feet. "That's enough." She sent a small tug on their bond. Then, she sent another to Lotus. She could hear the hooves closer. To her relief, Onyx backed away but still growled. Her eyes stayed on King Oberon. Clara could feel the hate coming off of his stare. It wasn't foreign to her. This only made her stand close to King Helios. "King Oberon. Your wife is alive and well. Your baby too. You need to calm down or you'll hurt her too."

King Oberon snarled. He got onto his feet. "I've had enough of this." He balled his hand into a fist. His skin turned stony. Crystals jutting out of his arm. "I'm ending this—"

"Put that down you stupid fool!" Queen Arebella's voice cut though the tension. All eyes on her.

Clara briefly turned to King Oberon. She watched the Sand Dwarf King's hatred melt away. A smile went on her lips as he rushed to Queen Arebella. Clara sent a mental message for Lotus to lower herself down. Her smile grew as King Oberon tenderly took his queen's hands before he wrapped them in a hug. In a brief moment, she saw her parents do the exact thing on their spring days.

Sniffles were soon heard by the Sand Dwarf couple. Soft exchanges barely heard by the sobs. The bittersweet moment ended as footsteps were heard.

Clara was surprised to see the soldiers were unharmed. *They must've decided to see if Queen Arebella is real.* She turned her attention back to King Helios. He was grimacing at her. Clara's heart twisted at the sight of the gash. It was far deeper up close. The wound ran from his hand to his elbow. Clara looked for something she could use. She turned to Lotus. She was about to ask if she could heal King Helios, but stopped short. Her face paled at the sight of Lotus's hind leg. Bloodied and swollen.

Before Clara could take a step, Lotus collapsed. The unicorn breathed hard. Clara ran to her side. She knelt down. Tears ran down her eyes. "Lotus!" She hugged her exhausted friend. "I'm so sorry... So... So sorry." Her body was shaking now. The dagger dropped from her hand with a clang. She didn't know how long she's been crying but a kind hand touched her shoulder. Clara looked up to see Queen Arebella's face.

"You've saved my life," Queen Arebella said. "Now let me return the favor." She turned to the Sand Dwarf closest to her. "Gather up the rest of the party. They're further down the tunnel. Be careful with the green Harpy. She's injured at the moment."

The guard nodded and took off. Clara watched as he muttered something to them before he disappeared into the darkness.

Clara was helped onto her feet. She could feel the world sway slightly under her. She took a deep breath. Queen Arabella's grip easing the strength back into her. Without a word, she allowed herself to be pulled by the monarch. To Clara's surprise, King Oberon lifted Lotus onto his shoulders.

The three of them were soon joined by King Helios. The walked further down the glowing tunnel. Bright quartz greeted them as they went further down. Footsteps echoed in against the cavernous walls. They finally arrived at an immense door. Iron and stone melded together. A basilisk and lion were tied together. Their jaws roaring at the skies. With a creek, the doors opened to reveal a beautiful city. The stone huts were crowned with amethysts. Small rivers laced next to the streets. Further back, was a castle made out of pure sandstone and red jasper.

Clara went breathless at the sight. "Marvelous…" Her cheeks went red the moment those words escaped her lips. She saw a few Sand Dwarves coming out of their homes. The children resembled the parents, but a little younger and shorter. All eyes turned to her. It made her shrink slightly. She looked at Queen Arebella.

The queen smiled at her. "Clara. Welcome to the Sand Dwarf Kingdom."

Chapter 21
Gemstones

All of the Sand Dwarves crowded around Clara and the monarchs. It felt strange having everyone so close to her. The mixture of expressions of the civilians ranged from joy to anger. Clara immediately turned her attention to Lotus. She sent a small ripple in their bond to see if Lotus was still awake. The response was weak and tired. *I'm sorry*, Clara sent back. Her sorrow bleed down the line like an ocean.

Before long, she saw Twitch, Shard and Iridescent in the crowd. Shard hissed, neck arched. His wings wrapped around Twitch protectively as if the Sand Dwarves would pluck a feather off of her body.

Iridescent was a mixture of colors. Orange with brown tints. The Reptilia scout pulled his tail inward. A few dwarf children giggled at this sight.

The castle grew more intimidating for Clara. The red jasper began to look like walls of blood. Her eyes frantically turned to Twitch every few seconds. Her heart twisted harder in her chest as they laid on Twitch's bleeding leg as it dragged against the dirt. She saw statues of the basilisk stand tall at the front door. One of them had broken horns and jagged tears of skin. They must be incredible statue makers, Clara thought. Their presence slowly calming her of her distress. They are so well carved that they almost look real.

Just as the group reached the door, she could've sworn that one of them blinked. Suddenly, the scarred basilisk let out a strange chirp and lowered its head to Queen Arebella. "Yikes!" Clara stepped back quickly. She bumped into King Helios before falling to the floor. "It's alive!" She tried her best to clamber onto her feet.

Queen Arebella laughed. "Our basilisks have been known to do that. Vixen was just excited to see me." She let out a soft coo as she hugged her basilisk. The creature's head was the size of Lotus. The pale yellow-green scales made it almost invisible in the sand. Molten orbs of amber gazed lovingly at their partner. The bird-like beak clacked softly.

Clara smiled at the sight. It made her heart twist even harder. She felt King Helios' scaly hands touch her shoulders. She looked up and took a small breath. She soon took noticed of a Sand Dwarf running to them.

The Sand Dwarf had rose quartz and sunstone hang down on her neck in thick cords. Her hair was a dull brown braided tightly. The dark tan of her skin complimented her thick set of muscles. Her garment was white from her head to her shoes. The symbols of the Earth God were sewn with green threads. It was as if the earth magic wanted to be known to all.

Queen Arebella smiled. "Ah. If it isn't my favorite healer. How are you, Quartz?"

Quartz breathed heavily. Her hands shaking. "I would be fine if your baby is still in one piece! If those Slave Traders did anything to you, I swear—" Crystals began to pop out of her arm.

Clara cringed. Her right hand trailed along the skin of her left. Goosebumps riddled it. Even Onyx let out a yip of surprise. She bit her lip. Her heart nearly jumped at her chest as Quartz looked at her.

"Who's this?" Quartz's skin slowly returned to normal. Then, her eyes went Lotus. Her spectacles ready to fall off the bridge of her nose. "Is that a unicorn?"

Queen Arebella grabbed a hold of the healer before she could do anything. "Quartz. Let's at least get inside and let you have a look at the injured."

Clara followed Quartz and the monarchs inside the castle. Onyx close to her heels. She allowed her hand to hold on to King Helios'. Their fingers interlocked as they made their way to an infirmary. Clara's eyes went wide as four of the ten beds were already taken up by castle guards.

"Okay. Lie down here, Queen Arebella." Quartz gestured to the bed on the farthest right, closest to a small hearth that was burning away. She relayed her instructions to King Oberon and King Helios.

Clara was about to sit down when Twitch came through the doorway. She glided over to Twitch and tucked herself under Twitch's wing. She and Shard led her to an occupied bed that was the closest to them. Once it was settled, Clara placed herself in a corner. Her legs tucked in. Onyx's weight giving her comfort as he curled up next to her. The world began to fade as she grew numb. The silence was the only thing she could take right now. Her bond with Lotus was quiet. A sense of terror crawled into Clara each time she wanted to tug it. Her mind could only go back to the field of flowers that she wanted to be in. The lilac and lavender billowing in the breeze. Her mother giggling as she made her flower crowns. Her father singing songs of the sky and earth. Rue folding a blanket as her duck quacked to the tunes. *I miss you all*, she thought bitterly.

"Excuse me..."

Clara jolted upright. Her head nearly bumping into someone. She looked up to see a startled Quartz before her.

"H-hello... My name's Quartz." Quartz adjusted her glasses. The lens revealed to be made out of clear quartz. "Your name is Clara?"

Clara nodded. She rubbed her eyes. Onyx let out a moan and shifted slightly beside her. She looked around to see that everyone seemed to be asleep. Soft breathing filled the room. Followed by an occasional snore. The lighting changed from fire to bluish-green glow from the same lanterns as before. Each of the occupants in bed had a peaceful expression on their face. In the farthest corner was Queen Arebella and King Oberon. Both monarchs held each other in their arms.

Clara turned her gaze back to Quartz. "How long was I out?"

"A few hours." Quartz yawned. She removed her glasses and rubbed her eyes. Replacing them she said, "I came here to see how you were doing. I also wanted you to know that I was very impressed with what you did."

"What I did?" Clara raised a brow in confusion.

"Queen Arebella told me that you managed to relink to her baby in assurance that the baby was okay."

"H-how is the baby?" Clara plastered her hands together. Her skin went cold at the mere idea that the babe would die from the stress after The Empty had activated their assault.

"Doing very well." A smile appeared on Quartz face. "I've never seen the life threads so intact. They were even strong enough to withstand a little more stress than normal in our pregnancy term."

"When will she have it?"

"In about a day or so." Quartz held out her hand. "You can rest on the cot for the evening. I can tell you the rest of—"

Clara immediately gazed at Lotus. Her lips pressed tighter. She cautiously touched the link to Lotus. She was only met with soft contentment. She let out a sigh of relief. Tears began to sting her eyes. She saw that Lotus' leg was bandaged. Clara felt tired once again. This time her limbs dragged as she made her way to the cot. Once she reached it, she laid down with ease. To her surprise, it was really comfortable on her back.

Onyx tried to climb up to join her. His enormous paws slipped, causing him to land on his tail. He snorted. His mind sent irritation rippling across their connection. He curled up beside her.

Clara put her hand on Onyx. She turned her head to look at Quartz. "Quartz... How did Lotus—" She found the healer on a pile of pillows followed by loud snores. Clara giggled. She closed her eyes. A smile planted on her face. A smile never thought to return.

Clara was back in the field again. Her parents singing to her. Rue laying on the ground, her gray hair now gone. Clara was eating some honeyed bread. To her surprise, Onyx and Lotus were there. The two creatures ran around the field with her parents' animals. Clara couldn't help but laugh at the sight. Her white hair swayed in the breeze. Dragons casting shadows above her head.

All of this didn't bother Clara. Her smile only grew wider as more creatures began to appear in her field. King Helios only made her smile the brightest in the world as he approached her. The regal Reptilia was steel gray in the sunlight. His blue eyes sparkled. His outfit was comprised of loose-fitting trousers and a light blue tunic. He knelt next to her. His claws held a white rose. Then, he cupped her chin and kissed her.

Suddenly, soft crying was heard in the distance. Clara looked around to see where it was coming from. A wet lick from Onyx felt too real. Onyx licked her again. Clara gasped and nearly fell out of her bed. She felt her arm being caught. Clara glanced up to see King Helios. Her cheeks went red at the sight of him again. The urge to kiss him made her heart hammer inside. The crying came again, but louder this time.

Twitch was at Clara's side in a matter of minutes. A bright smile on her face. "Glad to see you up, sleepy head."

"What's happened?" Clara asked. Her mind was still foggy from sleep. "Why do I hear crying? Did anyone get hurt?"

Twitch shook her head. "No. Actually... Someone just joined us a few hours ago."

Clara slowly got up from her spot. She followed King Helios and Twitch to the source of the sound. Her steps wobbled for a moment before they regained traction. As she got closer, she heard several coos. Clara nearly fell to her knees as her eyes laid on the most miraculous sight she's ever seen.

Queen Arebella was holding a tiny baby in her arms. It would've been mistaken as a doll at first glance. The eyes were steel gray instead of the traditional dark eyes. The skin dark as his mother's. Tiny hands balled up into fists. The mouth formed a small "o". His unfocused gaze followed the room.

King Oberon stared down at them. In the light of the hearth, his cheeks glittered. His eyes were puffy. He had a few bandages around his arm but nothing to severe. He let out a small chuckle. "Welcome to the world little one."

Queen Arebella glanced up at Clara. "Clara. I would like to introduce my son. Thanks to you, he's alive and well. His name would be Garnet. He's strong like the dark red stones in the earth." She gently kissed him.

King Oberon turned to Clara. He took Clara's hand in both of his. He knelt down and bowed his head. Each word that came out of him came out in painful sob. "Clara... Th-thank you so much for bringing them home. I'm so sorry for my treatment of you and King Helios. My people are desperate. I was just told earlier..." He sniffed. His whole body shook. "The Slave Traders came into our territory because they offered one of my men gold coins if he told them where to grab the Sand Dwarves. He's been executed for treason."

Clara turned to King Helios. Her heart sunk King Helios nodded his head. Clara bit her lip. Her mind went back to the crest she saw lying on the ground. *If those Slave Traders were human... Surely Duke Averence and Lady Maroona wouldn't resort to such...* She shook herself of those thoughts. Her free hand place on King Oberon's shoulder. She gazed at him. "Please... Don't be too hard on yourself. You're the king. As well as a husband and father..." Clara looked at Lotus.

Lotus was on all four hooves. Her eyes were bright. An eager ripple sent between them. The ears moving in every direction. The horn gleamed in the light.

Clara went back to King Oberon. "I only ask of you to make peace with the Reptilia and the Harpies." She bit her lips before she spoke again. "I don't blame you..." She looked at everyone else. "Any of you for hating humans. I've always hated myself for it."

A heavy silence hung in the air. Everyone just stood there. Eyes wide with disbelief. Then, Twitch hobbled over to Clara and hugged her. Shard joined in the embrace. Their feathers were a meld of browns and greens. Heads touched together.

"I think you're a great human," Twitch said.

"Just try not to be stupid on the enemies you take on," Shard spoke. He received a small bonk on the head by Twitch but he just laughed it off.

Clara also felt Onyx nudge her. His warm body pressed against her back. Lotus came into her view with a sense of assurance rippled between them. Clara felt her hand go to her side. Tears blinded her. Sobs wracked her body. The pain. The shame. The anger. All the feelings that she harbored all those years finally burst out of her being.

The wings entwined harder. There were no longer any armored plates on the Harpies. Only soft cloth pressed on Clara's head. Then, it soon ended. Twitch and Shard took a moment to pat her head.

Clara wiped her tears away. She took a moment to calm down. Clara laughed as Lotus licked her face. Onyx joining in as he got onto his powerful hind legs. Clara's laugh grew louder than ever before. She could feel her bonds echo out their joy. The words whispering, "everything will be okay."

Everyone chuckled at the sight. King Oberon turned to King Helios. "King Helios, shall we discuss things further after we all have something to eat. My wife and I would like to be alone with our soon."

King Helios nodded. He turned to Iridescent and pointed at the door. Then, King Helios walked over to Clara. He gently stroked her head before taking her hand in his. His fingers carefully wrapped around hers. The two walked out into the halls of the castle. Onyx close behind.

Clara turned around to glance at Lotus once more. The unicorn's bright eyes gave her the reassurance to continue. She followed King Helios and the servants deeper into the inner sanctums of the castle.

Clara had a small breakfast. It mostly comprised of Blue Heart Cactus and silver dates. They didn't have bread, but the water was decent. Onyx sent grumbling messages of wanting to eat meat, but was smacked on the snout when he tried to sneak a scrap from one of the servants. She took note that the servants were thin. Skin taut against bone. She stole a glance a King Helios. The Reptilia king had a grimace on his face.

Once done, Clara was about to follow a servant when King Helios stopped her. Clara found herself shivering in delight at the mere touch of her arm. She turned to face him. "What is it, King Helios?"

King Helios was silent for a moment. His eyes were starting to cloud with worry. "Clara, King Obcron had mentioned this shortage to me time and again…" He looked around the servants and guards. "I never even realized it's been that bad." His eyes narrowed. Clara could've sworn that his gaze held a spark of rage. "You do know it could mean one thing."

Clara gulped. The rumors were true. "The Empty are growing stronger. They're going to wipe out everyone. Aren't they?"

"I can't say for sure." Without warning, he hugged her.

Clara found herself shivering more. Her arms instinctively wrapped around him. She wanted to stay in this embrace. She could feel the cloth scratch her face. The smell of sand and jungle lingered in every scale.

King Helios broke his embrace. "I'm going to talk to King Oberon. We'll have to come up with a strategy of how to defeat The Empty once and for all. Right now, we need to keep a close eye if any changes occur." He left; his stride matched with the servant.

Clara stared at him longingly. Suddenly, she heard a soft humming behind her. Clara nearly jumped at seeing Twitch so close to her. Her cheeks went red.

Twitch just only smiled. "So… You got a crush on King Helios, huh?" She leaned forward, her face only inches from Clara's. "When are you going to kiss him?"

Clara nearly back pedaled. She saw the Sand Dwarf servant wave them over. She wrapped her arm around Twitch's hip and walked in the direction of the servant. Her face turned crimson at the mere idea of kissing in real life. She could even feel the invisible laughter coming from her animals. Behind her, she could hear Shard protesting and Iridescent muttering.

They soon arrived at their chambers. Large beds with silk sheet laid before them. Smells of Sulphur tickled

Clara's nose. She dragged Twitch to the nearest bed and set her down. Shard and Iridescent were sent into other rooms for the sake of preventing "unwanted activities". Onyx hopped onto Clara's bed. His long legs stretched out. Tongue lolled to one side.

Clara laughed at his contentment. She turned to see Lotus laying on her side. A special carpet laid out for the unicorn. Clara walked over to Lotus. She stroked their bond. *I promise. I'll break you free of this bond.* Suddenly, Lotus nickered. A puff of hot air tossed back Clara's hair. Clara blinked in surprise. She felt Lotus' response. A tight embrace Clara didn't want to fight off. Memories of joy during their time together rippled through her. The desire to continue this path grew stronger.

Clara stared back at Lotus. Her eyes were raw, but her heart ached in places she's never imagined. "You... want to stay... bonded to me?" She turned to Onyx. The heterochrome stare laid heavily on her. "What about you, Onyx?" Silence filled the air. It felt like an eternity until Onyx got up from his spot and licked her cheek. Lotus also followed. Clara giggled as they sent her vibrations similar to scolding a naughty child. "Okay, okay." She hugged them both. "Thank you."

Twitch looked around the room. She let out a soft sigh that catches Clara's attention. "So... What do we do now?"

Clara got up from her spot. "Well. Look around the room I guess." Clara frowned as a smile spread across Twitches face. "Uh... Twitch... What are you thinking up there? If it's something that will physically injure us, Shard will skin us both!"

"No. How about… we guess our partners!"

Clara tilted her head. "Partners? But we're not married yet."

Twitch laughed. "No. It's a game Harpies do. Mostly the females. We guess who our future mate is going to be based on what we know about the person next to us. Ready?"

Clara went red at this. She never talked about boys with anyone back at her village. Let alone discussed anything like that to Rue. She tried to open her mouth, but Twitch cut to the quick.

"I already who your perfect mate is."

Clara's face turned to a darker shade of red. "Y-you do? That's impossible. I haven't had any attraction to boys so—"

Twitch laughed. "Oh, come on. Don't be so modest. It's King Helios!"

At those words, Clara bit her lip. Too stunned at the words she wanted to say. She quickly sat down. Her world began to sway under her feet. She took a deep breath. Her heart still hammered in her chest, but it wasn't out of pain. It was something else entirely. Clara looked around the room to see if he was nearby. "What makes you say that?"

"It took me a while to realize it." Twitch leaned back in her bed. Her injured leg twitched slightly. "The way he looks at you. It was hard to tell how he feels about you because he's nearly expressionless. Then, I notice how tenderly he holds you. He even did that when we were being dragged back to his castle."

Clara blinked. "He-He was carrying me to the chambers this entire time?"

Twitch gave Clara a wicked grin. "Indeed." Then, she tapped her wing on her chin. "Now thinking about it, I think what make you two even more compatible is the fact that you have an air of a queen."

Clara fiddled with her fingers. Her cheeks slowly drained of color. *Me? A queen?* She could almost imagine everyone back home laughing at her. Lady Maroona's being the loudest. The sneers on their lips. Taunts of her being queen of such as savage people rang in her head. Then, it was met with a defiant wave from Onyx.

Clara took a deep breath. "O-ok. I guess it's my turn to guess your partner. It's Shard."

Twitch's feathers ruffled slightly. A blush crept into her cheeks. "Maayyybeeeee…"

Clara folded her arms. A deep frown on her face. "Well, you were the one who—"

A soft knock at the door drew their attention away from the door. Clara walked over to the door to see who it is. She soon saw Quartz standing before her. The healer did a small bow while holding a basket of glittering gemstones. Clara backed away to allow Quartz in. She closed the door behind her.

Clara's eyes focused on the basket. She's only seen gemstones in books so it was interesting to see them this close. She inched closer to the basket once it was set on the table. Her fingers intertwined each other, her mind holding back the desire to touch them. *They're important to the Sand Dwarves! They're important to the Sand Dwarves!*

Quartz stared at her with a perplexed expression. Her lips formed a frown. "What are you doing?"

"I-I'm sorry." Clara backed away. "Those jewels really are beautiful. However, due to the history of our respective peoples... I didn't want to touch without your permission. You know... The thefts."

Quartz silently moved her glasses against the bridge of her nose. Her right hand balled into a fist. Skin tight with fury. "I see you've heard of the infamous Red Sand Battle..."

Clara nodded. She folded her hands together. Her head raised high. "Forgive me, if I came across as extremely rude. I do find your gems beautiful. However, they're part of the customs of your people. I... just didn't want to be selfish about it."

Quartz's gaze soften. "That's the first time I've heard a human say that." She wiped the tears that leaked out of her eyes. "My father was involved in that battle. He and my cousin were part of the battalion that was meant to take down one of your mages. They were stronger than any of us could expect... He..."

Clara's heart twisted with pain once again. She took Quartz's hand. "I'm so sorry. You don't need to say anything." Clara quickly wiped her eyes. "Curse my fragile heart! I've been crying left and right." She was immediately surprised to see Quartz point to the basket.

"You can touch them," Quartz assured. Queen Arebella requested I have them sent to you."

Twitch sat up, intrigued by the conversation. She watched Clara head over to the basket.

Clara looked at the stones. For some reason, she felt a pull from some of them. It was as if they had a secret to share. Slowly, she picked a few stones that were in the basket. Two blue ones, a red one and one of the deepest green.

Quartz raised a brow. "Impressive. Why those?"

Clara fingered the stones. The power from them brushed against her fingers. Curious, she activated her vision to her shock, she could only see tiny green threads in the emerald. The others had the coloration of other elements. Clara blinked for a while to get her vision back to normal. She rubbed her eyes for a while.

Twitch slowly tried to get up. Her injured leg dangled over the edge as she moved. She was stopped as Clara raised a hand.

"It's okay, Twitch." Clara turned to Quartz. "These stones seem to carry the other elemental threads. How is that possible?"

Quartz pulled out a bag from her robe. She opened it. Pellets resembling gold fell out onto her hand. The material soon melted and morphed into a camel. It moved its head left and right. "You know how this world is made by threads right?"

Clara nodded. Her eyes focused on the camel.

"There's an old story amongst our people that after the Divine Battle, the earth god saw a few strands of elemental threads that lingered. Having no purpose to even speak of. Moved by pity, he took a few rock threads and merged it together with the other threads. They were his treasure. He was so enchanted that he cried tears of gold. The finer grains became the sands we knew now." Quartz twisted her fingers and the camel disappeared. The pellets lay in her hand once again.

Clara thought for a moment. Something about it was very familiar to her. Then, it occurred to her. "Rue used to tell me a similar story but with silver."

Quartz raised a brow. "Rue?"

Clara's heart ached. The loneliness setting back in. She shook herself. "Never mind." Then, she thought back to what Quartz said. "What can you tell me about Life Threads?"

Quartz walked over to Twitch. She removed the bandages with ease. Quartz slowly moved the leg back and forth. Small amounts of blood dribbled out of the Harpy leg. Quartz sighed as she reapplied the bandages. She turned to face Clara.

"Life Threads are far different from regular Elemental Threads as you can tell." Quartz slowly began to roll up her sleeve. "Only those with a Beast Heart, like the Wild Shepherdess, can be able to handle them properly." On her forearm was an elephant. The trunk was raised high in a regal manner.

Clara stared at it in surprise. She instinctively touched her back. Her fingers tracing the dragon's head. She could feel some of its magic simmering out from underneath it. "There... There's more than one?"

Quartz nodded. She rolled her sleeve back down. Thick hands dug into the pocket. She fished out a few leather bags. Drawstrings pulled, she looked into the contents. Quartz let out a low curse. "Dung beetles! Just our luck. We're tapped out." She went back to Twitch and rinsed the foot with hot water. Fresh bandages wrapped tenderly around a fragile bird leg. She then went over to Clara.

Clara knelt down to show her wounds. As the sleeves were pulled back, her amber eyes went wide at the sight before her. There were barely any scars on her arms. Smooth, pale skin glowed in the soft light of the oil lamp that hung in the farthest corner of the room. Clara blinked in dismay. She glanced over to Twitch, her shocked expression matching hers.

Quartz clicked her tongue. "Well... This is new. How long have you had this injury?"

"Only two days ago."

Quartz raised a brow in confusion. "So, how did you get them?"

Clara soon began to give the full details of what happened. Her fight with the slave traders. Twitch's capture. The controlled lion. Onyx's wounds. Finally, her skin paled as she described the threads that she pulled in order to save them.

When she was done, Quartz was pale. Her jaw slacked at what was being described to her. Even her glasses sat at the edge of her nose, ready to fall off. She opened her mouth. Then closed it. She paced around the room for a moment. Her feet made her twirl with ease. Clara was just getting dizzy watching it. Quartz stopped in front of Clara. She looked at Clara's arm once more.

Clara couldn't help but feel awkward about this. *Maybe this is too much for her. There were things I'm still dealing with.* She opened her mouth to say something.

"That's... amazing! If not reckless and terrifying." Quartz said. She adjusted her glasses once more.

"I'll say," Twitch added. Clara could feel her gaze turn hard on her.

Quartz pulled up a chair. She made Clara sit down. Her fingers measured the length of Clara's hair. Without Clara permission, she snatched the stones and began to fiddle with them.

Clara tried to turn her head around. She glanced at Quartz in confusion. "What are you doing? You didn't answer my question." Her cheeks squished in the palms. Her head was forced to face Twitch. Suddenly, she felt her hair being pulled. She froze in place. Her scalp stung a little from the tying knot.

A heavy silence settled between them. Their routine started to settle into a gentle rhythm. Pull and twirl. Pull and twirl. Every once in a while, Clara could feel a brush going down the length of her hair. Her heart felt steady. The sensation reminding her of the times Rue would do her hair for her. She nearly fell asleep. Eyelids began to droop.

"There!" Quartz's voice snapped Clara back to reality. "All done." She went in front of Clara. A small mirror in her hand.

Clara nearly tumbled out of her seat. She was stunned how much her hair has grown since her exile. With trembling hands, she held the mirror up. Her amber eyes were brighter than ever before, almost a shade of molten gold. Her silver hair was brushed out. It was now touching her shoulders. She took note that she had two thick braids that crowned her head. They were held up by the jewels she picked up from the basket.

Twitch let out a sharp whistle. "Clara… You… You look beautiful…"

Clara swallowed at those words. She's was called many things. Beautiful was like a bell beneath the waves. Distant but sweet. She tucked in her lips. She took a deep breath. *Don't cry*, she thought. *You've done enough crying for today.*

"It's a special custom we Sand Dwarves have," Quartz explained. She began to gather her things. "At the age of sixteen, the females would have gemstones braided in their hair. They pick the gemstones they feel the closest to." She gently took the mirror from Clara. She placed the mirror on a nightstand closest to Onyx. "As for Life Threads, controlling them is mostly considered a taboo amongst most of the kingdoms."

Clara raised her brow in shock. Then, she pressed her fingers together. Her skin crawled as she recalled what she did. "IIIIIII can see why…"

Quartz quickly turned to Clara. Her glasses on the verge of falling off her nose. "With a few exceptions of course." Suddenly, her eyes began to glow. Hers were a molten gold orbs. A faint image of her elephant appeared beneath the fabric.

Clara gasped. "I thought I was the only one to do that."

Quartz giggled. "Nah. It's just taking a lot of skill and a strong connection to the word. From what you've told me, that slave trader was probably given that power from someone else. A false connection to the world results in disastrous consequences. Basically, robbing an animal or other races their soul."

Clara clutched her arms. She bit her lip hard. They become something similar to the Empty. She gulped hard. "W-what are the exceptions to the taboo?" Her spine went cold as she thought of Arebella's baby. "Is the baby okay?"

Quartz nodded. "You did fine. If anything, you managed to reconnect the threads with Queen Arebella and her baby. Our bodies our tough but there were a few threads loose. That was the original source of the hysteria." As she said that, the glow disappeared.

Clara felt warmth return to her body. She leaned back into her chair. Onyx was at her side once again. Her fingers brushed his fur. Her heart eased for a little bit.

Quartz shifted her glasses. "Well… I'll leave you two alone now." She walked over to the door. Her hand on the handle. She briefly turned to Clara and Twitch. "By the way… What were you two shouting about?"

Clara's face went red at that. Her heart almost ready to burst. Here we go again.

Twitch grinned. "Do you have a man you've got eyes for?"

Chapter 22
Power

As the night finally dwindled down, Clara was enjoying the quiet of her surroundings. She looked over to see Twitch was fast asleep. Soft snores filled the room. Onyx grumbled softly in his sleep. Clara briefly caught an image of him chasing a rabbit around the fields. She giggled at the image. Then, her mind went back to Lotus. *I wonder how she's doing*, she thought.

Clara got out of bed. She crept over to the door. She twisted the knobs and shut the door as best as she could. Clara got only a few feet away from the room when she was met by an armored Sand Dwarf. For some reason, he bowed before her. She bowed back.

"What assistance can I help you with?" The Sand Dwarf guard asked. Something about his eyes were a little off. They were a bit glazed. His voice was slightly sluggish.

Clara thought for a moment. "Uh… Yes." Might as well get some help in finding where the healer's quarters are. "Can you show me the healer's quarters?"

The guard bowed. He went in the direction that she believed was the healer's quarters. Clara followed behind. Their footsteps echoed across the dreary halls. Torches barely lit the room. Clara could make out the basilisks that slithered along the pillars. Faint hisses filled the room. She could feel uncertainty from them. Even her bond with Onyx screamed with worry. Clara tried to send back reassuring waves to him, letting him know that she's all right.

She soon reached the healer's quarters. There weren't as many Sand Dwarves in it. The bed that Queen Arebella was supposed to be in was empty. *At least the queen is safe in her own bed now.* A faint smile crawled onto her lips. A soft knicker brought her back to reality. She felt an impatient tug from her bond. Clara giggled at Lotus.

The unicorn was now upright in a bed of straw. Her ears were flicked back with some form of annoyance. As if she knew what Clara and Onyx were doing the entire time. Her eyes bright. The hind leg was heavily wrapped in fresh bandages.

Clara knelt down and touched Lotus' let. The cloth was dry as a bone. *No ointment*, Clara thought. *The Empty really did a number on them.* She frowned deeply. *There must be some way to fix this.* Clara thought long and hard if there was an earth based spell that would revive all the plants. Suddenly, a shadow fell on her. However, she didn't feel any fear in her bond.

"Clara?"

Clara whirled around to see King Helios stand before her. The Reptilia King looked extremely tired. His eyes holding a dull glow. A small frown on his face. Onyx stood by his side. The black wolf gave a soured expression. King

Helios tilted his head. "What are you doing here? This place is notorious for being a maze."

"A castle guard showed me here," Clara answered.

"What guard?"

Clara was about to point out the castle guard, but found that he was gone. Clara blinked. "That's strange... He was right there a moment ago." She tried her best to shrug it off. *Best not to assume the worst.* "What brings you here?"

"I've just finished with my meeting." King Helios let out a tired sigh. He rubbed his face. "Right now I just want to sleep."

Clara got up from her crouching position. "Well... Do you want me to walk you to your guest chamber?" Without warning, she was gently scooped up into his arms. Her stomach growled loudly. Clara's cheeks flushed. She wrapped her arms around herself. "Sorry..."

King Helios shook his head. "It couldn't be helped. They plants they do have around her are barely alive."

Clara thought for a moment. *Maybe this is my chance to do some good for the Sand Dwarves.* "Can you show me what it looks like?"

King Helios was silent for a moment. His gaze never broke away from hers.

Clara bit her tongue in shock. Her cheeks going crimson. "I'm sorry... I just thought to help. They've been through a lot." She looked down at her hands.

King Helios let out a soft chuckle. "You have a wondrous heart, dear Clara." He set her down. "Very well.

I still have enough life in me to take make the journey back to the plant sanctuary." He strode over to Lotus.

Clara stared in shock as he picked Lotus up with ease. She soon began to notice that his back was starting to glow. A few dots that seemed form a lion roaring on its hind legs. She continued staring until Onyx's snort brought her back to reality. She shook herself. She followed King Helios down the halls. They were soon outside the palace. It felt strange being this far from Twitch and Shard.

As they continued down the path, Clara began to notice how empty the streets were. When she first came here, there were shocked gasps and whispers. A celebration would've been appropriate. However, several broken house were spotted. Crumbled down walls. A broken wagon. Even the crystalline window showed just how broken this proud race has truly become. Not a single soul aside from Clara, King Helios, Onyx and Lotus, were found to break this lonely atmosphere.

They came across what Clara had wanted to see. It looked like an underground garden. Fungus littered the ground. Dried up moss covered a few stalagmites, resembling fuzzy teeth on the cave floor. Wilted plants littered the majority of the floor. Smells of rotten vegetation filled the air. Above them was a hole that seemed to be fifty feet high.

Clara crinkled her nose at the stench. She covered her nostrils to minimize the fumes. Her vision soon activated. There were barely any threads at all. The majority of it was simply empty space. "This… is all what is left?"

King Helios grimly nodded. He lowered Lotus. "The Empty have slunk in here a few times. Mostly attacking the farmers. However, they never get close to the village."

Clara went over to the nearest plant. Her fingers curled against the limp stalk. *The gods asked me to help. So, let's see if I can without relying on Onyx or Lotus.* Clara sent a small link to Onyx and Lotus, letting them know of her plan. She waited for a response. After a while, she felt a reassurance between their link. Clara took a deep breath.

Her vision activated once again. The threads were there but in short scraps. Clara lightly touched the strings. They curled around her fingers with ease. She tied them together. The same technique she used in the past. The strings were slowly connected once again. She briefly turned her vision off. The stalk in her hand didn't appear as listless. However, it didn't look like an herb that would help. She went to the other plants.

Each plant received the same method. Each one didn't look as withered as they previously were. Clara gritted her teeth. Her body screamed. She slammed her fist into the ground in frustration. Her vision threatened to flicker out. *It's no use! I'm so useless without some form of help!* She could almost sense the other villagers taunting her. Lady Maroona standing over her, smirking. Words like weakling entered her ears, causing Clara to clamp her hands against her head.

She could feel Onyx and Lotus wanting to link with her. The desire to lend their power to her burned at her core. She took a deep breath. This time, she decide to send words to her link. *I'm grateful that you two have gotten me this far. I'm even happy that you want me to stay. However, I need to do this alone. My skills nearly cost you your lives. You've seen the damage. I can't risk taking you down and getting hurt any more.*

Clara rubbed her fingers against her hair. She felt the cold surface of the stones. She looked around for a reflective surface. She noticed that King Helios had his sword in his possession once again. The sheath cradled against the hip. "King Helios. Can you have your sword pulled out for a moment? I... know this will sound strange but I just need to see my reflection for a moment."

King Helios stared at her with a puzzled expression. After a few moments, he shrugged and pulled out his sword. There wasn't much light that leaked down from the hole above them, but it was enough for Clara to see.

Clara took note of the emerald that sat on her head. She closed her eyes. Her breathing slowed down. She opened her eyes once again to activate her vision. The blade began to resemble glass. The webbing thick enough to see her reflection clearly. She soon began to notice four glowing orbs above her head. The green one, no doubt the emerald, was the closest to her. *I wonder if I can tap into it.* Clara raised a finger to her head and pressed against the emerald.

A surge of power erupted into her body. She recalled what Quartz said that the origin of the gemstones. Clara twirled the thick strands around her fingers. It soon became clear to Clara as to why the humans stole the stones. *They're not just beautiful*, she thought. *They're another form of connection aside from beasts.* She soon recalled that Duke Averance and the other mages had medallions and necklaces compared to the rest of the villagers.

Clara felt her heart burn with anger. She closed her hand into a fist. *That's not fair*, she mentally hissed. She slowly turned to the wilted garden once again. Clara placed her hand onto the cave floor. She forced the threads of the emerald to push into the earth.

The room was soon filled with a green haze. Threads of green and brown moved in a frantic hurry. They twisted and stretched. Some were stitched together to form shapes. New forms began to peek through. Rumbling noises deafened around her. Clara immediately stopped what she was doing.

Once everything returned to normal, she deactivated her vision. Her body didn't scream as much. She looked up to see something beautiful. The garden was now replaced with living plants. Flowers from lilies to roses bloomed. A soft trickle of water echoed. Mighty oak trees and several palm trees with coconuts stood tall. Smells of herbs hung in the air.

Clara's eyes brightened at the sight of this. A smile reached her lips. Her body didn't scream as much. The taunts in her mind slowly died away to a dead hum. She went over to the herb that was known to treat open wounds. She plucked a white flower from a nearby bush.

Her fingers mashed it down to a past as she went back to Lotus.

She unbandaged the wound once more. It did look better than it was earlier. However, the ugly scabs were on the verge of leaking out pus. Clara rubbed the paste onto the leg. She hushed Lotus as the unicorn nickered softly. Once it was done, Clara gingerly wrapped the bandage back on.

A surge of pride radiated off of her. She was able to do her magic without hurting anyone. She stood up and smiled at King Helios. "I did it. I did it." She hopped with joy. She twirled around as if she could hear the invisible music playing. Laughter escaped her mouth. She immediately ran over to King Helios and hugged him.

In the embrace, they twirled for a moment. Clara's feet hovered slightly in the air. Her arms wrapped around his frame. The smell of sand and tropical rainforest wrapped into his scales. Once the spinning stopped, Clara looked up to him once again. Twitch's words entered her brain. Her skin turned pink as heat crawled into her. She slowly backed away.

King Helios simply stood there. His white spots seemed to glow as if the stars had fallen onto his body. His tail twitched back and forth. He cleared his throat. "We should go show this to King Oberon."

Clara nodded. She laughed as Onyx and Lotus rushed into the garden. Onyx took massive gulps of water. His tail wagged with pure joy. Lotus, on the other hand, was running at full speed. The horn gleamed like a piece of ivory in the light. Clara watched them for a while. Then, she called them over. "Onyx. Lotus. Time to head back."

Suddenly, a noise startled her out of her joy. It sounded like a whip of some sort. Clara turned around to see King Helios down, a large net covered him. "King Helios!" She ran over to him. Clara's hands fumbled against the knots. She soon noticed something. She looked closer to see that the fibers of the ropes were green. Plant-like. Her heart sunk.

"Clara!" King Helios roared. "You need to get out of here!"

Clara glanced around. She heard Onyx growl, his fury burned like an uncontrollable fire. Lotus neighed loudly. Several scuffling noises resounded. Clara briefly saw a few squat figures move out of a small cliff only a few feet above her. Her eyes widened. "Sand Dwarves? But I thought—" Something wiped out of the corner of her eye.

Clara dodged with barely enough speed. Her arm was wrapped in the net, an unwelcomed weight on top of her arm. She frantically pulled at it. She gritted her teeth. Clara turned her head to see King Helios being tugged away by several lean shapes. A glistened body following right behind them.

Clara reached out. "Helios!" Things went dark as a burlap sack covered her head.

Chapter 23
Dark Elf Territory

Clara scrambled to regain her steps. She could barely feel her arms. Her wrist bound tightly. Clara tried to fight back but firm hands hold her tight. She gave a hard kick. The tip of her toe made a hard impact on something soft, earning a scream.

Clara smirked with satisfaction. *At least I got a hit. I hope Onyx and Lotus are okay.* The last time she felt them, they were running toward the Sand Dwarf castle. Clara continued to struggle against their grasp. Throwing a kick every once in a while. She received a heavy hit on the back.

"This one sure is feisty," said one voice. It had a slight whistling tone as it spoke.

"Are you sure we grabbed the right one?" another asked.

"Of course," A third voice broke through the fray. "There's only one human in the world who'd have disgusting hair like that."

Clara's heart dropped to her stomach. *No... It couldn't be...* Her skin ran cold. She could feel her back aching greatly from the blow of the unknown object. She bit her tongue. All she could do for now was just listen.

The third voice continued to speak. "Are you sure that the potion was strong enough? The lizard looks like he's still conscious."

Clara tried to hold back her rage. A small growl escaped her throat. Her numb fingers made an attempt to ball up. She heard faint breathing in the midst of marching feet. *Helios?* She nearly jumped when something brushed against her ankle. It was sharp. Tiny claws raking her flesh.

The marching stopped almost entirely. Their grip on Clara's arms didn't loosen. However, they removed the bag from her head. King Helios' breathing was heard clearly in the near silent atmosphere.

Clara blinked at the suddenly light that hit her eyes. Several torches lined an iron gate. The tips were wicked spikes. Animal skulls of varying sizes and shapes draped over it. A faint odor of blood reached Clara's nose mixed with rain. Further behind it was a castle. This one had stone so black that it could almost blend into the night if the stars and moon weren't hovering above them.

Clara glanced around as she dared. There was a large mountain range looming over her. She soon realized that the air was cooler than it was in the cavern. Almost freezing. She shivered. Tall pine trees stood around them. Their bristles looking menacing than friendly. The dark blue sky barely held any stars. The moon gave her a cold gaze. She spotted King Helios in a cart. He wasn't moving, not even putting up a fight.

Clara twisted toward the direction of King Helios, but was grabbed harder by her captors. After a while of struggling, she could now see what they are. They had blackish-gray skin with back nails. Their hair was slightly white. Blood red eyes glared back at her. Pointed ears angled to the sky. *Dark Elves.*

"Well... Isn't this new?"

Clara whipped her head to the voice. She stared in horror at the owner of the third voice. "Basilini..."

Basilini had a portly build. His small glasses smashed against the bridge of his nose. His brown hair curled into places it shouldn't. His black eyes held no laughter even though a small smile ruled his lips. Around his neck were massive medallions that contained aventurine and peridot. He wore mages robes of dark green with a thick brown rope. By his side was a pale brown ox. The large animal wore an elegant saddle on its back. It grazed on some grass, but the movements almost had no life to them. "Hello, Clara. It's such... a pleasure to meet you." Every word he said was hollow.

Clara tried to hide the terror in her voice. "What's going on, Basilini? Why in all of Heartstrings would you align yourself to the Dark Elves? It's considered treason! You know their bargaining only ends things in ruin." She was met with a punch to the face. Her world spun for a moment. However, she was able to stand her ground. Eyes turned back to the boy.

"You're one to talk!" Bassilini hissed back. "You were getting cuddly with a lizard."

Clara took a step forward. Her face almost inches away from his. "King Helios had been kind to me.

Whatever hate you feel toward me, leave him out of it."
She leaned back as another punch came at her. Clara
thrashed her head forward, her skull made a heavy impact
on Basilini's nose with a sickening crack.

Basilini let out a loud wail. "You brat! How dare you
do this to me!" He covered his nose but it did little to hide
the blood seeping between his fingers. His glasses fell to
the ground. He waved his ox over. In a matter of minutes,
the mighty beast knelt down and allowed him to climb on.

Clara only gave him a defiant look. She could've
sworn she heard giggling behind her. She then noticed the
Sand Dwarf from earlier. The armor was gone. Only baggy
clothing clung to the stocky body. Clara gritted her teeth.
"You!" She watched the Sand Dwarf slowly turn his head.
"Yes, you! How could you do this? To me and your king?
Do you realize—" the rest of her words were cut off the
moment she saw a cold, blank stare.

A clicking nose drew Clara's attention away from the
Sand Dwarf. Walking toward her was Lady Maroona. The
daughter of Duke Averance was wearing a blood red
gown. The bodice riddled with rubies and blood stone. Red
hair tied back in a tight pony tail. A net of pearls adorned
her head. In her hand was her usual fan. Her basenji
walked beside her. It was wearing a color that held the
same gemstones as its master. Lady Maroona had the same
smile she used when she wanted to tear down Clara.

Clara straightened her back as best as she could. For
some strange reason, there was no dread the ruled over her
body. Instead, there was a burning sensation in her soul.

Of course, she'd be here, she thought. She narrowed her eyes. Her lips mashed together to hide her rage.

"Hello again, Clara," Lady Maroona said. Though her voice sounded friendly, her eyes were cold. "I see you've managed to survive your ordeal of being exiled. Most humans that are wouldn't last for more than a week." She giggled.

"And I see that you're just as disturbing as ever," Clara retorted. "That's why so many of your potential suitors would always run in a hurry." She tried to hide her own smile as Lady Maroona lost her smile. Normally she would shrink away from it, but for some reason it just made Lady Maroona seem smaller than she really is.

Lady Maroona tried to swing down her folded fan at Clara. Clara dodged this time. She bit the noble's hand, earning a shriek. Lady Maroona screamed. Her hands tried to punch Clara.

Clara held on. Her jaws becoming tight as Onyx's when he tore away at the meat he was given. She even growled. Her teeth dug in so deep that she could feel blood start to seep into her mouth. Finally, she let go after the two Dark Elves pulled her back. Clara took notice of the yodeling basenji. She let out a growl, causing the creature to whimper and hide behind Lady Maroona's skirt. The Sand Dwarf with the dulled gaze quickly joined them.

"By the blackened fires!" Lady Maroona let out a few string of curses that a lady her age shouldn't be allowed to say. Her eyes went harder at Clara. "You've also become more feral."

"What's the meaning of this, Lady Maroona?" Clara's voice began to heighten with word. "Why are you working with the Dark Elves? Haven't you forgotten the destruction they've caused? The deals they've broken. What does kidnapping me and King Helios accomplish? To boost your twisted ego."

Lady Maroona kept silent. She just turned on her heel. She walked away with a few grumbling words about Clara's beast leaving her. Her dog soon tailed behind her. Ears flat to his head, tail tucked in. Basilini had his ox quickly join them.

Clara was soon dragged away with them. Exhaustion was starting to settle into her body. She tried to look for King Helios, but entering the castle made her sick with dread. The castle was made out of pure black stone. Red tapestries hung over the archways and skeletons scattered along the floor. Some of them were human. Blood splattered against the pillars. Smells of rot hit her nose hard. She tried to fight back the urge to vomit. Behind her she heard the Dark Elves whispering to each other.

"That was hilarious!" The first Dark Elf chuckled. "I've never seen those brats scream so loudly before."

The second seemed to tried to hide his own mirth. "This one has some sturdy jaws to rival that of wolves. We shouldn't speak so lightly since those older humans are here."

Older humans? Clara found herself searching for any sign of other humans. The halls held a dull glow. The torches had an eerie blue glow. She was soon led to the dungeon. She coughed at the rancid stench that instantly hit her nose. Her hands were untied as they opened the door for her. Clara stumbled into the cell with one push.

"Better make yourself comfortable," the second Dark Elf said. He slammed the door shut. He grabbed his companion before any word could be uttered.

A heavy silence echoed in the dungeon. Save for a few drops of water hitting against the stone. Some scurrying noises were heard in the distance. The mountain cold moved into the drafts from above. The other cells were filled with moans of other prisoners.

Clara laid on the filthy floor. Her skin covered in goosebumps as she shivered constantly. Her breath began to appear in whisps. She tucked in her knees as she curled into a fetal position. Her ears strained to hear where King Helios will be. No sound.

At least Onyx and Lotus are far away from this gloomy place. Clara found herself thinking of Onyx's black fur wrapping around her as he would lay close to her. Lotus' muzzle touching her forehead to reassure her that she was still her. She found herself thinking about Twitch and Shard flying high in the sky. The warm, tropical air of the Reptilia Kingdom was something she wanted to feel again. Dragons roaming the ground and skies, hopefully away from The Empty.

Clara awoke the next morning. She didn't know how long she was curled up but the pain in her back indicated that it was a long time. To her surprise, there was something warm on top of her. She'd expected Onyx to be there, but instead it was a blanket of musty wool. Clara tried her best to hide her disgust for the smell that hovered in the air. She slowly got on to her feet, nausea ruling over her stomach. A soft thud echoed. Clara looked down to see a strange bag sat in the middle of the floor. A shadow loomed by her cell.

Standing in front of it was another human. She was a few years older than Clara. Her dress was black as night. Her black eyes held a cold gaze that made it feel like she was an embodiment of death. Skin as pale as hers. Cheekbones arched. Her hair black as night. "This should help. It should make you stop making those horrendous noises." She walked away before Clara could even utter a word of thanks.

Clara looked down at the bag. As another wave of nausea hit her stomach, she quickly took the bag. She held it close to her nose and sniffed. Scents of lilac and rosemary hit her nose. It slowly gave her a sense of relief. Her nostrils no longer burned. She looked around her cell. The stone walls were made of some form of mixture of onyx and a black stone that she's not familiar with. She touched her hair to see if the stones were taken from her while she was asleep. All of them were still present. She walked over to the bars. With one hand, she gave it a hard shake. It moved slightly.

Well. That helps with the planning how to get out of here. She noticed that a few of the torches were burnt out. Clara leaned forward to peer into the semi-darkness. She huffed with frustration. *Now, how am I going to see King*

Helios or the passages? She paced for a while. A rumble erupted from her stomach. She grimaced.

Clara looked down at the bag. She knelt down to pick it up. She tugged at the string. There she looked at the contents inside. Lilac and Rosemary were nestled inside the sack. Remembering that rosemary is edible, she took a small leaf. It quelled the gnawing pain of hunger. She cinched the bag up and continued her search. She peered into the darkness. Ears strained further. "Helios..." She tried her best to whisper, but the words hissed out. "Can you hear me?"

A sudden shuffling noise reached her. Her heart skipped a beat. *Is it him?* She quickly looked around for any signs of guards nearby. *I wonder how much the Dark Elves know about my power?* She decided to activate her vision once again. The threads were seen brightly despite the darkness. She moved her head slowly. She even placed herself between the bars just to have a better view. She soon spotted a cell that had a cluster of red, light blue and green. The shape slowly moved.

Clara gripped the bars tighter. "Helios! Are you okay?" She covered her mouth. She looked around for any of the guards nearby. No one in sight.

"C-Clara..." King Helios' words came out raspy. More shuffling occurred. The cluster of threads nearly collapsed before her. "Deactivate that before someone sees!"

Clara was reluctant. She didn't enjoy the idea of not seeing him in the darkness. She sighed. Her vision turned off. She spoke again. This time, lowering her voice. "Are you okay? Are you hurt anywhere?"

King Helios grunted. "Lightheaded. My body aches but I don't see any bruises on me. I do feel a blanket on me. Where are we?"

Clara sighed. "The Dark Elf Kingdom."

A loud shuffling noise erupted. Heavy breathing followed close behind. "Clara? Do you know anything about their king?"

Clara shook her head. "No. If anything, most of the villagers dread saying his name." She slowly looked around. *Now I know why*, she thought. But why would Duke Averance consider coming here?"

Footsteps echoed above them. Metal clinking against the stone walls. Mutters of contempt growing louder with each breath. Two Dark Elves soon appeared in the stairway. Their eyes burned with an unnamed fury. Both of them held the same blue-flamed torches.

"The other humans would like to have a talk with both of you," one of them said.

The second Elf had a scare that went diagonally across his face. It stretched from his right temple to his left chin. His hand was on the pommel of his sword.

Clara could feel unease in the pit of her stomach. She closed her hand into a fist. She tried to hide the shiver that ruled over her spine. She still felt weary through her body. Her eyes were orbs of molten gold. As best as she could, she hid the pocketed herbs into the pocked of her pant leg. "Well... Get on with it then."

The elves opened her cell door. Then, they went to King Helios'. Both of them were tied with rope and vines before they ventured up the stairway. A cool mountain breeze greeted them as they reached the main floor. The smell of death still hung in the air. Armored humans and elves walked around for a while. Nasty looks being exchanged to one another. Some gazes landed on Clara and King Helios.

Clara paid no mind with the glares. She tried to reach out to King Helios. The desire to comfort him grew stronger as she got a clear look of his face. She saw his concern and fear. She tried to reach out to him, but her arms were pinned back by one of the Dark Elves. She gritted her teeth in frustration. *If King Helios is this afraid*, Clara thought. *I can't imagine what it'll be like to meet him.*

High above the rafters, screeches were heard from above. Several thin shapes flickered in and out. Shiny eyes sparkled in the clumps of shadows that were made by the morning sun. Fluttering echoed above until one of the Dark Elves shouted at them.

They soon arrived at a banquet hall. A fire place was at the right of a long pine table. Over the mantle was a stuffed head of a mighty stag. The dead gaze staring at the guests that came into the room. Dangling above it was a chandelier made out of bone. Even the chairs themselves were made entirely out of bone. Sitting on them were Duke Averance and the Mage Counsel. Their beasts were with them, moving in a listless state. The children were with them too.

Clara found herself unable to move. Her hands balled into fists as she watched the humans, she had to give respect to were feasting like pigs. She could see rows upon rows of food before them. They were eating with greedy gusto. Their loud chewing, slurps and guttural grunts made her face twist in deep disgust. "I see you're enjoying your spoils." She could see all of them turned their attention to her. How she wanted to use the stones right now.

Duke Averance sat at the head of the table. His gray eyes focused on her. His dog growled loudly as if he was reflecting how his master felt. His wore a dark red suit with spikes along the shoulders. His thick brows scrunched down. Up close, his dark hair was braided to resemble small horns that peeked on his skull. It made him more menacing than his dog. "Clara... Never thought to see you here."

"Neither did I." Clara glanced at Lady Maroona. The gloves still remained on her hands. She snarled. "If anything, I'm surprised that all of you are here since many humans are forbidden to come near Dark Elf Kingdom."

The mages stiffened at this. Mage Oak was the first to speak. "How dare you talk to us this way!" He slowly rose out of his chair. His fingers started to glow with magic. "Do you have any idea what we're capable of?"

Clara raised a brow. "Do you have any idea what the Dark Elf King is capable of? If you're as wise as you claim to be then you shouldn't bring your children hear. Let alone your dear beasts." She pointed to the chandelier. She could hear the offensive hiss from one of the elves. She didn't care.

The group stayed where they were. Indignant looks on their faces. Even Basilini's tomato red face made it hard for Clara not to laugh. Especially at the fact that an ugly bruise landed on the bridge of his nose.

King Helios stared at this in apprehension and confusion. He turned to Clara. "Do you know them, Clara?"

Clara turned to him. A reassuring smile crept along her face. "In a matter of speaking. These are the 'humans' that tormented and belittled me all my life. Not only that but they were supposed to protect humanity from the outside kingdoms and the beasts." Her face then darkened. "I can't believe I was so foolish to be afraid of these pathetic souls."

At that Basilini got out of his chair. He charged at her with all his might. His shouts being heard at the distance. Before he could get any closer to Clara, a large shape appeared before them. It was a massive wall of black scales. A whip-like tail hit the young boy, causing him to fly across the room and hit a wall.

Lady Maroona snarled at Basilini. "That stupid idiot."

Clara stood in shock at the creature seen before her. It was as big as Gaia. The horns resembled that of mountain goats. The head bearing a mixture of a deer and a wolf. Red eyes turned to her. *A Shadow Dragon.* Clara froze in place. Her hands balled into fists. It didn't smell of death but it did smell of ash. A hot breath washed over as it tilted its head, wondering what to do with her. It gave a small bow and went to a small corner where there was barely any light.

Clara let out a small breath. *I better see what they're up to*, she thought. *I better not give away how much I've grown in power since they've exiled me. Except for my sharp tongue. Thanks so much, Shard.* "All the banter aside, why did you bring us here? For war?"

The water mage was the first to speak. Her dirty blonde hair came down in clumps. "No, dear. We're here to... Resolve this issue."

King Helios tried to take a step forward. "That being?" No one made a response to his question.

Clara felt a certain rage inside her. She took a deep breath. "He asked you a question. He's a king to his people. You should at least give him some respect."

"Shouldn't you give us respect?" The Air mage asked. His scrawny frame leaned back in a chair, he fiddled with his fork. His pale blue robe hung around him, giving him a ghostly presence.

Clara's face turned red at this. She could feel the threads around her. Even the ruby began to feel hot on her head. "Respect? I've been shouted at for messing up on the littlest things. I was asked to do chores that were supposed to be someone else. I've beaten, kicked and even had my hair cut by you and your demented spawn!" She could see their growing anger, but no fear was in her heart. Even Lady Maroona's expression made her face redder than hers. "Yet all of you have the gall to ask me to give you respect while I'm tied up against my will and have King Helios poisoned! He may not be human, but he deserves more respect than any of your sorry camel spit!"

Without warning, Lady Maroona threw her plate at Clara's head. She began to fiddle with her fingers. Her basenji yelped in pain. The dog suddenly went feral. Growling, teeth showed as it snarled. It charged at Clara. Their paws landed on her chest, knocking her over.

Clara was knocked onto the floor with a heavy thud. She tried to wiggle away, but the binding prevented her from doing that. Teeth sunk into her throat. The jaws were powerful enough to crush her windpipe, but there was enough force to make her wheeze. Stars began to appear above her. She could hear Lady Maroona cackling in the distance. She kicked as best as she could but the dog was in a position where she can't reach. Colors began to blur. Then, threads began to appear.

The one on the dog were pale red. Not like the blazing crimson that would come off of Onyx's body. If only I could reach, she thought. The world starting to fade. Then, the teeth and pressure were off of her. A faint "yip" was heard, followed by a hiss. She coughed as she sat up. Air slammed into her lungs. Small trickles of blood were felt along her neck. In front of her was King Helios. His tail coiled around her hips.

"You infidel! How dare you treat her this way? You're more of a mockery to human kind!" King Helios slowly turned to her. "Are you all right, Clara?"

"Don't ignore us lizard!" Lady Maroona grabbed her goblet when someone snatched her wrist from behind.

Clara stared in shock as she saw the same woman from before. She watched as the woman twisted Lady Maroona's wrist hard despite her thin frame. She slowly got onto her feet. Clara could feel her back ache, but right now she wanted to have a better look at King Helios. She caught a wild gaze in his eyes. The lion mark on his back began to glow slightly.

Duke Averance rose up from his spot. "Get your hands off my daughter, witch!" He made a lunge at her, but the black dragon let out an unnerving roar. Its head arched. He sat back down.

The woman slowly turned to the mages. "I think it's enough for today. It seems the audience you've requested had enough of you. Please kindly leave."

"We're not leaving until we've met with king," said the blue robed mage spoke. She took a deep breath. "Perhaps we should take a moment to head to our quarters and rest. It looks like these two have made this meal off putting."

With that, the others got out of their chairs and began to walk away. Their beasts following them. They all watched the black dragon with nervous glances. Even Lady Maroona was a bit apprehensive as her dog limped beside her. They vanished from view, but it took a few moments longer for their footsteps to silence.

One of the Dark Elves tried to pry King Helios away from Clara, but grew nervous as King Helios' grip on her grew tighter. He sighed. "We better take them back."

The woman raised her hand. "Just a moment." She walked over to Clara. Her thin fingers lightly touched her chin. She moved it left to right. She clicked her tongue in disapproval. "A few nicks but nothing serious."

Clara stared at her incredulously. *Nothing serious! Lady Maroona's dog tried to choke me to death!* She flinched as she felt something cold against her skin. A cloth wrapped around her neck. Once it was cinched comfortable, she and King Helios were taken back to the dungeon.

As the two walked back, Clara looked at the hallways again. She could make out several windows that might be potential blind spots. The rafters were crawling with wyverns. Then there was the shadow dragon. *If I remember right, shadow dragons have the strongest sense of smell. Best night vision as well as hunting in the dark.* She strained her ears to hear for any rats that might be crawling along the stone. There was some skittering but it didn't seem that there was enough to form a wall to distract the Dark Elves.

Once they reached the dungeon floor, the Dark Elves tried to separate the duo once again. King Helios' grip grew tighter around Clara. He growled and hissed. Even with his arms restrained, he gave one of the soldiers a solid headbutt. The other drew out his sword but King Helios dodged the blade. The Reptilia King bit hard into the armored arm. Blood leaked out the moment he let go and gave a hard kick.

Clara stood there. Her mouth opened into a small "o". "Where did you learn to fight like that?"

"Long story," King Helios answered. He coughed and wretched for a moment. "Curses! I've heard nightshade being a strong poison but I never dreamed that it could—" He pushed Clara out of the way as an axe almost cleaved her in two.

Clara grunted. "You really need to work on not pushing me to the ground." She soon remembered the herbs from her pocked. She moved her hand close to her side. She tangled their threads onto her fingers. The pocket burst as the pouch tumbled out. The greenery sprang out. The stone floor covered in a carpet of grass and flowers. Smells of fresh spring entered the room. Vines slithered between the thick fibers of rope and broke her bonds.

Clara formed a wall of stone as the second elf soldier charged at her. The weapon hit the rock with a loud clang. It echoed in the halls. Clara soon used the stone floor to create crafted prisons. Once it was done, her body began to feel weak. Her wrists ached from being bound for so long. She breathed heavily sweat beaded down her brow.

Clara looked at King Helios once again. She flinched as he began to heave. Disgust making her own stomach twist in knots. *I better go help him*, she thought. However, the nagging feeling that she wouldn't have much luck with it bounced in her brain. Clara walked over to him. Her knees wobbled as she continued to move. Her desire for food slowly grew stronger.

King Helios quickly held her up just as she was about to collapse. His breath reeked of vomit. "I'm all right. Nightshade only has an effect on mammals. Reptiles like me are only a little sickly to it." He groaned. His head bowed. He wiped some of the vomit that hung from his lip. "Ugh! Unfortunately, we're stuck with the smell. Sorry if my breath bothers you."

Clara looked around for something to use to break the bonds. She soon came across a dagger and pulled it out of a sheath that was on one of the guard's right hip. She cut the rope with ease as it fell away from King Helios' wrist. Clara was about to say something when several shuffling noises were heard from upstairs. She activated her vision. She saw at least ten clusters of purple threads heading their way. She bit her lip. She looked around for an opening or a duct. Then, she spotted something in a faraway corner. She slowly regained her step. She grabbed King Helios' wrist and pulled him in the direction of the corner.

They soon saw there was a hole in the wall. Big enough to fit a small child in. Clara knelt down and touched the rocks. The stones shifted slightly under her touch. She pushed them away. Clara and King Helios exchanged looks and soon pushed away the stones that were safe enough to move around without collapse. The hole grew bigger and bigger. As well as the sound of footsteps.

Clara's heart thundered in her chest. Her limbs growing weary, but the fear of being caught or killed only made her work faster. She pushed hard until she tumbled out with King Helios in tow. Her world spun temporarily as they rolled down hill. Rocks smacked her back and arms. Her right arm was suddenly snatch from her side. Her feet dangled in the air. After swinging for a moment, she soon realized that she almost fell into a deep ravine.

Her heart nearly stopped breathing. What a drop! A delay any longer and… She felt herself being pulled up. She put her hands on rock and roots that were strong enough for some footholds. Clara was soon able to stand on solid ground. She spotted King Helios laying on his side.

She knelt down by his side. She slithered her arm underneath his side to prop him up. Faint screeches were heard in the distance. Clara moved closer to him. She lifted him up. "Helios. We need to go. They'll be on top of us if we stay here any longer."

King Helios stared at her in pure amazement. He soon pulled his feet toward his body. He leaned forward, in sync with Clara's movements. His breathing was a little labored. His whole body shivered as the mountain breeze rushed at them. "L-let's get going then."

The two moved as quickly as they could. Leaves rustled with each step they took. The air filled with shouts and screeches. Flapping above them. Each step brought them down the mountain as best as they could. They soon found a hollowed-out tree that was big enough to hide in. They ducked into the entrance.

Clara hugged Helios as the sounds grew louder. Thundering hooves came around the corner. Her heart went still as she heard something slide. She bit her lips hard. She's heard of Dark Elves riding Mountain Striders before. Goat-like creatures that were bigger than a regular Mountain goat. A speed that could rival that of horses, it could easily match with the wind. Dark pelts that would blend into the night. Supposedly, one of the meanest creatures in all of Heartstrings. *Where's Lotus when you need her?*

"Search the area!" One voice barked. It was heavy with authority, no doubt the general. "They couldn't have gotten far."

"What should we do with them?" another voice asked.

Clara took in a sharp inhale. *No. No... It couldn't be.* She slowly let go and inched her way to the entrance. Clara had to grip the ground in order to conceal her rage. A few feet from the entrance were the Minotaur back at the Harpy's forest. He was dressed in the very same armor that he tried to kill her in. His name was foggy in her mind as she tried her best to remember it. She could feel the ruby in her hair being hot against her head. It was slowly turning her hair into flames.

The Minotaur had his back facing them. In his hand was a large halberd. His tail swished from side to side in pure annoyance.

"They were to meet King Noctral. He's to question them as well as see if we can gain new territory."

Clara gave a hushed growl. *Like that'll ever happen!* She felt being pulled closer to King Helios. His heart pressed against her ear. She began to calm down. Her breathing less tight as before.

The Minotaur bellowed and shuffling was followed.

"Make no mistake Promoths. I will turn your sorry hide into leather if I hear one more complaint out of you. Your friendship with a human maiden was bad enough. Do you want to disgrace your kin more?"

After a long pause, a heavy snort broke the silence. "No, sir." Hooves thumped against the ground. They began to move farther and farther away from Clara and King Helios.

"Move out!"

Shuffling of leaves and snapped twigs broke out in the forest. Even a few animal snorts were enough to put Clara in a tense state. Sometimes the sounds grew closer to the tree. After sometime they finally went away.

Clara was the first to crawl out. She bit her lip. She took a deep breath. Her fingers rubbed against the gemstones. The ruby was still hot, a deep shade of crimson that was on the verge of turning black. Her hands scrunched up the leaves in her hands. "Why… Why did this happen?" Tears began to sting her eyes.

She turned to seeing King Helios struggling to move. Clara wiped her eyes. *I better get a fire going.* She quickly gathered leaves and kindling. Her hands made a small moat around the mound of flammables. Clara touched the ruby once again. The heat of the red threads twirled around her fingers. She gently moved it over to the fire. Some smoke appeared for a while until a tiny flame appeared onto it.

King Helios dragged himself over to the heat. His claws raised against the flames. "I-is thissss the firsssst time ussssing f-fire magic?" His words were slurred. Eyes unable to focus of what he was seeing before him.

Clara moved over to him. She pressed her finger against the ruby once more. The heat returned to her fingers. She touched his arm. To her surprise, he flinched away from her. The movement almost putting out the fire.

"Clara, b-be careful. You could—" King Helios laid his head down against his claws.

Clara's heart twisted inside of her. She tucked her knees in and pressed her fingers together. "I'm sorry… I thought it might help." She pulled in herself tighter. "I wish Onyx and Lotus were here." She sat there for a moment longer. Then, something rippled in her bond. An eager sensation that rippled through her.

A loud rustling was heard from the bushes near the right. Clara quickly got up. She felt her limbs shaking. Her eyes darted from one spot to another. She balled her hands into a fist. Her breathing hitched. The noise grew louder and louder. Suddenly, a flash of black crashed into her. Clara fell back with a heavy thud.

Clara giggled as she felt a familiar wet tongue licking her. "Onyx!" She wrapped her arms around Onyx's thick neck. His muscles ripped with each movement. She buried her face into the nice black fur. A tinge of blood hit her nose. She felt something warm and wet hit her cheek. She got up and touched her face. On her fingers were droplet of blood. The scarlet liquid matched the color of the ruby.

The sound of hooves soon echoed across the way. Lotus soon appeared. Her white horn gleamed in the sunlight that had somehow leaked from the pine trees. On her back was a strange looking saddle equipped with several bags that hung from the side. Lotus' ears were perked forward. She bobbed her head up and down. Joy radiating off her bond.

"Lotus!" Clara was on her feet for a moment before she tumbled back onto her knees. She groaned as her stomach growled. "Just my luck!"

Lotus knickered as she knelt down. She nuzzled Clara's face. Her eyes sparkled with a light hidden in her eyes.

Clara pulled a flap open. To her surprise, there were some of the original supplies. There was even some dates and meat that was in there. As Clara pulled out the contents, she soon notice a note laying at the bottom. She pulled it out and unfolded it. She stared in surprise as she read the note:

You and King Helios were gone for a while. We started to search for you when we found Lotus and Onyx. One of the guards was walking dead. Saw a piece of Dark Elf armor on the ground. It didn't take long for me to figure out where you went. Hang on! Help is on the way!

Your dear friends,
Twitch, Shard and Iridescent

They're coming. Clara's heart warmed at those words. She turned to King Helios. Her friend was now wrapped around Onyx. She picked up a date and handed it to him. She nearly screamed when he snatched it from her hand.

King Helios munched on the fruit. Juice seeped out of his mouth. The moment he finished he glanced at Clara. Realization flashed in his eyes. His head turned away from her. "Sorry…"

Clara smiled. She bit into her own date. The little fire helped ease the chill on her bones. The juices bringing a sense of relief that she needed right now. However, one thing bothered in her mind. *Promoths knew my mother… and that Dark Elf said that he disgraced his kin by being friends with a human. What's going on?*

"That Promoths was a curious one," King Helios said. "He didn't sound too eager to find us."

Clara was silent for a moment. She began to notice that he wasn't as sluggish as before. If anything, he was starting to look a bit better. "How are you feeling?"

King Helios looked at her once again. Concern was in his eyes. "Less likely to vomit when we have to move again." He rotated his wrist for a moment. "The ache is gone too, but this cursed cold is going to be the death of me if we don't get out of here." He sneezed.

Clara laughed. She stared at the fire for a while. She brushed away any leaves or needles that would catch the small embers. She flinched as one ember hit her palm. She stared at the small burn for a while before smothering it. She looked at King Helios once more. "Thank you. It's the first time anyone stood up for me before."

King Helios lifted his head. His hand reached out to touch hers. "I couldn't just let them do that to you. I'm just sorry you've had to put up with it for so long." He stroked Onyx's black fur. His tail thumped the ground hard. "Were the other villagers were like this?"

Clara shook her head. "No. I had my mother, father and Rue..." She wiped away the tears that soon flooded down her cheeks. A sigh escaped her lips.

"Clara... I noticed you were tense earlier. Did... did you know Promoths?"

At those soft and sincere words, Clara couldn't hold back those feelings any more. She cried hard. She covered her mouth to make sure none of the other Dark Elves were in earshot. "He's the Minotaur that killed my mother." She sobbed. She found herself pulled into a tight hug.

King Helios wrapped his arms and tail around her. His cold scales pressed against her skin. His frame perfectly fitting hers. "Clara. I'm so sorry. I know exactly how you feel." After some time, he let go of their embrace. "I promise, that I'll do everything I can to never make sure no one makes you feel that way again."

Clara nodded. She hugged him once more. Then, she went back to eating what looked like to be a papaya. As she finished her fill, Lotus suddenly got up. Hooves stamped hard onto the ground. A wave of unease washed over her like black tar.

Onyx let out a low growl. Ears pinned back. Lips revealed gleaming white teeth despite the blood stained around his muzzle.

A fog began to roll in. Heavy and thicker than Clara had ever seen. She got up from her spot. She frantically looked for something in the bags that could help her. Her limbs didn't feel as numb and weak, but her magic wasn't in the best use at the moment. She soon found her dagger. The bronze hilt warm against the cold atmosphere. She heard several creaks. Clara turned around.

To her horror, the pine trees in front of them began to warp their branches. Needles raining down from the sky as branches intertwined with one another. Briars and thorns crept out from the ground like angry snakes. They formed a vicious ring around them. No escape. Silence hung in the air. The fog had become so thick that there was nothing but a wall of grayish white.

Footsteps crunched under the dead leaves and debris. A clinking of armor followed with it. A dark shape soon appeared before them. Black armor with wolves and ravens carved into the metal. The figure was tall. Taller than most of the Dark Elves. The helmet had three large spikes that jutted upward. On his side was a broad sword with an amethyst on the pommel. A chuckled vibrated out of the helmet. "So, these are the two prisoners that everyone is making a fuss about." The voice had a slight husk to it.

Clara raised her dagger up. Her hands gripped the hilt tightly. The warmth that she felt earlier was now replaced with a heavy chill running down her spine. "S-stay back!" She moved slowly to King Helios. She stood in between King Helios and their mysterious assailant. Onyx was by her side now. His fur began to show hints of orange.

"Clara don't—" King Helios got up. Barely dodged a branch trying to snatch him off the ground. He grabbed Clara and Onyx before a piece of bark turned into a spiked wall and fall on top of them. He hissed at the Dark Elf. "Who are you? What do you want?"

The armored Dark Elf tilted his head. "Ooohhh! Isn't this interesting? I've heard that Reptilia are supposed to be heartless. However... I've never seen a Reptilia be this protective with a human before." His unseen eyes turned to Clara. "Clara is it? That's a pretty name." He let out a low whistle. "The name alone means bright and clear." He pulled out his sword. He leveled it so the blade was aimed at Clara.

Lotus and Onyx shielded her. Their ears were pinned so far back that they were flat against their skull. Ripples of anger and desire to protect Clara rang true. Then, Onyx shifted his attention to the part of the mist.

An enormous shadow slinked against the trees. It huffed greatly as it moved toward the armored warrior. It was lizard-like with bat wings. A barb the size of a cart wheel flashed out, striking a tree in the process. The more it got near to its master, the more of its shape grew apparent. Moss green scales with a black underbelly. Ram horns that curled neatly around cow-like ears. Gray eyes focused on the intended prey. The long neck arched. There was no doubt that this was indeed a wyvern. The biggest in all of Heartstrings.

The armor warrior petted the wyvern as it lowered its head. "Let me introduce myself." He did a small bow. "My name's King Noctral of the Dark Elves. However, most humans would prefer to me as 'The Black King.'"

At that name, Clara let out a sharp gasp. She's heard of that name before. The Black King was said to be one of the most dangerous Monarchs in all the clans. He had once cut down forty men without so much effort. His chambers are said to hold bones of his enemies and put them on display. Clara raised her sword on him once again. "Don't come near us!"

King Noctral only laughed. "You think you can take me on with a dagger? By the looks of you, you've barely had any weapon training down." He took a step forward. Then, he tilted his head as his invisible gaze saw Onyx and Lotus' reaction. His voice began to sound amused. "Well. Well. A wolf and a unicorn protecting a human. That's something you don't see every day. I thought humans would want to stay away from such creatures with all that unstable magic nonsense." A flash of silver light leaked out of the visor of the helmet. His whole body stiffened. "So… You're a Beast Heart." He turned his gaze to King Helios. "The both of you."

Clara stared in shock. She whipped her head to King Helios. He's a Beast Heart? *Wait… It would explain why his back has that lion image!* "What about it? Are you going to kill us?" She activated her vision. Several threads of dark brown threads were before her. *I know I can't handle moving someone's life threads around, but if I can form a shield.* She pulled at the threads as best as she could. The earth rumbled and a small wave of rock came at King Noctral.

King Noctral showed no hesitation. He swung his sword at the rock. It cut through with ease. He charged at Clara, but was intercepted by King Helios. The Reptilia King grabbed his wrist and flung him to a wall of briar with all his might. A spear made of shadow soon sprung out of the ground, allowing the Dark Elf to grab it and flung back at them.

Onyx ran ahead. His fur began to glow brighter. Heterochronic eyes bright. Once King Noctral landed a few feet in front of Clara, Onyx leaped at him. Teeth crunched against the metal. Several pieces fell away. Onyx finally bit into soft skin before being torn away.

The wyvern screeched. The shockwave knocking back Clara and King Helios. It began to move forward until Lotus let out a beam of light. It shrieked in shock. The dragon-like creature turned its head toward Lotus. It snapped but missed. Two creatures caught in a dance. Whenever the wyvern lunged, Lotus would dodge with ease.

Clara tried to use her dagger in the spots that were exposed. The more she lunged, the more King Noctral avoid her. Her movements grew faster and frantic. She had to duck from the flying debris from the wyvern's collision into the briar and branches. She brushed away the needles that rained down on her. She barely had enough time to dodge a blade.

We can't keep this up, Clara thought. *We have to get out of here.* Exhaustion burned through her. The threads that she found in the ground weren't of much help. Even the emerald was starting to fail. *I'm not sure what I can do with both the lapis lazuli and sapphire would do. I know the ruby is associated with fire now, but it might cause a wildfire if it gets out of hand.* She noticed Onyx barking at something. She followed his gaze. There was a hole in the branches that were big enough to squeeze through. Clara blocked the broad sword with her dagger. The blow shattering her shoulder.

King Noctral's eyes gleamed in the visor. They were the same shade of violet as the gemstone. "You think your little antics will take me down? I've taken on enemies far more skilled than you." He kicked her hard in the stomach.

Clara gasped in shock. She fell back onto the ground. She coughed for a moment. Once a heavy shadow landed on her, Clara made a frantic attempt to crawl away from him. However, she felt strange. It felt like the strings inside her were being pulled upward. She was yanked back up, her body twisted in massive knots. She gritted as she was being stared down by the monster before her. The words she wanted to say were stuck in her throat. Her brain began to feel panic rush in. The only problem was it wasn't hers.

From the corner of her eye, Clara saw both Lotus and Onyx standing stock still. Their muscles twitched. Their eyes moving from one spot to the next. Next to them was the mighty wyvern. A barb tail coiled around them.

Clara soon turned her attention back to King Noctral. The visor was pulled back to reveal his face. She soon began to notice the scar that went from his left temple to his right chin. His breath smelled of mint. *If I wasn't in peril, I would find that kind of weird!*

King Noctral has his hands twisted in a way that looked like he was trying to hold on to multiple ropes at once. Blood tricked down from underneath his gauntlet. "Going to back to your question from earlier. No. I don't plane on killing you. Especially now that you and King Helios will play a far better role in my plans. Personally, I prefer you over—"

"Your Majestyyyyyy!"

A shrill cry erupted in the sky. A Dark Elf began to scramble out into the ring. The armor was stripped away. She was covered in blood. Her chest had a deep gash. "Run! Run!"

"What's the meaning of this?" King Noctral glared at the warrior. It turned to pure horror at the sight. Even his wyvern grew nervous.

"E-empty! Empty are coming—" Her words were cut off by a long, gleaming tentacle covered her mouth. She couldn't breathe as shapeless blob slithered up her body. It went up her spine. Then, it plunged into her mouth. She quivered and shook. A loud squelch was soon heard. She dropped to the floor. Her eyes upward in a glassy gaze. The Empty crawled out.

Mmm... Make me... Whole... It slowly crawled toward her.

Clara screamed. The Empty's voice echoed loudly in her mind. "No! NO! Get out of my head!"

King Noctral glanced around to see that several more Empty were crawling toward them. More loud screams were heard in the distance. Bellows crowning the treetops. Fire soon began to explode all around them. "Just my luck! Glin! Get to the castle!" His wyvern roared in protest. "Don't worry about me. I'll be fine."

Just as he said this, Clara activated her vision. She used all of her strength to pull the ultraviolet threads from King Nectral. He cried out and let her go. Clara's throat began to burn. The sight of the dead Dark Elf caused her to wretch for a moment. Flickers of flame began to appear within the trees. Animals and birds frantically running away. Smoke growing bigger and bigger.

Clara scrambled away from them. *It just like back at the village!* Her mind once again went to the scene of what happened all those years ago. Large flames consumed trees. Smoke that blackened the sky. Her father going into the heart of the village as commanded by the duke. Her mother told her to stay inside the house while she went to see what was going on outside. After a few minutes, a scream was heard. Clara ran out to see her mother dead. Promoths looming over her dead body.

She bumped her head into something. She soon realized that it was King Helios. Her eyes taking his. Clara grabbed his hand before he could even say a word. She pulled him toward Lotus, Onyx close behind them. She quickly got him up on the unicorn's back. With ease, she was able to get on. Her fingers locked into the mane.

She briefly turned back to see King Noctral hop onto his wyvern. They went into the sky and vanished into the smoke. Clara glanced at the Empty. Her heart hammered hard in fright. *It's now or never.* She looked ahead. The path was slowly being blocked by the Empty. "Lotus!" Her voice was barely heard over the crackling. "I'm going to need your help. Both you and Onyx."

King Helios gave her a worried look. "What are you planning?"

"Watch!" Clara sent a mental message to go. Lotus lurched forward. Then, she galloped at full speed. Onyx close to them at full speed. Clara activated her power once more. She pulled some of Lotus' golden threads and tied it with Onyx's red ones. She remembered that those threads needed to be handled with care. Then, she tied them to her own. Glowing white threads began to manifest around her. Their bond for the entire world to see. With a deep breath, Clara imagined all the light was giving them speed. The gemstones glowed brighter; their aura began to surround them.

Before long, Lotus galloped faster than ever before. She was able to plow through a row of the Empty with ease. Onyx protecting her by howling out soundwaves with all his might. Hooves and teeth tearing away at the Empty. Each step brought them farther and farther away from the flames and smoke. Plants growing in their wake.

Before long, Lotus and Onyx managed to reach to the bottom of a nearby ravine. A steady stream of water glowed under the morning sun. Both beasts breathed heavily, mists of their breath appearing from their nostrils.

Clara and King Helios slide down from Lotus' back. They clung to each other as they made their way to the stream. Clara slowly did her best to go down, but she slipped on a rock. She tried to hold on but King Helios tripped on his tail and the two splashed into the river.

"How many times are we going to fall into this kind of predicament?" King Helios sighed as he shifted himself to land. His body vibrated from the cold.

Clara also shivered. "I don't know. I hope the others will find us soon. I've only been here for... a day and already I want out of this demented kingdom." Her limbs began to grow weak once again as she clambered up the bank beside him.

The two looked up at the sky. Soft rustling of the trees above were the only things that calmed the frantic hearts. The clouds lined with silver. The light gave them a much needed comfort after what had seemed to be an eternity in darkness. Then, the two finally laughed.

"I can't believe that worked," Clara said. Her stomach still hurt from the kick, but she laughed anyway. "Quartz told me life threads were powerful, but I never imagined that I was able to do it a large magnitude."

"Probably due to your Beast Heart." King Helios slowly reached for Clara. "Still... Thank you for saving me." His hand wrapped around hers.

Clara felt tears stream down her eyes. "You saved me... I've... I..." She took a deep breath. Another thing crawled into her mind. She even remembered what Quartz showed her. "Helios?"

King Helios shifted his head toward her. His eyes were wide. "Y-yes..."

"Do you think there are more Beast Heart out there?" She slowly turned her head to him. "Are you really one too?"

King Helios was silent for a moment. "Yes. I didn't realize it at the time until I was trying to get back to the Reptilia kingdom in the cold."

"Were you starting to see threads? Sometimes moving ones?"

"Yes." King Helios moved forward. "And you?"

Clara stared at him for a moment. Her cheeks were still wet. She felt Onyx and Lotus lay down beside her. Their exhaustion radiating off their bodies. "When I was five... maybe six." She gave a heavy sigh as she felt a large burden being lifted off her shoulders. "Lady Maroona and her 'friends'... Though they're more of her pets than actual friends. They attacked me one day without warning. Next thing I knew... I was pulling green strings." She smiled. "You should've seen the look on their faces. They screamed like owls and ran away."

King Helios laughed. "I'm pretty all the clans would've loved to see that spoiled brat have something like that."

Clara smiled. Suddenly, increased rustling was heard a few feet from them. She immediately propped her elbows to see who it was. So far, there was no one. "Twitch? Shard?" The rustling started coming from the west. She turned to it. To her horror, shapeless blobs appeared from the undergrowth. They went to her at break neck speed. "No!"

Before anyone could react, The Empty were on top of them. The world around began to become a strange sheen. The plastic bodies began to morph and twist. Their grip tightened around their prey. Neck, legs and arms pinned. Screams and bellows were barely heard in the unforgiven mountains as The Empty have begun to form their malicious tasks.

Chapter 24
Voices of the Empty

Darkness. That's all Clara could see. She felt for her chest. The last thing she remembered before the world went black were the strings from her body being pulled apart. Her bond being severed from Onyx and Lotus. She could no longer feel their emotions. Their fears. King Helios' warm scales snatched from her hand. It felt strange. She wanted to be free of them ever since her bonding ceremony. Now, there was a strange emptiness flowing into her soul. Her heart began to unwind slowly.

She tried to reach out for something. She found her legs unable to move. Suddenly, she heard the voices from before. Hollow and unfeeling.

Make... us... whole... The words began to echo around her. It grew louder and louder. An unending plea. While their bodies weren't seen, Clara could feel them press against her.

Clara hyperventilated. Her hands clutched at her chest in a desperate effort to save her own heart to be taken. She tossed around. Twisting her hips and arms in hopes of shaking of them up. "S-stop! Stop it right now!"

W-w-why?

Clara looked up. Her throat almost made it impossible to speak as an invisible hand constricted against it. She gritted her teeth. Her heart beating loudly in the darkness. "B-becau-cause! You're hurting everyone! You're hurting me! Taking my heart won't change what you are! Empty!"

Just as it had begun, the constriction abruptly ended. Clara coughed. The air slowly went to her lungs. Once the coughing stopped, she started to breath slowly. She lightly rubbed her throat. Her legs were finally free to move. Clara adjusted into a kneeling position. Her eyes were on an Empty before her.

The creature had several dull threads sticking out of its body. A weird cooing noise came out of the strange being. Translucent skin apparent in the darkness. It didn't attack her. The only strange thing was that it began to create a pair of eyes from the broken threads. *P-please... Can't go on...*

Clara stared at the creature in great confusion. "Wait... what do you mean 'can't go on'?"

The dull threads began to move on their own. Black and white threads began to take on two strange forms. The white was the form of a creature with bird wings and long rabbit-like ears. The other had addax horns that graced his head. *L-long ago... Gods and Goddesses took turns... make individual beings...*

"But the Goddess of light and God of Darkness fought each other!" Clara couldn't understand this madness. First deities not bearing any human resemblance, then a goddess disappeared. Now there was an agreement between creations? *Things just get stranger and stranger.* "I know the Goddess of Light disappeared because of Nixon and his weird brother."

N-no... N-Nixon was making us... His brother... jealous... broke us, but cursed...

"Cursed? Broke?"

Before long, the threads began to play a scene. The white threads began to create what resembled humans. The black threads began to create something. It was a tiny orb of colors in the center of its hand. Then, a strange cluster of purple and black began to appear. Horns that resembled deer but had a thornier appearance. It let out a wicked screech, smashing the orb. All the colorful threads were scattered birds flying in the darkness. Two dark beings were fighting amongst each other.

The white tried to break up the fight but were hit by the cluster. Grays soon appeared in the white figure. The body slowly went stiff. Other colored threads that resembled some of the gods gathered. Heads bowed in mourning.

The black creature bellowed in response to the cluster. With a simple strike, the creatures were both ripped apart. Suddenly, a strange voice filled the sky.

Look for feathers of brown and green.

For you shall find the Harpy Queen.

Find in the sand for a mighty trunk.

Look to the sea where a Leviathan has sunk.

Find a Shepherdess with a hair of silver.

Reptilia king born a lion,
Will make the world bright.
Beware the girl of red.
Born of the spider, all will be dead.

Clara was sure there was more to the prophecy, but the lead Empty laid against its side. Soft wheezing was heard. Clara slowly moved toward the lead Empty. She stretched her arms out to the creature. She tenderly scooped up the creature. Clara was surprised at how soft the body was in her hands. The translucent skin made her hands sparkle underneath. The colorful eyes looked up at her.

The Empty. One of the most feared creatures of Heartstrings was also the most fragile thing in existence. Even though they were meant to be lacking emotion, Clara couldn't help but feel pity.

She soon recalled her own emptiness. The feeling of moving from place to place. No kind word. No greeting. Only cold stares and sneers. Whispers about her hair. The death of her parents didn't make anything better. It only grew larger and larger as the years went by. A few times she tried to change the color of her hair, but the ink would fall out. She straightened her back until her spine hurt. She did her best to be presentable at all times. Nothing worked. No one wanted her around.

Clara gently stroked the soft surface. "You've been alone all this time. Haven't you?"

The expressionless eyes only stared at her. Then, it lifted a sparkling tentacle to her. *Please… W-we're tired… No one heard us but you. Guide us… Shepherdess…*

Clara was about to touch when something pulled on her. A large hand snatching her away from the dark void she was in. She desperately held on to The Empty. "It's okay! I'm here!" She could feel the strength in her arms ready to give way. "No! I… I want to help." *Their… Their just as alone as I am!* A bright light flashed around her. Her fingers tried to move the threads in a frantic fashion. She only seemed to attend to the eyes. Their shape were perfect spheres. Then, the pull was so strong that she could no longer resist it.

"It's not time yet to make us whole again." A unison of voices spoke before her. A crowd of people, no doubt the souls of the dead, waved her goodbye. "Come to them when a full moon is high. Find us, Wild Shepherdess." The world soon began to spin rapidly.

Clara gasped. "Wait!" She reached out but there was nothing but air in front of her. She found herself in a small cave. The entrance opened to a field of treetops. A moonlit sky hung low. Owls and crickets played their nighttime tunes.

Clara shifted and realized that something was on her legs. She looked down to see a blanket made out of Mountain Strider fur lay on her lap. A soft crackling reached her ears. She saw a fire roaring before her. King Helios laid close to it. Onyx and Lotus were close to her side.

Clara gave them a confused look. They barely had an injury on them. Their bandages were mostly placed on the legs. Not one was found on their back. *But the Empty came down on us. I thought we were going to die. Unless... The lead Empty commanded them not to attack.* As she was thinking this, she heard heavy flapping. Something wrapped around her.

"Clara!" Twitch's wings covered Clara's face. The world temporarily consumed in green. "You're finally awake!"

Clara soon felt stings along her back and face. Even her own arms felt like needles were thrusted into his skin. She took a deep breath. As she opened her mouth, her chest began to feel like a small hammer hit it. "Ow... T-Twitch? What happened? Where are the Empty?"

Chapter 25
Twisted Mages

Twitch backed away from Clara. "You were so beat up. Somehow, you, your beasts and King Helios managed to get away from them." She grimaced at Clara's wounds. "How are you feeling?"

Clara gritted her teeth as pain ran down her spine. "Now that you mention it... My body hurts everywhere. Including my chest." She shook her head. "What about the Empty?"

Twitch raised a brow. "Aaaaarrrrrreeee you okay? You seem a little mixed up."

Clara took a deep breath. She slowly closed her fist. *She's going to find me a bit crazy.* She soon began to relay all the things that happened to her. The darkness. The inability to feel her bond with Onyx and Lotus. A story of the gods. The Empty's existence. When she finished, decided to feel for Onyx and Lotus. Nothing. Not even a speck of emotion. Worried, Clara put a shaky hand on Onyx. She shook Onyx hard.

Onyx gave a low moan. He lifted his head. His heterochromatic eyes stared back her. His gaze was confused.

Clara's heart dropped down to her stomach. She couldn't feel anything. Her mind went back to the threads ripped from her body. Tears rolled down her eyes. She covered her face into her hands. Sobs echoed throughout the cave. Before long, she felt a soft whine from Onyx. A howl soon followed.

Lotus shifted. She raised her graceful head. Her head tilted. Then, she placed her head on Clara's lap.

More flapping noises were soon heard. This time they were accompanied by some footsteps. Shard soon came into the entryway with Iridescent and Quartz in tow. They all stared in pure shock as Clara continued to cry.

Shard went over to Clara. "Clara? What's wrong? What happened?" He knelt down as best as he could without smothering her.

Clara hiccupped a few times before she could make a response. She moved her hands away to reveal her tearstained face. "I... I can't feel them..."

Shard and Twitch exchanged glances. The feathers on their heads were slightly raised. They went back on Clara. "Clara..." Twitch said. "What are you talking about?"

Clara could only hug herself in that moment. "I can't feel my bond with Onyx or Lotus." She went back to crying again. "I can't feel their emotions. I'm... empty inside." Tears rushed down her cheeks. She soon felt a wall of scales hug her tightly. She looked up to King Helios.

"Shhh..." King Helios whispered. "It's okay, Clara. Everything will be okay now."

Clara didn't have the words she wanted to say at the moment. She just cried on until the next dawn. Her body ached to a dull throb. She laid on her bed. Her hair splayed out. Onyx and Lotus both went out for a moment. A part of her yearned for sleep but the mere idea of her severed bond only left her feeling hollow.

Clara was soon handed a bowl of water by Quartz. Clara said nothing and drank. The mountain water felt a bit stale. However, it did remove the raw sensation of her throat from her crying and trying to explain all the events that had just happened.

Quartz started examining the wounds. She unwrapped the bandages along Clara's arms. It revealed several deep gashes that ran along Clara's pale skin. She grimaced. "They really nailed you! I surprised that you've lasted this long. Let alone survive."

Clara stared at the wounds. She slowly traced them. Her mind going back to the souls that were lost, wondering around this world instead of going to the next. The never-ending pain that The Empty were feeling at this very moment. She even recalled those prismatic eyes from the lead Empty. "I... promised them... I promised the lead Empty..."

She felt a strange tug on her hair. In the corner of her eye, she soon made out Quartz fixing the braids in her hair. The gemstones in place once more. She tried to activate her vision once more. Nothing happened. She could no longer see the strings. Her fingers twitched and moved at a certain angle. Nothing happened. Clara sighed.

Quartz finished the last of the braiding. She moved in front of Clara. Her fingers lightly took her chin. "Well... You seem to be in decent shape. Don't worry about your magic. You were only with them for a short time. I'm sure that you would be able to control threads again in no time."

Clara tried to smile but her lips refused to move. She looked at King Helios. The Reptilia King was able to use his powers to move a rock from one place to another, but it didn't make her situation any better. She touched the stones on her head. Her heart sank. She could no longer feel the sensation of the gemstones' power. Clara tried to get up. This time her limbs weren't screaming in agony. "I'm going to stretch my legs."

She felt her hand being grabbed. She looked at Quartz. The Sand Dwarf gave her a sincere look. "I won't stray from the cave." *I just wish someone would tell me about what the Empty have done now.* The cold air hit her skin as she exited the entrance. It was soon riddled with goosebumps, but she didn't care. All she wanted was to know where Onyx and Lotus have gone.

She walked a few feet. Her eyes looked to the pure blue sky. There were no signs of wyverns, dragons or minotaur nearby. She continued down the path. Her ears pinned against the silent atmosphere. Clara nearly tripped as she made her way down a small path. She soon smelled fresh blood. Clara turned her head to a nearby brush. She soon spotted Onyx pop his head out of the brush. In his jaws was a dead rabbit. Blood stained his muzzle.

He walked out with a happy stride. His tail wagged. He sat in front of her. Proud to show his prize.

Clara gave a small smile. The sight of the dead rabbit disturbed her, but at least Onyx had his freedom back. She gently rubbed his head. "I'm sure Shard and the others appreciate the hunt. I wonder if Lotus had any luck finding food." Just as she said those words, Lotus soon appeared before her.

The unicorn let out puffs of steam. Her sides heaving. She knelt down. Her forelegs tucked in. She looked at Clara.

Clara was puzzled by this gesture. Then, she recalled where she's seen it before. Her eyes lit up. "You want me to ride?"

Lotus moved her head up and down in a violent manner. Her mane flapped as she did so.

Before Clara could answer, Onyx shoved his head into her back. Clara stumbled for a moment. Her hand gripped Lotus' mane. She stared in shock. "Y-you sure? I… thought you'd want to go home for sure this time. It's going to be dangerous now. No doubt King Noctral will be searching for us."

Lotus only met her words by biting Clara's shirt and pulling her up as she got upright. Before Clara could protest, Lotus moved forward. Only in slow circles. For a while it continued like this until Clara finally swung a leg over to the other side.

Onyx tore into the rabbit meat. His eyes watched it all with silent amusement. In a matter of minutes, the meal was gone. He licked his lips and began to move in a circle with Lotus. His paws matched in stride.

After what seemed to be a while, Lotus began to take off. The trees and undergrowth moved past in a sudden blur. Her hooves tore at the earth. Her horn glowed in the hidden light. Every leap over the streams and tree root were timed perfectly. Moving down the steep edges of the mountain were handled with such grace, that Clara would be rocked in a smooth motion.

Clara stared in wonder. The chill of mountain air was gone. Only a warm rush entered her body. She felt the breeze pull back her hair. The impact of the earth started to feel nice. A smile crept on her face. She raised a hand. She tried to activate her vision again. Nothing happened. She frowned and pulled on Lotus' mane.

Lotus stopped. Her body nearly went into a hard lurch. Onyx nearly collided with her hocks. Lotus glanced back at Clara. She nickered. She tried to lick Clara's face, but she was pushed away.

Clara sighed. "I'm sorry… I know you're trying to cheer me up." Her eyes began to sting. She gave a small chuckle. "You know… When I first left the human kingdom, I thought that breaking the bond I have would make me feel normal again…" she sniffed. "I… never thought that I would… I would actually…" She rubbed her eyes, hoping to hold back the tears. "Curse it all. I'm such a sentimental fool." She felt her cheeks being licked. Clara looked at Lotus again. She gave a small smile. "Thank you for being there for me."

"Clara!"

Clara nearly fell off. Onyx growled and moved his head on a swivel. Lotus gave out a startled neigh. Before the group was Iridescent. The Reptilia scout was holding his arm close to his body. Blood seeping out between his fingers. His scales flashed orange and brown.

Iridescent panted a few times before he could talk. "We've got to move! Now!"

"What happened?" Clara reached out to him. With a certain amount of strength, she was able to help Iridescent onto Lotus. She gave a Lotus a light tap with her hand along the neck.

Iridescent grunted. "It's those crazy humans you've told us about. The one you called Lady Maroona and Duke Averance are now taking control of The Empty."

Clara paled at this. Even though she couldn't feel their emotions through her bond, she knew that the mere mention of them left them extremely uneasy. "What?" she whispered. So many questions rattled in her brain. How was that possible? No human was able to do so for thousands of years. Did they do something to the stray threads The Empty carried inside? Were they watching Clara somehow? *No, there's no way they'd known that. However, Lady Maroona taking control of them. It would mean that she'll cut down anyone that stood in her way. It would mean*: "We need to warn the others!" She tightened her grip on the mane.

Suddenly, a rustling was soon heard. A sparkling blob slowly crawled out of the bush. Colorful orbs stared at here. It quickly made its way from one branch to another. Gargling noises that sounded frantic.

Iridescent went bright orange. "Clara! Move!"

Clara turned to him. "It's okay, Iridescent. I know this one." She held out a hand as Lotus sped by. Cracking and several noises made her turn around. The trees and plants were turning pitch black. Wilting away as a glistening tidal wave came toward them. Clara tapped on Lotus' neck. This time a bit harder than normal. "Lotus go!"

Lotus neighed. Her hooves began to tear up the soil. She was reaching a clearing. Her body began to move closer to the trees.

Clara shifted her body. Arms outstretched. *If the lead Empty was able to get away, then it could mean that the mages don't have control on all the Empty as Iridescent originally believed.* She soon spotted the creature hanging over head. "Jump!"

"What?" Iridescent nearly lost his balance. He wrapped his tail around her. His hands reached for the mane. "Clara, have you gone mad?"

"Trust me," she shouted. Her eyes never took off the lead Empty. It hung on the branches for a moment longer. Then, it leaped off. Everything slowed for a moment. Onyx and Lotus running with every power in their legs. Her arms outreached. Stiff and certain. Clara nearly fell off as it hit her chest. She adjusted it as carefully as she could. The creature centered on her abdomen.

As they sped on to their hiding place, they soon spotted Twitch and Shard unleashing several gales. A large gust of wind hit them. They went back a few steps but managed to avoid the crumbling patch of earth. Sounds of fighting also sounded. Before long, several armed humans were coming at them. Dust raised into the air.

Lotus jumped as high as she could. A sword missing her stomach by a few inches. She bellowed. Her hooves stomped hard. She dodged left and right.

Clara peered through the maddened scene. More of the earth was rotting away. Shouts of incoherent curses and commands were heard. Armored animals letting out battle cries of their own. Clara couldn't help but wonder just how much were these poor creatures were truly connected to their human without their free will being stripped. Were her parents' animals being the same way? Rue's duck? Do the monarchs know? *I need to find King Helios and get back to the Human Kingdom.* She narrowed her eyes until she saw a fleck of gray moving against some mossy rock.

King Helios stood his ground. A blade in his hand. He blocked while trying to protect Quartz. The Sand Dwarf raised a bow and notched an arrow. King Helios slashed open the chest of one soldier while he bit into another's arm. Several animals came at him. They were on him with claws and teeth sunk into his scales. He cried out, trying to shake them off.

Quartz sent several arrows into the air. They hit their mark. Animals and humans going down in a matter of seconds. She pushed King Helios out of the way just as an ox charged at them.

Clara tapped on Lotus' neck. She reached out to King Helios. "King Helios! Hurry! The land is crumbling." Her hand outstretched. Every ounce of strength focused on her core. Her heart hammered hard. Relief filled her once she was able to grab his hand. With the help of Iridescent, Clara was able to pull him and Quartz up onto Lotus' back. She could feel Lotus begin to slow down a bit.

A roar sounded behind them. Clara turned around briefly to see that the Empty have formed a mal-shaped monster. It was a strange conglomeration of animal and people's faces. Limbs shifted in and out. Fins, wings and tails thrashed about. Trees fell upon impact. Rocks crushed underneath its mighty weight.

What... What in all of Heartstrings is that? Clara's heart thundered hard in her chest. A wave of disgust felt along her spine as she smelled rotten. This thing was a living symbol of death. Clara tapped Lotus as best as she could. She could feel Lotus' body lurch hard. "I know, girl. I know."

Clara soon spotted a small drop that led to a river. She bit her lip. Okay... *Here goes...* "Head for that drop over there."

"What?" Everyone screamed in unison. Their protests drowned out by more roaring. They tried to shake Clara but they couldn't.

Lotus was a full speed. Her ears pinned back in fright. Her hooves were practically invisible. Onyx was ahead of her, nothing more than a black blur.

Clara glanced up at the sky. She could make out several shapes flying overhead. She bit her lip. Clara let out a silent prayer to the Light Goddess to wherever she may be. She eyed the little Empty in front of her. "Tie us and don't let go."

As if the lead Empty had understood the words that she said, it unleashed several glimmering tentacles. They wrapped around Clara and the others with ease. It stuck to their hips in a firm grip. It even made a makeshift harness around Lotus' chest.

Clara and the others did their best to dodge the arrows that came at them. It was hard to tell who was hurt but there was a soft thunk sound. Before long, Lotus arrived at the drop. Air rushed around them. Screams and howls echoed in their fall.

The fall itself was like an eternity. The mountain scenery opened before an open sky of blue. The clouds were white and silver. A sign of rain that would come soon. Specks of what looked like deer and bison bustled around from the brush. Ribbons of blue river spread across the trees. A faint sound of a waterfall echoed.

Clara felt along the group for King Helios' hand. A set of scales soon clasped around her skin. She turned her head for a moment. King Helios appeared tired, but his eyes held a sense of defiance. Her fingers tightened around his. Her eyes went back to the earth that was coming at them in a pummeling speed.

Twitch appeared in front of them. She began to flap her wings in a frenzied state. A few of her feathers came off, forming an invisible road. Shard was at her side, his mighty wings strengthening the winds.

Lotus' hooves soon landed on the road. She nickered and began to move forward. Her mane flowed wildly in the breeze.

"Where were you?" Iridescent shouted. He shook his fists at them. His scales took on a dark color. "Is this a Harpy thing to be fashionable late or is it just you two?"

"Just shut up and hang on!" Shard gritted his teeth. His wings flared out like flames. His eyes landed on him. "Do you have any idea how hard it is to shake off a wyvern? Let alone avoid having arrows rain down on you."

"Quite fighting, you two." Twitch narrowly dodged an arrow. She angled her wings upward, the winds lifting the road that higher before.

Shard went behind and let out a tornado as a brigade of arrows came at the group. He even snatched a lance that almost pierced his heart. With all his might, he flung it back. It was unknown where it landed but it seemed to have distracted the humans down below.

Clara could feel Lotus begin to lose steam. The strides were shaky. The world slightly tilted as Lotus' legs threaten to give way. Clara shifted herself to look at the scenery down below. There was a clearing here and there. However, her heart sank at the sight of dead trees around them. They were menacing, but at least their leaves and needles would give a comforting scent. She couldn't help feel the dread at the idea that animal carcasses were going to spotted once they get down. Clara shook the feeling away. She had to focus on where she was.

Twitch followed her gaze. A deep frown plastered on her face. "Not much life down there." She sighed. "Clara. I'm so sorry that we kept this information from you." She faced Clara, her wings doing their usual flutter pattern. "While you were still unconscious, I went to see what The Empty were up to. When I did find them, they were acting a red haired human... Just like the one in the prophecy Elder Summer had told us."

Clara's face paled. "Lady Maroona..."

Twitch raised a brow. "You mean the Lady Maroona that always bullied you for no particular reason? That Lady Maroona?"

Clara nodded. "What did she do?"

"I can't really explain it... She had this strange red glow. Some of it was coming from her dog." Twitch's feathers were raised slightly. "Poor thing kept crying the entire time. While I don't like the concept of domestic animals, I think that dog was a little pretty." She shook her head. "Anyway. Lady Maroona used those strings to pull at them. She gave a few commands. Then, she walked over to some carriage."

Before Clara could ask for any more details, a tornado appeared. It was far larger than the tornados that she and Twitch have ever produced. Its deafening wail stretched out through the entire mountains. An invisible hand tried to pull them into its vortex. Lotus neighed and pulled back as best as she could. Onxy, however, wasn't as strong. The black wolf vanished into the vortex.

"Onyx!" Clara reached out. Her entire being beckoned for threads to spring out of her limbs and grab her friend. Nothing happened. Before she could say anything else, she and the others were soon thrusted into the tornado by a large geyser of water. The wailing of the winds stung her ears. Her arms soon flailed out. The world kept spinning. She couldn't see which way was up or down.

However, she didn't find herself being separated from Lotus. She heard a heavy grunting noise. She could see the lead Empty squinting its jewel eyes, holding in the pain. Then, she noticed something glinting in the light. It sped past her. A warm sensation hit her face. More screams were heard. Then, there were several noises of something being embedded in skin. Faint tendrils were spotted as they went into the center of the vortex.

Gales began to die down. The glinting objects were soon revealed to be arrows, sickles and daggers. Some were already dripped in blood. Before long, ground was visible to them. A carriage laid on its side. Several humans laid on the ground next to their dead animals. Laying at the center was a light blue robed figure. She was young no older than Clara. Strawberry blonde hair came off like a flowing river. Pale blue eyes stared in the distance. A pool of blood sat in front of her abdomen. Next to her was a duck, laying just as lifeless as she was.

Lotus laid down for a moment. Her sides heaving. Criss-crossed along her body were gashes that were thin as a needle.

Clara looked at the wounds in pure dismay. She turned her gaze at the others. Her skin began to turn ash white. Her friends were riddled with gashes along their arms and legs. Twitch laid on her side. Shard was at her side, but his breathing was far more labored. She then thought of Onyx. "Onyx? Onyx, where are you?" A soft whine reached her ears. She followed the source. She gasped at the sight before her.

Onyx stood tall. His shoulders were riddled with deep cuts. His left ear had a large tear. A gash ran between his eyes. His head held high as he tried to maintain his dignity. He walked over to them as best as he could.

Clara ran over to him. She wrapped her arms around his mighty neck. Tears welled up in her eyes. His blood mixing with hers. She began to tear up. "I'm sorry. I'm so sorry that I've failed you again." She buried her face into his fur. A faint groan shook her. Her gaze went back to Twitch.

A wave of sickness went over her. *Please... Please no...* Her legs threaten to give under her. Clara steeled herself as she walked toward Twitch. A puddle of blood was starting to form around her. She rolled Twitch over.

Twitch was in a more severe condition than Clara had originally thought. She had a large gash to her side. Her leg was almost severed off, muscle and tissue making a vain effort to hold it in place. Arrows were stuck to her back. What made it truly horrendous was the arrows that stuck into her side. Twitch cough up blood.

Clara held her head up. Her amber eyes met with the Harpy's green eyes. "Twitch! Don't move don't speak. Quartz is going to take a look at those wounds. I'm sure we can do something about them."

"C-Clara..." Twitch wheezed hard. "The carriage... Over there..." Twitch lifted a wing toward a carriage that was a few feet over where her group had landed. "I... think I saw... humans with metal bands on their heads." Twitch coughed once more. "Y-you said that your monarchs were something—"

Clara gently squeezed her wing. "Don't say anything else!" Tears rained down her eyes. "You're my first real friend in a long time. I'm not going to lose you!" She felt something on her back. She turned to see Shard. He was giving her the ever-defiant smirk when they first met.

"Hey... Don't worry about us..." Shard coughed up a small puddle of blood. "We've been through worse..."

Clara's breathing began to hitch. Her panic began to set in. She looked at the scene once again. She glanced at the carriage that stood. It was white with gold trimming. A symbol of a horse jumping over a large crown painted the side of the door. It was the royal seal of the monarchs. Clara let go of Twitch and ran over. Onyx followed right behind her. She went could make out two figures in the interior. She banged on the door. No answer.

"Hello!" Clara banged the door again. "Your majesties! Can you hear me?" She grabbed the handle. She yanked on it. "I'm Clara. I came from Snowdrop village. Please! Stop this madness. Try convincing the Mages to end this." Her mind went back to the tribes upon yank after yank on the handle.

The Harpies flying in the skies. Their wings maneuvering through the trees as if they were the winds themselves. The Reptilia with their spices and devotion to their land. The Sand Dwarves and their stoic service. Queen Arabella's baby that has been born. Harpy chicks that are trying to survive in a rotting forest. Animals of the wild that call this place home.

Finally, with one hard yank, the door gave way. Clara poked her head in. Smells of rot hit her nostrils. Clara coughed hard. Her stomach coiled. Once the coughing was done, she saw two corpses sitting in a seat to her right. She tried her best not to scream at the grim sight.

They were dressed in royal garments of green and gold. There was barely any skin left on them. Empty eye sockets looked onto Clara. Their mouths were held in a grimace as if Clara had rudely barged in on something she shouldn't. Maggots squirmed along the floor. Flies began to crawl around the scene. Their crowns were placed in an awkward position on their head. The gold was starting to corrode. The animalistic shapes began to have more warped features.

Clara could no longer hold back her revulsion. She stumbled away and got on to her hands and knees. She wretched hard. Her burning with each movement. Once she was done, Clara leaned back. She wiped the remaining vomit off her mouth. *What's going on? By the gods, what madness is this?*

Questions whirled around her head. How long have they've been like this? Are they really the king and queen? Were they just decoys to fool the enemy? Surely, they weren't dead for this long and the Mages didn't just lie about the king and queen for years. Right?

Clara felt something tap her shoulder. She turned to the lead Empty. Their sparkling eyes began to give a shade blue. It pointed to Lotus standing over the girl that had attacked them earlier.

Onyx was at Clara's side. His whined. Ears pulled back. His pupils got big and his tail was tucked in tightly.

Clara hugged him for a short period of time. She got up. Her hands balled up into fists. She marched toward the scene with anger in her eyes. Savage raged inside her. She picked up the wounded mage with all her might. Her nails dug into the sleeves but she didn't care. Her friends were dying and it was going to get worse from there. "What's the meaning of this?" Her voice cut through the sky as the sun sank low into the horizon, turning the land into an endless sea of blood. "Why are there corpses in the royal carriage? What are the mages planning? What is your mistress planning?"

No response came. The girl was simple staring at the blank space.

"Answer me!" Clara was now shaking the person in a frenzied manner. Her teeth clenched hard.

"Clara enough!" King Helios' voice snapped her out of her trance. "There's nothing you can say to-What in the great jungles?"

Clara watched in horror as the skin immediately decomposed. It was spreading all the way up to the head. Clara flung it back. Black ooze seeped from the mouth. The girl let out an ear-piercing shriek. The duck beside her did just that as well. Clara clamped her ears tightly.

The Empty hissed. Its eyes turned bright red. In one swift movement, it cut the head off the screaming corpse. Its glittering body rattled.

Clara stood there. Here mouth opened. She couldn't register what just happened. Her mind went blank. Questions piled into her head. The loudest one being: Why did this had to happen?

Clara slowly looked around. The blood red sky wasn't giving her any answers. She turned to the ruined trees. Their stumps sticking out of the ground. Clara then changed her sight to her friends bleeding on the ground. Their blood was starting to blend in with the scenery. How long they have until they died is unknown. She grabbed her shorts. "I… I don't know what do… I don't know what to do at all." Clara allowed the tears to fall from her eyes. They dripped to the ground. Sobs wracked her body once again. "There's no one to help us. Everyone's dying…"

"That's the most rational thing I've heard you say throughout your stay in this dreadful kingdom."

Clara jolted her head left to the person who made that comment. She saw it was the female head mage from before. She wore the same colors as the dead daughter. Behind the mage was Basilini and High Mage Oak. They all stared at her with unfeeling eyes. "High Mage Hurricane."

King Helios held Clara's shoulders. "What nonsense have you've dragged us into? What happened to that girl?" He gestured toward the dust that laid there.

"Oh." High Mage Hurricane held no change in expression. "My daughter had been dead for a long time. She's been rather useless as she got older. It's amazing that Duke Averance was able to revive her with just a few twisting of threads. Even the Empty have been a bit useful in collecting the threads for once."

Clara's eyes widened. "What?" Her stomach coiled tightly than ever before. *Her child was dead the entire time?* She glanced at Basilini. The young boy only grimaced at her gaze.

"The Empty have been growing in numbers. One of them had some large chunks of life threads." Mage Hurricane's voice was becoming more lifeless. She ignored the hiss from the lead Empty. "Some of them were enough to super power our babies. Our legacies would be stronger than ever before." Her gaze turned to her pigeon. It was listless on her shoulder. "More threads than we could get from any of these useless beasts in our kingdom. It's nice that most of those peasants take care of them."

An ugly picture began to form in Clara's mind. The beasts that she was so afraid. Her own Beast Heart sensing the threads around her. It began to make sense. The domesticated beasts back home barely had any life threads in them. Their lives were being sucked away the moment they were bonded to a human. She glanced to Lotus and Onyx. *Were they both suffering because of me? Was Rue's duck suffering too? Did her parents' beasts?*

Clara stamped her feet hard. "How can you possible say that about your own beast? The people you meant to protect?" She briefly glanced back at the carriage. The image of the corpses still burned in her mind. "What about those two corpses in that carriage? Where's the real High Duke and Duchess?"

"Dead." The word came out of Mage Hurricane, sharp and precise. The sky only turned redder as the sun hid in the mountains. Her own cloak turned red and brown with each passing minute.

Clara was on the verge of fainting. King Helios' fingers dug into her shoulder, keeping her steady. Her face became paler than ever before. All the color was flushed out of her cheeks. The blood on her skin became hard, crusting around the wounds.

"They've been for a long time actually." High Mage Hurricane kept talking despite the hard glare from High Mage Oak. "They were getting too close in learning what the Empty are and how to stop them. If they did that, well… all the magic we've gotten over the years would be for nothing. Duke Averance did a magnificent job with disposing them and their trusted servants." She looked up for a moment. Her gaze becoming somewhat thoughtful. "However, those servants took forever since they went—"

Before she could say anything else, Mage Oak went over to Hurricane and twisted her neck. A loud crack split the air. She collapsed in a heap. Her bird flapped on the ground for a bit, let out loud screeches. Then it lay still. Blood leaked out of its body.

"That's enough out of you." Mage Oak's voice was deep and lifeless. His hazel eyes turned over to the rest of the group. He soon pulled out an axe from under his cloak. "You know too much now."

King Helios growled from beside Clara. "Why tell us in the first place?"

"W-why kill her?" Clara asked.

Mage Oak raised his axe slightly, almost taking aim at King Helios. "She was annoying. The lot of them are." He looked at Basilini with a certain disdain. "My wife wanted a child. I certainly didn't want that. However, they just were a means for our kingdom. Hurricane decided that we should do a blood bath and figured to tell all of you since you're going to die anyway. Especially you, Clara." He took a step forward. His horse already pawing at the ground as if it wanted to unleash the final blow.

Clara backed away. Her legs threatening to give way. Her panic starting rise in her once again. *Is-is this how it was for my mother?* She readied for the blow to be delivered on to her. She could almost imagine the blade cleaving her and King Helios in two. She had no magic at her disposal, Twitch and Shard are probably dead and the Empty will continue to be tortured by their existence.

Lotus got between her and the mage. Her horn raised high. She let out a triumphant neigh. Her horn glowed a bright beam of light. A flash of light blinded everyone.

Clara had to shield her eyes for a moment. Shocked cries rang in her ears. A ferocious bark brought her back to reality. Her vision focused on Onyx. The black wolf ran up to the muscular mage. She took a step forward, hand extended. She couldn't help but stare in wonder as Onyx tore a chunk of flesh along Mage Oak's shoulder. It was disgusting, but it did allow enough time to let go of the axe.

Then, Basilini began to twirl his fingers. His ox began to let out a painful bellow. Green threads began to materialize. Basilini stuck his fingers into the ground. Dead tree roots sprang out from the dead soil.

Clara and King Helios dodged just as one was about to impaled them. Clara's panic reached to new heights. She glanced to see Onyx and Lotus trying to run away. *I got to find a weapon. It's too risky taking on plant magic head on. However, the plants are still vulnerable to being cut down.* She searched the ground for weapons. She took great care as the roots still came at her.

She gritted her teeth. The pain from the weapons were setting in. Every movement only made fresh blood leak out from the wounds. Clara finally found a weapon to use. A dagger with a simple nine-inch blade. She tackled to the ground. She rolled with ease. She turned to see King Helios fending off Mage Oak with a spear. His horse gave a light green aura.

Clara felt a burst of pain coming off of her arm. She looked down to see that a tree root had pierced right through it. She took the dagger. Her other arm ready to strike. Another root shot out. Clara screamed. She tried to move her body but it was held fast.

Clara's panic started to die as she heard footsteps. She was soon staring into the hateful eyes of Basilini. In his hand was a lance, the tip was made of pure silver. His grip on the wooden stock was so great, his hands were ready to break it. She soon noticed that black tar was starting to leak out of the corners of his mouth. Rot became more apparent as he was only a few feet away from her.

Basilini let out a crazed laugh. "Finally... Finally I have that miserable brat all to myself. Lady Maroona said I was just a filthy pig. A walking dead thing with no life what so ever. How I've longed to kill you. If I kill you right now, then she'll love me and my father will too." His eyes lit up as he said those words.

Clara couldn't help but feel more dread in her stomach. She tried to move but her limbs only bled out more. Her blood oozing down the roots, turning the plants into a deep crimson. Her body tingled greatly. It felt like her world was starting to fade. Exhaustion ruling over her.

This is it, Clara thought. Bitterness filled her mental words. *I'm finally going to die by Lady Maroona's hands. I don't understand why she hates me so much. I guess I really mess things up... Don't I?* She watched the blade aim at her.

"Now it's your turn to be a dead thing," Basilini sneered. He arched the lance. His eyes were filled with glee. He was about to thrust it forward when Onyx attacked him. He screamed as the giant wolf bit into his arm. Basilini clawed at Onyx's strong jaws, thick fingers making a vain effort to pry them open.

Then, the lead Empty let out a loud screech and landed on Basilini's face. Glimmering tentacles sprang out and pierced his arms and legs. Green threads appearing around his body. It only lasted for a few seconds as the lead Empty was pulled away and tossed to the ground.

His ox let out a loud bellow. Hooves smashed against the ground. Bright green threads slowly began to turn black. The creature tried to smash the lead Empty but it was too fast for the bulky frame.

Clara was soon freed from her wooded prison. She grunted as the blood began to seep out in faster than before. Exhaustion ruling over her once more. Then, to her horror, she saw Basilini punched Onyx away and pick up the lance. It was aimed at Onyx, ready to impale him.

"No!" Clara renewed her strength. She tightened her grip of her dagger. With one swift motion, Clara plunged the dagger deep into his ribs. She ducked as he swung the lance at her. She got up. The dagger was now aimed at his chest. To her surprise, it went into his chest with ease.

Basilini stood there. A stunned expression written on his face. "Wha... Why di-did you defend that wolf?" He weakly pointed a finger at a distance. "Are-aren't you bonded to that unicorn over there?"

Clara followed his gaze. In the mad haste, she had completely forgotten about Lotus and King Helios. She found King Helios on Lotus back. Both creatures fighting with all their might, dodging the swings while piercing Mage Oak and his horse. A smile crept on her face. Her pride became apparent in her eyes as she looked back at Basilini. "Yes. I was bonded to a unicorn. Her name is Lotus. She's a loyal friend to me and not even being cut by your steel can phase her." She dug the blade deeper as she spoke. "I was also bonded to a black wolf and his name is Onyx. They accepted me despite their dislike of humans. They protected me even when I didn't force me too. They knew my fear and comforted me in my despair."

She pulled the blade out. Clara watched Basilini fall back. She picked up the lead Empty, allowing its shapeless body to nestle on her shoulder. "I'm sorry you've lived such a desolate life that forced you to follow Lady Maroona around. I can't imagine that kind of pain, but I know what it's like to be on the outside. Wanting to prove yourself." She knelt down beside Basilini. Her fingers lightly touched his skin as it began to yellow. She lifted them up and lightly placed them on his chest. "Go. You may have been Lady Maroona's pet, but you don't deserve to be in your father's shadow any longer."

Basilini didn't say anything. His lips formed a bittersweet smile. His tears leaked out before they were replaced by ooze. "M-magic…" He said at last. His words unleashed more of the ooze from his lips. "Y-you have real magic…" Then, he turned to dust. His ox let out a low bellow and collapsed beside it.

Clara found pity in the pile of ashes of her former tormentor. He always stood on the side. A few times she would see him struggle with his magic on her way home. Sometimes with his cold father standing over him. She gave a heavy sigh.

Onyx was beside her, panting heavily. Some of the black substance stained his teeth. He tried licking his mouth but it only made it worse.

A neigh broke their concentration. Clara once again turned her gaze to Lotus. Her heart sunk once again. Lotus developed a deep gash that went from her back to hip. Unicorn blood spilled onto the ground. In it, plants slowly started to grow back.

King Helios was trying to fight back. This time Iridescent had accompanied him. The two Reptilia fought off the large weapon. Iridescent sunk a lance into the thick hide of the Clydesdale. The muscled horse bellowed loudly, it reared up. Mage Oak was soon flung down from his spot. Axe sunk deep into the dead soil.

Finally, King Helios got up on Lotus' back. He looked like a performer from a distance. A sword in hand, he leaped from his spot. Everything slowed. King Helios roared as his weapon drew closer and closer in its intended target. Mage Oak's eyes widening in shock as he was about to witness his own demise. The blade dug into the High Mage's chest. King Helios backed away.

Mage Oak writhed in pain. He looked less like a muscular human and resembled more of a dying bear. His hands made a feeble effort to cover the hole as blood seeped out. Little by little, he started to move less and less. He took one last deep breath and laid still. His horse kicked Lotus hard as the stallion collapsed. Both of their eyes turned glassy, a never-ending stare into a dark abyss.

Clara simply walked over to the dead bodies. Each movement became slow since the blood became saturated into the fabric. Her vision began to blur for a moment. As she laid her gaze on Mage Oak, she felt nothing. No sadness. No anger. Just an emptiness that fit his own heart. *He didn't care about his son...* She recalled Mage Hurricane's unfeeling words. Not even a sign of kneeling down to mourn her daughter. *None of them did... The children of the mages are nothing but tools.*

A heavy thud broke her deep thoughts. Clara turned her attention to Lotus. The unicorn was now on her side. Clara tried her best to go over there, but her legs gave out. Every ounce of her strength was used to crawl over to her dear friend. "L-Lotus... Th-thank you... Thank you for getting me out of that horrible kingdom." She coughed. Her own mouth began to taste of blood. Some stained her teeth.

Onyx whined. He got under Clara. He lifted her up. His fur was slick with blood. As he walked, Clara could feel the limping motion.

Clara felt her arms getting weak. Then, she felt the Lead Empty lifting her up. The cool sensation of its skin gave a sense of relief to her hot skin. Strands of her hair hung limply, but the gemstones still remained where they were. Once she reached Lotus, her vision began to blur once more. The colors fade away. Darkness was starting to rule over her eyes despite being able to feel Lotus' bloody flank.

Suddenly, she saw it. The threads. They were dulled. Scattered and broken. She soon noticed Lotus' bright golden threads. They were fragile as before. The color dimming to a pale-yellow color. She lightly touched the spot where the threads were separated by a large hole. Fingering the hole was a cluster of silver threads.

Clara lifted her hand. Her life threads were glimmering above her face. It was as if she was made entirely out of stars. She recalled what Basilini said before he died. *Magic? Did he saw the threads?* Slowly she remembered what Quartz and Gaia said about Life Threads. *Green and browns represent earth, red for fire, light blue for air, gold for light... I can restore a tree, but the last time I ever restored a living being... Which means...* She placed her hand on Lotus flank again.

The lift threads soon knitted back together. It was slow and it only fixed only a third of the gash. Clara could feel her strength waning. She breathed hard, her lungs turning to stone. *This is worse than Onyx's wound. I can't do this alone.*

Help... The lead Empty's voice rang in her head. She saw several threads attach to her arms. A surge of energy flowed through her. Giving her enough strength to get into a kneeing position.

Clara soon heard footsteps coming behind her. Her name being called out. She tried to wave them off with a weak hand. "I'll be fine. Just take care of Twitch and Shard." She soon saw more threads appear before her. Greens and blues. Faint hands were now covering the hole.

Clara looked up to see what looked like a Harpy and a strange seal-like creature staring back at her. They both held a smile on their faces. Feeling a sense of trust from them, Clara forced her threads to mix with Lotus'. They began to knit together than ever before. Onyx's nose pressed against her shoulder. His red threads began to mingle among the silver threads.

"Clara…" Iridescent's voice cut through the chasm. "Twitch and Shard are dead."

Clara froze from what she was doing. Her hands trembled at the news. She remembered Shard's stubbornness and Twitch's taste for life. "No. They don't go down that easily. They've battled so many humans. Never even given up on me." She pressed the threads to heal Lotus. The unicorn's wounds started to stitch back together faster than expected.

Clara pulled away from Lotus and began to sink the rest of the threads into the ground. Her vision began to expand beyond her position. She then could make out completely dulled threads of light blue. Not even a small glimmer could be found. Clara tightened her fists. She turned to the Lead Empty. "My friend. One who takes the threads, are they truly dead?"

The Lead Empty's prism eyes turned golden as it shook in a manner of saying no.

Clara dug her fingers into the earth. Her threads woven into the ground. "Lend me your power to bring them back." She thrusted all of her soul into it. A pair of invisible wings sprung from her back. Clara raised her head and let out an earth-shattering roar. Bright lights flooded before her. Colors of various shades and hue exploded around her.

Clara moved her limbs. The threads obeying her command. She knitted and curled. Even though she could no longer see, she could sense life coming back to the land. Once she was able to regain her sight, she saw green grass underneath her. She turned her eyes to the sky. It was already purple with tints of dark blue. Several stars dotted the sky. She rolled to her side as exhaustion ruled her body. Her mind in a fuzzy haze.

"Clara!" King Helios was at her side. He cupped her face in his hands. "Y-your skin…" Behind him, Iridescent was staring at his arm. The Reptilia scout was stunned that his injury was gone.

Clara took a moment to swallow. "Huh? What about my—" She lifted them up to her face. She gasped. The wounds were completely gone. Not a single scar was etched in. She got up with King Helios' help.

"Clara!" Quartz ran over to them. Her eyes wide with shock. Her glasses were almost ready to come flying off her nose. "Come quick! Twitch and Shar—" Her mouth dropped open at the sight of Clara. "What in all of the golden sands?"

Clara heaved a sigh. "What is it now?"

"You! Dress! What's going on?" Quartz smacked herself.

Clara once again looked down. She was now in a silver dress. A cold breeze hit her on the diamond shaped hole on the back. She looked over her shoulder. Her birthmark was brighter than normal. "My Beast Heart activated." She picked up the Lead Empty. "Thank you. Now, I'm going to return the favor."

"Clara! Clara!" Twitch hovered into view. Her skin and feathers were now healed. Even her leg was back to its original state. Shard close behind her. "You did it! You did! I don't know how, but you've managed to heal us." She landed in front of Clara. Her wings wrapped Clara into a warm embrace. "I'm so glad you're okay." She quickly backed away. "What are you wearing?"

Shard landed beside her. "The bigger question would be: did you find your human leaders?"

Clara went silent. Then, she sighed. "Follow me." She walked over to the carriage. It had a few tree saplings around it. Clara grimaced as she was hit with the rotten odor again. Even the lead Empty crawled onto her shoulder in a feeble attempt to stay out of the stench's reach. Behind her, everyone gagged loudly.

"Wild winds," Twitch shouted. She quickly covered her nose.

"What a stench!" Shard backed away.

Quartz peeked her head inside. She cringed at the same sight Clara had the misfortune to deal with. She backed away. Then, the Sand Dwarf healer was on her hands and knees. She coughed for a few moments before she let out a trail of vomit.

A concerned Iridescent knelt down. He pulled out a handkerchief. His scales gave hints of red and orange as Quartz took it in gratitude.

The group stared at the carriage for a while longer. Onyx and Lotus both back away from the carriage. The two of them had their ears pulled back. The night air being filled with soft winds and crickets. Then, they backed away.

"So…" Shard was the first to speak. His head feathers raised up as more of his anger started to show. "Your human leaders are dead and those insane High Mages and Duke are now stringing everyone along of harvesting threads from living beast." He turned his head to the lead Empty. "No doubt, one of the reasons why those things are ravaging our lands."

Clara sighed. She soon recalled the meeting with the gods and goddesses. What the lead Empty had shown her. Then, High Mage Hurricane's confession. She even tried her best not to throw up as she described Basilini's death and Mage Hurricane's daughter decaying before her very eyes.

Once she was done, everyone held grim expression. Twitch's face paled, her pointed teeth peeking out of her lips. Shard had become so angry that his feathers turned bright red under the rising moon. Quartz turned to the direction of where the moonlight was beaming down. Iridescent and King Helios crossed their arms with grim expressions. The lead Empty even moved with unease.

King Helios was the first to speak after a long period of silence. "I've heard a story about tainted threads used to create Zomoinecs. They appear alive, but are a result of corrupted souls mixed with slaughtered wild beasts."

Quartz turned back to the group. "I've also heard of the prophecy too. Actually, there's…" She adjusted her glasses. "Clara… What kind of moon do you need to find the Empty at?"

Clara rubbed her neck. "When the full moon is high. I don't know why that is though." She froze. Eyes went wide. "Isn't the moon considered the portal to all the light threads? Next to the sun?"

"Technically, light and dar—" Quartz's glasses slide to the edge of her nose. "Oh, no…"

Clara immediately got to her feet. "We need to stop them! They're after all the elemental threads!" She picked up the lead Empty. She gave a small smile. "I think I know how we can take them down and find a way out of here."

Chapter 26
Freedom

Clara and Twitch hid deep in the underbrush. They watched several Minotaurs stand guard the gate of a strange ruin. Several statues of dark dragons dotted the area. Their armor gleamed in the light, but their faces held a certain bitterness that Clara could easily name.

"This isn't going to be easy," Twitch whispered. She shifted from leg to leg. She had to make sure her head didn't hit a tree branch. "They look like they might tear apart the sun."

Clara turned her head at an angle. She could make out her friend's silhouette. Despite having to be stuck in Dark Elf Territory a little more than she would like, Clara knew that if she doesn't stop Lady Maroona and the High Mages from taking all the threads that had once belonged to the dead, then all the kingdoms will fall under their wicked rule. "It will work. It just has to." She looked over to where King Helios was hidden. She could make out his outline in the tangled branches.

A black-pelted Minotaur spoke up, "What is this foolish world coming to?"

Another with white fur nodded. "Our kingdom fell apart and now we have to follow the orders of a few dark eyes and a red-haired brat."

The black Minotaur chuckled. "Don't get me started on her! She's absolutely insane. She twirls her fingers around and the other young just follow her along."

"I even noticed her own hound is reluctant to obey her every command."

The black Minotaur went into a full-blown laugh. "Really? I thought a well-bred would do everything a human tells them."

Suddenly, a one-eyed Dark Elf marched over. Her teeth clenched together. "Quit talking you overgrown cows! King Noctral ordered us on high alert. The lead Empty is not around. If it's not obtained, it won't end well for anyone."

"Madame." The white Minotaur bowed his head low. "It's a miracle that they are even controlled at all." He was met with a slap.

"Don't get smart with me." The Dark Elf's dark eye had a small glimmer of hate. "I don't like these disgusting humans here as much as you do. However, King Noctral made an agreement with them. The human land for the Empty."

Clara bit her lip. She was glad to have the lead Empty on top of Lotus. She gave Lotus mental instructions to go by Onyx's signal. She held up her dagger. It was slightly damaged from the fall, but the blade was clean enough to send a signal if needed. She watched as the Dark Elf soldier stalk off. Then, she heard a few steps south of where they are. No doubt that it was Iridescent.

One of the Minotaurs bellowed. He pointed a spear at an invisible adversary. His companion looked on in annoyance. Then, the partner also let out a low bellow. The two were poking and prodding. Some even threw fireballs. They grunted, smacking boulders as they go.

Iridescent appeared before them. He gave a wide grin, but Clara knew that he was trying to hide the brown that was creeping up his scales. "Hello, gentleman. My what a fine evening isn't it? Plenty chilly for your hot-headed wits." He crept back slowly as they started to move toward him. Eyes glowering. "Guess I should go. Ta Ta!" He vanished in a heartbeat.

"Get him!" The black Minotaur charged. His head lowered down. His partner followed him suit. They charged at the air. Dust rising as they continued to unleash their fire magic.

Clara had to lean back as one fireball almost hit her. Clara let out a low breath. Her heart hammering. *Rue wasn't kidding*, she thought. *Minotaurs really are powerful with their fire magic. I better learn water magic when I get the chance.* She could barely make out anything in the dust. She heard punches being exchanged. A rustle soon followed and Clara could make out King Helios jumping down from the trees with grace. A sword in hand.

Shouts filled the air. Spears went flying out. After sometime, King Helios popped out of the cloud with Iridescent at his side. The two Reptilia ran to west. The two Minotaur guards chased after them. All was slightly silent after that.

Clara peeked her head out. She scanned the area for anything that might resemble a Shadow Elf guard or sniper nearby. *Shadow Elves are deceptive as well as cunning.* She repeated the words from Rue used to tell her every night. *They hid in thick underbrush. Due to the mountains it gave them easy leverage due to the terrain. However, they do have a way of showing them through lower leveled soldiers.* She narrowed her eyes. The lighting of the moon made the pine trees become menacing. It did allow her to see if there were orbs of purple light leaking out. One of the few things that Dark Elves had to be careful in their deceit were their eyes. Since those with purple eyes have a tendency to glow, it causes their shadows to become slightly visible.

Clara walked out of the brush. She waved Twitch over. "It's all clear."

Twitch walked out of the bushes. She huffed in frustration as leaves were stuck to her feathers. She preened them just as Shard flew in.

Shard held several spears and swords in his talons. He had a grin on his face. He was wearing a brand-new tunic that seemed to have belong to a Dark Elf scout, but was torn in a few places to make it more accommodating to his wings and talons. He lowered himself as he set the weapons down. "You're cue, Clara."

Clara tilted her head back and let out a howled. It was low and clear. To her surprise, wolf howls rose through the trees. Clara felt a blush creep up along her cheeks. "Oops… I guess I didn't think there would be other wolves in the mountains."

Twitch spat out the last of the leaves. "Well, as our old Harpy proverbs would say. When you're tasked that requires a flock, summon one."

Clara shook herself. "Can you at least check where Lotus and Onyx are?"

Twitch jumped into the air for a moment. She hovered, her wings invisible to the naked eye. She fluttered back down with ease. "Onyx is head toward our direction. Lotus is leading away some of the Dark Elves and humans away. They took the bait."

Shard laughed. "I'm surprised they'd chase her considering I took most of their weapons."

Clara turned to Shard. "Where's Quartz? I thought she was with you."

Shard sighed. "She had to pack some of the herbs from the mountain she stole along with food supplies."

"Did you leave her with at least one weapon?" Clara crossed her arms.

Shard nodded. "Yeah. A short sword, but she insisted on her own axe and that weird jar." He shrugged. "Let's get going."

Clara nodded. The three of them went past the archway that held the ruin. It held stone carvings of dragons holding various objects that represented the elements. She soon heard paw steps in her direction. She faced south to see Onyx running at her, the lead Empty on his back. She patted his head as he came close.

As they moved deeper into the ruins, they heard a hissing growl. They walked a little further to see lines drawn into the soil. Tied up with thick, colorful ropes, was the massive Empty beast. The multiple faces and limbs writhed in a mass. It tried to bite and claw, but it resulted in a massive shock to the creature.

Clara felt nervous by the massive monster before her. She could hear the multiple voices inside her head. The anger. The despair. It sent chills down her spine. She activated her vision again. There were threads beneath them. She knelt down and placed her hands on the cool stone floor. Suddenly, she was lifted up into the sky. A fireball missed by an inch below her feet.

Clara sucked in a breath. *Where did that come from?* She could feel her own heart beating fast. A yelp made her look over to see Onyx knocked to the ground, but unharmed. His black fur wet from water. However, the lead Empty was trying to get away from the other mage children. It hissed and flung its tentacles at them. Clara tried to summon the earth threads to cause the shift in the ground.

Twitch cried out. Her talons let go of Clara as she was thrusted down. She unleashed several small tornados to hold herself up. Her wings strained with effort.

Clara quickly summoned a few tornados and thick moss to soften her landing. It helped for a little while. Then, something began to snag at her core. It felt like she was being held up by invisible strings like a puppet. She gritted her teeth. A dry laugh reached her ears. Clara moved her eyes, but she found herself on her knees and her arms pinned back. Her entire body felt like burning at this point.

A scream exploded around them. Then, it was followed by footsteps. The click of fancy slippers was all too familiar with Clara. "What a pain," grumbled a voice.

Lady Maroona soon came into view. In her hands was the lead Empty, weak and nearly lifeless. The tentacles looked bizarre against her silk gloves. She looked down at the creature in pure disgust. Her lip curled into a snarl. Her dog was at her side. Its head hung low. The entire body trembling.

Clara couldn't help but feel sorry for the Basenji. "M-Maroona…" Each word was getting harder to breathe. The air being slowly squeezed out of her lungs. "You and your father won't get away with this madness." She struggled but her arms were still pinned back.

Maroona gave a perplexed stare at Clara. "What are you talking about?" She lifted the Lead Empty up to her face. She curled her fingers into the translucent surface, earning a hiss. She rotated it slightly before looking at Clara once again. "We're just freeing this world from one less vermin that we humans have to worry about."

At this, Twitch managed to set herself in a sitting position. "S-Save it! We know about your dead rulers! You've been deceiving your kind after all this time. Plus, we know that you're going after wild beasts and trying to figure out how to harness their power." She choked for a moment as an invisible pressure rested on her neck.

Duke Averance soon appeared beside his daughter. His dog was at his side. He gave an exhausted sigh. "I should've put a tighter leash on Hurricane's mouth. I wouldn't be too surprised that Oak took care of her. He makes good on his tasks." He gave a dark chuckle. "Unlike his useless son."

Clara growled. "You've cheated his life. You made him some fake creature that wasn't supposed to exist."

Maroona dug her fingers deep into the lead Empty's body. This time, a scream was heard. After a short period, it laid limp against her hands. She sneered at Clara. "Funny. I should say the same thing about you." She walked over to the alter and set the lead Empty down.

Just as she did so, King Helios and Iridescent were dragged to the scene by Promoths. Shard was trapped in an orb of water, thrashing about to break free. Dark Elves brought Quartz over, her hands bound tightly behind her back. King Noctral behind them. One of the Dark Elves was holding on to what looked like a strange creature that Clara had never seen before. It had the body of an antelope with a cricket's head and wings.

Maroona paid them no mind. She began to twist her fingers, the threads began to become more visible around her glove. Some of the red threads were blending into the gloves. She snarled as if she was in pain. Maroona let out a frustrated huff and peeled her gloves off. It soon revealed a strange marking that consists of three animals. A moth, a scorpion and a spider were circled together. Their arms locked together in a sinister circle. Shades of pink and red danced on her skin.

Clara and the others were stunned by this. *Was she a Beast Heart?* Clara thought for a moment. She activated her power for a moment. She nearly screamed to what she was seeing before her. It was a strange being behind Maroona. She couldn't smell rot but the skeletal appearance was enough to unnerve her. Her stomach rolled at the soulless eyes that were turning toward her. *No... She's something else...*

"So..." Maroona's voice began to become cold as she spoke these words. Her eyes held a dark shadow. What was even more terrifying was her eyes took on a deep red color. Her lips twitched as if she was ready to bite Clara at any given moment. "You have the Thread Sight. I guess that's what happens when you're born a Beast Heart." She turned her gaze to Duke Averance. "Isn't that right papa?"

Duke Averance gave an exasperated sigh. "I should've known that Clara was going to be more trouble than she's truly worth." He crossed his arms. He turned his gaze to Clara. "I really thought by removing you from the human kingdom, you'd be eaten by now. However, I think your resilience was far stronger than I originally imagined. Even your parents were a nuisance."

A cord struck hard in Clara. The ruby on her head began to burn. She even noticed that Promoths giving her a sympathetic look. She had to breathe in through her nose, fighting off her anger. She slowly deactivated her sight.

Duke Averance continued with his story. "The winter you were born in was deplorable. I had to negotiate with these Dark Elves here. Conniving as they are, they have the best materials in all the lands."

"Wouldn't your higher royals be upset for pulling such a dangerous deal like that," Quartz asked. However, her voice took on a taunt. She smirked as he glared at her.

"They've died when I became Duke," Duke Averance answered. He paid no attention to the Sand Dwarf. "As far as everyone knew, a fire broke out and killed everyone but two servants. They somehow escaped. For your parents, well… They came across an Empty that we managed to capture." He soon pulled out a bag of gold. "I tried to give them some gold, but…" He pulled out a gold coin. On it was the royal symbol. It immediately burst into flame. "A disagreement broke out."

Clara growled. Onyx was at her side from what she saw from the corner of her eye. Spears and swords were trained on him. Hackles raised. Teeth bared. Ears flat against his head. Even though she couldn't sense the bond, she knew he was angry.

In her mind, she could imagine what happened. Her parents found out about the dead rulers of their kingdom and the corruption of the magocracy. Her father was a well-known blacksmith when he was alive. Her mother was a simple bread maker. They would've spread word of what was going on through town. Wait… She looked at King Noctral. "Did Duke Averance want you to attack my village?"

King Noctral didn't say anything, but his eyes seemed to hold some form of regret. His grip on his captor loosened only slightly.

Clara forced her gaze onto Promoths. She could see the sorrow in his eyes. This time, her anger was reaching to a boil. "Do you have any idea what you've done to your fellow humans? How much loss was caused by you? My parents didn't deserve—" Her lungs began to collapse. She started to have a hard time breathing.

Onyx yipped at the sight. He growled, his black fur gave off shades of red and oranges. It appeared like veins draped around him. He moved as fast as he could. He bit into the blade of a nearby sword. The moment he bit down, the metal melted in an instant. He went for the closest Dark Elf. However, he could only bite only a few inches from his face. Red threads began to tie him down. He was pinned in an instant.

Clara tried to yell but her throat was still constricted. She wriggled, but it was all in vain. She felt her hair being grabbed hard. She was dragged away by a strangely strong Maroona.

"Enough talking," Maroona said. She tossed Clara in front of the two Empty. She walked further away to allow some space. She flicked her hands toward the group. "Let's just get this ceremony going before anything else happens." She smirked as she watched everyone move away from her and the monsters.

Clara watched her friends being dragged away. They were lined up in a strange fashion. Almost circular. She looked ahead at the lead Empty. The colorful eyes turned blue in sorrow. She wanted to pet the little creature's head to reassure that everything will be okay. *But it's not*, she thought. *Everyone is pinned down. My plan back fired. Now everyone will die by this thing.* Tears burned her cheeks.

Maroona's wicked laugh reached her ears. "Too bad your one horned donkey isn't here to see this." She could even hear a yelp from Maroona's dog. "Shut up! You're getting really annoying now."

Clara could fill her body being ripped apart. Her heart was ready to be plucked out. She could see a glowing center on her chest. Tentacles began to grapple along her body. Threads tying her up by the wrists and ankles. She tried to pull her body away but the force only put more strain on her body. Suddenly, she heard a neigh in a distance. She looked up at a ledge to see a flash of white running. In that moment, she felt something. A wave of fear, but assurance that she wasn't going to face this alone.

Clara thought back to the times she was with her friends. Twitch sharing her home. Shard teaching her wind magic. Quartz braiding her hair. Then, the moment she thought of King Helios, her birthmark on her back began to glow brightly. She remembered that she saved a baby from dying. She stopped Slave Traders from doing any more harm to the Reptilia Kingdom. Each thought brought a smile to her face.

She got up from her spot. The threads that bound her broke away. She opened her hand. She took a deep breath, her heart clamed. Clara reached out to the Empty. She watched the large monster. It stared at her warily. The lead Empty, on the other hand, took her hands in pure gratitude. Without warning, it disappeared in a flash of light. Threads exploded into her hand.

    The monster reared up. Its roar shook the ground. Stone structures began to crumble. Everyone that gathered immediately backed away. The monster continued to thrash. A few times began to cry out in undistinguishable jabber. Multiple limbs thrashed and stretched to break its bond. All of its eyes were on Clara.

    Clara lifted her hands higher. The glowing light bathed her arms. The tips of her fingers touched a lion-like face. She sent soothing ripples down her mind and into the mass. She could see the creature began to calm. Suddenly a faint whoosh was heard. A spear had clipped her leg, tearing a piece of her dress. She turned around to see Maroona in a slight crouch, arm extended. Clara found a sense of satisfaction in Maroona's feral gaze. To her own joy, she could feel Onyx's growing excitement as well.

    A horn jutted out from the shoulder of a Dark Elf shoulder that was holding on to Twitch. It tossed the warrior into the air and crash onto the ground. Lotus reared up, her horn slick with blood. She kicked another Dark Elf away. She headed straight for Maroona.

    Maroona twisted her fingers. Her dog yelped. Then, it jumped at Lotus. Before the both of them could collide, Twitch grabbed the Basenji dog. The talons wrapped on them tightly. Maroona had no choice but had to jump away. She snarled as her red threads vanished.

Onyx immediately got off the ground. His fur blazed. He let out a ferocious howl. Several howls followed. This time, they were much closer. Onyx ran toward Clara. Lotus close behind. Before long, wolves popped out. Pelts of white, black, brown and ginger blurred in the mass.

Clara hopped onto Lotus' back with ease. She and Lotus unleashed bright lights before the group. Clara moved her fingers. The earth obeyed. It created several quicksands, trapping the captors. She summoned several winds that lifted dust into King Noctral's eyes.

She could sense the emotions of so many creatures. It was easy to see why so many humans would want this power. *Even so*, she thought. *I need to stop this nightmare. The Empty will devour everything and everyone until there's nothing left.* She looked at her arms again. She activated her vision and could sense the lead Empty. She recalled how it looked at her. How it responded. It was almost... alive. *I think I know how to fix this.* She sent her mental plans to Lotus and Onyx.

Onyx went ahead. The other wolves avoided him, but the soldiers weren't as luck. They screamed and rolled as they were trying to choke the flames. Lotus sped on. She jumped and leaped away from the water and fire. The animals tried to cut her path. Duke Averance's dog snarling as they came forward. Just as they were about to pounce, the wolves snatched them by their teeth. Onyx and Lotus leaped over them with ease.

Clara looked over her shoulder. She could see Quartz using sand to blind her enemies as she made her way to the strange bug creature. King Helios punching alongside Iridescent. Shard picking up his enemies and tossing them down. Suddenly, Maroona exploded from the group. She seemed to be controlling a crazed Mountain Strider.

Clara sent a small order to go faster. She pulled at the threads with a small tilt of her hand. "Everyone get out of the way!" The moment she said those words, the threads that were holding the large monster broken in a matter of seconds. The Empty monster let out another loud roar and charged forward. Clara forced the earth to pull her friends away to avoid the contact.

All the soldiers, both human and Dark Elf scrambled away as best as they could. A few Minotaurs were injured by the large monster. Duke Averance cried out as one of the stray tails, a barbed on, sliced his stomach. The other two high mages tried to fight the creature but were smacked around by the flailing limbs. The Empty monster roared at them, then it turned to follow Clara.

Clara adjusted her seating. She let out a small fire go in the palm of her hand. She raised it high. "Hey!" She used every ounce of her energy to call them. "Here! Here! Come get me!" Once she saw the creature move closer, Clara turned her attention to Maroona. She saw that her deranged pursuer wasn't there. Suddenly, she felt something ram into her side from the right. Her world spun as she and Lotus tumbled down a slope.

Clara was starting to feel sick. She made a frantic attempt at reaching for something to hold her in place. Suddenly, she felt a hard tree stump. Her body jarred for a moment. Her heart hammered hard. She could feel the strength of the lead Empty digging its threads into the ground. Clara glanced at the slope. It was steep with a few rocks at the bottom. *That's way too close for comfort*, she thought. *I better find Lotus and reach the bottom. Its large size should be at a disadvantage there.*

She reached out to where Lotus was. Her ears heard a faint whinny. She looked to her left. A few feet away from her, balancing on a dead trunk that was ready to collapse at any moment, was Lotus. Clara regained her footing on the uneven ground. She clambered to where Lotus was.

Clara calmed her heart. Her eyes focused on Lotus. She took a deep breath. *It's okay, girl.* Her mental words floated down her bond. *I'm going to hop over.* She leaped as she heard the trees groan. Clara hugged Lotus neck just in time to see the Empty monster looming over them.

The monster stared at them with its ever-moving heads. Multiple limbs were holding onto the trees, but they were decaying by the touch. It gave off a low rumbling sound. Then, it hissed when Maroona came into view astride a Mountain Strider.

They were balanced on the slope. The loose rock barely phased them. In Maroona's hand was a spear. Blood began to drip from her arms. Her red hair was now in a massive disarray. Her mouth formed a feral snarl. She aimed it at Clara. "I'm taking this thing and I'll kill you first." She gave a dark laugh. "I should've killed you long ago. However, papa warned me that too many questions would rise up." She shrugged. "Not that it would matter."

Clara got onto Lotus' back. Her eyes held a defiant gaze at her former tormentor. "I'm not going to letting you get away with this, Maroona."

"What happened to Lady Maroona?" Maroona tilted her head. "I thought you were to address me as such."

Clara sat far taller than she had ever done before. Her frown deep. "I only used that title as a form of respect for you." Her fingers went deep into Lotus' mane. "You're not worthy of it. You're just a glorified brat surrounded by living corpses that are nothing more than mere puppets!"

Maroona laughed. "You think you're better than me? You have a disgusting marking on your back. You've bonded with a unicorn. Though it's pretty weird why that wolf follows you around." She pointed to Onyx as the wolf ambled toward them. "Plus, you think those ugly creatures will be of help to you?"

Clara's face turned red. She flicked her wrist, igniting a small flame. She hurled it at Maroona. It was blocked, but the rage inside her made her twist her wrist. The flame came back and it formed into the face of a small wolf.

Maroona stared at it in an unimpressed manner. She curled her fingers in. The flame dissipated, barely an ember landed on her dress. She turned to face the creature once again. Maroona activated the threads once again. She pulled with all her might. The blood was spurting out of her forearms.

Clara could feel the knots in her stomach at the sight of this. *I have to stop this! I need to sever the link or these creatures will have their life threads destroyed.* "Go Lotus! Get ready!" She lightly tapped the stones on her forehead. The lapis lazul grew bright along with the ruby and emerald. She could feel the threads twirl around her hand. Clara imagined a dragon's claws.

Lotus and Onyx leaped forward. In turn Maroona's steed leaped as well, her spear held high. In a brief second, they collided. Lotus plunged her horn deep into the Mountain Strider. Onyx bit into the hind leg while avoiding the claws. Maroona tried to strike with her spear, but silver threads appeared out of nowhere and coiled around the weapon.

Clara glared at Maroona. Her mouth twisted into a snarl. "Get your filthy weapon away from my beasts!" She unleashed a fireball onto Maroona's shoulder. Her fury burned with the same fire. She was no longer afraid of Maroona. All she could see was a wretched creature that would call herself when all the young noble has ever done was harm everyone and everything that moved. Clara thought of the dog once more. It maybe too late to save the poor beasts that are bonded to her friends, but she might save the canine from a gruesome fate. She unleashed her silver threads into Maroona's life threads.

She could feel the link between Maroona and her dog. It was weak. She could barely hear the dog's plea to have food or let it run around when it wanted to. No. When she wanted to. The dog had a name. Clara allowed Onyx,

Lotus and the lead Empty to join in on the link. She could feel their fury. Their pity. She thought back to the poor ox and duck that were bonded by their respective owners. Clara couldn't save them, but she could save at least one dog. *Well, I guess all of us should break this bond. Ready?* Her life threads sharpened and wove together with the others. It soon formed a sword of pure light.

Clara swung her sword down. It caught Maroona's face, creating several gashes on her opponent's cheeks. She shoved Maroona off the Mountain Strider and landed on the other side. She heard a rumble. Clara lifted her head to see several boulders were heading toward them. It was ready come down on them. The monster began to tumble forward. "Just my luck," Clara muttered under her breath.

She felt her heart twist as Lotus and Onyx began to run downhill. The loose rocks underneath were making it hard to become stable enough to avoid hitting a few trees. *Ow,* she mentally cried. *I'm going to be bruising for the next several days.* Her eyes widened as the bottom of the slope was rapidly approaching. Time for a quick landing! Clara forced her vision to activate. She found a few threads to use. She summoned enough moss, grass and lichen to form a thick bed. Tree branches stretched beyond belief.

Clara separated herself from Lotus as they began to lose their footing. She and her beasts landed on the earthy carpet hard. Clara groaned. Then, she saw the Empty falling straight at them. Clara scrambled to get up. She grabbed Onyx and Lotus and tried to pull them out of the way. The two beasts were able to get onto their feet. All three ran a few feet before a heavy thud from the Empty cause them to tumble down from the shockwave.

Clara was back on the ground once again. Her breathing ragged as exhaustion set in. She found herself scratched up in a few places along her arms. Her fingers felt raw. *If Rue were here, she'd yell at me for being careless with my magic.* She slowly got up from her spot. Her limbs ached. She yelped as she felt a sharp pain along her back. She felt blood trickled down to her hip. *Oh great! Now my back is mess up!*

She gritted her teeth as she got back up. Clara ignored the sharp pain. She turned around to see the Empty being a writhing mass. A few smaller empties were scattered on the ground. She took a deep breath. Her hands curled up into fists. She looked around for any signs of Maroona. So far, she saw the Mountain Strider limping away. There were no other signs of Maroona. Not even a drop of blood. Above Clara, the moon was high in the sky. "Time to end this."

Clara walked over to the Empty. Her arms glowed once again. She raised them high into the air. She kicked away the debris scattered around her. Clara turned her gaze back at the Empty. They all hissed at her. "It's okay," she whispered. She felt her heart going inward. She revealed her life threads to the Empty.

The Empty were a little hesitant. Even though they didn't have eyes, Clara could easily sense their uncertainty. Then, they stretched out their tentacles. Their bodies glittered brightly under the full moon. Multiple colors surrounded them. One by one, they all vanished as Clara walked toward them. The monster raised its multiple head once more. Their mouths opened in a gurgling roar. The limbs thrashed but not as violently as earlier.

Clara put her hands on the creature. She braced for any dangerous response. Instead, she was met by faint whimpers. Clara looked up to see tears trickle down its multiple eyes. She could sense the exhaustion in it. Its sorrow of roaming this world. Its anger of not finding a reason to live. Its never-ending hunger.

She felt her own eyes water with tears. In some way, she's lived like that too. Wondering in her own kingdom. Never noticed for her true worth. Given tasks that made her doomed to fail. She wiped away her tears. A warm sensation ruled her back. She leaned against the smooth skin of the Empty monster. "It's okay now. I'll fix this."

In a burst of light, threads of varying shades of color floated all around her. She couldn't even see her own face. Suddenly, several specs of light appeared. They twirled and stretched. Before long, they soon revealed to be a large crowd comprised of animals, Humans, Dark Elves, Harpies and a few Sand Dwarves. They all had relaxed expressions. It was as if they were finally freed from the burden they were suck with so many years ago. One human stepped toward her. His dark hair stood out against his burly clothes.

Clara was stunned. Her heart ached as she realized who it was. "Father..." Even though it's been ten years, she still remembers him well. His joyous songs, His soured expressions when he at the most bitter fruit in all the land.

"Hello, Clara," her father, Gabrielidan, gave her a soft smile. "Thank you for freeing me."

"And me as well."

Clara turned around to see her mother stand before her. "Mama!" She flung her arms around her. She sobbed uncontrollably. Her shoulders scrunched up from the effort. "I'm sorry! I wish I could've used my magic earlier to save you." She felt a pair of warm arms wrapped around her. She looked between her parents as they encircled her.

Manna adjusted her auburn hair as she faced Clara. "It wasn't your fault. What happened that day was beyond any of our control."

Clara sniffed. "Duke Averance had the Minotaurs kill you and father, didn't he?"

A heavy silence hung in the air. Her parents exchanged glances at her then at her. Their eyes were grim. Lines taught into a thin line. They broke their embrace and held Clara's hands.

"Yes and no," her father answered. "Duke Averance did stage the raid on our village, but he was the one to kill us."

Clara's eyes widened at this. "But why would he do that? What would he gain from killing you?" Her fingers were squeezed gently.

Manna sighed. "There isn't much time left. You must breathe life into the Empty." She looked Clara square in the eye. "In terms of why he killed us, all you need to know is that he wanted to silence us."

Clara's mind clicked into place. Her lips tightened, almost hard to speak. "You know the truth of the High royals."

Her parents nodded. Then her mother said, "We confronted him about his lies, but he threatened us. He was trying to control the Empty and the village children were part of his experiments." She soon began to fade. "Clara! We've been wondering this world for so long. The Empty contain the Life Threads of the dead. If we don't get out soon, we'll never move on."

Tears came back to Clara's eyes. "But… I just got you back." She received a hug once more. Suddenly, a soft barking was heard in the fog. It was Onyx. She could feel his concern reach her along with Lotus'. She immediately realized that she wasn't alone. She took a deep breath and showed her friends where she is. They soon appeared at her side. "Okay…" she wiped her tears, she presented her friends. "These are the beasts I'm bonded too. I know they're not a dog or a regular horse, but they've been by my side since my exile."

Her parents smiled at them. Her mother patted Onyx's head. Her father gave Lotus' muzzle a stroke. Then, they hugged Clara one final time. They backed away and joined the group.

Clara took a deep breath. She glanced at her beasts. *Ready?* She laughed as they got onto their hind legs. She looked at the Life Threads before her. The Empty need a form. Something that makes them stand out from among the rest. Clara looked up at the sky. The moon was clear, but she could make out the black strands that were blocking the path to the world of gods. She tightened her grip and started to pull at the threads.

The threads twisted and turned with each movement. She curled her fingers up. She began weaving. Her Life Threads creating a solid bond with the dead to the moon. As she did so, she began to move higher and higher into the sky. She made careful work of wrapping Lotus and Onyx powers together. The light of Lotus acting like lanterns while Onyx's fire gave the warmth they needed. Before long, she created a rainbow-colored bridge that stretched from the ground to the moon.

She took the threads that still remained in her hand. Her heart swelled with gratitude and sorrow as she watched the souls that were stuck for so long having the ability to go home. Even Onyx's and Lotus' content eased her strain. *I best hurry and do something about The Empty*, she thought. She was only a few feet from the ground when she stopped in her tracks. *No... They're not like that. They're so much more.* Clara began to weave the remaining threads.

In her mind's eye, she decided what sort of shape they should take. They took a piece of Heartstrings. The animals, the plants. Everything that was connected to nature. She began to think of what would seem an ideal case. Clara created the head and made her way down their bodies. As the threads were woven together, she could see the same translucent skin from the Empty. However, it began to glow like a star. Rainbow veins fluttered underneath. Limbs started to stretch out. A long tail curved into a "s". Each attempt made Clara's body begin to weaken. Her legs threatening to cave under her. Once she was able put her feet on the ground, Clara had enough strength to hold Lotus neck.

The moon was gone, but a ribbon of sunlight peeked over the mountain tops. A soft breeze went through the ravine carrying the sweet smell of flowers. The ground now had grass sprouting from the barren spot. Ferns and marigolds dotted the area. Standing only four feet tall was a creature that all of Heartstrings has never seen before.

The head of the creatures resembled that of a lemur. Their hands and limbs were like that of a frog. Butterfly wings graced their backs while moth antennas hung over their eyes like snowdrops. Their long tails curled and flexed. Their eyes were spheres of various colors. Some even resembled that of opals. They all looked at Clara.

Clara gave a weak smile. She sat down with the help of Lotus as the unicorn lowered her neck. "There. You're no longer burdened by your curse. You can now live freely the way you wish."

The largest of the strange cluster stared at her. His eyes turned to a shade of light blue. His lemur face stared at her in admiration. Then, he bowed at her. "We're whole now. Thanks to you, Clara of the Snowdrop village."

Clara sighed. The ache in her heart lingered for a moment, but it was over for the most part. Her arms began to ache greatly. She looked down to see that some of her earlier scrapes and bruises that came from her fall were now being cleared away. Clara looked up to the morning sky. "I'm just glad that life can move forward again."

"Don't celebrate yet."

Clara whipped her head around to see Promoths standing only a few feet from where she was. She took note that the Minotaur had some of his armor sheared off. He had blood trickling from a nicked ear and nostrils. His tired eyes were trained on her. *What does he want?* He soon took a few more steps toward her.

Clara began to grow nervous. She tried to inch away but exhaustion ruled her body once more. Her muscles caved, making her landing face first in the dirt. She only moved her arm a few inches from her side. Clara could hear Onyx growling and Lotus stamping her hoof on the ground. Clara tried to say what she wanted to say, but her mouth was too dry at this point. Then, she found herself being carried bridal style.

The lead former Empty hissed. His wings flared out on his back. His eyes turned to a shade of red. "What's the meaning of this? How dare you try to hurt the Wild Shepherdess!" He arched his back.

Promoths stared in curiosity. "What are you exactly? Your hiss resembled the Empty but you appear different somehow." Then, he pulled out something that was hidden beneath his remaining armor. It was a leather flask. It swished slightly as he held it up for Clara to see. His attention turned to her, filled with concern. "Here. Drink this."

Clara stared at it. Her hands frozen in hesitation. She looked to Onyx. Her wolf was sitting there, he was unsure what Promoths is doing but he didn't smell any poison in the flask. She turned her attention to Lotus. The unicorn only eyed the cow-headed creature. *Well... I know that Duke Averance killed my parents, not Promoths.* She swallowed hard. *I'll just give him the benefit of the doubt.* She wrapped her fingers around the flask. She pressed her mouth against the lip. The water trickled down her mouth.

Before Clara could stop herself, she began to gulp down the water hard. The sweet taste felt so refreshing on her throat. In an instant, the fatigue was gone. She was starting to feel strength in her legs to hold her up. Once she was done, Clara remembered where she was. Her face immediately went crimson.

Promoths walked over to Lotus and set her down on her back. "You best move now. Before anyone else gets down here. I don't think the Duke will take well to the state you put his daughter in." He backed away from Lotus and started to walk forward. "Follow me. I know a short cut."

Clara looked at Lotus. Then at the former lead Empty. Her lips pursed with thought. "Let's get going." She sighed. She tapped Lotus' shoulder and they walked on. Onyx was at their side, his eyes not taking off of Promoths. As they continued down the path, Clara began to notice a few things as morning light came in.

The trees looked gentle. Its thorns were smaller than normal. Wyvern were spotted to the right but they didn't seem to be interested in Clara and her friends. Tiny goldenrods and violets peeked through the grass and rock. Moss carpeted the dead trees. In the shadows of the underbrush were a few baby shadow dragons. The air smelled of summer. The sun's warmth spread through a clearing that held a herd of elk.

Lotus suddenly stopped. Clara lurched slightly and glanced at her. She saw her unicorn being more alert than she's been ever since they restored the Empty. Ears pointed forward, but moving in a different direction slightly.

Clara soon heard muffled voices talking. She narrowed her eyes to have a better look. Faint figures stood in the clearing. They seemed to be talking amongst themselves. She tapped Lotus closer. Once she did, she soon recognized the faces before her. She swung leg off Lotus' back and began running toward them. She waved at them. "Hey! Hey!"

Her heart leaped with joy as she saw two flying shapes coming at her. "Twitch! Shard!" Her arms extended wide as they came nearer. She was soon embraced by a wall of green feathers. However, she could see a few brown feathers peeking out. "You made it!"

Twitch laughed. "Of course, we did! It'll take more than a bunch of spears and lances to knock us down."

Shard tried to look angry but his lips were betraying him. "Where have you been? We lost you after you made

Lotus vanish into the woods. We thought for sure you fell off a cliff." Just as he said this, he soon noticed the former Empty walking over to them. He raised his feathered brow. "Uh… Who are they? Where did you find them?"

Clara was freed from Twitch's embrace and walked over to the glittering creatures. She extended a hand before them. She was grinning from ear to ear as King Helios, Iridescent and Quartz walked up to them. "Everyone, I would like you to meet the creatures that had once been the Empty."

Everyone stared at the former Empty with wide eyes. Quartz's glasses threatened to slide off her nose. Iridescent's mouth dropped low enough to show his tongue. A heavy silence held in the air for a moment.

Clara couldn't help but giggle at their reaction. She told them everything that happened to her, Lotus and Onyx. The dangerous chase. The fall. Clara's face-off with Maroona. As she was talking about her parents, her voice began to broke. "I… I knew Duke Averance was cruel… but I never realized he would go that far to…" She took a deep breath before she could talk again. Before she could do anything else, the lead Empty soon stepped in.

"Miss Clara made us whole with the remaining Life threads that were a part of us." He gave a small bow. "We are forever in her services."

Clara sniffed for a moment. On instinct, she rubbed her eyes to avoid any onslaught of tears. She took a moment to calm herself further. Suddenly, a large hand patted her head. She turned to see Promoths staring down at her.

"I'm sorry, Clara." Promoths voice was filled with sorrow. His eyes glistened. "I knew that Duke Averance was planning something when he tasked us with raiding Snowdrop village. I wanted to ask why, but he wouldn't say anything. I got concerned about Mana so I went to warn her." He knelt down to face her stare her square in the eye. "By the time I got there... She was already gone." He gave a heavy sigh. He got up and was about to walk away.

Clara took his hand. "The human you supposedly befriended..." She bit her lip. "That was my mother, wasn't it?"

Promoths didn't respond. He only nodded. Promoths slipped his hand away from Clara's. He pointed to a set of twin mountain peaks that was only a few feet away from them. "Go down between those peaks. There's a slope that'll lead you to Selkie territory." He walked away. His eyes to the skies. "It'd be best if you lot run now. It will be only a matter of time before they reach you." He continued walking. "Farewell."

Everyone stared at him for a moment. No one knew what else to say to their strange guide. The elk cries were the only thing that broke the silence. Suddenly, a faint roar echoed in a far distance.

Quartz made a dash for her bizarre creature. Her short legs making quick work of the distance. "Time to go!" She climbed onto the creature with ease. "Hyah!" With a firm kick, the creature got up and bolted down the path were Promoths pointed.

"Wait for us!" Twitch called back. She turned to Clara. "Do you think Lotus has enough strength to carry you back?"

Clara turned back to Lotus. She could see exhaustion written on the unicorn's face. She sent a mental message down the bond. *We're going to have to do one more sprint. Just go a little farther and you'll be able to rest. I promise.* In response, Lotus snorted and reared up. Determination rippled down the bond. Clara laughed as she got on.

She soon saw a few shapes that started to grow bigger with each passing minute. Clara found herself eager. A wild grin spread on her face. The thought of this challenge sent shivers of delight down her spine. She glanced to the lead Empty once more. *I better take them with me.* She climbed back onto Lotus' back and extended a hand. "Come with us, Wild Kin."

The leader blinked. "What… What did you call us?"

Clara picked him up. He was shockingly light for his size. "Wild Kin." She patted his head. There were tufts of blue fur sticking out of his head. "You were connected to nature through the threads. What you did was considered wild and uncontrollable. Back when you were the Empty, you were a force of destruction. The name 'Wild Kin' means that you're truly part of nature. As for you, your name will be Orion. It means 'brave one'." She quickly got on. She also sent a mental message for Onyx to let a few

Wild Kin climb onto his back. Then, she sent another command to a different animal close by.

Before long, the nearby elk walked over to King Helios and bowed down. King Helios stared at the creature in great surprise. "Clara? What did you do?"

Iridescent began to push his king toward the bowing creature. "Uh... Your Majesty... I think we should save those questions for later." He pointed toward the sky as the dark spots were now starting to take solid shape. He quickly hopped onto another elk and went away.

Clara gave him a small smile. "I'm doing what a shepherdess does. Bringing sheep and other creatures to safety." She clicked her tongue for Lotus to go. As she began to speed forward, she turned her head to see King Helios hop onto his elk. She grinned as she saw him by his side.

More elk started to appear. Cows and bulls alike having a Wild Kin on their backs. Their hooves thundered almost as the roar that came upon them. They picked up their pace. The path before them was getting much closer. Up ahead, Twitch was carrying Maroona's basenji in her claws. Shard was flying beside her. It was hard for Clara to see if he was giving her a dirty look, but she didn't care as long as they were able be together.

Clara stared at the path before her. The road to Selkie territory. A path to a new life. A path that will help her unlock the mysteries that still reside in the world. Where was the goddess of light? What happened to the first Wild Shepherdess? What other Beast Hearts were there? She wasn't sure, but one thing still rang true. She had company now. Two Harpies, a Sand Dwarf, a gaggle of Wild Kin and two Reptilia. One Reptilia that made her heart skip. She couldn't help but grin as he came riding beside her.

I'll be okay, she thought. *I'm not alone anymore and I'll never be alone.* Clara raised her hands high. Her Beast Heart beating with every moment that counted.